OUTSTANDING PRAISE FOR THE NOVELS OF ELLEN MARIE WISEMAN!

THE PLUM TREE

"The meticulous hand-crafted detail and emotional intensity of *The Plum Tree* immersed me in Germany during its darkest hours and the ordeals its citizens had to face. A must-read for WWII fiction aficionados—and any reader who loves a transporting story."
—Jenna Blum, *New York Times* bestselling author of *Those Who Save Us*

"Ellen Marie Wiseman's provocative and realistic images of a small German village are exquisite. *The Plum Tree* will find good company on the shelves of those who appreciated *Skeletons at the Feast* by Chris Bohjalian, *Sarah's Key* by Tatiana de Rosnay, and *Night* by Elie Wiesel." —*NY Journal of Books*

"Her characters are not just victims, but flesh-and-blood people. If you care about humanity, you must read *The Plum Tree*."
—Sandra Dallas, author of *The Patchwork Bride*

WHAT SHE LEFT BEHIND

"A real page-turner." —*Historical Novel Society*

"A great read!" —*The San Francisco Book Review*

COAL RIVER

"Wiseman offers heartbreaking and historically accurate depictions. . . . The richly developed coal town acts as a separate, complex character; readers will want to look away even as they're drawn into a powerful quest for purpose and redemption . . . a powerful story."
—*Publishers Weekly*

"Heartrending and strongly drawn." —*Booklist*

THE LIFE SHE WAS GIVEN

"Wiseman has crafted a can't-put-it-down novel of family secrets involving two young girls who only seek to be loved. Perfect for book clubs and readers who admired Sara Gruen's *Like Water for Elephants*." —*Library Journal,* Starred Review

Books by Ellen Marie Wiseman

THE PLUM TREE

WHAT SHE LEFT BEHIND

COAL RIVER

THE LIFE SHE WAS GIVEN

THE ORPHAN COLLECTOR

Published by Kensington Publishing Corporation

The PLUM TREE

ELLEN MARIE WISEMAN

KENSINGTON BOOKS
www.kensingtonbooks.com

For my mother, Sigrid,
the strongest woman I know—
with much love and admiration.

In memory of my beloved sister, Cathy.
I miss you every day.

ACKNOWLEDGMENTS

One of my fondest fantasies during the endless solitary hours spent writing this novel was the prospect of honoring the people who supported and believed in me along the way. I do so now, in no particular order, with great joy.

Thank you to my friends and family for not saying I was crazy when I told you I was working on a book, and for understanding when I didn't call or pick up the phone. To all who are not mentioned here by name, please know that you have touched me and helped me along this journey and will have my love and gratitude always.

For reading earlier drafts and bolstering my confidence, thank you to Douglas Towne, Jana Chavoustie, Debbie Battista, and Mary Giaquinto, DVM. Thank you to Gary Chavoustie for igniting the spark that led to the idea and for being my "longest" friend. Thank you to Sophie Perinot, author of *The Sister Queens,* for your friendship and excellent advice, and to all my author friends over at Book Pregnant, for always being there whenever I need someone who understands this wild ride. BP rocks!

I am especially grateful to my kind and brilliant agent, Michael Carr, for taking a chance on me and for helping me revise the manuscript. Without you, I would not have been able to achieve this final step of publication. I hope we can have lunch again someday. Next time I won't be nervous! I'd also like to thank Michael's associate, Katherine Boyle, for helping this novel find a home.

I am forever indebted to my gracious and insightful editor, John Scognamiglio, for making my dream come true. John's expert editorial guidance, along with the sharp eye of my copy editor, Debra Roth Kane, strengthened the book in ways I couldn't have imagined. Many thanks also to the rest of the Kensington team for all your hard work turning my manuscript into a real live book.

I will never find adequate words to thank my mentor, William

Kowalski, award-winning author of *Eddie's Bastard,* without whose formidable talent and immeasurable patience this novel would not exist. Thank you for teaching me to "Always Return To The Right Foot" and how to be a storyteller. I will be forever grateful for your gentle guidance, your kindness and generosity and, most of all, your friendship.

To my beloved mother, Sigrid, thank you for giving me a rock to stand on. You raised me with love, instilled in me an appreciation for hard work, and taught me that with determination, all things are possible. You are an inspiration to all who know you. I hope you're half as proud to be my mother as I am to be your daughter. Thank you for tirelessly sharing your stories and always believing that I have what it takes to share them with the world. This novel serves as a love letter to the beautiful place where you grew up and to the memory of sweet Oma and Opa. I hope it does them justice. To my father, Ted, thank you for always being there, and for giving me the love and security I needed to have a childhood with the freedom to dream. Thank you for the many trips to Germany, for sharing your love of the lake, and for all the incredible family memories.

Thank you to my big brother, Bill, one of the best men I know, for always being someone I can count on. You and I have gone through a lot together, and I love you with all my heart. To my sister-in-law, Yvonne, thank you for your love and support, and for listening.

Dear sweet Bill, my husband, my best friend, my partner in crime. You're the kindest, most generous person I know, and I'm proud to be your wife. Thank you for unquestioningly and unhesitatingly supporting me during the years I was working on this novel and for not complaining about the numerous times we had soup and sandwiches for dinner. Thank you for your steadfast love, for riding this roller coaster with me, for enduring years of ceaseless babbling about WWII and Nazis, and for never faltering in your belief in me, especially when I didn't believe in myself. I'm proud of us, and I'll love you until the day I die.

And finally, a most heartfelt thanks to my wonderful children,

Ben, Jessie, and Shanae, and my precious grandchildren, Rylee and Harper, for making me proud and loving and supporting me, no matter what. Not a day goes by that I don't celebrate the magnificent gift of being your mother and grandmother. You are my life, my world, my universe, and I love you with everything that I am.

By appointing Hitler Chancellor of the Reich you have handed over our sacred German fatherland to one of the greatest demagogues of all time. I prophesy to you this evil man will plunge our Reich into the abyss and will inflict immeasurable woe on our nation. Future generations will curse you in your grave for this action.

—Former general Erich Ludendorff,
in a telegram to President Paul von Hindenburg

CHAPTER 1

Germany

For seventeen-year-old Christine Bölz, the war began with a surprise invitation to the Bauermans' holiday party. On that brilliant fall day in 1938, it was impossible to imagine the horrors to come. The air was as crisp and sweet as the crimson apples hanging in the orchards that lined the gentle foothills of the Kocher River valley. The sun was shining in a blue September sky quilted with tall, cottony clouds that swept rolling shadows over the countryside. It was quiet in the hills, except for the scolding jays and scurrying squirrels as they gathered seeds and nuts for the coming winter. Wood smoke and the mossy scent of spruce intermingled to produce a smoldering, earthy aroma that, despite the fall chill in the air, gave the morning depth and texture.

Due to a shortage of rain that year, the leaf-covered trails of the forest were dry, and Christine could have run along the steep, rocky sections without fear of slipping. Instead, she took Isaac Bauerman's hand and let him help her down the lichen-covered boulder, wondering what he'd think if he knew how much time she spent in the woods. Normally, she would have leapt off the side of Devil's Rock as if she were immortal, landing squarely on the slippery layers of pine needles and spongy earth, knees bent to keep from tumbling forward. But she didn't jump this time, because she didn't want him to think she was a lumbering tomboy who lacked class or manners or grace. Worse than that, she didn't want him to think that she didn't have the sense to realize that the legend about the boulder—that some boys playing hooky from church had once been struck and killed by lightning there—was nothing more than a spooky fable. He'd laughed when she told him, but after, as they gripped the boulder's cracks and fissures and moved down its ancient side, she wished she hadn't bored him with such a foolish childhood tale.

"How did you know where I . . ." she said. "I mean . . . How did you find . . ."

"I looked in my father's desk for your wage records and got your address," he said. "I hope you don't mind that I invited myself over and joined you on your walk."

She walked faster, so he wouldn't see her smile. "It's all right with me," she said. It was more than all right with her; it meant that the hollow sensation she felt whenever they were apart had disappeared. For now, at least. As soon as she had woken up that day, she'd started counting the hours until she could go to her job at his house. After a breakfast of warm goat's milk and brown bread with plum jam, she had done her chores, then tried to read, but it was no use. She couldn't stay at home another minute. Instead of watching the clock, she decided to go into the hills to search for edelweiss and alpine roses for Oma and Opa's anniversary table.

"But what would your parents think if they knew you were here?" she asked.

"They wouldn't think anything," he said. He hurried ahead, then walked backwards in front of her, acting as if she were going to step on his toes and hopping out of the way just in time. He laughed, and she smiled, mesmerized by his playful grin.

She knew that Isaac spent hours reading and studying and could probably recite the Latin names for the strawberries and hazelnuts that grew wild along the grassy knolls. More than likely, he could identify each species of bird, even in flight, and the different animals that had left paw tracks in the soft earth. But his knowledge came from pictures in books, while hers came from observation and years of folklore. She'd spent her childhood exploring the rolling hills and black forests that surrounded their hometown of Hessental. She was familiar with every winding trail and ancient tree, knew every cave and stream. What had begun as an early morning chore, collecting the edible mushrooms that her father had patiently taught her to identify, soon became her favorite pastime. She loved to escape the village, to walk along the edges of fields, cross the railroad tracks, and follow the rutted wagon trails until they tapered into narrow, wooded paths. It was her time alone, time to let her thoughts roam free.

She couldn't count the number of times she'd climbed to the thirteenth-century cathedral ruins in the heart of the forest, to daydream in the protected nest of soft grass formed by its three ancient, crumbling walls. The flying buttresses lent no support and the cathedral windows were empty now, serving as nothing more than stone frames for evergreen boughs, milky skies, or twinkling stars cradled in the white sickle of a quarter moon. But she often stood where she estimated the altar would have been, trying to imagine the lives of those who had prayed and married and cried beneath the church's soaring arches: knights in shining armor and priests with long beards, baronesses roped in jewels, and ladies-in-waiting trailing behind.

Her favorite time to hike to the highest point of the hill was early sunrise in the summer, when the dew extracted earthy scents from the soil, and the air filled with the fragrance of pine. She loved the first hushed day of winter too, when the world had settled into a slumber, and newly fallen snow sugarcoated the sheared yellow wheat fields and the gray, bare branches of trees. She was at home here, deep within the high-skirted evergreens, where the sunlight barely broke through to the musty forest floor, while Isaac was at home in a gabled mansion on the other side of town, where iron gates were flanked by trimmed hedges, and mammoth doors stood beneath ancient archways carved with stone gargoyles and medieval saints.

"Well," she said. "What would Luisa Freiberg think of you being here?"

"I don't know what she would think," he said, falling in beside her. "And I don't care."

If she'd known he was going to show up at her family's house on Schellergasse Strasse that morning, waiting in silence on the stone steps behind her until she closed the oversized wrought iron latch on her front door, she would have worn her Sunday coat, not the tan wool overcoat that hung down to her ankles. It was thick and warm, a Christmas present from her beloved Oma, but its stiff collar and frayed pockets did little to hide the fact that in its former life it had been a carriage blanket.

Now, as she led Isaac through the forest and down the hill toward the apple and pear orchards, she kept touching the coat's buttons, running her fingers along its overlapped front, to make sure it concealed the old play clothes she had on underneath. The gathered arms of her childhood dress were too short, the stitch-less hem too high, the unbuttoned bust too tight, and the navy gingham too childish. Her leggings, held up by straps buttoned to her undershirt, were gray and nappy, covered by hundreds of pills and snags from catching on bushes and ragged bark. But it was what she always wore to hike, because, before today, she'd always come alone. In this outfit, she didn't need to worry about ruining her clothes when she knelt in the dirt to pick wild mushrooms from beneath a damp fern or had to crawl on the ground to gather beechnuts for cooking oil.

Like those of everyone else in her family, nearly all her clothes were reconstructed from printed cotton sheets or hand-me-downs. And until she'd started working for the Bauermans, she'd thought nothing of it. The majority of girls and women in her village dressed as she did, in worn dresses and skirts, starched aprons with mended pockets, and high, lace-up shoes. But now, when she went to her afternoon job at Isaac's house, she always wore one of her two Sunday dresses. They were the best she owned, bartered for with brown eggs and goat's milk at the local clothing shop.

This upset Mutti—her mother's name was Rose—who'd been working full-time at the Bauermans' for the past ten years. The dresses were for church, not for dishes, washing clothes, and polishing silver. But Christine wore them anyway, ignoring Mutti's hard look when she walked into the Bauermans' beige-tiled kitchen. Sometimes, Christine borrowed a dress from her best friend, Kate, to wear to work, with promises to return it unsoiled. And when getting ready, she was always careful to brush and re-braid her hair, making sure the blond plaits were straight and even. But this morning, when Isaac had surprised her, her hair was in a haphazard braid down her back.

To her relief, Isaac was wearing his brown work pants, suspenders, and a blue flannel shirt, the clothes he wore for cutting grass or chopping wood, instead of the pressed black trousers, white shirt, and navy vest he wore to *Universität*. Because, even though the Bauermans were one of the last wealthy families in town, Isaac's father made certain that his children knew the virtues of labor. He gave Isaac and his younger sister, Gabriella, regular chores.

"I know what your parents would think," Christine said, keeping her eyes on the red dirt path.

They made their way out of the dark interior of the forest, through thinning trees and gangly saplings, and emerged at the grassy edge of the highest apple orchard. Six white sheep were in the clearing, their woolly heads rising in unison at Christine and Isaac's sudden appearance. Christine stopped and held up her hand, signaling Isaac to stand still. The sheep gazed back at them, then resumed their job of trimming the grass in the orchard. Satisfied that the sheep weren't going to run off, Christine dropped her hand and moved forward, but Isaac grabbed it and pulled her back.

He was over six-foot, with broad shoulders and muscular arms, a giant compared to her petite frame. And now that they were face-to-face, she felt blood rise in her cheeks as she looked up into his shining, chestnut eyes. She knew each feature by heart, the dark waves of hair that fell across his forehead, the chiseled jaw, the smooth, tanned skin of his brawny neck.

"And how would you know what my parents think?" he said, grinning. "Did you and my mother sit down over coffee and cake, so she could tell you all about it?"

"Nein," Christine said, laughing. "Your mother didn't invite me for coffee."

Isaac's mother, Nina, was a fair and generous employer, occasionally sending home gifts for Christine's family: *Lindzertorte* cookies, *Apfelstrudel,* or *Pflaumenkuchen,* plum cake. At first, Mutti had tried to object to Nina's gifts, but it was no use. Nina would shake her head and insist, saying it made her feel good to help the less fortunate. At the Bauermans' they had real coffee, not *Ersatz Kaffee,* or chicory, and every so often, Isaac's mother sent a pound home with Christine. But it wasn't Nina Bauerman's policy to sit down and drink from her best china with the help.

"Mutti said it was understood about you and Luisa," Christine said, distracted by the strength of his wide, warm hand gripping hers. She pulled her hand away and started walking again, her heart pounding.

"There's no understanding," he said, following her. "And I don't care what anyone thinks. Besides, I thought you knew. Luisa is leaving for the Sorbonne."

"But she'll be back. Right? And Mutti told me . . . Frau Bauerman always says: 'Use the best silverware tonight, Rose. Luisa and her family are coming for dinner.' And just last week, 'It's Luisa's birthday, so please buy the best herrings to make *Matjesheringe in Rahmsosse;* it's her favorite. And make sure that Isaac and Luisa are seated next to each other for afternoon coffee and cake.' "

"It's only because our families are close. My mother grew up with Luisa's mother."

"Your parents are hoping . . ."

"My mother knows how I feel. And so does Luisa."

"And your father?"

"My father can't say anything. His parents protested his engagement to my mother because she wasn't a practicing Jew. But he ignored them and got married anyway. He's not going to tell me what to do."

"And what are you doing?" she said, shoving her hands deep in the pockets of her coat.

"I'm enjoying a hike on a beautiful day with a beautiful girl," he said. "Is there something wrong with that?"

His words sent a thrill coursing through her. She turned away and strolled downhill, past the last row of twisted apple trees to a wooden bench, its thick supports buried in the sloped earth. She gathered her coat around her legs and sat down, hoping he wouldn't notice the trembling of her hands and knees. Isaac sat next to her, elbows propped on the short backrest, legs outstretched.

From here, they could see where the train tracks left the station, then bent along a wide, slow curve before running parallel to the hills. Beyond the tracks, neatly plowed fields rolled out in brown furrows toward the village, huddled on one end of the vast, green-and-brown patchwork valley. Wood smoke curled from chimneys toward hills patterned with trees, their leaves turning to autumn's red, yellow, and gold. The silver ribbon of the Kocher River meandered through the center of town, its winding curves banked by high stone walls, its length cut into sections by covered bridges. They could see the spherical stone steeple of the Gothic church of St. Michael's, soaring high above the market square. To the east, the pointed, brownstone steeple of the Lutheran church, across the street from Christine's house, rose tall and noble above a congregation of clay-tiled rooftops. Each steeple sheltered a trio of massive iron bells that rang each daylight hour and echoed through the Sunday morning streets with the majestic peals of an ancient call to worship. Beneath the sea of orange clay rooftops turned the life of the village.

Within a crooked maze of cobblestoned streets and stepped alleys, between centuries-old fountains and ivy-covered statues, children laughed and ran, kicking balls and jumping rope. The village bakery filled the cool fall air with the aromas of freshly baked pretzels, rolls, and *Schwarzwälder Kirschtorte,* Black Forest cherry tarts. Chimney sweeps walked from house to house in top hats and soot-covered clothes, their oversized black brooms carried over their shoulders like bottlebrushes for giants. Inside the *Metzgerei,* or butcher shop, apron-clad women counted out their coins, inspecting and selecting fresh *Wurst* and *Braten* for the midday meal and sharing news and greetings in front of the impeccably clean white counter. Beneath a gathering of striped umbrellas in the spacious market square, farmers' wives arranged crates of apples and purple turnips in preparation for the open-air market. They organized buckets of pink and violet zinnias beside sunflowers, and stacked wooden cages of clucking brown hens and white ducks beside mounds of pumpkins. At the Krone, on the corner, old men sat in worn, wooden booths and sipped warm, dark beer, elaborating on the stories of their lives. It had always seemed to Christine that there was an urgency to their reminiscing, as if they were afraid of forgetting the important details, or afraid of being forgotten themselves. Behind tall, sandstone houses, compact, fenced-in yards housed flocks of chickens, tidy vegetable gardens, and two or three pear or plum trees. In medieval barns, hard-working farmers piled hay and fed beet scraps and withered potatoes to wallowing pigs. The second-story windows of each Bavarian half-timbered house were pushed wide open, spilling out feather beds to freshen in the sun.

Christine couldn't explain why, but this scene filled her with a mixture of resentment and love. She'd never dream of telling anyone, but there were times when she found it boring and predictable. Just as they were certain of night turning to day, everyone knew that at the end of the month, the whole village would gather in the town square to celebrate the Fall Wine Festival. And every spring, on the first of May, the Maypole would signal the start of the Bakery Festival. In the summer, the front of the town hall and the marketplace fountain would be overgrown with grapevines and ivy, and the young girls and boys would put on their red-and-white outfits to celebrate the Salz-Sieder Festival.

At the same time, Christine was aware of the simple beauty of her homeland—the hills, the vineyards, the castles—and understood that there would never be another place where she felt so loved and secure. This centuries-old Schwäbisch village, known for Hohenlohe wines and salt springs, symbolized home and family, and would always be part of who she was. Here, she knew where her place was. Like her younger sister, Maria, and two little brothers, Heinrich and Karl, she knew where she belonged in the order of things.

Until today.

Isaac's sudden appearance on her doorstep felt like a previously hidden clue on a treasure map, or a newly discovered fork in a familiar road. Something was about to change. She could feel it in the cool fall breeze.

Restless, she jumped to her feet and plucked two gleaming apples from the branches of the nearest tree. Isaac stood, and she tossed one in his direction. He snatched it from the air and dropped it into his pocket. Then he started toward her, and she ran, from one row of trees to the next, her long coat gathered up in her hands.

Isaac shouted and caught up to her, then grabbed her around the waist and spun her off the ground, twirling her around and around, as if she weighed no more than a child. The startled sheep scattered in all directions, then gathered, panting and staring, beneath an oak on the edge of the orchard. Finally, Isaac stopped spinning. Christine laughed and struggled to get away, but he wouldn't let go. Then she gave in, and he let her down, holding her close until her feet touched the ground. She looked into his eyes, her chest flushing with heat, her knees trembling. He wrapped her arms behind her back and drew her closer. Inhaling the intoxicating fragrance that was uniquely his—fresh-cut wood, spice soap, and clean pine—she swallowed, feeling his warm breath on her lips.

"I don't want to be with Luisa," he said. "She's nothing more than another little sister to me. Besides, she loves herring too much. She's starting to smell like a fish." He smiled down at Christine, and she lowered her eyes.

"But we're from two different worlds," she said in a quiet voice. "My mother says . . ."

He lifted her chin, put his fingers over her lips, and said, "It doesn't matter."

But Christine knew it mattered. Maybe not to her, and maybe not to him, but somewhere along the way, it would matter. According to her mother, she was wasting her time looking for affection from someone like him. He was the son of a wealthy lawyer, and she was the daughter of a poor mason. His mother grew roses and raised money for charity, while her mother scrubbed his family's floors and washed their clothes. He had attended school for twelve years and was now in *Universität,* studying to be a doctor or a lawyer; he hadn't decided which. She'd loved school and had received good grades, as long as she and her fellow students weren't being pulled out of class to gather a late harvest or pluck potato bugs from the farmers' fields.

Looking back, she found it ironic how hard she'd studied. Her foolish hope had been to be a teacher or a nurse. It wasn't until she was eleven, when she found out that it cost money to go to school for more than eight years, that she gave up on her dreams of being anything more than a good mother and a hard-working wife. Her parents, like the majority of the people in her village, didn't have the extra ten marks per month for middle school, or twenty per month, plus the cost of books, for high school. Bloom where you're planted, Oma always said. But Christine's roots were restless, wondering what it would be like in more fertile soil.

Isaac talked to her of classical music, culture, and politics as she stood at the ironing board starching his father's shirts. He talked to her while she worked in the garden, telling her he'd been to Berlin, to see operas and theater. He described the world—Africa, China, America—as if he'd seen it himself, using colorful descriptions of landscapes and people. He was fluent in English and had taught her a few words, and had read every book in the family library, some of them twice.

And then, there was the fact that the Bauermans were Jewish.

Isaac's father, Abraham, was fully Jewish. Nina was half-Jewish, half-Lutheran. It didn't matter that the Bauermans were non-practicing. Most of the people in the village saw them as Jewish. And anyone who was a member of the Nazi Party—although it was sometimes hard to tell who was and who wasn't—considered them Jews. Isaac had explained that, while his father would have liked his children to embrace his religion, his mother wasn't the type of woman who had the time or inclination to follow anyone else's rules. She didn't feel any more Jewish than she did Lutheran, so she wasn't about to force Isaac and his sister into making choices before they were old enough to make up their own minds. But in the Nazis' eyes, they were all Jews, and Christine knew that some of the people in her village would look down on the fact that he was a Jew and she was a Christian.

"Why are you looking so sad?" he said.

"I'm not," she said, trying to smile. Then he lowered his mouth to hers and kissed her, and she couldn't remember how to breathe.

After a few blissful moments, he drew away, breathing hard. "I told you," he said. "Luisa knows how I feel. We laugh about our parents trying so hard to make us a couple. She knows how I feel about you, and she wants me to be happy. And I have a confession to make. The real reason I came to see you today is because my father has given me permission to bring a date to our holiday celebration. And I'll feel a fool if you don't say yes."

Christine stared at him, wide-eyed, her heart leaping in her chest, making her think of the startled sheep bounding across the grass.

The Bauermans' December celebration was an important occasion, the one social gathering where all village officials, dignitaries, and lawyers, along with other influential people from nearby cities, always made an appearance. Christine didn't personally know anyone who had attended the party as a guest, because the people she knew were factory workers, farmers, butchers, and masons.

But last year, Mutti had allowed her to help in the kitchen with the caterers, arranging expensive cheese and teaspoons of black caviar on crudités and scalloped crackers. Delivering the food to the servers at the end of the hall, she'd been mesmerized by what she'd seen and heard, the colorful scene reminding her of picture pages from a fairy tale. The sound of violins filled the air, and sparkling champagne overflowed in crystal glasses. Men in their finest tuxedos and women in long, shimmering gowns seemed to float as they waltzed across marble floors, like flowers that had pulled up their roots from the cold winter garden and glided into the light and warmth of the grand house. A million tiny lights twinkled on every banister and molding, and a shining menorah lit every decorated room. A huge evergreen tree, covered in silver and gold, towered to the ceiling in the foyer. Mutti kept reminding Christine she was there to work, not to stand there, eyes wide and mouth open, bewitched like a silly schoolgirl.

Now Isaac was asking her to be his date at the biggest celebration in the village, not to arrange sandwiches and drinks on a silver tray, but to attend as one of those women wearing an elegant, flowing gown. His question hung in the air between them, and she had no idea what to say. As if to punctuate her hesitation, the rhythmic chop of a wood ax echoed from the valley below. Finally, the shrill whistle of a train declaring its arrival at the village station broke her trance.

"Aren't you going to say anything?" he asked.

"We used to watch from across the street," she said, smiling.

"What do you mean?"

"We used to watch you. Me and my sister, Maria, and my best friend, Kate. We used to watch the rich people stepping out of their automobiles in their fancy clothes to come to your parents' party. We saw you and your little sister greeting people at the door."

"Ugh," he said, rolling his eyes. "I hated that. All the ladies wanted a hug. And all the men patted me on the head like a dog. Even now, I'm taller than most of them, but they still insist on whacking me on the shoulder, saying things like . . . good boy, good boy, or your father's a good man, a good man."

"But you were so handsome in your black tuxedo. Kate and Maria thought so too. And little Gabriella is the spitting image of your mother, with her auburn hair and dark brown eyes."

"Well, I don't have to do that this year. Besides, Gabriella loves the job. She'll be happy to have it to herself. She loves the attention." Then, to Christine's surprise, his face went dark. "But I'm afraid there won't be as many people as usual."

"Why not?" she asked, suddenly afraid it had something to do with the reason he'd invited her.

"A lot of my parents' Jewish friends have left the country," he said. "Their invitations came back marked: 'Return to sender. *Adresse Unbekannt.*' "

The sudden change in his mood surprised her, and she tried to change the subject. She didn't want this glorious moment to be ruined. "I don't see how I can say yes," she said. "I don't have a nice enough dress."

"We'll find a dress," he said, reaching for her. "My mother has a closet full of them. And if you can't find one you like, I'll take you shopping. Either way, you'll be the most beautiful girl at the party." Then he kissed her again, and the rest of world, along with its cares and worries, disappeared.

A half hour later, they walked hand-in-hand out of the hills. In the fields, local farmers spread manure from horse-drawn wagons and tilled the remnants of summer wheat into the ground, using giant gray oxen to pull their plows.

To the east, a train was approaching, having passed through the village, its black length growing short and squat as it rounded the wide curve. Christine and Isaac stood near the crossing, his arms around her waist, to watch it pass. The locomotive picked up speed as it turned into the straightaway, then thundered past, hot currents of air pulling on their clothes and hair. Great swells of gray smoke billowed out from the hot stack, and the smell of burning coal filled the air. The giant cast-iron wheels clacked along the tracks, insistent and loud, consuming all other noise in the train's frantic, mighty rush toward its next destination. Christine laughed and waved to the passengers behind the glass windows, trying to imagine what distant and exciting places they were headed to. After the last car passed, she and Isaac ran all the way back to the village.

CHAPTER 2

Christine rubbed her thumb over the smooth surface of the stone inside her coat pocket as she walked, trying to remember every word Isaac had said. She wanted to memorize the strength of his arms around her waist, and the warmth of his kiss, so she could tell Kate every detail. If she hadn't been in such a hurry to get to her best friend's house, she would have stopped on the edge of the cobblestone street to take the stone out and look at it more closely. Instead, she smiled, pleased that he trusted her with something that meant so much to him. He'd kissed her again before they'd parted ways at the end of Haller Bridge, making her promise to find him when she came to work that afternoon, because he wanted to be with her when she told her mother that she wouldn't be able to work at the holiday party this year.

"I'll be in the garden," he'd said. "Trimming the blackberry bush and repairing the limestone fence."

"But how am I supposed to get out there? I have to pass through the house, and my mother will be waiting. . . ."

She could picture Mutti now—her spotless white apron, her red hair in a French twist—working at the massive oak island in the Bauermans' tiled kitchen, the wood-fired stove behind her, turbulent and hissing with sputtering copper pots and steaming kettles.

She imagined her mother's face when she looked up from kneading dough to see Isaac standing beside Christine, possibly holding her hand. Mutti would either smile and ask what was going on, or turn, her face blank, pretending to tend to a pot on the woodstove. If she turned away, it would be her way of showing disapproval, and Christine wasn't ready for anyone to ruin her day. Maybe they should wait. After all, the party was months away.

"There's an old access door in the stone wall on the west side, along Brimbach Strasse," he'd said. "I'll unlock it from the inside."

"But what if someone sees me and wonders what I'm doing?"

"Just open the door and slip inside," he'd said. "No one will notice." Then he reached in his pocket and folded something cool and hard into the palm of her hand. "Here," he said. "I want you to bring this to me this afternoon. It's a lucky stone my father gave me when I was eight. I was a big collector when I was little, dead insects, snail shells, pebbles, acorns, that kind of thing. But this is special. My father said it's from the Triassic period. See, it's got a snail fossil on one side. Maybe it's foolish, but I keep it in my pocket all the time, because that's when I first realized that there's a whole world out there, waiting for me to learn about and explore it."

She turned the stone over in her hand, smooth as silk on one side and indented with an intricate spherical pattern on the other, and said, "I don't think it's foolish."

"Well, you'd better bring it back to me, first thing, or my luck might run out. You wouldn't want to be responsible for me cutting my hand with the hacksaw or dropping a rock on my foot, would you?" Then he started across the bridge, sprinting in the other direction. "I'll be waiting for it," he called over his shoulder.

Now, she walked faster, bursting at the seams to share her news with Kate before going home to change. She and her best friend, Katya Hirsch, were only two weeks apart in age. Their mothers had been friends before they were born, and as newborns, they'd slept together in prams, bouncing along cobblestone streets on the way to market. As toddlers, they'd played together on a blanket in the sunny yard while their mothers picked plums. And as adolescents, they jumped rope for hours on end, dared each other to wade beneath Hangman's Bridge, cut each other's hair, and scared themselves silly with tales of the "Black Monk of Orlach," who haunted the woods, or the "Water Girls," who tricked people into falling into the river. Christine couldn't wait to tell Kate that she was in love.

As she made her way along the sidewalk, she smiled, listening to the comforting noises of the bustling village. The rhythmic scratch of birch tree brooms on stone sidewalks and the flap of clothes in the breeze was accompanied by chickens clucking in dooryards, roosters crowing from their perches on garden gates and Dutch doors, and cows thumping against the inside walls of half-timbered barns. Wagon horses clip-clopped along the cobblestones, while sows and hogs grunted and squealed, rooting in sour-smelling pens built between sidewalks and buildings. The high-pitched clang of metal striking metal and the smoky aroma of hot fires rose from farmyards, where blacksmiths shoed horses and farmers repaired harnesses and tools. Mothers called out back doors for their children, and snippets of laughter and conversation drifted from open windows, along with the smell of baking bread and frying *Schnitzel*.

Christine skirted the old and middle-aged women trudging along in front of her, wondering if they could remember the giddy thrill of passion before life had forced them to rush through their days without seeing the world. Wearing dark scarves around their worry-lined faces, they pulled miniature wooden wagons with chapped, calloused hands, wobbly spoke-wheels click-clacking along the cobblestones behind them. Their carts held barrels of cider or tins of fresh milk, burlap bags of cabbage or potatoes, or, if they were lucky, the carcass of a rabbit or a slab of smoked pork.

She hurried past little girls playing make-believe on front door stoops, their soft curls falling from knitted caps, their thin arms clutching tattered dolls as they poured imaginary tea and nibbled on pretend *Lebkuchen* and *Springerle* cookies. A group of shouting, ruddy-cheeked boys ran by, kicking a dented can, their scuffed shoes and short, patched trousers making them look like a band of orphans. She felt sorry for all of them, not just because of their hardship, but because they had to go on with their ordinary, everyday lives while hers had been forever changed.

It wasn't their fault the way things were. Opa recounted stories of the devastation and poverty in postwar Germany. In the years following the country's defeat, people had lived on bread made from rutabagas and sawdust, and typhus and tuberculosis were everywhere. Stores and shops had nothing but empty shelves, but it didn't matter, because even if they'd had the goods no one could afford to buy a potato, a bar of soap, or a spool of thread. Oma told Christine that they used to take baskets full of paper money to the store to buy a pound of butter, but even then it wasn't enough. The German mark had been worth little more than dirt, and instead of toys, children were given hundred-Reichsmark coins to play hopscotch and checkers.

Even now, people were without jobs, without food, frightened and desperate for relief. In these times, nothing went to waste, not a crust of bread, not a snip of cloth. Oma joked that when a farmer in Germany butchered a pig, he used everything but the squeal.

Almost everyone Christine knew, acquaintances and friends, struggled in the same situation or worse. She'd seen the hardships faced by others less fortunate than her own family, people without backyards for a flock of chickens or a patch for a vegetable garden. While Hitler and the Nazi Party promised freedom and bread, the necessities— bread, flour, sugar, meat, and clothing—were in short supply. A bag of sugar had to last six months, and when rye flour was available, Christine's mother and Oma baked huge loaves of crusty brown bread and hid them in a cool dresser drawer, like safely guarded treasures.

Mutti worked almost as hard keeping the chickens and goats alive as she did her children, because she knew how important they were to her family's survival. Vegetable scraps, fruit seeds, hard rinds of cheese, half-eaten crusts of bread, every leftover morsel was fed to them, especially when the ground was covered with snow or frozen and unyielding to chickens scratching for bugs. Christine and Maria cried when Mutti butchered a baby goat to feed the family, but they ate it anyway, because they never knew when there'd be meat on the table again. On weekends, people came out of the cities to barter with the farmers, trading their prized possessions—clocks, jewelry, furniture—for a dozen eggs, a slab of butter, or a scrawny chicken. Christine had even heard stories about city women being forced to search garbage for leftovers to feed their hungry children.

Thinking of this, she suddenly remembered how lucky she and her mother were to have steady jobs at the Bauermans', and a quivering shadow of anxiety passed through her. Her *Vater,* Dietrich, was forced to search for a new stonemason job every time one was finished, so his income level changed from month to month. In the past few years, there'd been less and less construction. For weeks at a time, he could do little more than hunt for rabbits, or plow a farmer's field in exchange for a burlap bag of old potatoes or a bushel of sugar beets Christine's mother could boil down into syrup to use for sweetener. There were more mason jobs in the large cities, but even if he was lucky enough to get the work ahead of a hundred other men, it took nearly all his pay to ride the train there and back.

This past year, Christine knew that her part-time wages had made a difference in her family's life, buying a crate of apples or a wheelbarrow full of coal. What if Isaac's parents let her go just to keep them apart? What if they let her mother go too? She slowed, wondering again if their class difference would be what mattered in the end. But Isaac had promised her that it wasn't important. More than anything, she wanted to believe him, so she pushed the thought out of her mind and walked faster.

Now, a block from Kate's house, she looked down at her shoes, hoping they hadn't gotten too dirty from her hike in the hills. It'd taken her parents over a year to save enough money to buy them, and she'd only had them for two months. Her mother wouldn't be happy if they were scuffed up and grimy. Her previous pair had been on her feet since she was thirteen, until her toes hung over the worn sole and the seams gave out. The new shoes she had on now were the same practical, high lace-up style everyone wore, but she loved the feel and look of the shiny black leather. As happy as she was to have them, she still felt bad having to pass down her "worn-down-in-all-the-wrong-places" shoes to fifteen-year-old Maria, who'd have to wear them that way until the shoemaker came to repair them with his miniature hammer and polish-stained hands.

Realizing that now, along with everything else, she had to clean and polish her shoes too, Christine started to run, remembering that she wanted to tell Maria, at home helping Oma care for six-year-old Heinrich and four-year-old Karl, about Isaac as well. As it was, Christine barely had time to tell Kate about the kiss and the invitation, and she was hoping to ask if she could borrow another dress before rushing home to change and clean up.

Kate's three-story house sat at the very edge of the sidewalk, sandwiched between two equally large stone houses, pink-and-red geranium petals from six green window boxes speckling the cobblestones out front. Christine looked up, hoping to shout through an open window, but the red-painted panes were pulled closed. She knocked on the door and stepped back, running her fingers and thumbs over her long braid again and again, like a spinner twisting wool into yarn.

After what seemed forever, the door opened, and Kate stood there, smiling, in a ruffled peasant blouse and blue dirndl, the bodice and hem embroidered with white edelweiss and purple hearts. Christine thought it odd that she was wearing an outfit usually reserved for weddings and festivals, and wondered where she was going. Then she noticed that Kate's pale, porcelain complexion was pinked with the easy flush of red-haired girls, and her green eyes looked glassy. She seemed out of breath, and, with one slender arm out to the side, looked like she was holding something out of Christine's view.

"What are you doing here?" Kate said, pushing stray pieces of hair from her damp forehead. She stole a glance to the side, then giggled in a high, unnatural squeal.

"What's going on?" Christine said. "Who's in there with you?"

"I really don't have time to talk right now," Kate said. From inside, a male voice mumbled, and Kate giggled again. Then, changing her mind, she said, "Promise you won't tell? You know Mutti would have the vapors if she knew."

Kate was an only child, fussed over by a fragile mother prone to headaches and dizzy spells that could only be cured by long hours in a dark bedroom. Her father, who owned a bakery and was older than Christine's father by fifteen years, did little more than roll his eyes at his wife's tendency toward drama and overprotectiveness.

"You know I won't," Christine said, wishing she'd gone straight home.

Smiling as if she'd won a grand prize, Kate pulled the young man into view, her pale hand gripping the open collar of his white shirt. His light blond hair was tousled, his thick lips red and chafed. Wearing black trousers and a navy vest similar to the outfit Isaac wore to *Universität,* he wrapped his arms around Kate's waist, resting his chin on her shoulder, and studied Christine with brackish-blue eyes.

"This is Stefan Eichmann," Kate said. "He was in fifth grade when we were in third, remember? He moved to Berlin the summer before sixth grade. But, lucky for me, he just moved back."

Christine held out a hand. *"Guten Tag,"* she said. "I'm sorry. I don't remember you."

"I don't remember you either," Stefan said, ignoring her outstretched hand. Dreamy-eyed, he pulled Kate closer, nuzzling her ear. Christine buried her hands in her coat pockets and squeezed Isaac's stone in her fist.

"Stefan and I ran into each other at the butcher shop yesterday," Kate said, playfully batting Stefan's lips away from her ear. "We found out we've got a lot in common. He's teaching me English, and he's promised to take me to the theater in Berlin!"

"How lucky for you," Christine said. "Well, it was nice to meet..."

"He can get free tickets!" Kate interrupted, squealing and practically bouncing up and down. "His father used to run one of the theaters there!"

"Your father must be an important man," Christine said, trying to think of an excuse to leave.

But then, Kate froze and bit her lip. She glanced back at Stefan. "Stefan's father died last year," she said, her voice flat. "That's why he and his mother moved back here."

Christine felt her face growing warm. "I'm sorry," she said. *"Bitte,* accept my sympathy for your loss."

Stefan straightened and jerked his head to one side, as if trying to work out a kink in his neck. "He left me and my mother penniless," he said, screwing up his mouth as if the words were laced with arsenic. "It was no loss."

Christine couldn't think of anything to say. She'd never heard anyone say such things about one of his or her parents, especially a *dead* parent. "Well," she said, turning to make her escape. "I really should be going. I'm sorry I dropped by unannounced. It was nice to meet you, Stefan."

"Wait," Kate said. "What did you want?"

"It was nothing," Christine said, hurrying down the steps. "I'll talk to you tomorrow."

"All right," Kate said. *"Auf Wiedersehen!"*

Christine ran the four blocks toward home, then hurried around the corner onto the main thoroughfare that intersected the top of her street. Kate was impulsive, so it shouldn't have surprised Christine to find her kissing a boy she barely knew. But there was something else about Kate's reckless behavior that bothered her, and, at first, she couldn't quite put her finger on it. Then it hit her. Finding Kate alone with Stefan, the two of them acting as if they'd been dating for months, made Christine realize that Kate would never understand how much it had meant when Isaac kissed her for the first time. *Maybe I'll just keep it to myself for now,* she thought, turning at the top of Schellergasse Strasse.

A manure-filled wagon harnessed to a team of oxen filled the steep, narrow street, blocking her way. Christine stopped in her tracks and groaned, thinking about how much time she would lose having to go around the block. The farmer, in overalls and muddy boots, was out of his driver's seat, pushing against the yoke and thrashing the animals with a leafy branch. The oxen snorted and stomped their hooves, struggling to pull the overloaded wagon up the hill, but they were only able to move it a few inches at a time. To Christine's relief, the farmer saw her and paused, waiting for her to pass. She nodded her gratitude and hurried forward, worried that her hair was going to stink like manure. She squeezed between the wagon and the weathered barn that abutted her parents' woodshed at the barn's back corner, careful to stay as far away from the sour-smelling muck as possible.

Then she noticed that sometime since she'd left that morning, a poster had been attached to the barn's dry timbers. "First Regulation to the Reich Citizenship Law," the title said in Gothic letters. After clearing the wagon, she waited for the farmer to inch the oxen forward, then went back to read the black-and-white poster. Beneath the title, in bold print: **"No Jew can be a Reich Citizen."** The center of the poster showed crude outlines of men, women, and children, below the questions: "Who is a German citizen? Who is a Jew?" The human figures were shaded black for Jew, white for German, and gray for *"Mischlinge"* or mixed race. Lined diagrams showed family trees, explaining who would be considered German or Jewish by the crossing of blacks, whites, and grays. Beneath that were drawings of banks, post offices, and restaurants, with signs that read: *"Verboten!"* with black and gray figures standing outside the doors. And then the warning: "Any person who acts contrary to the prohibition of section 1, 2, or 3 will be punished with hard labor, imprisonment, and/or a fine." Below that was paragraph after paragraph of fine print.

Isaac had told her that things were changing for Jews, but until now, she hadn't taken it seriously. Life in their hometown had always been ordinary and peaceful, and she didn't see how having a new chancellor could change that.

At first, Isaac's father and other visiting members of the family—uncles, grandfathers, and cousins—had agreed Hitler was another dirty politician, put into power by President von Hindenburg, Vice Chancellor von Papen, and conservative members of the aristocratic ruling class, along with big bankers and industrialists. These men wanted Hitler in a position to put an end to the republic and to return Germany to the days of the Kaiser. But then the chancellor had become dictator, putting himself and his followers above the law, and now, they were using that power to strip the Jews of their rights. In the past few months, anyone considered a Jew had been required to carry an identity card and register all wealth, property, and businesses. And as a result, in the Bauerman household, the loud exchanges had changed into hushed whispers, because it was too dangerous to discuss such things out loud.

Christine stared at the poster with clenched teeth, feeling angry pressure beneath her jaw. The manure wagon had crested the hill and turned the corner, so she ran back to the top of the street and looked both ways, searching the length of the main thoroughfare for other flat surfaces: buildings and high fences, any stone, wood, or stucco façade. Then she put her hand over her heart, certain it was turning to lead. Every hundred yards or so was another poster, but she'd been too busy thinking about Kate and Stefan to notice.

She returned to the announcement on the barn and examined the shaded figures again, trying to clear her mind long enough to remember the lineage of Isaac's family. According to the notice, a second-degree *Mischlinge* was a person with one Jewish grandparent. A first-degree *Mischlinge* had two, but didn't practice the Jewish faith or wasn't married to a Jew. Isaac had three Jewish grandparents: a full Jew.

But Herr Bauerman was an important lawyer. Surely that would matter. Just the other day, Isaac had told her how upset he'd been that his father had no choice but to do legal work for a Nazi officer from Stuttgart. Would these same people tell him that he and his family weren't allowed in banks and restaurants? Then she remembered Isaac telling her that some of his father's Jewish friends—doctors, lawyers, and bankers—had already left the country. Icy dread settled in her chest. What if Isaac and his family left too?

She scanned the wooden fence that surrounded her family's vegetable garden. On this side of the road, after the weathered barn and starting with her house, the row of homes and barns sat back from the street, leaving a rectangle of open space that allowed for front courtyards and sidewalk gardens. Her parents' garden filled the corner created by the end of the weathered barn and the length of their woodshed and house, and took up their entire front yard. It wasn't a tenth as big as the Bauermans', and there were no stepping-stones, hidden statues, or stone fountains, but it provided the produce necessary for her family's survival. Besides that, it was a source of pride to her mother, the patches of orange marigolds, yellow strawflowers, and blue snapdragons neatly planted between leafy rows of turnips, beans, potatoes, and leeks. Her father had even built a stone walk down the center and hung a bell on the garden gate, which was directly across from their front door and flanked on either side by plum trees.

To her relief, there were no warnings hung on their garden fence. She didn't want ugly posters to spoil her family's hard work, and she was certain her parents wouldn't want them either. Her parents' home was a three-story fieldstone and half-timbered house, handed down through the generations by her mother's family. Once a week, the stained-glass window in the upper half of the front door was washed and polished, the three hallways and two sets of wooden stairs between each floor brushed and mopped. The sidewalks were always swept, the garden always weeded. Even the winter storage room off the first-floor hallway was impeccable. Empty glass jars, waiting to be filled with produce or homemade jam, and cans filled with homemade liverwurst were neatly arranged on paper-lined shelves. In the small cellar, wooden bins, used to store apples, potatoes, turnips, beets, and carrots, lined the whitewashed walls.

A barn shared the roof and south wall of their house, which shared a roof with another barn, which shared a roof with their neighbor's house. The timber and stone façades on this side of her block were bare, devoid of Nazi propaganda, but across the street, the church sat on higher ground, and another poster hung on the stone retaining wall, next to the stairway opening.

Breathing hard, Christine scanned the windows of the surrounding houses, trying to decide if she should run across the street and tear down the poster. But an elderly gentleman, Herr Eggers, was leaning out his window, smoking his pipe and watching her. Not knowing if he was a member of the Nazi Party or not, she couldn't take the chance. The last thing she wanted, when things seemed finally to be going her way, was to be turned in for destroying Nazi property.

Instead, she hurried along the stone walkway between her house and the garden, pushed open the front entrance, and slipped inside, leaning against the heavy door to make sure it was latched and locked. In the first-floor hall, she slipped off her shoes and hurried past her grandparents' bedroom, then took the stairs two at a time. The smell of fried onions filled the house, and she knew that Oma would be in the second-floor kitchen, frying *Bratwurst* and *Spätzle* for *Mittag Essen,* the midday meal. If Christine was going to change and leave again without being pestered to take time for lunch, she had to get in and out without being noticed, because Oma's self-appointed mission in life was to get people to eat.

Christine tiptoed down the narrow corridor of the second floor landing, hurrying past the closed doors of the kitchen and front room with her shoulders hunched. She unbuttoned her coat and crept up the next set of stairs, careful to sidestep the squeaky first and third boards. When the kitchen door opened below her, she froze.

"Christine?" someone called above the sizzle of onions and the crackle of the wood-fired stove.

"Mutti?" Christine said, her throat suddenly hard. She went down the steps and stopped on the landing, gripping the banister with one hand. "What are you doing here?"

"I need to talk to you," Mutti said. "*Bitte,* come in here and sit down."

Christine moved from the bottom of the stairs, searching her mother's eyes as she entered the warm kitchen. Mutti closed the door behind her, took the pan from the fire, and set it aside.

For as long as she lived, the smell of cinnamon and sugar-glazed gingerbread would remind Christine of her mother's kitchen. The cast iron woodstove dominated one flower-stenciled yellow wall, massive and black next to a pile of split firewood. Kitty-corner to the stove, French doors led out to a balcony on the side of the house, created by using the roof of the woodshed. Opa had built a railing around the balcony, and it was protected between the house and the high wall of the weathered barn next door, the perfect spot for stringing a clothesline and for starting vegetable seeds in the spring. Along the opposite wall of the kitchen, a porcelain sink and high oak cupboards ran beside hinged casement windows covered by eyelet curtains. The push-out windows looked over a stone terrace and fenced backyard, home to brown chickens and a cluster of pear and plum trees. The enclosed area next to the back wall of the house was home to three brown dairy goats and their occasional kids, with an entrance to their indoor shelter, a converted cement-walled room next to Opa and Oma's sleeping quarters.

The evening and midday meals, *Vesper* and *Mittag Essen,* were eaten in the front room down the hall, but for breakfast, the entire family squeezed around the corner nook in the kitchen, the children on the booth's cloth-covered seats, the grandparents and parents on the short wooden benches. The scratched, pockmarked table, covered with a green and white oilcloth, had a large drawer in the center that contained mismatched silverware, a glass salt-shaker, and a crusty brown loaf of the daily bread. At this cozy corner nook, the morning coffee and warm bread with jam were savored, the dough for noodles and bread kneaded, the garden vegetables cut and sorted, and in the winter, when the kitchen was the warmest room in the house, it was where the family laughed and played games. And today, Christine had the feeling, it would be the place where she learned bad news.

Trying to slow her hammering heart, she slid into the booth, one hand in the pocket of her coat, fingers gripping Isaac's stone. Oma had done laundry that morning; the smell of lye soap lingered in the air, and the windows were still moist with condensation. Mutti sat down across from her, her blue eyes and the soft lines of her face unnaturally hard, her lips pressed together. She was wearing her house apron over a nut-brown dress, a dress normally reserved for work at the Bauermans'. Christine watched her mother fold her calloused, oven-scarred hands on the table in front of her, and felt beads of perspiration spring out on her forehead.

"We will no longer be working for the Bauermans," Mutti said, an uncharacteristic tremor in her voice.

Christine stiffened. "What? Why?"

"There are new laws," Mutti continued. "One of the laws forbids German women to work for Jewish families."

For a fraction of a second, Christine relaxed, realizing that the news had nothing to do with her and Isaac. Then she remembered the posters outside.

"Is that what those ridiculous posters say?" she said. "I'm not going to let some stupid law tell me where I can or can't work!" She stood, ready to bolt, but Mutti caught her wrist and held it.

"Christine, listen to me. We can't go to the Bauermans'. It's against the law. It's dangerous."

"I need to talk to Isaac," Christine said, pulling away and heading toward the door.

"Nein!" her mother shouted. "I forbid it."

Christine wasn't sure if it was the odd trace of fear or the determination in her mother's voice, but something made her stop.

"Herr Bauerman has been forced to abandon his office in town," her mother continued, her tone softer now. "He's no longer allowed to practice law. If you're caught going over there, you'll be arrested. The Gestapo knows we work there."

Christine said nothing. She just stood there, willing it not to be true. Her mother got up and put her hands on Christine's shoulders.

"Christine, look at me," she said, her eyes watery but stern. "One of the new laws also forbids any relationships between Germans and Jews. I know you care for Isaac, but you have to stay away from him."

"But he's not really Jewish!"

"It wouldn't matter to me even if he was. But it matters to the Nazis, and they're the ones making the laws. We have to do as we're told. I have permission to go there now, one last time, to pick up our pay. We'll need the money. But you're not going with me, do you understand?"

Christine lowered her head, covering her flooding eyes with her hands. How could this be happening? Everything had been so perfect. She thought of Kate and Stefan, happy and oblivious to all that had changed, their only concern Kate's overprotective mother. And then she had an idea. She wiped her eyes and looked at her mother.

"Will you take a note to Isaac for me?"

Mutti pressed her lips together, her forehead constricting further. After a long moment, she reached up to brush Christine's hair from her forehead.

"I suppose that won't hurt," she said. "Write the note quickly now, I don't have much time. But until things are back as they should be, you're not to see him." Christine started to turn, but her mother held her arm. "You're not to see him. Do you understand?"

"*Ja*, Mutti," Christine said.

"Hurry now."

Christine ran upstairs to her bedroom and closed the door. A few days earlier, she'd decorated the multipaned window in her room with fall leaves, a different species glued to each thick square of swirled glass: gold beechnut, yellow oak, red maple, and orange hickory. It all seemed so childish now. Now, the sparse room reflected the way she felt, bone-cold and empty as a cave, the cool drafts of the coming winter already making their way through the invisible crevices in the fieldstone and mortar walls and the undetectable cracks in the thick, dry timber. A pine armoire, her narrow bed, and a wooden desk and chair were the only furniture, and the threadbare rug on the tiled floor did little to ward off the chill.

She took Isaac's stone out of her pocket and held it in a fist over her heart while she searched her desk. Two sheets of leftover school paper were folded near the back of the drawer, and she found a stubby pencil between a stack of old books and her aged Steiff teddy bear, which used to growl when she squeezed his stomach but no longer uttered so much as a moan. She tucked the stone into the front right-hand corner of the drawer, took a book off the shelf, and held it beneath the paper. Then she sat on her bed and stared at the blank sheet, blinking through her tears. Finally, she wiped her eyes and began to write.

> *Dearest Isaac,*
> *This morning, I was so happy. But now, I'm frightened and sad. You were right about everything you tried to tell me about Hitler and the Nazi discrimination against the Jewish people. I apologize for not taking you more seriously. My mother just told me that we can no longer work for your family because of another new law. She says we can't see each other. I don't understand what's happening. Please tell me that we'll find a way to be together. I miss you already.*
> *Love,*
> *Christine*

She folded the letter into a wrinkled envelope she found in one of her books, sealed it, and took it to her mother.

"*Bitte,* set the table," Mutti said. She hung her apron on the back of the kitchen door and shoved her arms into her black wool coat. "The *Wurst* and onions are finished. Cover the pan and leave it on the edge of the stove to stay warm." She opened her handbag and slid the letter between her change purse and a pair of gray gloves. "If I'm not back within the hour, start without me."

Christine stood in the hall and watched her mother hurry down the steps, fear and anger pressing into her stomach like a slab of cold granite. It wasn't like her mother to fidget with her scarf and the collar of her coat, and the hard heels of her shoes clacked down the front hall even faster than usual. After Christine heard the front door close with a heavy thud, she made her way into the front room.

The front room doubled as the family and dining room, with an antique maple sideboard that held books, dishes, and tablecloths, an oak dining table and eight mismatched chairs, a horsehair couch, an end table for the radio, and a wood- and coal-burning stove. On the wall between the two front windows overlooking the garden and the cobblestone street was her mother's treasured tapestry, an embroidered landscape of snow-covered Alps, dark forests, and running elk. The wall hanging came from Austria, a souvenir from her parents' honeymoon. The only other decoration in the room was a cherry regulator with a gold pendulum that once belonged to Christine's *Ur-Ur Grossmutti,* great-great grandmother.

Oma was sitting on the couch, darning a sock from a tangled pile of leggings and undergarments that sat in her aproned lap like a multicolored cat. Her silver hair was braided and pinned in a neat circle around her head, her veined hands working in a steady rhythm. Beside her, the radio crackled and squawked, a man's commanding voice announcing more rules and regulations from the Führer. When Oma saw Christine, she turned off the radio, put down her needle and thread, and patted the couch cushion.

"Come sit by me, good girl," she said. "*Du bist ein gutes Mädchen.* Did you see your mother?"

"*Ja,*" Christine said, falling into the couch beside her.

"It's another sad day in Germany," Oma said.

Christine leaned against her, searching for comfort in her soft shoulder and familiar smell of lavender soap and rye bread. It was Oma who had taught her and Maria how to knit and sew, and Christine had fond memories of sitting next to her on the couch, working the yarn and cloth into doll clothes and miniature blankets while Oma hummed church hymns. Growing up, Christine had always looked to Oma for solace, whether to dry tears from a skinned knee, or to soothe a bruised ego from the rare parental scolding. It wasn't that her mother was cold or insensitive, but she was too busy, cleaning, cooking, and trying to keep food on the table for a family of eight. Oma would sit with Christine for hours, her soft, papery fingers caressing Christine's flushed cheeks and brushing stray hair from her furrowed brow.

But today it was impossible to find relief. Christine stood and looked out the window.

"Where is everyone?"

"Maria and the boys went to the railroad tracks to look for coal. And I sent Opa to the fields to find dandelion greens for one last salad before winter."

Christine pictured Opa in the countryside wearing his green Tyrolean hat, his hands shaking as he leaned on his hiking pole to pull edible weeds from the cold fall ground. He was probably talking to himself, or singing like he did in the kitchen whenever he fixed a chair or loose cupboard door just so he could be near Oma while she cooked and baked. By the time he finished his repair, there'd be flour on his shirt and nose and cheeks, left there by Oma shooing him out of her way.

"Should I go look for him?" Christine asked.

"Maria and the boys will bring him back in time for *Mittag Essen*," Oma said, dropping the wooden darning egg into a tattered sock.

Christine recognized the sock as her own, one of a thick wool pair she wore to bed in the winter, when she had to wear layers to bed because there was never enough coal to burn through the night. Her *Deckbed*, bedcover, was getting thin, and would stay that way until they had enough money to buy another bag of goose feathers from Farmer Klause. And if she had to run down the hall in the middle of the night to use the toilet, the frigid floorboards seeped through her socks like ice, making her shiver until she was tucked back beneath her covers. Food was scarcer in the winter too, with no fresh vegetables from the garden, milk from the goats, or eggs from the chickens. Now, without the extra income from their jobs, not only would she be waking up cold, she'd be waking up hungry too.

She bit her lip and turned away from the window, then went to the sideboard and pulled out eight dinner plates, wondering how long it would be before Isaac read her note. Today at least there *was* food.

CHAPTER 3

Christine took a deep breath and backed up to the dining room door, the oval serving platter full of browned onions and sizzling *Bratwurst* balanced in her hands. She pressed the handle down with her elbow and entered the noisy room, hoping her mother would be there, home from the Bauermans' and waiting at the table with the rest of the family.

In the back of her mind, she knew that Mutti would have come into the kitchen first, to put on her apron and help with the food. But today, she couldn't be sure of anything. Her thoughts were scattered, and the simplest tasks—setting out silverware, washing the field dandelions Opa had picked, mixing oil and vinegar for the dressing, reheating the meat on the stove—had taken all her concentration. Mutti had been gone twice as long as Christine had expected. What if her mother had changed her mind about giving Isaac the note? What if he wasn't home? What if he didn't write back? What if the Gestapo had arrested Mutti for going to his house? What if they found the note, arrested Isaac, and were on their way to arrest her?

On shaky legs, she carried the serving platter to the dining table. The jumbled clamor of Opa's deep laugh, Oma and Maria's banter, Heinrich and Karl's teasing, and her father's monotone droned like the chaos of a hundred kindergartners stuck inside on a rainy day. She tripped over Opa's hiking pole, which he'd propped against the corner of the table, sending it to the wooden floor in a clatter. Clenching her jaw, she set the platter on the table, the din from her family going on and on, as if she were invisible, then she set the hiking pole in the corner and went to the window to check for her mother. Heinrich and Karl were laughing and poking each other, and it was all she could do not to pound on the table and yell at them to be quiet.

"Come sit down, Christine," her father said. "Your mother will be home soon enough."

Christine did as she was told. She glanced at Vater, searching his black hair for the gray tint of cement dust, the telltale sign that he'd found a job. But his strong, tanned face and calloused hands were clean, his brown eyes hard with anxiety.

Unlike Mutti's family, who could trace their German roots back for centuries, Vater was originally from Italy, which explained his and Heinrich's dark features. The freckle-faced baby of the family, Karl, like Christine, had blond hair and blue eyes, as Oma and Opa used to, before age and hardship had turned them gray. It was a mystery to everyone where Mutti had inherited her red mane, but she had passed the reddish tint to Maria, whose waist-length hair was a shiny strawberry blond.

"Heinrich, Karl, it's time to be still," her father said. "Oma needs to say *Danksagung*."

The boys stopped wiggling and turned to face the table, obediently folding their palms on their laps. Maria had spent a good half hour scrubbing their hands and faces, but their fingernails were still black around the edges, with only six jagged pieces of coal to show for their efforts. Vater waited in silence, watching until they settled, then gave Oma a nod. Christine lowered her head. She dug a thumbnail into the hollow space between her knuckles, listening for the sound of her mother's footsteps on the stairs.

"Der Herr," Oma began.

A heavy thud-thud on the front door made Christine jump and Oma stop mid-prayer. Everyone had the same wide-eyed look of surprise, because even though they were late having lunch, it was unusual for anyone to come to the door at this hour. All across Germany, the hours between noon and two were set aside for the most important meal of the day, *Mittag Essen.* Shops and businesses wouldn't reopen even one minute before two o'clock. Christine and her father stood at the same time.

"I'll see who it is," Vater said. "Stay here, Christine. Everyone start eating. We've delayed long enough."

Christine sat back down and tried to breathe normally, wondering if the Gestapo would bother to knock. Maria dished a hot *Bratwurst* and a forkful of onions onto Oma's and Opa's plates. Christine picked up the dandelion salad and passed it to Oma, keeping her eyes on her father. As soon as he was out of the room, she went to the window.

A black army truck was parked on the street, gray columns of smoke spewing from the shuddering upright pipes behind the high cab, the white outline of the Iron Cross painted on the doors, a red flag with a black *Hakenkreuz,* or swastika, draped over the covered truck bed. Two men in Barbarossa helmets and black uniforms were unloading dark cubes from the back of the truck, handing them out to four other soldiers. Christine recognized them as SS, or Schutzstaffel, Hitler's Nazi security, and breathed a sigh of relief. It wasn't the Gestapo. She pushed open the window and looked down at the walkway between the garden and the front of her house. One of the men was at their door, talking to her father. From where she was, she could see that the dark cube in the SS man's hands was a radio.

"*Nein,*" she heard her father say. Then she saw him take the radio. "*Danke schön,*" he said.

"*Heil* Hitler," the soldier said, raising his arm in salute. She wasn't surprised that she didn't hear her father reply. The SS man took long, purposeful strides back to the truck.

Christine watched the other SS going door-to-door, identical radios in hand. Three of the men came back to the truck with old radios, just like the one her family had sitting on a white doily on the end table next to the couch. After a few minutes, all the men converged on the armored vehicle like rats to a hunk of Limburger cheese, disappearing into the passenger-side door and the canvas-covered back. The driver gunned the engine and started up the hill, thick-treaded tires gripping the cobblestones like oversized caterpillars inching their way along the street.

Just then, Mutti came around the corner of the weathered barn, purse hooked over her arm, eyes glued to the unfamiliar vehicle in the road. As quickly as it had arrived, the truck left, and Christine pulled the window closed. Should she just sit down and try to eat, or go and meet her mother at the door? Vater was aware of the new rules and regulations. It was his belief that if they just did as they were told, they'd be left alone. He'd be angry if he found out Christine had written a note to Isaac, and he'd be even more upset that Mutti had agreed to take it.

"Christine," Maria said. "Your food is getting cold."

Christine pulled out her chair and sat, certain that everyone could see her heart thumping beneath her dress. She looked around the table, wondering why, all of a sudden, everyone was so quiet. Opa sat with his head bent over his plate and gummed his food. Oma was cutting Karl's meat, while both boys swung their socked feet under their chairs and nibbled on fried *Bratwurst*. Maria was the only one looking in her direction, brows lowered as she chewed on a mouthful of dandelion leaves.

Maria wiped her lips with her napkin and whispered, "What's wrong with you?"

Before Christine could answer, her father came into the room, the new walnut-brown radio in his hands. He stood at the end of the table, shaking his head. Everyone stopped eating and waited.

"Unplug the radio, Christine," he said. He set the new radio on the table.

"What's going on?" Oma said.

Christine got up and unplugged the old radio. Then Vater lifted it off the end table and set it on the couch.

"Read this for us," Vater told her. He held out the bright orange tag that had been tied to one of the new radio's dials.

"The People's Radio," Christine read out loud. "Think about this. Listening to foreign broadcasts is a crime against the National Security of our people. Disobeying the Führer's order is punishable by prison and hard labor." She looked at her father, waiting for him to comment, but he said nothing, his face set in hard anger.

"What does it mean?" Maria said.

Just then, Mutti burst into the room, tying the strings of her apron around her back. Her face was flushed, her eyes watery and red, but she smiled at her family.

"Can I get anyone a cup of hot tea?" she said. When she saw her husband and Christine standing on the other side of the table, she stopped. "Is something wrong? What were the SS doing outside?"

"Come sit down," Vater said. "We have everything we need."

"Did you get out of work early today?" Maria said.

"We'll talk about that in a minute," Mutti said, running a hand over Karl's head.

Christine stared at her mother, hoping for some kind of sign that she'd given Isaac the note, that he'd written back, anything to let her know that Mutti had seen him. Their eyes met for a split second, but her mother looked away, pulled out a chair, and sat down.

"We've had a visit from some of Hitler's puppets," Vater said. "They were handing out these radios. The old shortwave can be tuned to stations from all over Europe. But this one can only be tuned to two channels, both run by the Nazi Party. They asked if we had any other radios. I told them no." He turned to face Heinrich and Karl. "Do you know why I told them no?" The boys shook their heads. "I told them no because we can use this old radio for firewood. We're not allowed to have it anymore. If they find out we still have it, they'll put us in jail. I'll go burn it in the kitchen stove right now, to heat the water for the dirty dishes." He picked up the old radio and left the room.

Christine knew what he was doing: What Heinrich and Karl didn't know couldn't hurt them or their family. They were too young to keep a secret. Vater was taking the radio to hide it. The idea made her light-headed. She picked up the platter of *Bratwurst*.

"Would you like me to reheat this for you?" she asked her mother, hoping she could get her into the kitchen alone.

"Nein, danke," Mutti said, taking the serving dish. "I'm sure it's fine." She pierced the sausage with her fork and scraped the rest of

the onions onto her plate, her pinched face a curious struggle between misery and an attempt to put on a happy smile for her family.

"Did you have any trouble?" Oma asked in a quiet voice.

"Nein," Mutti said. "Herr Bauerman was having problems getting our paychecks organized, that's all. And Frau Bauerman is beside herself. All but three servants have been let go. She asked me to make lists of what was in the root cellar and the pantry, that kind of thing. Everything took longer than I'd thought." She finally made eye contact with Christine. "Isaac was there, helping bring all the paperwork in from his father's office."

Christine braced herself. "Did you talk to him?"

Mutti opened her mouth to answer, but Vater came back in the room. She picked up her silverware and began to eat instead. Her father sat down, face red, shoulders hunched in frustration.

"If the other parties hadn't been so busy fighting," he said, "and if the country hadn't been in such economic turmoil, we wouldn't be in this mess! Hindenburg was too old and tired to put up a fight, otherwise he would have never appointed Hitler chancellor. That madman wasn't elected by the people! And now that he's arrested or murdered the opposition, he's selling National Socialism like a preacher sells religion. You do not question. You obey. If not, then they'll just get rid of you!" He slammed his fist on the table, and everyone jumped. The plates and dishes rattled, and Oma put a hand over her heart. Christine's mother put her arm around Karl, who started to cry.

"We just have to hope for the best and keep going," she said.

"But he allows the Gestapo to arrest anyone who criticizes him. Soon they'll control everything! They already control what we read, and now, they want to control what we hear. There are no newspapers but the Nazi newspapers, and now they control the radio too!"

Mutti cleared her throat and frowned at him. "Right now it's time to be together, share a meal, and be grateful for our family."

"And they'll throw you in jail for talking like that," Opa said, gesturing with his gnarled, blue-veined hands.

Opa's warning reminded Christine of the notice she'd read in the Nazi newspaper, *Völkischer Beobachter,* The People's Observer:

"Let everyone be aware that whoever dares to raise his hand against the State is sure to die."

Her father had always been outspoken, but until today, she hadn't thought anything of it. Then she remembered her mother having a talk with her and Maria a few months ago. She'd told them to keep quiet about their opinions, to be careful what they talked about in public. They should keep their conversations light, talk about the weather, the latest gossip, even boys, anything but politics. At the time, Christine had shrugged it off, wondering why her mother would think that two young girls would care about a subject so boring.

Vater sighed. "I'm sorry. Your mother's right. Now is not the time to talk about the problems of the world." He sawed a slice from his cold *Bratwurst,* put it in his mouth, and made an attempt to smile.

"Vater," Heinrich said in a small voice. "In school yesterday we were told we had to put together a family tree. The teacher said the Führer wants to know if there are any Jews in our family. He said we should do as we're told because we don't want to attract the wrong kind of attention. And our parents should bring in papers about birth, marriage, and baptism."

Vater stopped chewing and shook his head in disgust. Opa took another helping of dandelion salad, then passed the bowl to Vater, acting as if he hadn't heard a thing.

"Don't worry," Mutti said. "We'll help you."

Vater agreed, and they all finished their meals in silence. Christine forced herself to eat, then sat on her hands, waiting for Mutti to start clearing the table. As soon as her mother wiped her mouth and stood, Christine picked up the serving platters and followed her into the kitchen.

"I have a note from Isaac," Mutti said. She reached into the pocket of her coat on the back of the door. "But it will be the last one. Your father is to know nothing about it. And I told Isaac the same thing I told you. The two of you are not to be in contact again until this is over, do I make myself clear?"

"*Ja,* Mutti. *Vielen danke,*" Christine said. She held the note tight in her fist. "May I go to my room now?"

"Go ahead. It's been a long day for everyone."

Christine ran up to her room and shut the door. She sat on her bed and tore open the envelope.

> *My beautiful Christine,*
> *Meet me in the alley behind the Market Café,*
> *tonight at eleven o'clock. Be careful. Don't let any-*
> *one see you.*
> *Love,*
> *Isaac*

Christine fell back on her bed, the note clutched to her chest. How would she get through the next eight hours?

A few minutes later, just as Christine was pushing Isaac's tightly-rolled note through a loose seam in her Steiff teddy bear, someone knocked on her bedroom door. She jumped and forced the message into the bear's stuffing with one finger, then placed the tattered animal back on her desk and wiped her cheeks. She took a deep breath.

"*Ja?*" she said, trying to sound calm.

"It's me," Maria said in a soft voice. "Can I come in?"

Christine opened her armoire and pretended to straighten her clothes. "Come in! The door is open!"

Maria slipped into the room, closed the door behind her, and sat on the edge of the bed, arms folded to ward off the chill. "What's going on?" she said. "You were acting like a nervous chicken during *Mittag Essen*. And now you're up here hiding in your room."

Christine pulled a dress from her armoire and draped it over the back of her chair. "I'm not hiding. I'm just doing a little rearranging, that's all. I think I might have a couple dresses to hand down to you. I'm getting so tired of wearing the same old thing!"

Maria stood and took the dress from the chair. "*Ja?* Like this one? Your favorite?"

Christine looked at the outfit in her sister's hands. It was her blue Sunday dress, the soft cotton one with the gathered waist and embroidered collar. She loved that dress. And Maria knew it.

"*Nein,*" she said, taking the frock from her sister. "Not that one. I told you, I'm just rearranging my clothes."

"Mutti told me why she was home from work early," Maria said. "But that doesn't explain why you were so on edge."

"The Gestapo could have been at the Bauermans'!" Christine said, hoping her frown looked convincing. "They could have arrested Mutti!"

"But she's home now," Maria said. "She's safe." Maria moved closer and put a hand on Christine's arm, her head tilted, her eyes soft. "Remember that time everyone was supposed to bring a pear branch and three marks to school? Your teacher was going to have the branches carved into flutes, so everyone could learn how to play. You had the pear branch, but Mutti and Vater didn't have three marks to spare. Everyone in your class had a flute except you. Instead of crying, you polished the banisters and swept the stairs, even though they'd just been cleaned a day earlier. Mutti thought you were being helpful, but I knew. I saw the sadness in your eyes. You were keeping yourself busy so you wouldn't sit down and cry. Besides, you and I both know you barely have enough clothes to rearrange, let alone extras to give to me. I know you're sick of them, but Oma won't be making more anytime soon. Now tell me, what's really going on?"

Christine's shoulders dropped, and she sat down hard on the bed, her blue Sunday dress clutched to her chest. "Isaac loves me," she said, an overwhelming rush of joy and misery making it hard to breathe.

Maria gasped. "How do you know? How did you find out?"

"He told me. This morning."

Maria laughed and plopped down beside her. "Did you tell him you love him too?"

"Shhh ...!" Christine cupped a hand over her sister's mouth. "Vater might hear!"

Maria pulled Christine's hand away. "I'm sorry," she whispered. "So? Did you tell him? Did he kiss you?"

Christine bit her lip, smiling and nodding, her vision blurring with fresh tears.

"He kissed you!!" Maria practically squealed. "How many times? What was it like?"

"Shhh!" Christine said again.

Maria rolled her eyes. "I'm sorry!" she whispered. "I'm just excited and thought you would be too!" Then she noticed Christine's tears, and her face went dark. She grabbed Christine's arm. "Did Isaac say or do something to hurt you? Gestapo or no Gestapo, I'll go over there and straighten him out if he did!"

Christine shook her head. *"Nein,"* she said. "It's nothing like that."

"Well then, I don't understand. I thought you'd be happy!"

A lump formed in Christine's throat. How do you explain the best and worst day of your life happening at the same time? Maria had known all along how Christine felt about Isaac; she'd guessed her older sister was in love the same day Christine had realized it herself. Christine had come home that afternoon, daydreaming about Isaac's chestnut eyes and deep voice, remembering the way he'd smiled at her in the sunlit garden. With a warm, pleasant glow filling her abdomen, she'd been lost in thought, unusually quiet while helping Maria peel potatoes in the kitchen. Eventually, Maria nudged her and said, "What's his name?"

"Whose name?" Christine said, coming out of her trance.

"Whoever put that silly, glazed look in your eyes," Maria said, laughing.

In the end, Christine had admitted everything, swearing her sister to secrecy in their usual way: "Promise to God, all included, nothing counts." The made-up phrase meant Maria had sworn to God, with no way out because it included everyone in the room and discounted the power of crossed fingers or whispered confessions to take it back. It was their private way of knowing a promise was real. So far, Maria had stuck to her oath about Isaac, just like she'd stuck to her promise not to tell when twelve-year-old Christine and Kate had snuck off to get their fortunes read by gypsies camping in the forest, or the time Christine had spilled Mutti's only bottle of perfume on the bedroom rug. But that had been a long time ago, in a different world, back when they were children, before the Nazis made the rules. Things were different now. People's freedoms, and very possibly their lives, were at stake.

Christine thought of Isaac's note, hidden inside her silent teddy bear. The thought of meeting Isaac later, in secret, sent an electrifying current of excitement and fear through her body. She could barely contain herself and wished Maria would go back downstairs before she revealed everything. She wondered if this was what it felt like to be insane, ecstatic and miserable all at the same time, ready to weep one minute and rejoice the next, unable to explain it to anyone. More than anything, she wanted to tell Maria about the message and the secret meeting, but in the fear-charged atmosphere the Nazis had created, she was afraid Maria would try to keep her safe by telling her parents. Instead, she told her sister about the kiss in the orchard, about Isaac's strong hands and soft lips, about the surprise invitation to the holiday party she'd never be able to attend. It was difficult not having someone to confide in, but even "Promise to God, all included, nothing counts" wouldn't work this time. Christine couldn't risk it.

"Just because you can't work for his family doesn't mean you can't see him!" Maria said. "When you're in love, you can't let anything stop you!"

"The Nazis aren't just anything."

"What do you mean?"

"Mutti didn't tell you about the other new law?" Christine said. "The one that forbids us to be together because Isaac is Jewish?"

Maria's eyes widened, and her mouth fell open. "Oh *nein!*" she said, pounding her fists on her knees. "How is that possible? Who do those *Scheisse* head Nazis think they are?"

Despite her heartache, a small, half crazy-sounding chuckle erupted from Christine's lips. Maria never swore. She tried to be a good Christian in every way, from never missing church to reminding them all to say their prayers every night. And she always admonished Vater for cussing. It was like hearing Oma use bad language.

"Why are you laughing?" Maria said.

"I'm sorry," Christine said. "It's just, hearing you call the Nazis names . . ."

"Well, they are *Scheisse* heads, are they not?"

"*Ja,*" Christine said. "They're worse than that. But be careful. Don't let anyone outside the family hear you say things like that."

"I know," Maria said, pulling Christine close. "This just makes me so mad! I don't understand any of it!"

"Me either," Christine said. Ever so slightly, Maria rocked her big sister back and forth, and Christine found herself thinking again what a wonderful mother Maria was going to make someday. There was no doubt Maria would smother her babies with love. Of all the members of their family, her little sister was always the first to hand out hugs and kisses. Whether welcoming their father home from work, or kissing her little brothers' bumps and bruises, she was the most physically affectionate person Christine had ever known. But now, Christine could tell, hugs were the only comfort her sister could offer. Like everyone else, Maria didn't know what to say when it came to the unbelievable things the Nazis were doing.

"Don't worry," Maria said. "This won't last forever. It can't. It just can't. And besides, love conquers all, right?"

CHAPTER 4

At ten forty-five that night, Christine opened her bedroom door and listened, her heart in her throat, Isaac's lucky stone clenched in her fist. At first, she thought the house was silent, her family sound asleep in their beds, but then, her stomach dropped. The radio was still on in the living room, a tinny, frenzied voice chiding the quiet hours of darkness. For the first time in recent memory, her parents were up past ten.

Two hours before, she'd gone downstairs to say good night, certain that everyone would be getting ready for bed. To her surprise, she'd found Mutti and Vater in the living room with Oma and Opa. They were sharing a warm beer, another bottle warming on the woodstove, and listening to the new radio, her father and Opa at the table, Oma and Mutti on the couch. Christine stood beside Vater's chair and listened to Hitler's brusque voice, wishing he'd end his tirade so her parents and grandparents would go to bed.

"I am personally taking over command of all armed forces," Hitler shouted. "We have successfully completed the Anschluss, the annexation of Austria into Germany, and so, my homeland has finally come home. After years of persecution and oppression, ethnic Germans in the Sudetenland have become part of greater Germany. Soon, the master Aryan race will have the *Lebensraum*, 'living space,' we deserve!"

"That madman wants to take over the whole world," Opa said.

Oma shushed him and leaned forward. Mutti looked up at Christine, her eyes tired and puffy.

"Are the boys asleep?" she whispered.

"*Ja,* and Maria too," Christine said, hoping Mutti wouldn't notice her quick, short breathing. She'd thought that by the time she wanted to sneak out later, everyone would be fast asleep, but here they were, so engrossed in the radio they looked like they were going to be up all night.

"You look tired," Mutti said. "Why aren't you in bed?"

"I'm going up now. I just wanted to say *gute Nacht.*"

Mutti stood and gave her a hug. "Don't be worried if you hear the sound of the old radio coming from our room," she whispered in Christine's ear. "But let us know if it's too loud."

"I will," Christine said, wishing her father had burnt the old radio in the kitchen stove. Instead, her parents had hidden the radio beneath their bed, in a small wooden storage box with a folded blanket over the top, to make it look like a chest full of linens. It was just one more thing to worry about. She already felt shaky and out of control, tossed about by the twists and turns of life, like a broken twig swept away on a raging current.

Pretending to be interested and trying not to fidget, she forced herself to listen for a few more minutes, afraid they would ask what was wrong. When she couldn't stand it another second, she said good night and went up to her bedroom, crawling beneath the covers in her dress, just in case her mother came in to see if she was all right.

That afternoon and early evening had been the longest of her life, even though she'd tried to keep herself busy by cleaning out the chicken coop and pulling the dead plants and fall weeds from the garden. Now, peering out into the dark hall, she realized that someone could come out of the living room and catch her sneaking down the stairs. Her heart thumped against her ribs as she waited for her eyes to adjust. Then, holding her breath, she gripped the banister and crept down the flight of steps. Every creak echoed like a gunshot through the empty halls, and she froze with each squeak, ready to run if the living room door opened. Forever passed before she reached the first floor. Behind the bottom staircase, she stood on her tiptoes and reached for the extra key hidden above the cellar door, her fingers blindly searching the narrow lip of the wooden doorframe. Once she found it, she slipped on her shoes, unlocked the front door, and slid outside into the cool hours of darkness.

At last, she was free in the moonlit night, hurrying down the street on her tiptoes, stealing glances over her shoulder to make sure she'd escaped undiscovered. Her breath plumed out into the cold night air, misty vapors swirling past her as she ran, like the vanishing remnants of lost spirits. Avoiding the pools of yellow light cast on the glistening cobblestones by street lamps, she turned left at the bottom of the hill, then slowed, a safe distance from her house. Here and there, light burned in the windows of half-timbered houses, and she could see hunched silhouettes gathered around radios, smoking and drinking and gesturing, like animated storybook characters drawn on living room walls. She hurried from one tall, gabled house to the next, keeping close to the edges of deep doorways and granite balustrades.

For the next six blocks, her lone footsteps echoed along the stone avenues. Suddenly, she felt the presence of someone behind her. She slowed and held her breath, ready to turn and run. Then a cat yowled, and she let out a sigh of relief, turning to see the marmalade-colored feline behind her, tail up, back arched, legs stretched, as if padding along the sidewalk on its tiptoes. She shooed it away. It took off across the street and disappeared down a dark alley.

At the end of the last block, she moved to the other side of the village square, entered the narrow street beside the Market Café, then turned into the shadows behind it. Scattered puddles from the evening's earlier rainfall gathered in the uneven cobblestone alley, where they shimmered like pools of black oil. Isaac was sitting on the steps leading into the back of the café, the full moon reflected in a puddle at his feet. He stood when he saw her.

"Are you all right?" he asked.

She ran into his arms. "I am now," she said, breathing hard. The anxiety-filled hours leading up to this moment melted away as he kissed her on the cheek, the forehead, and finally, the mouth. When he released her, she could barely see his face, his familiar features obscured by the deep gloom. Behind him, a blue shaft of moonlight angled across the alley wall. She pulled him toward it.

"What are you doing?" he said, resisting.

"Come into the light. I want to see your face."

"*Nein.* Someone might see us."

"Oh," she said, moving toward him. "I'm sorry. I didn't think of that."

"Did anyone see you?"

"*Nein.* The streets are empty."

"And you didn't tell anyone about this."

"Of course not. Don't you trust me?"

"It's not that," he said, pulling her close again. "Right after your mother left, the Gestapo came to our house. They asked the remaining help for their identity cards to make sure only Jews were left under my parents' employment. They took my father's papers, legal files, letters, addresses, everything."

"But it won't stay this way," she said. "People won't put up with it. Things will be back to normal soon."

"*Nein,* Christine, they won't. My father is trying to talk my mother into leaving for America. My uncle is there, and my grandparents, aunts, and cousins went back to Poland. But she won't go. Her parents and sisters are still in Berlin, and her brother is in Hamburg. She thinks because we're half-Christian and German, they won't do anything to us."

"See, she's right. Why would Hitler do anything to German citizens?"

"It's dangerous just for you to be here with me!" he said too loudly. Then, catching himself, he lowered his voice. "There are laws against relationships between Germans and Jews."

"I know," she said, laying her head against his chest. "My mother told me. But it doesn't make any sense. Like your mother said, you're half-Christian, and you're still German. Your grandparents' religious beliefs can't change that."

"The Nazis don't see it that way."

"What are we going to do?" she said. "I have to see you."

"I don't know," he said, the unmistakable chafe of frustration in his voice.

She looked up, trying to read his eyes hidden in his shadow-covered face. Before she knew what was happening, his lips were on hers again, and she trembled with a confusing mixture of fear and ecstasy. When they parted, she spoke first, breathless.

"We'll meet right here, every night."

"*Nein,* it's too risky." She didn't want to let go, but he pulled away and leaned against the stucco wall of the café. She held her breath, dreading what he was going to say next. Finally, he sighed and said, "Once a week will have to be enough. Even then, we're taking a big risk. But first, you have to tell me that you realize how much danger you're putting yourself in. I have to know that you understand. You can't tell anyone, not your best friend, not even your sister."

"I won't tell anyone. And I won't get caught."

He reached for her, and she leaned into him, her hands gripping his muscular shoulders. "When we're together," he whispered, "we'll only see each other, not the ugliness around us." Then he kissed her again, with a hungry, open mouth. She wanted to disappear into his arms, carried away to another time and place, back to this morning when she'd thought that everything was right with the world. But then he pulled away and said, "You'd better go."

"Wait," she said, reaching into her pocket. "Your stone."

"Keep it. So you don't forget me."

"I could never forget you." She folded the stone into his hand. "You said it was your lucky stone. Right now, you need it more than I do."

He kissed her again, then put the stone in his pocket. "Hopefully, all of this will be nothing but a memory someday, just like the snail who left the fossil in that rock. We'll meet here at the same time next week. Can you do it?"

"I'll be here."

Then they kissed again, long and hard, and she wished for it not to end. When it was over, he turned and walked toward the opposite end of the narrow corridor, disappearing around the gray stone corner of the café. She lingered, shivering, and listened to his fading footsteps, hoping he would turn around and come back. But little by little, the quiet night grew silent, and she knew he was gone. With the cold fingers of fear and loneliness wrapped around her heart, she made her way out of the alley, crossed the empty square, and hurried home.

A million flickering stars dappled the sky above her house as she stood looking up toward her parents' living room window. The light was still on, and she could see faint shadows high on the wall, her father leaning back in his chair, Opa's head bent, chin to his chest, as he dozed. What would they think if they knew she was not in her bed, but out here, alone, in the dark street? What would they think if they knew she'd just met Isaac in a cold, wet alley?

Back in the house, she moved in slow motion, locking the heavy front door and taking the stairs one at a time. She paused between each step to listen for any sign she'd been heard, surprised that her parents were still awake, listening to the insistent, tinny voice of Hitler. Instead of subsiding once she was safely back inside, the miserable clutch of fear settled in her stomach, like an ancient boulder at the bottom of a lake.

CHAPTER 5

Over the next few weeks, more and more posters went up in the village, one claiming "All of Germany listens to the Führer on the People's Radio." Another showed Hitler—shoulders back, a hand on one hip—staring into the distance above the words: "One People, One Reich, One Führer." The newest poster hung outside the bakery, the butcher shop, and every church and store. It showed a handsome blond couple with two flaxen-haired, rosy-cheeked children, above the slogan: "Marry well—for race, health, and party membership!" When Christine saw the perfect Aryan family smiling merrily on every wall, it made her think of the latest directive the Nazis had issued: the list of unacceptable baby names. *What will be next?* she wondered. *Will they tell the German citizens what to eat and wear?*

At night, as she made her way along the deserted streets to meet Isaac, the Nazi posters shimmered in the dark, like birthday candles in a tomb. She thought about ripping them down, taking them home, burning them in the woodstove. If she got caught, she could always use the excuse that they were out of firewood and coal. But fear outweighed anger, so she tried to ignore them and move on.

Dwelling on her thoughts wouldn't change anything. Time was the only thing she had on her side, because it was the only power that could command change. They'd have to wait this out and hope someone would overthrow Hitler, or that somehow the Nazis would come to their senses. She thought it ironic how, only weeks before, she couldn't wait, had been downright impatient in fact, to know what adventures lay before her. If someone had told her that her life would include middle of the night rendezvous because it was illegal to love someone, she never would have believed it. But she refused to surrender to bitterness or self-pity.

Instead, she counted the days between their secret meetings, remembering Isaac's gentle kisses and the way his mouth cocked to one side when he smiled. Even though they'd openly professed their love for one another, their first few encounters had been brief and awkward, filled with self-conscious moments of silence until they thought of something else to say after the initial "hello" and "I missed you." The world had changed by leaps and bounds in a matter of weeks, and it seemed pointless to talk about everyday things. The only thing that made sense, the only thing they understood, was what they were feeling for each other. And for that, they needed few words. Each time they met, they felt more at ease. It wasn't long before conversation became easier, silences became more comfortable, embraces more familiar, and kisses more urgent.

"It seems almost too easy to walk the streets at night without being seen," she said at their fourth meeting. "They're always deserted." They were holding hands, side-by-side on the café steps, hunched together against the cool nighttime breeze.

"People arc keeping to themselves," Isaac said. "They only leave home to do important errands and shopping. Everyone's afraid of being stopped and questioned. I've been thinking we should meet closer to your house. I don't mind walking a little farther."

"But why?" she said. "I'm not worried about getting caught. I could just let my eyes water and tell them that I was out letting off steam because I had a fight with my parents."

"Because it's less suspicious for a man to be out late. It's too dangerous for a woman. I'd never forgive myself if something happened to you."

"But what about you? Once they check your papers . . ."

"If the Gestapo comes into the village at night," he interrupted, "I'll hear their vehicles. I'll have time to run and hide."

"Oh," she said, teasing him. "So you think I can't run?"

"Not as fast as I can."

"Would you care to prove it?" She stood and let go of his hand.

"Nein," he said. "Sit back down."

"Ach nein," she said. "You can't get away with saying something like that and not have the courage to prove it."

He stood and wrapped his arms around her waist, squeezing tight. "Go ahead and run," he said. "I'm right behind you."

She tried to pry his arms open, but it was no use. He was too strong. "That's not fair."

"See how helpless you are?"

"It's your fault."

And then they were kissing, any worries about running and hiding melting away.

A week later, Christine's confidence in her ability to fool the Gestapo received a crushing blow when she overheard Vater telling Mutti about a friend he used to work with, a Catholic man married to a Jewish woman.

"I was in the hall," Christine told Isaac. "I don't know why I didn't just go into the kitchen. It wasn't as if they were trying not to be heard. I guess I just felt . . ."

"Guilty?" he said.

"I was going to say scared."

"What did he say?"

"Vater's friend had taken the train to Stuttgart to visit his sister on her birthday. When he arrived on the platform, a man stopped him and said he was with the Geheime Staatspolizei, Secret State Police. But he was in plainclothes. He asked Vater's friend where he was from and where he was going. The friend showed his papers, and the policeman said to follow him to the Gestapo building opposite the train station. Inside, a second officer took the presents Vater's friend had brought for his sister, mint tea from his wife's garden and a tin of goat cheese. They accused him of stealing these things and told him he couldn't ride the train anymore. They said if they saw him at the station again, he and his Jewish wife would be sent to a work camp."

"What are you saying?" Isaac said. "Do you want to stop seeing me?"

"That's not it at all. I'm not saying anything. I just wanted to tell you. Vater said the Gestapo know everything."

"Did you hear the announcement on the radio?" he asked. "It's the law now. Everyone has to use the official greeting 'Heil Hitler.' "

"I heard it," she said. "Everyone raises their arms and does what they're told."

"And you? Are you doing what you're told?"

She looked at him, trying to read his face. Would he be offended if she said yes? "At first, I felt ridiculous and refused. But now, after hearing Vater's story . . ."

"You'd better do it," he said. "You don't want to draw attention."

Within two months, they'd relocated their secret meetings closer to her house, to a wine and root cellar tunneled into the side of a hill. The tree- and shrub-covered mound ran behind a row of shops and cafés on the other side of the road that intersected the bottom of her street, in a rutted, woodsy area cut by a creek used to power the local grain mill. The cellar belonged to Herr Weiler, the butcher, but he shared the storage space with the other restaurants and cafés. A rusty padlock that Isaac opened without struggle, or evidence of their break-in, secured the recessed, moss-covered door. Inside the stone room, oak wine barrels and timber shelves lined with dusty bottles ran the length of one curved wall. The back of the long, narrow space was filled with crates full of turnips and potatoes.

As tempting as it was to open the spigot of a wine barrel and have their fill, they touched nothing, simply grateful to have a hidden place, protected from the cold winds of the approaching winter, where they could talk and kiss without worrying about being seen. Christine brought a short candle that, when lit, let off a thin trail of gray smoke that drifted up toward the square airhole in the curved ceiling, where it disappeared into the night. Sometimes Isaac brought cheese and fruit, or slices of his mother's famous *Pflau-menkuchen*. They tipped over an empty wine barrel, covered it with a red-and-white checkered tablecloth, and turned the root cellar into a romantic, isolated hideaway.

While the world outside churned in chaos, they talked and laughed, swaying to the music he softly hummed, dry and hidden in the dirt-floored tunnel. They made plans for a time when the world would be sane again, praying it wouldn't be too long. But as the weeks went by, they began to wonder if it would ever happen.

"They said it was a spontaneous reaction to the murder of a German Embassy official by a Polish Jew," Isaac told her in late November, during their discussion of the past few weeks. "But my father and I agree that it was planned and deliberate. It wasn't civilians angry about what happened. It was the SS dressed in civilian clothing. They're the ones who looted Jewish-owned businesses and beat Jews in the streets."

They were sitting on their coats, leaning against the potato crates, her legs folded beneath her skirt to avoid the chill radiating out of the dirt floor. He had his arm around her shoulders, his chin resting on top of her head.

"The paper showed pictures of synagogues on fire in Berlin," she said.

"They're calling it Kristallnacht, because of all the broken glass. Ninety-one Jews killed and twenty thousand thrown in jail."

She looked up at him in surprise. "For what? Fighting back?"

"Who knows? The SS don't need a reason." He clenched his jaw and scraped the heel of his shoe along the dark, packed earth, as if he wanted to kick or punch someone. "If Hitler had his way, he'd run the Jews out of Europe. My parents had to pull Gabriella from school because now it's illegal for Jewish children to attend non-Jewish schools. Jews will have nothing," he said, his voice at once angry and sad. "I've had to stop attending *Universität*. My parents are using their savings just to keep food on the table. I feel like I'm being watched when I go to the grocery store. I can't fight back. I can't do anything. I'm not going to have a job, or money, or an education. I'm not going to have anything. I love you, Christine, but how will you ever make a life with me?"

She put her hand on his cheek. "You're forgetting something. I don't have anything now. My parents are poor, but they're together. And I've never been happier in my life. I haven't changed my mind. The only thing I want is to be your wife."

At that, he smiled and pulled her close, kissing her and guiding her backwards until they lay on their coats side-by-side. She started to shiver, despite not being cold. He pulled the edges of his coat over her upper arms, hovering above her on his elbows. His chestnut eyes were soft, filled with love, and she was overcome by the warmth and depth of his affection. She wrapped her arms around him, and he kissed her, open-mouthed and breathing hard, his heart pounding against her breasts. Then she was pulling at his shirt, fumbling for the buttons, her own breath coming heavy and fast. His warm hand moved from her waist to the back of her thigh, squeezing and groping on the outside of her skirt. He kissed her neck, the pale, deep hollow above her collarbone, the warm, soft mound of her cleavage. And then, without warning, he stopped and shook his head.

"We can't do this," he said, panting. "If you were to get pregnant . . ."

Her stomach tightened, then she wilted, the suppression of desire making her entire body ache. "I know," she breathed.

He laid his head on her chest, and she could feel his body trembling. "If they found out you were carrying a Jewish child, they'd send us to prison. You, me, and our baby."

"I know. I know. I know. Just hold me."

She gritted her teeth, trying to calm her thundering heart. Isaac's breathing slowed, and she felt his body loosen and relax. Then, all of a sudden, the weight of his head on her chest made her think of a baby lying there: Isaac's child, his infant son or newborn daughter, nuzzling her breasts, looking for comfort and nourishment. *Will it ever be?* she wondered. *Will we ever be allowed to be together, to live like everyone else, happily married, with a house and children, to enjoy the most basic human rights?* Tears sprang to her eyes, and she wrapped her arms tighter around him, clutching his shirt in her hands, wishing she could spend the rest of her life in his embrace, suddenly afraid that somehow, somewhere, he was going to be taken away from her. *How did it come to this? How did I find myself living in a world where a person can be thrown in jail for loving someone? Where an innocent baby, a new life created by two people willing to work and sacrifice to give that child whatever it needs, can be locked away or worse, just because one or both of its parents are Jewish? This is a nightmare,* she thought. *It must be. Any minute now I'm going to wake up and find out none of this is real.*

She pinched her hand, but nothing happened. She was still hiding in a root cellar, lying on a dirt floor, the love of her life in her arms, both of them considered criminals. She stared at the amber glow of the candle flickering across the curved ceiling, suddenly aware of the icy cold seeping up through the earth, through her coat and into her skin, seeking her muscle and bones, searching for her heart, a heart that suddenly felt hollow with sorrow and fear. *What's going to happen to us?* she thought, tears soaking her hair.

That winter was the worst in recent memory, with furious snowstorms every few weeks and howling winds that blew flurries sideways, creating towering drifts in the streets. It was days before the horse-pulled plows were able to clear the network of narrow avenues and winding boulevards, just in time for the next big storm to fill them up again.

Christine's mother pulled the shutters closed, lined them with old newspapers, and hung tablecloths and sheets over the inside of the front windows. But the dry, powdery snow still found its way inside, to form tiny drifts, like miniature sand dunes, on the wooden floor. As soon as the sun went down, Mutti stopped feeding coal to the stove and gave them each a blanket to wrap around their shoulders during dinner. Once the coal burned down to nothing but a pulsing mound of black and orange embers, they went to bed wearing hats, mittens, and extra layers of clothes.

As 1938 turned into 1939, Christine found herself cursing the weather. There were times when the snow was so high that she and Isaac could only stand outside the root cellar, shivering and hugging until he told her to go home. To add to her misery, he decided they should only meet once a month, because even though they did their best to stir up the snow and wipe out the evidence, they were leaving tracks and footprints on private property. It wouldn't be long before someone got suspicious.

Even when the snow started to melt, Isaac insisted they keep to the once a month schedule, because the secret police were making regular sweeps of the village now, going door-to-door to see that everyone had the proper papers. When people were this afraid, seeing someone on the street at night might cause panic. And what if someone recognized them?

Two days before the official start of spring, the radio announced that Hitler had sent troops into Bohemia and Moravia, and the Führer had personally arrived in Prague eight hours later. By the time the tulips and crocuses were up, detained Communists, Socialists, labor leaders, and enemies of the state were being sent to a new work camp in southern Germany called Dachau. In May, there was an announcement that any child below the age of three who was suspected of suffering from a serious hereditary disease was required to be registered with the state.

Christine moved through the weeks in a trance, counting the long hours until she could see Isaac again. During the day, she walked to the mill and the store with her head down, certain that people would read the secret in her eyes. Once, a military truck drove through the open-air farmer's market, and it was all she could do to keep her hands from shaking as she counted out coins for a tin of cheese.

According to Christine's mother, Kate was officially dating Stefan. To everyone's surprise, Kate's mother was thrilled, and she'd asked Mutti to tell Christine that her daughter was too busy to get together. In truth, Christine was relieved. She wouldn't have been able to listen to Kate's swooning, giggle-filled stories without bursting into tears. When Christine saw Kate and Stefan walking in the streets hand in hand, she spun around and went the other way, or ducked into the nearest alley and ran out the other side.

Through it all, Christine was grateful to have Maria, a sister who would always be there for her, no matter what. While they worked side by side, preparing the garden for planting, beating the feather beds in the backyard, hanging sausage to dry on broomsticks balanced across open shutters, it was comforting to know someone understood why her eyes sometimes filled for no reason. Christine purposely avoided talking about Isaac because she was afraid she'd accidentally reveal their secret, and, thankfully, Maria never pushed the subject.

Still, Maria knew her sister's heart. On more than one occasion, she squeezed Christine's hand under the dinner table, seeing that she was close to tears while the rest of the family talked and laughed. For now, it was enough to know that someone understood she loved and missed Isaac with every fiber of her being. To relieve her guilt for not telling Maria the truth, Christine told herself that someday she'd tell her everything, hopefully someday soon.

During the first week of hot weather, the Führer boasted of his demand for Danzig to be returned to Germany, despite the fact that France and Britain were ready to defend Poland. At the same time, Poland and Russia amassed troops on German borders, and Christine overheard people whispering at the butcher shop and in the bakery that war was not far off. Everyone she knew hoped there was still a chance for peace, despite the distressing news. As the crisis escalated, rumors circulated about the rationing of food and supplies. Christine tried not to think about the stories Opa had told her about women and children starving during the last war.

On September first, Hitler made the announcement that Poland had fired on German territory, and, in self-defense, German troops had returned fire. Bombs would be met with bombs. On the same day, an eight o'clock curfew was put into effect for all German Jews.

Christine felt like a noose was tightening around her neck.

For the next few nights, she tossed and turned until dawn, worrying that Isaac might put an end to their meetings because of the new curfew, and trying not to think about war. But she couldn't stop the images of flying bullets and bombs dropping on her village, at the same time trying to convince herself that it couldn't possibly happen in such a small, unimportant place. Worst of all, she wouldn't know if the curfew had changed Isaac's mind for another three weeks and four days, because their last meeting had been only two days earlier, the night before France and Britain declared war.

During the three long weeks before she saw Isaac, the radio announced that the Royal Air Force had bombed the German cities of Cuxhaven and Wilhelmshaven, and that German troops were making their way into Warsaw. The first casualties of war appeared in the paper, a list of those who had died for their fatherland, along with a new decree that threatened the death penalty for anyone endangering the defensive power of the German people.

When she finally met Isaac in the wine cellar, Christine tried to remember all the news, because the SS had taken the Bauermans' radio. According to the daily list of new rules and restrictions for Jews in the newspaper—no shaving soap was to be sold to a Jew, no tobacco, no fish, no tortes, no flowers—it was now illegal for them to own a radio.

"There were eight of them, and they went through everything," Isaac told her. "They pushed my father around and swatted me on the ears, then stole what they wanted, candles, soap, meat, butter, bread, books, suitcases, my mother's jewelry and furs, my sister's dolls. The next day they came with a truck and took our paintings, our good furniture, our china, our silver. Even our menorah. They made us carry it all out and load it up, then my father had to sign a paper saying he had voluntarily handed everything over to the German Red Cross."

"How can they do that?" she said. "How can they just steal people's possessions in broad daylight?"

"Who's going to stop them?"

Christine shrugged and shook her head, tears welling up in her eyes. "I don't know."

"They told us we should just turn on the gas, or go hang ourselves."

"*Ach* Gott." She took his hand. "I'm so sorry. Do you have anything left?"

"My father hid some money beneath the floorboards behind the toilet in the upstairs bathroom. They didn't find it."

"Is there anything you need? Something I can get for you and your family?"

"A one-way ticket out of the country?"

Christine stiffened. She knew Isaac and his family would be safer someplace else, but she needed him here. She needed to see his face, to hear his voice, to feel his strong arms around her. The minute the thought crossed her mind, she hated herself for being so selfish. "Have you heard from any of your relatives?" she asked.

"My father's sister sent a letter from Lodz three weeks ago, but we didn't receive it until yesterday. She said at first, Polish Jews were ordered to wear armbands with the Star of David, but then they were forced into ghettos. Men who tried to resist were shot, and her husband was one of them. She and her three children were sharing a bedroom with eight others. She wanted to know if there was anything we could do to get them out of there. She said it would be her last letter, because they were no longer allowed to receive or send mail. My father sat down and cried, and my mother wouldn't even look at him. She still thinks things are going back to normal. She thinks Hitler will be too busy with his war to bother with us, and we'll be all right as long as we do what we're told."

"And what do you think?"

He lowered his eyes. "I think we have to stop this."

His words fell over her like an icy veil. "Stop what?"

"We have to stop meeting. If we get caught, it'll be over. For both of us. With the curfew, it's just too dangerous. Someone might follow me. We can't do this. I won't come anymore."

Christine covered her face with her hands. She had known this day would come. Still, she felt nauseous when he said it out loud, like she'd been punched in the stomach. His voice sounded cold and harsh, but when she looked up, his eyes were glistening.

"We'll be together again soon," he said, taking her in his arms. "And nothing will keep us apart. I'll get in touch with you somehow. When it's safe. I promise."

She drew away and went to the overturned wine barrel, where she pulled off the red-and-white tablecloth and spread it out over the dirt-packed floor. Then, she stepped into the center of it, tears filling her eyes, and unbuttoned the blouse of her dress. He stood watching her, his lips pressed together, his head tilted to one side. She slid the top of her dress from her shoulders, pulled her arms from the sleeves, and let it fall to her waist. When she started to undo the thin belt of her gathered skirt, a low, tortured groan escaped Isaac's lips. He rushed forward and buried his face in her neck, his strong arms crushing her arms to her sides.

"We can't," he mumbled, his breath warm against her skin. "As much as I want to, we can't."

"If I can't see you," she whispered in his ear, "I want this moment. I need something to remember you by, something to get me through this."

He pulled the blouse of her dress over her shoulders and backed away. "I won't," he said. "I won't put you in jeopardy. Someday we'll be together, but not now. Not here. Not like this."

Christine wrapped her arms around herself and sank to the ground, head hanging and shoulders convulsing. He went to her and pulled her to her feet, then held her and rocked her back and forth, as if she were a child. After a few minutes, he helped her put her arms back in her sleeves, buttoned the front of her dress, and wiped her wet cheeks with his thumbs. Then he picked up the tablecloth, turned it over on the ground, and got down on his knees.

"What are you doing?" she said, wiping her eyes.

He pulled a box of matches out of his pocket and lit one, waiting until it almost burned his fingers before blowing out the flame. Then, in the right-hand corner of the tablecloth, he used the burnt stick to write an oversized *C,* going over it again and again until the charred, black wood of the match was used up. She knelt beside him, her hand resting on his broad back, feeling his muscles tense and relax as he worked. He lit another match and added "& I," then used six more to finish "C & I." Beneath that: "1939."

"Someday, we'll come back here, together," he said. "In the light of day. We won't worry about anyone seeing us, and we'll get this tablecloth. And when we get married, we'll have it on our wedding table, beneath a giant cake and a thousand flowers."

Christine nodded, swift tears falling from her swollen eyes. They stood and folded it, corner-to-corner and end-to-end, looking into each other's faces as if burning each feature to memory. She pressed her lips together to stifle a sob, watching as he took his lucky stone from his pocket and pushed it between the folds of the tablecloth, then shoved the whole thing between the cold cement wall and the farthermost corner of a wooden potato bin.

CHAPTER 6

In the middle of November, ration cards were delivered to every household by hand, names taken, papers inspected, and heads counted by two somber young men in camel-colored uniforms and nut-brown hats. The sheets of perforated paper were color-coded: red for meat, yellow for sugar and flour, white for dairy, brown for bread. They couldn't be saved and used when needed, because they expired monthly, and they couldn't be traded. Each family member was allowed, if the family could afford it, one pound of meat, nine ounces of sugar, fourteen ounces of coffee substitute, four pounds of bread, ten ounces of butter substitute, three ounces of jam, one and a half ounces of cheese, and one egg per week. Whole milk was reserved for children and expectant mothers, and anyone under fourteen was allowed slightly bigger rations. The somber men warned Christine's mother that it was illegal to buy and butcher a pig, and that doing so would result in the termination of their meat ration cards.

They also informed them that to buy shoes and clothing, people had to apply for a permit. When Mutti asked how it was done, the men said that she shouldn't bother, because permission was seldom granted. They left instructions for every household to gather scrap metal, paper, bones, rags, and empty tubes, then drop them off at the post office. It was crucial that all resources went toward the war effort, and it was every German's patriotic duty to sacrifice.

As her family began getting used to the new system, Christine slowly stopped crying herself to sleep every night. But the instant she opened her eyes every morning and remembered that she didn't know when she'd see Isaac again, misery plowed into her all over again. There were times when it took a good hour before she could crawl out of bed, her legs and arms weighed down with grief. During the day, she shoveled snow, scrubbed floors, washed windows, took over Opa's job of bringing up firewood, and volunteered to stand in the ration lines for hours on end. It was all an effort to exhaust herself, so she'd be too tired to picture Isaac's face, or think about what he might be doing, so she could sleep. It didn't help.

In December, Christine and Maria got Farmer Klause's permission to cut a Weihnachts *Baum*, Christmas tree, from the woods behind his barn. Hoping to surprise their brothers, they woke early on the morning of Christmas Eve to a fresh snowfall, every rooftop and branch fattened by thick, white clumps. They tiptoed downstairs and put Vater's work shirts and pants on over their dresses and wool stockings, pushed their feet into extra socks, tugged thick hats over their heads, and draped knitted scarves over their noses. They helped each other get ready, the layers of bulky clothes making it nearly impossible to tie their shoes and button their coats. After they pulled on each other's mittens, Maria waited in the hall while Christine retrieved a small ax from the cellar.

Outside, the sisters grinned at each other, an unspoken agreement to enjoy the quiet morning in silence. The air was cold and still, the only sounds the snow crunching beneath their feet and the distant chirp of winter birds. The sun sparkled like millions of tiny mirrors on the white expanse of blanketed streets, every post and fence topped by a plump, powdery cap. Without a word, the sisters trudged through the heavy snow to the end of their road, where, all at once, Maria burst out laughing.

"I don't think Heinrich and Karl would recognize us even if they did see us leaving!"

"I know!" Christine said. "You look like a fat old man!"

"I feel like one!" Maria said. "I can barely move with all these clothes on!"

Christine laughed too, surprised how good it felt to have a light moment. For a second, she felt guilty; how could she laugh when there was a war going on, when she had no idea if or when she'd see Isaac again? But surely Isaac smiled and laughed occasionally; surely he enjoyed time with his family. If there was one thing she needed to learn, it was to live in the moment. Isaac would want that for her. She made up her mind to try now.

"I hope the boys have a good Christmas, despite everything," she said. "I wonder what we can do to make it special."

"Let's look for the biggest tree we can find!" Maria said.

"They would love that!" Christine said. "Remember the time Heinrich picked out that gigantic tree, then stood there crying because Mutti said it would never fit in the living room?"

"It was twelve feet tall!" Maria said.

"I know, and Heinrich howled until we let him pick out another one."

"Then he picked out a tiny one because he insisted on dragging it home by himself. Wasn't he only about four years old at the time?"

"*Ja,* but he was already a little man, trying so hard to be big and strong like Vater. Remember the Christmas we all piled in Farmer Klause's horse-drawn sleigh and drove through the countryside?"

Maria smiled. "I'll never forget it. It was magical. I can still hear the bells jingling!"

"You'd been begging for a horse, and it was the closest thing Vater could get to surprise you."

"It was the best Christmas ever. Maybe we can do that for Heinrich and Karl. They'd love to go for a sleigh ride! The weather is perfect and the snow is deep enough!"

"I'm afraid Farmer Klause sold his sleigh a long time ago. He needed the money."

"Oh," Maria said, her shoulders dropping. "It was the most beautiful sleigh I'd ever seen. Remember it was shiny and black, with gold trim and red cushions?"

"*Ja,* it was beautiful," Christine said. "My best Christmas memory was when I was eight. I was going to the dressmaker's with Mutti on Christmas Eve. It was just the two of us, and we were picking up some new material. You're probably too young to remember, but Oma made us matching dresses that year. I was so excited about Christmas, and about picking out the material with Mutti. On the way to the shop it started snowing—these huge, slow flakes drifted down from the sky—and I just remember feeling so happy."

Maria took Christine's mittened hand in her own. "Don't worry, you'll feel that way again someday. I promise."

Christine forced herself to smile, blinking against the moisture in her eyes. She didn't want to ruin the moment. It felt good to bring up happy memories, almost giving her hope that somehow, everything would work out in the end. "Remember the time Mutti dressed up as Christkindl?" she said. "She was giggling so hard her nose was running. We all knew it was her!"

Maria laughed. "*Ja!* She borrowed Herr Weiler's long, red nightcap and used rags to make a beard. I don't think I've ever seen her laugh so hard. She wasn't very good at fooling us, but it was a wonderful time. Oh! That gives me an idea! Let's use ashes from the woodstove to leave footprints next to the tree. We'll tell the boys Christkindl left them when he brought their presents!"

Christine nodded, and the sisters walked faster, hurried on by their growing excitement. At the edge of town, they crossed a snow-covered field toward Farmer Klause's woods. Inside the forest, loose flakes drifted down from the towering spruce, encircling the girls in a quiet, soft snowfall. Christine and Maria examined every evergreen, scrutinizing the shape of the branches from every angle, looking them up and down to find the perfect specimen. Following rabbit and fox trails, they found a clearing, and, right in the center, a wide, young spruce.

"This is the one!" Maria said. "It will fill the entire corner of the living room!"

"Heinrich and Karl will love it!" Christine said, kneeling to examine the trunk.

Maria held the lower branches out of Christine's way and, after several practiced blows, the tree was down in minutes. Each sister grabbed a low limb, and they dragged the spruce across the field, the stiff branches scratching a wide path through the drifts. Trying to synchronize their strides as they hauled the heavy tree up a hill, they had to stop every few minutes to catch their breath. Every now and then, one of them would lose her balance and fall to her knees, while the other laughed and helped her up out of the snow. Eventually, they took off their scarves and stuffed them in their coat pockets, sweating from the exertion.

After dragging the Christmas tree home through the snowy streets, the sisters set it up in the corner of the front room, wrapping a white sheet around its base to look like snow. Normally, they would have had a short evergreen, one that would sit on the end table and, even with the star on top, still fall short of touching the ceiling. This spruce went from the ceiling to the floor, its branches nearly reaching the dining table.

When the boys came into the room, Heinrich's eyes went wide. "It's the biggest Christmas tree ever!" he shouted.

Karl put his hands over his open mouth and edged closer to the evergreen, moving in slow motion, as if he wanted to make the moment last.

Maria knelt beside him. "Do you like it?" she asked, putting her arm around his small shoulders.

Karl smiled and nodded. "Can I touch it?" he said.

Maria kissed him on the cheek. "Of course you can! It's your tree!"

"I'll bet we've got the biggest Christmas tree in Germany!" Heinrich said, his voice filled with pride.

"That's because you're the best brothers in Germany," Christine said, standing behind him and wrapping her arms around his shoulders.

"Danke," he said, turning to look up at her. She hugged him, one hand reaching out to Karl and Maria. Karl did his best to wrap his short arms around them both, and Maria joined in by hugging everyone. As the siblings embraced in front of the tree, Christine's eyes filled, and she glanced at Maria, who looked back with shining eyes.

"Fröliche Weihnachten," Christine said. "Merry Christmas, my loves."

"Fröliche Weihnachten!!" the boys and Maria said at the same time, and everyone laughed.

On Christmas Eve, after Christine and Maria used ashes to leave footprints on the floor next to the giant spruce, Mutti and Oma decorated the fragrant boughs with white candles, tinsel, and straw stars. Christine, Maria, Heinrich, and Karl waited outside in the hall until the grown-ups shut off the lights and rang a bell that signaled *"Bescherung"*—that Christkindl had left and the children could enter the glowing room to see their presents. Heinrich hurried toward the tree, then stopped short, pointing at the floor.

"Look, Karl!" he said. "Christkindl left footprints!"

Karl gasped, staring at the oversized, ashy prints.

"That *sorglose* Christkindl!" Mutti said. "I told him to wipe his boots!"

"It's all right, Mutti," Heinrich said, winking. "We'll help you clean them up."

Christine and Maria looked at each other. Heinrich knew it was a trick. For some reason, the thought that he no longer believed in Christkindl made Christine's chest constrict. She had been hoping her brothers still believed in magic. Someone had to. It reminded her of the morning she'd spent in the hills with Isaac, how naïve and idealistic she'd been, how, in what felt like a matter of minutes, she'd been forced to face reality. Everything was shifting too fast. There was a war going on; her brothers would be forced to grow up soon enough. Now, no matter how hard she tried to recapture the joy of this special day, this Christmas Eve with her family and the biggest tree they'd ever had, the lighthearted moment was gone. Her heart sank.

Before they could open their presents, the entire family gathered around the flickering tree to pray and sing carols. Oma cried as usual, her wrinkled, watery eyes shining as she stared at the tree and sang *"Stille Nacht"*—"Silent Night"—in her soft, quavering voice. It was almost more than Christine could bear. Now more than ever, she understood why Oma wept when she sang the familiar carols. Christmas was an enduring milestone that came and went, while the world forever changed. She bit down on her lip and closed her eyes, trying not to burst into tears and run out of the room. She pictured Isaac's family without a menorah or a tree, and she mourned the invitation to the holiday celebration that had long ago been canceled.

When her family opened their gifts, she forced herself to "oh" and "ah" at the mittens knitted by Oma and the pink marzipan pigs Mutti had bought before the war. Karl and Heinrich got tops and yo-yos, carved by Opa and Vater, and they didn't waste any time before sending the toys spiraling across the floor. Despite herself, Christine smiled as she watched them play, her heartache momentarily eased by their shouts and laughter.

Keeping with tradition, all year long Mutti had set aside sugar, spices, nuts, and seasonings, so they each could have their own plate of gingerbread men, roasted chestnuts, and sugarcoated *Pfeffernüsse* cookies, a rare holiday treat to eat between meals. On the woodstove, a kettle of *Gluehwein,* spiced red wine, simmered, filling the room with the smells of cinnamon and clove. Mutti ladled the steaming liquid into red, etched glasses, then passed them around, along with a kiss planted in the middle of everyone's forehead. She always saved Vater for last because she knew he'd grab her, swing her onto his lap, and say *"Fröliche Weihnachten und Prost!"* before giving her a big kiss on the lips.

Everyone sat around the room eating and laughing, and Christine did her best to join in. To her surprise, Mutti left her place beside Vater and sat with her on the couch, putting an arm around her and whispering in her ear.

"I know you miss him," Mutti said. "But you'll see him again when this madness is over. I'm sure of it. There's a time for everything, you know. A time for work, a time for play, a time for worry, and a time for rest. Right now, enjoy this time with your family. We never know what tomorrow brings."

"*Danke,* Mutti," Christine said, smiling and wiping her eyes. Maria came over and sat on the other side.

"I love you," Maria said, taking her hand in hers.

"I love you too," Christine said. She took her mother's hand, holding it on her lap with Maria's. "Both of you. So much."

On New Year's Eve, the traditional midnight church bells were ordered silent, and pubs and restaurants were to be closed by 1 a.m. Christine snuck out of the house at twelve-fifteen and walked to the wine cellar, hoping, by some miracle, that Isaac would be there.

A full moon cast a luminescent glow over a drift of snow that stretched away from the far edge of the cellar door, like the high, white tail of an ethereal dragon. The expanse of white ground leading up to the entrance was untouched, and she could tell no one had been there. Her heart sank, and she turned to leave, then changed her mind and pulled open the rusty lock. Inside, she sat on the cold floor, rocking back and forth, praying he'd read her mind and show up. Two hours later, so cold she couldn't stop shaking, she put the heavy padlock in the latch and left. On her way home, the cavernous sky made every star look crystal clear, and she felt like she could see the entire universe. She wrapped her arms around herself and tried to imagine other places in the world, where people were allowed to say and do as they pleased. Did they have any idea what was happening here? Would they even care?

Near the end of the long winter of 1940, the rationing of cigarettes and coal was put into effect, and the punishment for any German citizen caught listening to foreign radio transmissions was increased to six years in a maximum-security prison, or death. On the radio, Hitler warned there could be total war because France and England wouldn't accept his offer of peace. Christine's father just shook his head and said that Hitler wanted to blame everyone but himself for the war.

Throughout the rest of winter and into spring, Nazi reports of Wehrmacht victories and the sinking of enemy ships interrupted radio broadcasts on a regular basis. Every account was followed by the soaring melodies of Richard Wagner, and Christine got tired of hearing the same music over and over. In bold, black headlines, the newspaper announced that the Luftwaffe, under the head of Hermann Goering, had bombed France, Belgium, and the Netherlands, and in retaliation, the RAF bombed the German cities of Essen, Cologne, Düsseldorf, Kiel, Hamburg, and Bremen.

The radio was always on, trumpeting every detail, but to Christine and her family, the actual conflict seemed worlds away. Whether intentionally or not she wasn't sure, but they rarely talked about what was happening. In the ration lines, people talked about the weather, their relatives, upcoming weddings and birthdays, everything but war. It seemed to Christine that the only people excited about what was happening were the announcers on the radio. She started to wonder if people avoided the subject because they didn't want to think about hiding in their cellars while bombs and anti-aircraft fire blasted above their heads.

In April, she made the decision to go to the other side of town, to walk by Isaac's house to see if he and his family were still there. When she reached his residence, she walked fast and stayed on the opposite side of the road, looking straight ahead, as if she belonged in the neighborhood and had someplace important to go. She went around the block three times, staring at the windows of his house out of the corner of her eyes until her head hurt.

The once splendid home looked empty and sad, curtains drawn above flower boxes that held nothing but dirt and a few straggling vines. In the garden, the purple lilacs were starting to bloom and the forsythia was thick with yellow leaves, but the yard had a wild quality to it, with scraggly bushes, fruit trees in need of pruning, and a vegetable plot choked with pricker bushes and dried thistles. When she saw the unkempt garden, a gnawing, hollow cavity swelled inside her stomach. The Bauermans were gone.

On her fourth turn around the block, her heartbeat finally slowed and her knees stopped quivering. She crossed to the other side of the street, wondering if she should check the garden access door on Brimbach Strasse. And then she saw him. Through the twisting, brown trunks of a close stand of fruit trees, the dark figure of a man was bent over the vegetable garden. Her heart leapt in her chest. She stopped and looked up and down the street, then moved closer to the retaining wall surrounding the Bauermans' property. The figure straightened and turned, one hand held over the small of his back, the other lifting a burlap sack over his shoulder. It was Herr Bauerman, looking as shriveled and gray as the potatoes he was searching for in the hard, dry earth. His clothes were wrinkled and dirty, as if they hadn't been changed in weeks. Christine remembered that Jews weren't allowed to send their laundry out, and imagined poor Frau Bauerman trying to wash clothes by hand, something she'd never done in her life.

She thought about climbing over the low wall and hurrying through the fruit trees to ask Herr Bauerman if she could see Isaac, knowing full well she'd be putting herself and his family at risk. But the urge to see him was so strong it clouded her reason, and it didn't take long for her to convince herself it would be all right. It would only be for a minute, she reasoned, and besides, who would know? Was there a law against saying hello? She clenched her teeth and bent down, pretending to tie her shoe. She didn't know what to do. What if Herr Bauerman told her to go away? What if Isaac refused to see her? But she had to try. Her mind made up, she straightened, ready to make a move. Just then, as she put her hands on the retaining wall to hoist herself up, a smiling couple came around the corner arm in arm, a blond woman wearing a long fur coat, and a man in a black SS uniform. Christine drew in a sharp breath and hurried to the other side of the road, content for now, at least, with the knowledge that Isaac was still there.

On May 11, the newspaper headlines read: "Chief Warmonger Churchill Becomes Prime Minister." There were two papers for sale in Christine's village now, the *Völkischer Beobachter* and the newspaper used to promote anti-Semitism: *Der Stürmer,* "The Stormer." Christine's father bought the *Völkischer Beobachter* because it was the only one available, but he wouldn't read the other one, even if it'd been handed out for free. Christine didn't want to read it either, but she couldn't help noticing *Der Stürmer's* disturbing headlines, splashed across the displays in store windows.

On a rainy afternoon near the end of May, too miserable to be trapped inside, Christine went for a walk without an umbrella. The air smelled clean, with a hint of fragrance from the white and pink petals of blossoming fruit trees. Just as her mood started to lift, she went by the greengrocer's and spotted a quote written in bold type by *Der Stürmer's* editor: **"The time is near when a machine will go** into motion which is going to prepare a grave for the world's criminal—Judah—from which there will be no resurrection."

In place of hope, a greasy fear stirred in her stomach. She stared through the glass and reread the quote four times, blinking against the raindrops on her lashes. *What does it mean?* she thought.

"Christine!" someone shouted. She jumped and turned to see Kate hurrying toward her, shoulders hunched to avoid the curtain of rain falling from the edge of her black umbrella. "What are you doing?" she yelled above the thrumming downpour.

"Um," Christine said, looking down at her wet, empty hands. "I came to the store to get salt. There isn't any."

Kate moved closer and held the umbrella over Christine's head. "Oh," she said. Her red hair was snarled, her eyes bloodshot and swollen. She looked as bad as Christine felt.

Christine searched for something to say. "Where's Stefan?" she asked finally.

Kate's face crumpled in on itself, and tears welled in her eyes. "He's been drafted," she cried. "He left six days ago."

"I'm sorry," Christine said. "I didn't know."

"But my mother told your mother."

"I don't think so. Maybe your mother forgot. I'm sure she's busy."

"Maybe your mother didn't tell you. I was wondering why you didn't come see me."

Christine shook her head, trying to clear it. *What does any of this matter?*

"Why don't we go inside and have a cup of tea or an Italian ice?" she said, pointing at the café next door.

Kate drew the back of her hand under her nose like a three-year-old. "I didn't bring any money," she said. "I was just out walking. . . ." She trailed off, her voice hitching as if she might break down again.

"I've saved a few coins for a rainy day," Christine said. Then, trying to muster a smile, she held a cupped hand outside the umbrella. Within seconds her palm was full of water. "I'd say this is a rainy day. Come on. Let's treat ourselves. We deserve it."

"All right," Kate said, sniffing.

A sign on the door said *"Jude Verboten!"* and, at first, Christine hesitated. Then she noticed two SS seated inside, next to the wide front window. The skin on her neck grew hot. The two soldiers were leaning back in their chairs, watching her and Kate through the glass. Their black uniforms had the *Siegrunen,* or double *S* runes—like twin lightning bolts—on their lapels, the Iron Cross at their collars, the silver skull and crossbones on the black bands of their peaked hats. If she turned around and left now, it would be too obvious. She followed Kate through the glass door, keeping her eyes straight ahead, then stood by the entrance, waiting while Kate closed her dripping umbrella. Even with her back to them, she could feel the SS watching.

Had it been just a year ago, every table would have been filled with couples and families having lunch or afternoon coffee and *Kuchen.* But today, there were only five other people in the cozy establishment: the officers; the owner and chef, Herr Schmidt; his wife and the only waitress, Frau Schmidt; and a wrinkled old gentleman in a gray shirt and worn *Lederhosen.*

Christine followed Kate to the back of the room, toward a round, glass table in a corner decorated with blue-and-white Delft windmill plates and Hummel pictures of cherubic children holding geese and baby lambs. They passed the old man reading a newspaper, his walking cane leaning against the other empty chair, his coffee and a half-eaten *Bratwurst* on the table in front of him. Christine watched him lift his ersatz coffee to his thin lips, his hand shaking so badly she was sure he would spill it. Somehow he managed to get it up to his mouth and down again, without losing so much as a drop. She made her way to the back table, her insides quivering like the old man's hands.

She slid into her chair, stealing a glance toward the officers at the front of the café. To her relief, they were getting up to leave, adjusting their hats and pushing their arms into the sleeves of their long greatcoats. Against the gray backdrop of rain in the front window, their black uniforms looked like the dark silhouettes of jumbo marionettes.

"I don't want anything," Kate said, slumping in her chair.

"Come on," Christine said. "It'll do you good to have a little treat."

"But I miss him so much already!" Kate said. "What if he never comes back?" Her face contorted again, and Christine feared she was going to wail out loud.

"I know you feel helpless," Christine said. "But you need to think positive. I have to keep telling myself over and over that I'll see Isaac again. The only way I can keep going is by telling myself we'll be together someday."

Kate blew her nose into a saturated handkerchief and frowned at Christine, her face soaked with tears. "Isaac?" she said. "But he's a Jew!"

Christine went rigid. She looked at the officers, her stomach in knots. They were paying their bill at the counter, oblivious to what Kate had said. In the center of the glass tabletop, a yellow menu leaned against a vase of blue coneflowers and red poppies. Christine picked it up, trying to find her voice. It was all she could do not to get up and walk out.

She cleared her throat. "What should we order?" she said finally, wondering if Kate had been reading *Der Stürmer* in the time they'd spent apart.

"Since Stefan left, I haven't had much of an appetite."

"I'm sorry about Stefan," she said. "But you just have to trust he'll be all right."

Christine didn't believe her own words. For all she knew, a hundred men had died since the two of them had entered the café. Stefan could have very well been one of them. Every day the list of names in the paper grew.

"It's hard to be optimistic," Kate said. "Everyone's saying it's going to be a long war."

"I don't think anyone can predict what's going to happen."

"Stefan says the war is their fault."

"Whose fault?"

"You know," Kate said. "The Jews." She lowered her voice and leaned forward. "I thought Isaac was a schoolgirl crush. You know, the rich, handsome boy you knew you could never have. And now, with the new laws . . . Well, anyway, it's not like he ever knew you existed. I mean, nothing ever came of it, right?"

Christine felt her eyes flooding. The temptation to tell Kate that she and Isaac were in love, that they'd been meeting secretly, was so intense she almost blurted the words out. Instead, she stared at the menu, biting down on the inside of her cheek. "I've known him longer than you've known Stefan," she said.

"You had a crush on him. It's not the same thing."

Christine swallowed, fighting the urge to tell Kate everything just so she'd shut up. "I still miss him."

Kate rolled her eyes. "I'm sorry. I know you miss working at his house and seeing him. But you've got to forget about him."

Just then, Frau Schmidt appeared at their table, ready to take their order. They stopped talking and sat up straight. Christine couldn't take her eyes off Kate. *Who is this person?* she wondered.

"A cherry Italian ice, *bitte,*" Kate said.

"I'll have the same, *bitte,*" Christine said. Her head reeled, as she wondered what had possessed her to ask Kate to come in here. She should have made an excuse and kept walking.

Kate drummed her fingers on the table, waiting as Frau Schmidt wrote down the order. When she was gone, Kate leaned forward again.

"She got the telegram last week," she said, nodding in Frau Schmidt's direction as she ambled away. "Her son died in battle outside of Paris."

Christine felt her heart constrict. "The poor woman," she said. Out of the corner of her eye, she saw the officers moving toward the back of the café. Pretending not to notice, she forced herself to smile at Kate.

The officers stopped at the old man's table, waiting in silence until he realized they were standing over him. Finally, he looked up from his lunch.

"Hauptscharführer Kruger and I are from De Rasse und Sied-lungshauptamt, Race and Settlement Department of the SS," one of the officers said. He was tall and thin, his pointed nose like the beak of a bird on his angular face. "Your papers, *bitte.*"

The other officer, Hauptscharführer Kruger, snatched the newspaper out of the old man's hand, checked the front page, then threw it on the table. *"Mach schnell!"* he shouted.

The old man turned in his chair and fumbled for his coat. He searched his pockets with shaking hands. Finally, he pulled his *Ausweis* out of his coat pocket, but then he dropped it on the floor. A frustrated grunt escaped his lips, and he bent over to pick it up, his thin arms and legs shuddering. The identity booklet had fallen between his boots, and he couldn't see it. Christine got up and started across the room.

"Halt!" Hauptscharführer Kruger said, holding up a gloved hand in her direction.

Christine stopped in her tracks.

"Are you a Jewish sympathizer, *Fräulein?*" he asked her. "Or are you a Jew?"

"He dropped his identification," she said, pointing at the floor. "I was just going to help him."

"Mind your business!" Kruger said. "Or we'll arrest you for interfering with matters of the Reich!"

Christine dropped her eyes, but she didn't go back to her chair. She had no idea what she would do if they mistreated the old man further, but she knew she couldn't just stand by and do nothing. The bird-beaked officer bent over to pull the green identity booklet out from between the old man's feet, then straightened, nodding once in Christine's direction, and opened the *Ausweis*.

"He's all right," he said to Kruger. He dropped the booklet on the table, tipped his hat toward the old man, and headed toward the door. But Hauptscharführer Kruger stayed put, frowning at Christine, as if trying to decide if she was worth his time. Christine looked at him and held her breath. The bird-beaked officer stopped at the door and turned around.

"We have more important business to attend to, Hauptscharführer Kruger," he said.

Kruger stared at her for a few more seconds, then spun around and left. Christine exhaled and went back to her table, holding the glass edge for support and lowering herself into her chair. Kate stared at her, eyes as wide as the blue-and-white plates on the wall behind her head. Without a word, Frau Schmidt delivered the red Italian ices in crystal dishes, her face blank and staring.

"What's wrong with you?" Kate hissed. "Do you want to go to jail?"

"Are they going to put me in jail for picking something up off the floor for an old man?"

"If he was a Jew they would have," Kate said. Then, whispering, "Do you remember the Goldsteins who lived next door to us? The ones with the two dachshunds I used to take care of when they went to Poland to visit Frau Goldstein's parents?"

"*Ja,*" Christine said, feeling nauseous.

"A few months ago they disappeared. Someone found the dogs loose in the street. A week later, Mr. Goldstein came back, but he wouldn't tell anyone where he'd been, or what had happened. He just held on to those little dogs and cried. A month later he was gone too."

Christine swallowed. "What do you think happened?"

"I've heard they're rounding up Jews."

Something twisted in Christine's chest. "And doing what with them?"

"I don't know. But Stefan said Hitler won't be happy until they're all gone." As if suddenly ravenous, Kate took a big, dripping spoonful of cherry ice and shoved it in her mouth. She grimaced at the sudden cold against her teeth, then held her lips open, as if it were hot, her tongue and the inside of her cheeks bloodred.

CHAPTER 7

In June, the radio newscaster proclaimed in a frenzied voice that France had surrendered. When the "Horst-Wessel-Lied," the Nazi anthem, played afterward, Christine pictured a giant Nazi flag draped over the Eiffel Tower, and long lines of German soldiers goose-stepping past the Paris cafés. As spring turned to summer, the Luftwaffe began the first air raids on London, and the RAF started bombing Berlin.

The nightly attacks on the German capital lasted for weeks, and never-ending news of destroyed apartment houses and civilian casualties gave Christine nightmares about women and children being buried alive. She could barely stand it when she heard people talking about pulverized buildings and the speed at which fires had burned through attic after attic of attached houses, like flaming matches dropped on piles of dried hay.

As summer came and went, more and more of the men in the village were called away. Even without asking, Christine could tell, by the dark shroud of fear and the heavy pull of worry on the women's faces, whose husbands and sons had been called off to war.

A few weeks into fall, Heinrich and Karl announced that they were expected to bring scrap metal and chunks of coal to school, and that their teachers were keeping track of who brought what. Christine and Maria took them for walks through the village, looking for pieces of wire, thrown horseshoes, dropped nails, broken chain links, anything to help the boys meet their quota. But the streets were picked clean, and when they couldn't find any metal, Heinrich and Karl picked up cigarette stubs to glean tobacco for Opa's pipe instead.

On a brilliant Saturday afternoon near the end of September, the sisters walked behind their brothers, holding their scarves closed at their chins with gloved hands. Despite the sun, the breeze was raw, the sky filled with low, scudding clouds.

"Get that out of your mouth!" Christine shouted at Karl, who was half a block ahead of her and Maria, pretending to smoke a broken cigarette he'd found between the sidewalk and an old barn. Maria ran ahead and swatted the muddy filter from Karl's lips.

"It's just broken!" Karl whined. "It hasn't been smoked!"

Maria picked the cigarette up off the ground, holding it out at arm's length as if it were a rotten potato, and dropped it in Heinrich's bag. "Someone probably had it in his mouth!" she scolded.

"And that might not have been mud on the filter!" Heinrich teased, laughing and sticking out his tongue, like he was going to throw up. Maria shushed him.

Karl scuffed his shoe on the sidewalk and put his hands in the pockets of his *Lederhosen*. "I was just pretending."

"We know," Christine said, catching up to them. She wiped his mouth with the edge of her scarf and pulled his hat over his ears. "But you don't want to get sick, do you?"

"Nein," Karl said. He looked up at his sisters, his eyes filling. Maria cupped his chin in her hand.

"It's all right. We're not mad. Just don't put things like that in your mouth! Now run along. We're right behind you." Karl wiped his cheeks and followed Heinrich up the street. The girls resumed walking.

"I've never seen a little boy get upset so easily," Christine said.

"I know," Maria said. "It seems like he starts crying the minute you look at him cross-eyed."

"It's funny how different they are," Christine said.

"Ja," Maria said. "Heinrich acts older than we do sometimes."

"I wish Karl could be a little stronger," Christine said. "Being that emotional is just going to make his life more difficult." She watched her brothers wander back and forth along the sidewalk. Heinrich walked with his head down, diligently searching every crack and crevice, while Karl only glanced down every few steps, intent instead on looking at the houses and trees and clouds. "I hope this war is over soon. I can't imagine what will happen if the fighting comes to our village, how it will affect the boys."

Maria stopped and stared at her, her face suddenly white. "You don't think that will happen, do you?" she said, her voice tight. "I mean, we don't have anything to do with the war. There aren't any weapon factories here or anything. The Allies don't have any reason to bomb our village."

Christine clenched her jaw, wishing she'd kept her mouth shut. Maria had been a constant source of support to her, to everyone really; the last thing she wanted was to make Maria worry.

"You're right," she said. "I never thought of it that way."

"I know a lot of people are getting killed in the cities," Maria said. "But that's just by accident, right? The Allies are bombing military targets, and sometimes they miss. Right?"

Christine hooked an arm through her sister's and led her up the walk. *"Ja,* I'm sure it was an accident. Besides, the whole thing will probably be over in a few months."

"Do you really think so?"

"Of course," Christine said. She lowered her voice. "They can't fight forever, can they? Someone will win soon, hopefully not Hitler."

Maria pulled her close. "Then you and Isaac can be together," she whispered.

Christine nodded, forcing herself to smile, wondering if, like her own, the grin on her sister's face was fake.

On the first day of winter, a swarm of Wehrmacht soldiers in *feldgrauer,* field gray, uniforms, driving and riding in horse-drawn wagons, descended on the village. Like a scourge of locusts, they dismantled iron fences and metal railings from around houses, churches, and cemeteries. They pilfered flagpoles, streetlamps, and ornamental signs from inns and bars, all of it to be hauled away and melted down, made into bullets and bombs. Before they left, they went door-to-door collecting pots and pans, along with any other metal they might have overlooked.

After a quick discussion with Oma to decide which of their few worn utensils they could live without, Mutti held her tongue when she handed the soldier at their door a battered saucepan. Christine stood in the doorway beside her and saw her mother's face drop when she noticed the hanging bell from her garden gate in the soldier's hand.

A few days later, Christine and her family stood shivering in front of their house, hands in their coat pockets, watching a group of soldiers lower their church's bells onto a horse-drawn wagon. Oma cried when the soldiers shouted, "Yah! Yah!" and whipped the thin horses struggling to move the heavy load. Finally, the wheels creaked and turned. The animals dropped their heads, harnesses clinking and hooves sliding across the cobblestones, and dragged the wagon to the top of the hill. Mutti put her arm around Oma, who buried her face in her hands. Later, Vater said it'd be impossible for the soldiers to take the carillon from the steeple of St. Michael's, due to the sheer height of the bell tower and the fact that the largest of the three bells weighed over four tons.

On the Sunday before Christmas, a silent snowfall greeted the family as they stepped out the front door on their way to church. Karl and Heinrich whooped and shouted, spinning in circles on the road, squinting toward the sky and holding out their tongues to catch the thick, slow-moving flakes. Christine and Maria went into the snow-covered street to join their brothers while their parents and grandparents stood near the garden fence, taking a moment to watch the four children twirl together in the snow, their long, dark coats spiraling around them like whirlpools of cocoa being stirred into milk. Laughter reached Christine's ears, and for a fraction of a second, she imagined she was getting used to the heavy ache of loss anchored to her heart.

But then, the tranquility of the moment was destroyed by the accelerated growl of an army truck. The vehicle careened around the corner and headed toward them at high speed. Christine and Maria pulled the boys out of the way, gripping their coats and hurrying toward their parents. They all stared, trying to catch their breath, as the truck slid to a stop in the slush and the passenger door flew open. A soldier in a black uniform jumped out and approached the family, a rifle over his shoulder, his face void of emotion. He stopped in front of Vater and raised a gloved hand in the air.

"*Heil* Hitler!" he said, clicking his heels together. He held out a white envelope stamped with a black, spread-winged eagle atop a swastika inside a wreath of oak leaves.

"*Heil* Hitler," Vater muttered, briefly raising his hand.

"Welcome to Hitler's army, Herr Bölz!" the soldier shouted. "You are to report to headquarters in Stuttgart tomorrow morning, at nine o'clock sharp! *Heil* Hitler!" Then, without waiting for a response, the soldier spun around and climbed back into the vehicle.

The army truck bucked and roared, notched tires slipping and catching on the snow-covered cobblestones. Christine and her family stood huddled together, hunched shoulders and winter hats dappled white by growing layers of snow. Vater stood motionless, staring at the envelope in his hand. Eventually, he put an arm around Mutti, who leaned into him, eyes closed, fingers pressed to her trembling lips.

"Do you have to go, Vater?" Maria asked.

"I have no choice," Vater said, stuffing the unopened envelope into his jacket pocket and kissing his wife on the forehead. Christine could tell her mother was trying hard not to cry, but her chin started to quiver and tears slipped from her eyes. Karl and Heinrich clung to Mutti's wool coat.

"Don't cry," Vater said. "Everything will be fine." He patted Karl and Heinrich on their heads, smiled at Oma and Opa, then touched Christine and Maria on the cheeks. "Come now. It's time for church."

Vater put his arm around Mutti and led her across the street. Maria took the boys' hands and followed her parents up the sandstone staircase to the raised churchyard, along the front walk, and through the entrance. Christine followed partway, then stopped, feet rooted outside the oak doors.

"Come, Christine," Opa said, putting his arms around her and Oma. Heinrich held the door open, and they walked inside as a family, holding onto one another as if one of them might blow away at any minute.

In stark contrast to the cold, gray day outside, the inside of the church was warm and glowing, filled with candlelight and the smell of aged wood and melting beeswax. Unlike the Gothic cathedral of St. Michael's, this modest church had been built with rough-hewn pillars and timber beams. Inside, it resembled a half-timbered barn, with exposed rafters, oversized trusses, straw-colored stucco walls, painted ceilings, and a plank wood floor. A rear staircase led to second-floor balconies made from girders and joists that extended out over the nave.

For over five hundred years, this small, solid church had endured. Christine tried to imagine the people who had once sat where she was sitting now, praying for strength and peace and a loved one's safe return. She ran her hand over the worn, varnished surface of the wooden pew, wishing she could channel the spirit of someone who'd lived a hundred years ago. Someone to guide her and tell her she'd survive this pain, no matter what. Someone to tell her that everything would be all right in the end. Besides wars and plagues and funerals, the church had seen centuries of weddings and baptisms, Easters and Christmases. Its beams and rafters had been decorated with flowers and candles, fragrant evergreen branches, swaying boughs of ribbons and berries. She closed her eyes and tried to draw strength from the thickset walls, the towering windows, the sturdy pews, the sacred altar.

Just then, the immense pipe organ began to play, and the voices of the choir swelled around her, filling the church with ancient hymns. Hymns that had been sung before she was born, and before this war. Hymns that would continue to be sung long after the war was over. Would her father be alive then? Would any of them be? The hair rose on her arms, and her heart swelled in her chest, overwhelmed by love and fear and wonder and sorrow. She thought about the thousands of people who had sung and played and listened to the same songs before her, people who had lived through the pleasures and hardships of life and were now at rest in the village cemetery.

Every day, thousands of soldiers were dying on the battlefield. Thousands of civilians were being killed by bombs. Why should her family be any different? Why would her father, or any of them, out of the millions suffering, be spared? They were nothing but numbers to the people who had started this war. The hymn's chorus came to a crescendo, and she couldn't control her emotions any longer. Hot tears fell. Her world was falling apart, and there was nothing she could do about it.

CHAPTER 8

At the beginning of 1941, the fierce battles of war had not yet reached Christine's village. But everyone could feel them coming, like a storm in the distance that rumbled and swelled in the clouds.

During the month of January, the nearby villages of Wurzburg, Karlsruhe, and Pforzheim were bombed. Now, people on the streets looked at each other with anxious eyes that said: "Did you hear? Do you think we're next? Will tonight be the night?"

From the third floor window in the hall outside her bedroom, Christine could see the flickering glow of burning cities, like red, pulsating mushrooms along the night horizon. If the wind was right and she opened the window, she could hear the hollow thump-thump of dropping bombs echoing through the earth, like the giant fists of an angry god.

During the first days of February, new posters went up along the stone walls and stucco façades of the winding avenues, to warn people that traitors—those who listened to enemy broadcasts, read enemy newspapers, or believed enemy propaganda—would be sent to the gallows. In the daily ration lines, where Christine sometimes stood for hours only to find that everything was gone, everyone looked over both shoulders before whispering to the person stand-

ing next to him or her. She was shocked when she heard people repeat the newest jingle: "Dear Gott, make me dumb, that I may not
to Dachau come."

The first letter from her father arrived in the middle of March,
and Mutti read it to the family in a trembling voice.

> *My dearest Rose and family,*
>   *Words cannot express how much I miss all of you.*
> *I pray that you are well. I want you to know that I'm*
> *in good health. Our training is vigorous, but we get*
> *plenty to eat. Even so, I can still taste the liverwurst*
> *and Griebenschmalz sandwich you made for my*
> *train ride to Stuttgart. Now that my instruction pe-*
> *riod is complete, I will be sent to the Eastern Front*
> *to lay communication wires for the advancing Sixth*
> *Army, along with the Corps of Engineers who must*
> *change the railroad tracks to the correct gauge to fa-*
> *cilitate our supply trains. I've signed up for a compul-*
> *sory savings plan, which we've been told will give us*
> *a good return at the successful conclusion of this war.*
> *Take care of each other. I will write as often as I can.*
> *I love you, and will see you again soon.*
> *Heil Hitler,*
> *Dietrich*

They were sitting around the table, eating the bland meal that
had become the core of their winter diet: watered-down goat's
milk, boiled potatoes, and turnip soup. Though no one could believe it, they missed the days when Mutti used to leave cow's milk in
an earthen crock on the cellar steps for three days, until it soured
and turned into the consistency of pudding. When it was just right,
they'd all sit around the table, the crock in the middle, to dip their
spoons in the cream, alternating this with bites of boiled potatoes
and salt. The boys used to grumble and grouse, but now that it'd
been over a year since they'd had cow's milk, Christine was certain
the curdled milk would have seemed like a treat.

"Why did Vater sign '*Heil* Hitler'?" Maria asked.

"He had to," Opa said. "Soldiers' letters are read before they're mailed."

"When is he coming home?" Karl whimpered.

"He'll come as soon as he can," Mutti said.

"Mutti," Christine said. "Someone stole our rooster. He was here last night, but now he's gone."

Mutti folded the letter into the envelope and slid it into her apron pocket, her lips pressed together. "Well then," she said, "there'll be no new chicks this spring, and no chicken stock or meat until we get another one."

As winter turned to spring, Mutti checked the mailbox on the front of the house every day, hoping there'd be another letter from Vater. Eventually she checked only every three days. Finally, she asked Christine to do it, because she couldn't take the disappointment.

On her way to pick up their rations, Christine took a different route every day, checking backyards and the open doors of chicken coops to see if she could spot their missing rooster. She found it hard to believe that any of their neighbors would take it, but during war, it seemed, the old rules didn't apply.

By the end of May, over half the fields surrounding the village lay unplowed and unplanted, because the only men who hadn't been drafted into war were too old to walk behind plow horses or carry heavy seeders for any length of time. A few farmers' wives were doing their best to keep the farms running, with the one horse they were allowed to keep and the help of a Polish *Kriegsgefangener*, POW, or a fourteen- or fifteen-year-old girl from the Labor Service Camp outside Sulzbach.

Christine felt sorry for the young girls riding their bicycles back and forth to the camp in their matching blue work dresses, their eyes downcast, their hands and faces scraped and smudged with dirt. They were from the Stuttgart Bund Deutscher Mädel, League of German Girls, a Nazi group for single girls aged fourteen to seventeen. Called "Labor-year girls," the city girls were required to spend part of spring and all of summer in government service, the young ones working on farms and living in camps run by women who belonged to the Nazi Party, while the older ones became air raid wardens or auxiliary firefighters.

There was a small group of Bund Deutscher Mädel in Hessental that met at the high school, but thanks to Christine's father's being born in Italy, she and her sister weren't allowed to sign up. The enlisted girls wore uniforms and had meetings in the school once a week, to put together care packages for soldiers and make straw slippers to send to hospitals. Christine and Maria agreed that they wouldn't mind helping the soldiers, but they were relieved not to be eligible, because it was the BDM girl's duty to pledge her allegiance to Hitler and the Nazi Party.

Sometimes Christine saw the Deutsches Jungvolk, for boys aged ten to fourteen, and the Hitler Jugend, Hitler Youth, for boys aged fourteen and up, line up for roll call in the school yard wearing their brown shirts, dark ties, and swastika armbands. Their duties included clearing the streets in winter, carrying mail, singing patriotic songs, hiking, playing war games, and, once they hit a certain age, being drafted into the Wehrmacht. Parents were warned that if their children were eligible and did not join one of Hitler's youth groups, they'd be put into an orphanage.

In June, Hitler invaded Russia, and within a week, posters went up depicting Russians as fat, slovenly men with a bottle of vodka in one hand and a whip in the other. At the beginning of summer, the government announced a meager monthly payment to German women for mending military uniforms. Once a week, Christine and Maria walked to the train station to pick up wicker baskets full of ruined jackets, overcoats, shirts, and pants, their arms and shoulders aching by the time they carried the heavy load back home. For hours on end, the women sat together in the living room, repairing the shredded trousers, torn shirts, and riddled jackets. The types and colors ranged from black to green to brown, with different variations of cut and design. But the majority of uniforms in need of repair were green, the color of the *Heer,* or regular army, and the *Frontkämpfer,* battlefront soldiers. Opa pointed out that there were no uniforms from the *Goldfasan,* or golden pheasants, the derogatory term the old men had come up with for the high-ranking Nazi Party members who wore brown-and-red uniforms and spent the war in relative peace and luxury at home.

Christine concentrated on making perfect, tiny stitches, trying not to think about the man who'd been wearing the uniform. But the more she struggled to keep her mind on something else, the harder it was to keep the nameless faces from forming in her mind. *What became of this poor soldier? Is he as damaged and torn as this sleeve or this trouser? Is he dead? Do his mother, his sister, his wife know what has happened? Could this have been my father's uniform?* By evening, Oma would nod off, mouth open, hands poised in mid-stitch. At first, one boxcar on every length of cars was filled with damaged uniforms. By the end of the summer, there were four boxcars full on every train.

On a gray morning in early September, a fine mist hung in the air. Christine made her way to the end of the bread ration line, squinting against the cold condensation on her lashes and brows. In her haste to get to the bakery before the bread was gone, she hadn't bothered to grab her coat, because the previous four days had been unseasonably warm and sunny, the last efforts of a hot summer. She gathered her sweater beneath her neck with one hand, embarrassed to see that everyone else had long coats and umbrellas. But then something else caught her eye, and she forgot about being cold. In the ration lines, there were people with yellow cloth sewn to their jackets, old women and young girls, teenagers, babies, toddlers hanging on to their mothers' hands, all of them with the yellow stars over their left breast. Christine hurried to the end of the row and tapped the shoemaker's wife, Frau Unger, on the shoulder.

"What's going on?" she asked. "Why are they wearing stars on their coats?"

"Didn't you hear the announcement last night?" Frau Unger said. "Starting today, it's against the law for German Jews to go out in public without wearing the Star of David."

"But why? What does it mean?"

Frau Unger shrugged. "How do I know? I can't keep up with the rules. There are too many. My poor husband nearly got arrested for shooting a wood duck. Can you imagine, throwing an old man in jail for trying to find his supper? Apparently, Himmler likes wood ducks."

Christine pictured Isaac and his family, standing in a ration line on the other side of town with stars on their coats. She looked up the long line in front of her. From behind, the people all looked the same. "I didn't know the Kleins and the Leibermanns were Jewish," she said.

"It's too late for them now," Frau Unger said, shaking her head.

"What do you mean?"

"They can't leave the country. One day, Hitler says to get rid of the Jews. The next day, he says they can't leave."

Christine remembered the letter from Isaac's aunt in Poland, and a hard knot formed in her stomach. After the stars came the ghettos. Is that what Hitler's plan was for the German Jews too? It was already prohibited for them to deal with Aryan tradesmen, shopkeepers, butchers, doctors, cobblers, and barbers. The Nazis had even gone as far as making it mandatory for them to turn in their hair clippers, scissors, and combs. There had been a reduction in rations for the Jews; at the same time it was illegal for them to stockpile food. Hitler was making it impossible for them to survive. Now he wasn't going to let them leave?

Her first thought was to leave the ration line and hurry to the other side of town, to find out if Isaac and his family were still living there, or if his father had finally convinced his mother to leave the country. But she had to get bread for her family, because for the past week, the bakery and the store had been out. Regardless, she felt like a coward because she hadn't gone to the other side of town since seeing the SS in the café. *The Bauermans must have left by now,* she told herself. *With everything that's been happening, I'm sure Isaac's mother was finally scared enough to listen.* With that thought, the knot of fear in her stomach uncoiled and crawled past her lungs, where it wrapped itself around her heart in a cold, tight ball of throbbing heartache.

A few days later, another letter arrived from her father. This time, Mutti read it to everyone at the breakfast nook in the kitchen.

> *Dearest Rose, Christine, Maria, Heinrich, Karl,*
> *Oma, and Opa,*
>   *I'm sorry I haven't written, but we've been on the*
> *move for months and have finally made camp for a*
> *few days. I pray that all of you are well and in good*
> *spirits. Did you get a plentiful harvest from the gar-*
> *den this year? I wish I could be home to help pick*
> *the pears and plums. What I wouldn't give for a slice*
> *of brown bread spread with your fresh plum jam. If*
> *you haven't already done so, don't forget to tell Herr*
> *Oertel that he still owes you two bushels of firewood*
> *for the work I did for him last year. Tell him you'll*
> *need it to get through the winter.*
>   *Right now, I'm sitting in an anti-tank trench with*
> *five hundred other men. We dug the mile-long ditch*
> *this afternoon, and this is where we'll sleep. We're*
> *deep in the Ukraine and are being told that the*
> *northern troops will take Moscow before winter.*
> *Everyone here is hoping for an early end to the war,*
> *so we can get back to Germany before the Russian*
> *winter hits. Hopefully, the war will be over and I'll*
> *be home with you by spring. Much love to you all.*
> *Heil Hitler,*
> *Dietrich*

Mutti passed the letter to Maria, who read it again and passed it to Oma, who passed it to Christine. Christine placed her thumb on a dark smudge in the lower left-hand corner, imagining it was her father's thumbprint, from where he held the letter and reread it before folding it into the envelope. She imagined him sitting there, thousands of miles from home, leaning against the red Russian soil, exhausted and homesick. The anguish of missing someone she loved was as familiar to Christine as hunger and cold, but she couldn't imagine the torture of being taken from her family and not knowing if she'd die before she got the chance to see them again. Blinking against her tears, she reread the letter.

"What's that?" Heinrich said, pointing at the French doors, his nose crumpled as if he smelled something rotten. Everyone looked. A cluster of white paper hung flat and wet on the dew-covered glass. As they watched, a second wrinkled wad slapped itself against another pane farther up. Then, a half dozen sheets came out of nowhere and stuck to the glass in a haphazard pattern, like the fall leaves Christine used to glue to her bedroom window. Mutti stood and opened the door, and a flurry of paper drifted lazily out of the sky and landed on the balcony, like a bizarre storm of jumbo snowflakes. The family hurried outside and snatched the falling papers from the air. Some of the sheets were blank, but most had lettering, and some were black and burnt around the edges, as if they'd been near a fire.

"This is from Heilbronn," Mutti said, holding out the sheet of paper so everyone could see. "It says, 'From the desk of the *Bürgermeister* of Heilbronn.'"

"This is too," Maria said, holding the surviving half of a scorched page. "It's from the school."

"Look," Karl said, pointing toward the road.

Down in the street, hundreds of scorched papers littered the cobblestones, while still more drifted from the sky. A swirl of pages caught in the breeze, traveled across the road, and landed against the garden fence in a shifting pile of paper and ash.

"How far away is Heilbronn?" Christine asked.

"About thirty-five miles," Opa said. "If it's still there."

CHAPTER 9

By the middle of the third long winter of war, the United States had joined the war against Germany, and the Russians had launched a brutal counterattack. Rumors circulated through the village that Hitler had been so certain of a swift victory that the soldiers didn't have the proper provisions or clothing to survive the Russian winter. Instead of dying in battle, they were losing their lives to typhus, exposure, starvation, and frostbite.

To lose loved ones to war was one thing, but to lose them because the leaders who sent them cared so little they didn't provide the necessary protection to survive? And to think that Vater had left with nothing more than the clothes on his back, despite Mutti's insistence that he take a change of clothes, his long underwear, his good hat, and winter gloves. The army offered no news, and Christine's mother, out of self-preservation, chose to accept that as a good sign, and she expected her family to do the same.

Mutti took "The People's Radio" into the kitchen so she could listen for news from the Eastern Front while she worked. At night, they left it playing to hide the voices of the Atlantiksender, the enemy radio station broadcasting announcements in German, on the old radio hidden upstairs beneath Mutti and Vater's bed. Christine, Mutti, and Maria sat on the floor to listen to the illegal shortwave, their backs against the wall, blankets around their shoulders, the volume turned down. After German military music and official-sounding broadcasts, the announcer said in perfect high German that Hitler was lying to his people, that the Third Reich was losing the war, and that German soldiers were surrendering by the thousands and being sent to work in America, where they earned large wages. The Kriegsmarine in U-boats were encouraged to surface and surrender while they still had the chance. Glancing at each other with wide, dark eyes, Christine, Maria, and Mutti listened in silence until the newscasts were over.

Within a month, the underground transmission found a way to broadcast over German frequencies, and the Nazis scrambled to counteract their efforts by beginning all broadcasts with a special announcement: "The enemy is broadcasting counterfeit instructions on German frequencies. Do not be misled. Here is an official announcement of the Reich authority."

With the arrival of warmer days, anti-American posters went up beside the rest, showing a black-and-white drawing of a six-armed giant made of airplane parts and riveted metal limbs. Beneath capitalized letters that spelled KULTUR-TERROR, the monster's head was a pointed, white hood above a collar imprinted with the letters KKK. One arm was that of a convict holding a machine gun; the other held the U.S. flag in reverse. The torso was made up of a birdcage and held a black couple dancing above a belt that read: Jitterbug. A bass drum formed the pelvis, with a Jewish flag dangling between legs that looked like bloody bombs, stomping over the picturesque landscape of a German village. Christine wondered if the Americans put up posters that depicted Germans as monsters.

On a warm morning in early April, Christine grabbed the egg basket and started out to the henhouse. In the past few weeks, she'd found three brown eggs in the nests of yellow straw. But now the weather had warmed, and she knew she'd find a half dozen or more. She was looking forward to surprising everyone with his or her own soft-boiled egg, a rare, large breakfast after the long, sparse winter. But when she pushed open the back door and stepped outside, she froze. The earth seemed to vibrate beneath her feet. A distant, rolling thunder—punctuated by strangled groans, metallic grinding, and mechanical screeches—came from the center of town. Instead of gathering eggs, she hurried back inside, set down the basket, and went out the front door.

As Christine moved closer to the village square, the snarling and grinding grew to a chaotic roar punctuated by the rhythmic pounding of boots and hammers. From this side of town, two roads entered the square from the crest of a hill. The Gothic cathedral of St. Michael's sat between the two roads, dominating the plaza with rows of arched windows, soaring barbed spikes, and a steep, orange-tiled roof. She entered the rear courtyard and followed the sidewalk along the towering sandstone walls until she reached the front of the church, where a granite cascade of fifty-four steps led down to the fanned cobblestones of the market square.

At the top of the steps, she pressed her hands over her ears and surveyed the chaos below. Beneath swirling clouds of dust, a writhing swarm of *Panzerkampfwagen,* armored tanks, trucks, motorcycles, soldiers carrying rifles and bayonets, and *Panje,* horse-drawn wagons hauling anti-aircraft guns, crowded the open area. A colossal red-and-white flag with a black swastika in the center covered the middle three stories of city hall, with two smaller flags covering the gabled buildings on either side. Engines revved, wagon wheels banged across the uneven cobblestones, and horses' hooves hit the street in uneven rhythm with the soldiers' jackboots as they marched in black columns across the square. The tanks growled and vibrated, their giant tracks screeching and shuddering like massive, rattling chains trying to tear holes in the earth.

Christine wanted to watch but she couldn't stand the noise, so she turned and hurried into the church. The wooden front doors were as tall and thick as the trunks of ancient trees, and when she pushed them closed, the chaos in the square muted to a rumble. Inside, the vaulted stone ceilings looked like a giant network of painted spiderwebs held up by row after row of slim, gray pillars, each four stories high. The cavernous cathedral smelled like incense and wet stone, and it was cool and quiet, like the inner depths of a watery cave.

The damp aroma brought back memories of childhood, when

she and Kate used to come inside the cathedral to escape the summer heat. They'd meander through the gargantuan stone edifice, looking up at the high walls and exploring the side rooms, speculating about the long-dead people who'd carved and painted stone into saints and angels, but had also melted black iron into screaming skulls and twisted snakes. Behind the altar, an open pit in the stone floor was filled with bones from the cemetery that had been moved to build the church, the skulls and femurs and clavicles stacked in neat brown piles.

Now, she turned right, through a squat, arched door just past the inner recess of the main entrance, and climbed a wooden staircase. Halfway up, the stairway narrowed as it circled around the bells and gears of the massive carillon. Staying close to the stone walls because there was no railing, she climbed faster and faster, hoping the bells wouldn't ring before she reached the top. On the last step, she went out a narrow door onto the enclosed octagon catwalk, the highest point in the village. She hadn't climbed up there in years, but it used to be one of her favorite places to sit on hot summer days, to catch the cool breezes that blew above the crowded buildings and narrow streets of the stifling village.

From here, she could see over the roof of city hall and the five-story gabled houses enclosing the village square, toward the succession of green and blue hills that swept over the earth like a vast, rolling sea. Despite the swirling mass of dirt and dust below, the air at the top of the steeple was clear, and she could see for miles. To the west, the forest spilled down from the hills and across the valley until it hit the edge of the village, where it swelled and spread like a green, leafy wave. The wooded land was elevated just enough to see beneath the trees, and Christine could make out soldiers working on airframes, and row after row of wing panels and propellers. They were assembling airplanes beneath the dense camouflage canopy.

To the south, a long line of tanks and military vehicles coiled out toward the open end of the valley, like a trembling black snake surrounded by plumes of grayish-yellow smoke. The tail of the snake disappeared behind the last foothill, but the dark head was moving toward town, a bottleneck building up at Haller Bridge. She could see the old air base in the center of the valley and a line of dark

planes along a long swath of flattened green. Insect-sized men un-
loaded what looked like wooden X's from tiny trucks and made a
fence around the base, like a row of black cross-stitch in the grass.

Down in the square, a group of soldiers used hammers and saws
to build a wooden platform off the steps of city hall. Another handful erected metal flagpoles topped by eagles and swastikas, the Ho-
heitsabzeichen, the national insignia, along the front of the stage.
More stacked piles of wood on either side. The side streets and
some sections of the square were cordoned off with ropes and
metal barriers. Christine watched for a few more minutes, then
raced down the steps and hurried home, her hope that the war had
forgotten this quiet village shattered.

She ran along the sidewalks, shocked to see that people were
still going about their business, as if tanks and soldiers weren't
overtaking their village. *Don't they know that bombs and bullets
will be next?* Until now, she hadn't realized that she'd expected
panic, people running through the streets, boarding up windows
and doors, loading belongings into carts and suitcases and fleeing
town.

Then she remembered Heilbronn. She slowed to a walk, every
breath burning in her chest. *No one is leaving because there's nowhere to go,* she thought. Every village and city she'd ever heard of
had already been attacked. Heilbronn was the closest town. The
day after she and her family had seen the burnt papers falling from
the sky, the radio announced that fifty thousand people had been
bombed out of their homes and seven thousand had died. She
wrapped her arms around herself, her legs shaking as she skirted
around others on the sidewalk.

At her house, two soldiers towered above her mother in the
open doorway, their broad backs toward the street. Mutti's face
floated between them, a white oval flanked by two pitch-black statues carrying submachine guns and Lugers. Christine moved along
the fence until she was close enough to see the tight knit of their
black uniforms and the reflection of the sun in their metal helmets
and leather boots.

"Frau Bölz," one of the soldiers said in a firm voice. "When the
alarm sounds, you need to find immediate shelter for your family.

Keep buckets of sand and water on your staircase, in case your house catches fire. You must cover every window with black cloth, block out any light, so the enemy planes can't see the village from the sky. Wardens will conduct checks at night, and failure to comply will result in severe punishment. There is a National Socialist rally tonight, and all citizens are required to attend. Soldiers will be in the streets, to make sure all residents come out of their homes. Failure to cooperate will result in your arrest! *Heil* Hitler!" Before Mutti could respond, the soldiers turned on their heels in unison and walked to the next house. Christine hurried toward her mother.

"What else did they say?" Christine asked her.

"They came to warn us," Mutti said, her eyes glued on the soldiers knocking on their neighbor's door. "They're using the old air base behind the village, and it won't be long before enemy planes start bombing it. We need to find a place to hide when the air raid siren goes off."

"Where can we go?" Christine asked. *And if Isaac and his family are still here, where will they hide?* she thought.

Mutti stood thinking, forearms crossed limply over her chest, scratching her wrist and staring at the sidewalk. "Our cellar is too small for all of us," she said in a lifeless voice. "We should talk to the butcher, Herr Weiler. His root cellar is big, and it's the closest." She turned into the foyer and hurried toward the bottom of the stairs. "Maria!" she called up the steps. "Christine and I have to run downtown. Be mindful of Heinrich and Karl, will you?"

Christine and her mother rushed toward the shops at the bottom of her street, where people were finally starting to act like things had changed. Outdoor tables and chairs were pulled inside cafés, two old men were boarding up the windows of the bakery, and Frau Nussbaum was taking in her potted geraniums while her husband nailed their shutters closed. Two soldiers were putting up posters while people crowded around to see what they said. Christine and Mutti stopped to look.

In jagged letters, the black and gray poster warned: *Der Feind sieht Dein Licht! Verdunkeln!* "The Enemy sees your light! Black out!" Below the words, a giant skeleton with an evil grin rode an Allied plane through a stormy night, a bomb raised in one bony hand, ready to hurl death and destruction on the German village below. Christine's stomach lurched. She'd never seen anything so frightening in her life. Mutti grabbed her hand and pulled her away, nearly running as she led her along the sidewalk.

When Christine and her mother reached Herr Weiler's root cellar in the side of the hill, a few storeowners were already inside, setting up benches and placing mattresses over the potato bins.

"*Grüss* Gott, Frau Bölz and Christine," Herr Weiler said in a loud voice. He was old and rotund, with a red face that was wide and flat. But he was always in good spirits, and setting up a bomb shelter was no exception. "You and your family are welcome here! There's plenty of room! We think we can squeeze in quite a number of people, and no one should hide in their house cellars alone. At times like this, we need each other!"

"*Danke,* Herr Weiler," Mutti said, wringing her hands.

Christine didn't hear the rest of their exchange. Instead, she was looking toward the back of the shelter, at a piece of cloth that looked like it was starting to slip from its hiding place behind the last potato bin. Her eyes watered, staring at the dusty, wrinkled corner of her and Isaac's red-and-white tablecloth.

CHAPTER 10

At dusk that evening, four armed SS yelled instructions from the road in front of Christine's house. More soldiers shouted in the next street over. Bullhorns caused their voices to overlap and echo along the narrow avenues and stone houses, making their terse instructions hard to understand.

"*Achtung,* citizens!" they barked. "Come out of your houses! It is *verboten* to remain in your rooms! You must attend the rally in the town square at precisely eight o'clock."

At seven-fifty, Christine and her family held each other's hands and followed their fellow villagers into the town square, everyone looking around, wondering what they were about to see. When they arrived, shouting soldiers herded the throng of old people, women, and children into place behind the metal barriers until the entire populace stood shoulder to shoulder, filling every available space. Maria hooked arms with Oma and Opa, and Mutti picked up Karl, holding him on one hip. Christine lifted Heinrich onto her back, her arms hooked beneath his knees, piggyback style. They struggled to stay together, shoved and jostled by hundreds of confused people who couldn't hear each other calling out to one another above the pounding of jackboots, drums, and military parade music. A sea of handheld torches cast flickering light on the gathering, while orange flames from two bonfires licked the sky, lighting up the red-and-white Nazi banners that covered the buildings behind the stage.

Once they'd moved forward as far as they could, Christine's racing heart did double-time as she read the pamphlet they'd each been handed when they entered the square. The black and yellow cover said: *Wenn du dieses Zeichen siehst,* "When you see this symbol," above the yellow Star of David. Inside, page after page explained that the Jews had unleashed war on the German people and that the Wehrmacht would ensure that world Jewry's terrible plan would never become reality. It went on to explain that Jewry was an organized criminality, and that the Jewish danger would only be eliminated when Jewry throughout the world had ceased to exist.

"What is it?" Heinrich said in her ear.

"It's nothing," Christine said. *It's a book full of lies,* she thought. *Nothing but Nazi lies.*

Her mother had the pamphlet folded in her hand, but she hadn't looked at it yet, and Maria held hers, along with Oma's and Opa's, curled in her fist. Christine glanced around to make sure no one was watching, then twisted the hateful paper in her hands and let it fall to the ground, where she crushed it beneath her heel. She reached for her mother's, but her hand froze when the music stopped, as if someone had seen what she'd done. She looked around, waiting for one of the soldiers to push his way through the crowd and take her away. But nothing happened. Then, a single toll from a heavy bell rang through the air.

The throng stood in silence, listening to the massive bells of St. Michael's chime the hour of eight o'clock, each tone echoing across the crowded square. After the last toll sounded, a military band began playing the "Horst-Wessel-Lied," trumpets blaring, a chorus of men's voices singing in strong, proud baritones. Thousands of black-helmeted soldiers carrying silver-tipped guns and Nazi flags goose-stepped into the plaza, making the cobblestones throb beneath Christine's feet, like the hard thump-thump-thump of the planet's pulse. In perfect precision, they lined up in front of the podium, their chins held high, their arms raised in salute. The tops of their helmets were at the same height, like row after row of identical tin soldiers. Christine wondered if they were a special unit, perfectly proportioned for an impressive display.

Another dozen soldiers walked along the roped-off aisles between the crowds, arms held high in salute, making sure everyone in the audience did the same. Christine clenched her jaw and raised her arm. There was a commotion at the end of her line, and a woman screamed. Christine saw a soldier grab a man by the collar and drag him out of the crowd, a female hand clawing at his sleeve. She couldn't be sure, but the dainty halo of gray braids on the woman's head reminded her of poor, heartbroken Frau Schmidt from the café.

After the last note of the Nazi anthem tapered off, four officers and another dozen soldiers in jodhpurs and high boots walked onto the platform. The clusters of medals on the officers' chests reflected the flames of the bonfires, giving the illusion of thumping, bleeding hearts. They turned on their heels and raised their arms in salute, and then, a squat, hunched figure with a dark mustache walked onto center stage.

"Sieg Heil! Sieg Heil! Sieg Heil!" the throng shouted. The skin on Christine's arms turned to gooseflesh. She could hardly believe what she was seeing. The man at the podium was Hitler. The crowd roared in a distorted drone that rose and fell like the howl of the wind in a wild storm. Hitler looked shorter than she'd imagined, and even from here, she could see his scowling mouth. The soldiers in the aisles clapped and shouted, encouraging everyone to follow along, their eyes scanning the masses for anyone who didn't comply. As they made their way along the edge of the crowd, a sea of arms lowered and people applauded, standing on their tiptoes and craning their necks to get a better view of the Führer. Christine thought she heard jeers among the applause and hurrahs. Up on stage, Hitler lowered his head and put his fist over the center of his chest. Then, he stood, motionless, waiting for the crowd to quiet. Only when there was complete silence did he look up and begin to speak.

"My German fellow countrymen and women, my comrades! Now the three great Have-Nots are united, and now we shall see who gains in this struggle, those who have nothing to lose, but everything to gain, or those who have everything to lose and nothing to gain. For what does England want to gain? What does America want to gain?" Hitler shook his fist in the air. "They have so much that they do not know what to do with what they have. We have never done anything to England or France. We have never done anything to America!" Hitler swung his arm over the people in the square. "Nevertheless now there is the declaration of war. Now you must, out of my whole history, understand me. I once said something that foreign countries did not understand. I said: If the war is inevitable, then I should rather be the one to conduct it, not because I thirst after this fame, on the contrary, I renounce that fame, which is in my eyes no fame at all. My fame, if providence preserves my life, will consist in works of peace, which I still intend to create. But I think that if destiny has already disposed that I can do what must be done according to the inscrutable will of fate, then I can at least just ask providence to entrust to me the burden of this war, to load it on me. I *will bear it!*" he shouted, pounding his fist on his chest.

Christine had never been to the opera, but she imagined that this was how the tragedies would be played out. She looked around to examine the faces of those around her, wondering if anyone else could see Hitler's malevolent soul coming through in his authoritarian words and exaggerated movements. Red and black shadows danced over the sea of upturned faces, making facial features indistinguishable. She had the unsettling image of a horde of lost souls standing at the gates of hell. Hitler went on.

"I will shrink from no responsibility. In every hour I will take this burden upon me. I will bear every duty, just as I have always borne them. I have the greatest authority among the populace. The people know me. They know that I had endless plans in those years before the war. They see everywhere the signs of works begun, and sometimes also the documents of completion. I know that the German people trust me. I am happy to know it. But the German people may be persuaded also of one thing, that the year 1918, as long as I live, will never return!" He looked toward the sky, then stood back from the podium and bowed his head, his gesturing hand held captive beneath his arm, as he listened to the crowd roar. Then he puffed out his chest and stepped forward, his fist above his head. "When the English and Americans attack our cities, we will raze their cities to the ground. When they drop three thousand kilograms of bombs, we will, in one raid, drop three hundred thousand! Now you, the citizens of Hessental, are being called up for service. . . ."

Maria stared at Christine with wide eyes, and Heinrich's arms stiffened around Christine's neck. His legs clenched around her waist. She wished she could say something to comfort them, to tell them they didn't need to worry about bombs, but reassuring words escaped her. *Three thousand kilograms of bombs? In one raid?* She thought of the wooden door on the root cellar, the few yards of tree-rooted earth between the top of the shelter and the open sky. *How will we ever survive?* She gripped Heinrich's legs, suddenly light-headed and worried she might drop him.

On stage, Hitler had changed the subject. "At every decision you make," he said, "think, how would the Führer decide? Is this compatible with the National Socialist conscience of the German people? The Jewish youth waits for hours on end, spying on the un-suspicious German girl he plans to seduce. He wants to contaminate her blood and remove her from the bosom of her own people. The Jews hate the white race and want to lower its cultural level, so the Jew might dominate. Was there any filth or crime without one Jew involved in it? None but members of the nation shall be citizens of the state. None but those of German blood may be members of the nation. Thus the home front need not be warned, and the prayer of this priest of the devil, the wish that Europe may be punished with Bolshevism, will not be fulfilled, but rather that our prayer may be fulfilled. Lord God, give us the strength that we may retain our liberty for our children and our children's children, not only for ourselves but also for the other peoples of Europe, for this is a war which we all wage, this time, not for our German people alone. It is a war for all of Europe and with it, in the long run, for all of mankind."

Christine felt her mother's trembling hand slip into her own. She turned to look at her. Mutti's eyes were glassy.

"Can we go home now?" Karl said. "I don't like it here."

Someone tapped Christine on the shoulder. At first, she ignored it, thinking it was Heinrich. But then, a strong hand gripped her arm, and she turned. The SS soldier towered above her, his face void of emotion. A rush of panic plowed through her chest. She glanced back at her mother, who was staring back at her, wide eyes in a pale face.

"Fräulein?" the soldier said to Christine. "You are to come with me."

"Why?" she said, trying to read the soldier's eyes beneath the dark shadow of his helmet. "What did I do?" Heinrich released his grip around her neck and slid down her back. Her mother gripped her arm with such force that she almost cried out.

"You've been chosen for a special task," he said. "You'll be reunited with your family as soon as you're finished."

Christine looked past him, down the line of spellbound people. Two more soldiers stood with a group of young women in the open aisle, most in Bund Deutscher Mädel uniforms, all of them blond.

"But I . . ." Christine started.

"It's best to do as you're told," the soldier said. "Follow me."

Mutti's hand fell away as Christine followed the black uniform through the crowd, the villagers stepping back to make room, their staring eyes filled with curiosity and pity. In the aisle, she recognized two girls from Maria's school days, one from a farm on the edge of the village, another she'd seen at the train station picking up uniforms. The soldiers led the girls along the aisles toward the wall of military lined up in front of the stage.

"What's going on? Why did they choose us?" Christine asked the girl in front of her.

"Don't you know?" the girl said, her voice filled with excitement. "Look at us. We're perfect examples of the Aryan race!"

A soldier appeared beside them. "No talking!"

On their way to the stage, Christine saw a flash of red hair on a girl standing on the other side of the rope. As she drew closer, the redhead turned, and Christine had a clear view of her face. It was Kate, smiling and waving a miniature flag. When Kate noticed the group of girls being led toward the Führer, her eyebrows lowered, and her face went dark. She crossed her arms and looked every girl up and down, as if to see why they had been selected instead of her. When she saw Christine, her face snapped forward, but not before Christine saw her mouth drop open.

The soldiers lined the girls up in front of the stage, instructing them to stand up straight and smile, feet together and chin up. Christine was last in the row. Behind them, Hitler made another announcement.

"The Aryan girls you see before me are pure treasures of the German state. You must keep them safe from the criminals looking to steal their German purity. They are the future mothers of the master race!"

The throng applauded, and the soldiers snapped to attention and shouted, "*Heil* Hitler!" When the band started to play another military march, Hitler made his way down the stairs on the side of the stage, waving and smiling to his adoring crowd. The four decorated officers followed him. Starting on the other end of the line, Hitler shook each girl's hand and touched her cheek. Christine's pulse thumped in her neck, the flames of the bonfires so close it felt like they were singeing the back of her head. She searched the crowd for her family, but it was no use. From here, it was impossible to recognize a face among the masses.

Now, Hitler was only three feet away. Christine couldn't help staring at his pasty cheeks and wattle neck, wiggling like a bowl of clotted cream when he shook hands. His thin-lipped mouth reminded her of rolled herring as he made his way down the line, mumbling a repeated phrase to every girl. He looked nothing like he did on posters, where he had smooth skin and a broad chin. In every picture or photograph she'd ever seen, he looked six foot tall. But in person, he was the same height as the girls, with a narrow chest and rounded shoulders.

Christine's mouth went dry when Hitler moved in front of her and offered his hand. For a split second, she couldn't move. His blue eyes locked with hers. She noticed that one of them was bigger than the other, as if the left half of his brain were bulging in its socket, pushing his eyeball out past its lid. His lip twitched, his glued-on smile faltering when she didn't respond. Christine noticed one of the officers moving toward her, hands out, ready to whisk her away for her crime. Finally, she remembered what to do, and her arm shot out. Hitler grabbed her hand, his warm palm soggy against her skin. A nauseating jolt leapt though her body, and it was all she could do not to yank her hand away. When he reached up to touch her cheek, she tried not to flinch.

"You are the essence of the German people," he said, his sour breath filling her nostrils, like someone had opened a bag of rotten potatoes at her feet. "I want to personally extend an invitation to you to join our Lebensborn program. The Third Reich will spare no expense to help German girls fulfill their duty to expand the master race, along with the fine men of our SS. Make your fatherland proud. We fight this war for you. And we will win, of that you can be sure."

At first, Christine wanted nothing more than for Hitler to let go of her hand, but then she gripped his tighter, fighting the urge to yank him closer so she could spit into his face. He gazed at her, his eyes looking but not seeing, and finished his rehearsed greeting. When she refused to let go, his muddy eyes cleared. He looked straight at her. *You've ruined millions of people's lives,* she thought, staring at him. *And I hope you pay. There's a place for murderers. It's called hell.* Hitler's shoulders went back, and his chin lifted, as if he'd heard her thoughts. A small sound escaped his lips, like the grunt of a burrowing animal. Then he laughed, shaking her hand with more energy.

"I appreciate your admiration, *Fräulein,*" he said. "But I must be on my way. I'm an important man, you know." He chuckled again and looked at the officer beside him, who laughed with him.

Christine let go of Hitler's hand and lowered her eyes. Behind him, the multitudes cheered. A black Mercedes-Benz convertible decorated with Nazi flags pulled up, and the driver got out and opened the door. Hitler smiled at the row of girls, then turned and climbed into the car. He stood in the passenger seat, his arm held high above the roaring crowd. After the car moved out of the square and disappeared down a narrow side street, an officer gestured that the girls were free to go. Christine hurried down the aisle to look for her family. The military band kept playing as the soldiers marched out of the square and the crowd dispersed. Christine saw Oma, Opa, Mutti, and Maria hurrying toward her, Karl and Heinrich in tow.

"Are you all right?" Mutti said.

"I'm fine," Christine said. "I just want to go home."

Maria slipped her arm through Christine's, and Karl reached for her right hand. She flinched and drew away.

"Don't touch me," she said, and kept walking.

Later, after everyone had gone to bed, Christine snuck down to the kitchen in her nightgown, wearing a wool sweater and a thick pair of socks. After the rally, a storm had blown in, making it feel like winter was starting all over again. Howling gusts rattled the shutters, and rain tapped against the windowpanes like icy fingernails. Christine lit a candle and set it near the sink, then went to the woodstove and felt the teakettle. It was still warm, but not warm enough. She opened the door to the oven and threw in another log, hoping to revive the dying fire, then rummaged in the cupboard for a stiff brush and bar of lye soap. After she found what she was looking for, she filled the sink with a few inches of water, then paced the room, waiting.

A few minutes later, bursts of steam erupted from the spout of the teakettle. Christine took off her sweater and rolled up the sleeves of her nightgown. She poured half the hot water into the sink, wet her hands and cheek, and then, using the lye soap and the stiff brush, built up a pungent-smelling lather on her skin. She'd washed her hands and face as soon as she had gotten home from the rally, and again before changing into her bedclothes, but it wasn't good enough. She could still feel Hitler's soggy hand in her own, his slimy fingers touching her cheek, as if somehow, through his secretions, through his tainted touch, she'd been contaminated, poisoned in some way. She kept picturing his sweat mixing with her own, his evil essence coursing through her blood, corrupting her body and soul. It was if the devil himself had laid hands on her, and now she was doomed to certain damnation. She closed her eyes and grimaced, scrubbing as hard as she could, tears building up behind her lids. The brush tore at her skin, the lye soap burning the tiny abrasions. After a few minutes, she went to the stove, retrieved the teakettle, and went back to the sink.

Just as she was getting ready to pour the boiling water over her hand, Maria came into the kitchen.

"What are you doing?" she said, her eyes wide. She grabbed the teakettle out of Christine's grip. "Stop! You'll get burned!"

"Bitte," Christine said. "I'm nearly done. It will be all right."

"Nein!" Maria said. She put the teakettle back on the stove. "Have you lost your mind?"

"I just need to wash. I need to sterilize my skin."

"He's just a man," Maria said, her voice hard. "An evil man, to be sure, but a man just the same. He can't hurt you by touching your hand! He doesn't have special powers!"

"How do you know?" Christine said, her eyes filling. "He has brainwashed so many people! How else could he still have so many followers, no matter what he does?" Even as she heard her own words, Christine knew they sounded crazy. She also knew Maria was the only one she could say them to.

Maria took Christine by the wrist and turned her toward the sink. "Here, I'll help you," she said. "But you're not going to pour boiling water on yourself." Maria let the soapy water out of the sink and refilled it partway, adding enough hot water from the teakettle to make it warm, then gently rinsed Christine's cheek and hands. "You've broken the skin in a few places," she said, her forehead furrowed.

"I can barely feel it," Christine said, letting Maria douse the lather from her irritated skin. "I'm sorry I scared you, it's just . . ."

"I understand," Maria said. "Not only did Hitler act like a madman up on that stage, he wants to kill the man you love. I'd probably do the same thing if he touched me."

"Danke for being such a good sister," Christine said. "I don't know what I'd do without you."

"Well, I don't know what I'd do without you either, so you'd better start taking better care of yourself. What if you'd been badly burned and got an infection or something? You know there's no medicine for civilians! You know everything is going to the soldiers at the front!" Maria retrieved a clean dish towel from a kitchen drawer and gently dried Christine's hands and face, her eyes growing moist.

"I know," Christine said. "It was stupid. I wasn't thinking straight."

Maria pressed her lips together, tears spilling from her eyes.

"Why are you crying?" Christine said. "I'm all right, really!"

"I know," Maria said, wiping a hand under her nose. "I'm just scared, that's all. I keep waiting and wondering what's going to happen next."

Christine wrapped her arms around Maria's shoulders, scolding herself for wallowing in her own foolish fears. Evil secretions coursing through her blood, indeed! What was she thinking? Her family, her little brothers and her little sister, needed her. She had to be strong, no matter what crazy thoughts went through her head.

"Everything is going to be fine," she said. "I'll always be here for you. We'll get through this together, all of us."

"Promise?" Maria said in a small voice.

"Promise."

"Promise to God, all included, nothing counts?"

"Promise to God, all included, nothing counts," Christine said, wondering if it was a mistake to make an oath she had no idea if she'd be able to keep.

CHAPTER 11

At seven o'clock the next morning, the first planes of the Luftwaffe took off from the air base, the low rumble like the growl of a beast lumbering across the valley. Christine was in the kitchen with Mutti, setting the table and boiling eggs on the woodstove, the two of them waiting for the rest of the family to come trickling in for breakfast.

Her mother was sitting on the edge of the table bench, cutting the last four slices of *Roggenbrot,* rye bread, into eight even pieces, her forehead furrowed, her lips held in a determined line. Christine hated seeing her mother that way, the wrinkles of her face deepened by exhaustion, her eyes dulled by worry. Mutti had lost weight; her cheeks were pale and hollow, the back of her dress hanging loose over her frame. Christine knew her mother was probably eating less so there'd be more food for her children, but from now on, Christine was going to keep track. And when she faced her mother with the facts, she'd appeal to Mutti's practical side. Mutti had to take care of herself too, because how would any of them survive without her? She was the one who knew to grow Swiss chard between tomato plants, knew marigolds would repel garden pests, knew how to bargain with the mill owner for another gram of cooking oil, could stretch the flour into the most loaves of bread, and could tell if the chickens needed more protein or fewer greens just by looking at the yolks of their eggs. She was the key to their survival and the last thread to anything familiar and normal. From food in their stomachs to clean clothes and warm baths, their mother provided the only bits of comfort to be had.

Just as these thoughts crossed Christine's mind, the heavy planes of the Luftwaffe flew over the village, and everything started to vibrate: the silverware in the drawer, the dishes in the cupboards, the windows, the furniture, the house. Karl and Heinrich burst through the kitchen door and scrambled into Mutti's lap, burying their faces in her apron. Maria rushed in behind them, still in her nightgown, her braids disheveled and half undone.

"I thought there was going to be a warning siren!" she screamed, putting her hands over her ears.

"It's our planes taking off!" Mutti yelled. She rubbed Karl's and Heinrich's shoulders. "It's all right. It's just loud because they're right over us."

Oma waddled into the kitchen holding Opa's hand. They all looked at each other, waiting. When it was finally over, Opa was the first to speak.

"That'll rattle your bedpan!" he said, and everyone laughed. Christine wondered if any of them would be laughing next week or next month or next year.

For the rest of the day and into the evening, the growling planes flew over the village. By the third day, Christine and her family were starting to get used to it. At first, there'd be the low snarling rumble; then the sound would grow louder and louder, until finally, when the roar sounded like a monster steam engine about to come rushing through the walls of the house, they all stopped what they were doing and held on to a piece of furniture or put a hand over the trembling dishes, waiting for it to pass. At the end of the week, two days went by without aircraft flying overhead, and in the relative quiet, Christine heard ringing in her ears when she tried to sleep.

After the rally, tanks and army trucks became a constant presence in the village. Officers helped themselves to rolls and bread from the bakery, pork and sausage from the butchers, and plums and apples from the trees. The Nazis appointed a new mayor, and every civilian saluted and greeted each other with *"Heil* Hitler." The "Welcome" signs in the windows of the Krone, the bakery, the tailor, and the shoemaker were replaced with notices that read: JUDEN VERBOTEN! An announcement hanging from the bulletin board at city hall stated that, in the interest of public security and order, and on suspicion of treasonable activities detrimental to the state, several village officials and clergymen—including the minister from Christine's church—had been taken into "protective custody" by the Gestapo.

The first time someone asked to shake her hand because she'd touched the Führer, Christine didn't understand what was happening. She stopped in her tracks, ready to run away from the person rushing toward her. When she finally understood what they were after, their eyes shining, their smiles wide, she pretended to act proud that she'd met Hitler face-to-face, hoping they wouldn't notice the raw scratches and dry skin where she'd scrubbed her hand and face. They were mainly the boys from the Hitler Youth, but there were young girls too, giggling and curtsying as if she were their personal connection to the man they'd seen on stage. But there were also people, mainly old men and middle-aged women, who no longer smiled and said hello when she passed.

Two weeks later, at one o'clock in the morning, Christine was pulled from her sleep by a hollow, anguished wail. Before she was fully awake, an image flashed through her mind: Mutti with a telegram clutched to her chest, screaming because her husband was dead. Christine's heart seized beneath her ribcage. She looked around her dark bedroom, the echoing wail growing higher and stronger, rising and falling, like the lament of a thousand mourners. And then it hit her. It was the air raid siren.

She threw on her clothes, the whooping howl of the siren going on and on and on. It sounded far away and yet impossibly close, as if it were coming from inside her room. She heard the door to her mother's room slam, her brothers crying in the hallway. Her fingers fumbled over the buttons on the front of her dress, and she pushed into her shoes, the siren crawling under her skin and settling into her bones, like the icy wind of a sudden blizzard. She grabbed her coat and ran into the hall.

Mutti was waiting near the top of the stairs, her hair loose on her shoulders, the waist of her dress skewed to one side. She was breathing hard, holding the boys by their hands. Maria came out her bedroom door, one shoe on and one off. Christine held her steady while she finished putting on her shoe, pulling her braids out of the collar of her coat.

"When we get to the first floor," Mutti yelled, "you two take the boys and run ahead. I'll help Oma and Opa."

"I can help them," Christine shouted. "You go with Heinrich and Karl!"

"Just do as I say!" Mutti said.

Christine reached for Karl's hand, but he shook his head and leaned toward his mother.

"It's too hard for the three of you to go down together," Christine said to him. "It'll be faster if you come with me."

He looked up at Mutti, who nodded in agreement. Karl timidly reached for Christine's hand. Then they heard the drone of approaching aircraft, and horrifying comprehension coupled with sheer panic forced them down the stairs. On the first floor, Oma and Opa were just coming out of their bedroom. Maria grabbed Heinrich's hand, and she and Christine ran ahead with the boys, out into the dark street and the deafening, undulating keen of the air raid siren.

The streets were filled with running people, some still in bedclothes, everyone wide-eyed and glancing up at the sky. Halfway down the hill, Christine looked over her shoulder and saw her mother and grandparents moving down the street in a shuffling half walk, half run. Opa's balding head bobbed up and down as he hurried behind his wife as fast as his aging body would carry him. She ran with her siblings across the street and behind the shops, pushed forward by the knock of anti-aircraft fire and the first high-pitched whistles of dropping bombs. In the distance, the probing beams of searchlights swung in the sky, capturing airplanes and bursts of exploding flak in circles of bright light. Christine could see bombs falling from the bellies of the planes, like seeds tumbling from a farmer's hand. She craned her neck to see if the rest of her family was almost there, yanked open the door of the bomb shelter, and shoved her sister and brothers inside.

"I'll be right back," she said to Maria. Maria opened her mouth to protest, but Christine turned and ran back down the alley. Her mother and grandparents were still on the other side of the road, Opa hunched over and breathless. A hollow thud-thud followed by cyclic explosions shook the earth. Oma hesitated at the edge of the sidewalk. Christine ran over and took her hand, and Mutti stepped back to help Opa.

"Come on," Christine shouted. "We've still got time. They're over the air base." When they reached the middle of the street, a line of airplanes flew directly overhead. Christine and her family stopped and looked up, frozen. She could see the bombers' dark underbellies, like enormous pregnant fish swimming through the night sky. The roar of the engines hurt her ears, and everyone grimaced and ducked. Then the planes were gone as fast as they came, disappearing into the gray and black smear of night sky. Christine hooked her arm through Oma's and helped her across the cobblestones and down the alley.

Inside the bomb shelter, a quiet gathering of shadowy figures waited in the gloom, some sitting on benches, some standing, some crouched against the walls. Two oil lamps hung from the ceiling, casting flickering silhouettes along the curved walls. Everyone looked at each other without speaking, their wide, panic-filled eyes expressing everything. A handful of people shifted on the bench, making room for Oma and Opa to sit down. Christine moved toward the rear of the shelter, where Heinrich and Karl, along with a group of other children, sat on mattresses thrown over the potato bins. She glanced toward the back wall of the cellar, behind the slat of the last crate, but the edge of her and Isaac's tablecloth was no longer visible.

Maria was there, leaning against the wall, arms wrapped around her waist, staring at her shoes.

"Are you all right?" Christine asked her.

Maria looked up and shook her head, her eyes flooding. "How long do you think we'll have to stay in here?"

"I don't know, not long." Maria pressed her lips together, and Christine pulled her close, whispering in her ear, "Don't worry, we'll be all right." Maria squeezed Christine's arm with both hands and leaned into her shoulder, head down and eyes closed, as if trying to make herself smaller. Christine could feel her shaking. "It'll be over soon," she said, praying it was true.

Just then, a bomb hit close by, making everyone duck. Jagged chunks of cement fell from the ceiling. Maria jumped and dug her nails into Christine's skin. Heinrich and Karl put their hands over their ears and squeezed their eyes shut. Several people cried out. Some of the children started to whimper and weep, burying their faces in each other's shoulders. The oil lamps swung back and forth, like pendulums counting down the seconds of their lives.

"Try not to worry," Christine told her sister, a raw flicker of panic rising in her throat. "They're bombing the air base, not us."

"But what if they miss?" Maria said, tears spilling from her eyes. She wiped them away and glanced at the boys, who were watching with furrowed brows, their arms wrapped around their knees, as if they wanted to curl up and disappear. The sisters reached out, and the boys jumped down from the mattresses and scrambled toward them, burying their faces in their skirts.

"They won't," Christine said, trying to keep her voice from catching.

"How do you *know?*"

I don't, Christine thought, realizing there was nothing she could say to ease her sister's fears. *But maybe if I say it, it'll be true.* Maria picked up Karl, whose small limbs shuddered with fear.

Just then, Mutti appeared, the corners of her lips twitching as she tried to smile. She reached out and, one at a time, caressed her children's cheeks. Karl practically leapt into her arms. Christine thought about the love and care her mother had put into raising them, baby bonnets to protect them from the sun, soap and kisses on bee stings and scraped knees, hands held while crossing the streets. How helpless she must feel, waiting to see if Hitler's war would be the death of her children.

"I'll have that fixed tomorrow," Herr Weiler said to the crowd. He pointed toward the new cracks and holes in the ceiling.

"We won't be here tomorrow," a woman said in a small voice.

"Of course we will," Herr Weiler said, putting an arm around his weeping wife. "And we..."

Another bomb exploded close by, cutting Herr Weiler off mid-sentence. It was followed by the roar of bombers passing over, so close it seemed they might crash down through the dirt at any second.

For the next half hour, no one spoke. They sat with their heads down and their shoulders hunched, listening to anti-aircraft fire and explosions in the distance. Christine held her breath with every bomb, some that sounded right over their heads. At first, she tried to count the number of explosions, but the blasts grew too numerous and close together, as if God were having a tantrum and stomping His feet on the earth. The air in the shelter grew thick with sulfur, smoke, and the sour odor of sweat and human fear.

It was impossible now, in the confines of the root-cellar-turned-bomb-shelter, to believe in the hopeful plans she and Isaac had made while meeting here. Back then, the scent of dark soil had intermingled with the smell of oak barrels, aged wine, and cold storage potatoes, to create a rich, earthy aroma. Now, the floor smelled like a rotting grave; the concrete walls reminded Christine of a tomb. Her mouth went dry, and she fixed her eyes on the wine barrel they'd used for a table, wondering if it'd be the last thing she saw before she died.

Eventually, the rumbling explosions grew further and further apart, and the people in the shelter began talking in quiet voices. To Christine's surprise, a couple of the old men lifted their heads and made jokes.

"Good old Goering," one of them said. "At the beginning of the war he boasted that the Reich capital would never be subjected to a single enemy bomb. If an enemy bomb reaches the capital, he said, then my name is not Hermann Goering; you can call me Meier! Well, Reichsmarschal Meier, there have been one hundred and nine air attacks on Berlin since the beginning of the year, so now we will call the air raid siren Meier's Trumpeters!"

"And Hitler says he's only bombing England because Churchill called him weak," another called out.

"The morning after the war is over, I'm going to go on a walking tour of Germany," a man said. "But I haven't figured out what I'm going to do in the afternoon."

A few people laughed out loud, but most only chuckled quietly or said nothing. At first, Christine worried that the men were taking a chance voicing their opinions out loud, but then she realized there were no Hitler Youth in the shelter. On the other hand, maybe the isolation of the bomb shelter and the electrifying fear of imminent death had given them the sudden feeling of liberation. Then, the man who had made the joke about Goering stood. There was a yellow star on his jacket.

"The Nazis say Germany's problems are because of the Jews," he said. "But who will they blame their problems on after they get rid of us?"

"Sit down, old man," a woman said. "You've got enough troubles."

Herr Weiler pushed himself up from the bench and looked around, his shiny face glistening in the dim yellow glow of the oil lamps. "This is my root cellar," he said, scanning the crowd. "In here, we're just Germans. If you don't like that rule, you can find somewhere else to hide."

After that, people grew quiet again. Between the silences outside, they heard sporadic gunfire and distant shouting. Herr Weiler and the Jewish man stood at the wooden doorway, two old men ready to defend the shelter full of women and children. After a solid hour of stillness, punctuated by the thump-thump of faraway bombs hitting their targets, a long blast from the siren sounded to signal the all clear. Christine's family and the rest of the villagers crept from the shelter, eyes cautious and blinking.

Black smoke rose over distant sections of the village, and in the direction of the air base, the hazy glow of burning fires reddened the dark sky. But this section of town looked undamaged.

Christine linked her arm through Oma's and held Karl's hand, then followed the rest of her family through streets littered with scorched paper and roof tiles. The weak glow of a smoky quarter moon illuminated the riddled stucco of nearby houses, along with wooden doors and window boxes pockmarked by flak and shrapnel.

Halfway up the hill, Mutti stopped in the middle of the street and hung her head in quiet prayer. Their house was unharmed. As they moved closer, they saw shrapnel in the shutters, but the roof and walls were intact, as were the barns and houses in the immediate area. Inside, Mutti built a fire in the kitchen stove while the somber family gathered around the corner nook. After everyone drank a cup of warmed goat's milk to calm down, they went back to their rooms.

An hour later, Christine was still awake and staring at the ceiling, praying that Isaac and his family had survived the air raid. She tried to forget the last few hours in the shelter: the shrinking walls, the bone-chilling cold, the relentless fear. In its place, she tried to recall the day on the hill with Isaac. She imagined the warmth of his hand in hers, the soft skin of his lips. She tried to relax her muscles and take long, slow breaths. Finally, she started to fall asleep, dreams of sunny meadows and flocks of sheep playing in her mind. Isaac was chasing her. Then her eyes shot open. The air raid siren was going off again.

CHAPTER 12

By the end of May, the Americans had joined the English in the bombing campaign. As a result, the air raid siren howled during the day too. While the lilacs bloomed and the birds built nests in the trees, helplessness and despair seemed to cling to everyone. In the ration lines and on the streets, people hardly spoke, their eyes hollowed by anxiety and hunger, their faces drawn by misery. Fear had become part of who they were, and it showed in their hunched shoulders and hurried pace.

Throughout the rest of spring and into summer, warplanes droned in and out of the valley with as much regularity as the trains that used to arrive and depart. Without the air raid siren to warn them, it would have been impossible for the villagers to tell the difference between enemy planes and the Luftwaffe.

Christine's grandparents wanted to believe the bombs were meant for the air base, but every attack left houses and shops in ruins. In the sections of town left intact after an air raid, laundry hung shredded by shrapnel; trees and gardens were black and scorched. Outside of town, fields were pockmarked with craters, trees were toppled and burned, and sheep and cattle lay dead in scorched pastures.

Karl and Heinrich complained of earaches and hid under Heinrich's bed at night, their feather bedcovers pulled over their heads, legs curled to their chests like infants. The first time Mutti went into their room and saw their empty beds, she ran into the hall yelling, frantic that they'd been kidnapped or had run away. When the boys clambered out from beneath the bed frame, Mutti was so relieved to see them that she fell to her knees and sobbed.

By the end of summer, it was a rare night that they weren't jolted awake by the air raid siren. On most nights, the warning sounded two or three times, sometimes more. The boys grew so exhausted that Mutti and Christine had to force them awake and pull them from bed, to half carry, half drag them through the dark streets. Mutti worried about how they would ever get up in time for school once it started. But then the announcement was made that school would remain closed until further notice because there were no bomb shelters in the buildings.

When the raids had first started, everyone in Christine's family had gotten dressed when the sirens went off. After a few weeks, they just threw their coats on over their nightclothes. But as summer turned into fall and the number and intensity of the night raids increased, they wore their clothes, and sometimes their shoes, to bed. Despite Christine's protests, Mutti remained adamant that the children run ahead, while she helped Oma and Opa down the hill, through the alley, and into the shelter. It seemed to take longer and longer each time before they appeared at the door, breathless and disheveled.

Eventually, Karl developed a fear of the siren itself. In the middle of the day, the first rising wail sent him on a panicky search for his mother. And it had awakened him from his fitful sleep so many times that he started to hear it in his nightmares. He'd start for the shelter before he was fully awake, stumbling down the steps in his bare feet. Twice in one week, Mutti reached him just in time to stop him from going out the front door. After that, she let the boys sleep in her room, so she could calm them when they threw back their covers, terrified and ready to run.

Even though he was nine years old, Mutti ordered Heinrich to stay in the garden or backyard with Karl during the day, so she would know where they were if the sirens went off. They were allowed to play ball in the street, but only if they stayed in front of the house, where Mutti could look out a front window to see them. Heinrich begged his mother to let him run with his friends, to play war or catch frogs in the rain-filled bomb craters. But Mutti was having none of it. And she made no bones about telling everyone that the other mothers were out of their minds letting their sons run loose in the village while there was a war going on. The mayor helped her argument when the Hitler Youth delivered written cautions about unexploded bombs, with instructions to report anything that looked unfamiliar.

On a sunny day in early September, her mother's rules and the mayor's notice were foremost on Christine's mind as she walked beside Heinrich through a bombed-out section of town on the opposite end of the village. For three and a half blocks, there was nothing but jagged walls, half floors suspended in mid-air, cracked staircases that led nowhere, and vacant windows. Her stomach turned as she imagined charred bones among the ruins and ash. On the second floor of the last house on the block, the scorched remains of a blue curtain fluttered in the breeze of an empty window. She instructed Heinrich to stay in the center of the street and keep walking, unable to take her eyes off the ruins that ran the length of the sidewalk like a row of rotted, black teeth.

They were on their way to the Klause farm, just outside the north edge of the village, carrying their mother's treasured Austrian tapestry, rolled up in their arms like a giant cigar. Heinrich was on one end, Christine on the other. She could have handled the cloth wall hanging on her own, but Heinrich had begged Mutti to let him come, crying that he was sick and tired of being confined to the yard. Christine could understand how he felt, but because he was with her, her plans to go by Isaac's on the way home were ruined.

Earlier that day, Mutti had asked Christine to climb on the couch to help take down the tapestry. At first, Christine had thought her mother wanted to put the hanging in the first-floor hall, along with the two suitcases packed with extra clothes, important papers, and what few sentimental belongings they had, to be grabbed by Christine and Maria when the siren went off. She'd climbed on the couch and lifted the corner loops off the nails, thinking it odd that her mother would want to struggle with such a cumbersome object on their flight to the shelter. The recent decision to take the suitcases made sense, because the contents would be all they had left if their house was destroyed. But taking the wall hanging would be too difficult. Who would carry it? Christine and Maria already had their hands full, with a brother in one hand and a suitcase in the other. And Mutti had to help Oma and Opa. But just as Christine was getting ready to suggest that Herr Weiler might let them store it in the cellar, her mother's face crumpled in on itself.

"Frau Klause always commented on how beautiful this was."

"What's the matter?" Christine said. She thought of her father, wondering if her mother would tell them right away, or spare them from bad news as long as possible.

"Nothing," Mutti said. "I'll be all right. It's just an object, a material possession, nothing more."

"But why are you crying? Because it makes you think of Vater?"

Mutti set the rolled-up tapestry on the table and looked at Christine. "We need a rooster," she said. "I spoke to Frau Klause yesterday. She has three."

"You're going to trade the tapestry for a rooster?"

"I have the memories of my honeymoon with your father. Nothing can take those away."

"But there has to be something else we can use," Christine said. "Wouldn't she like some plums or a pound of potatoes?" Christine looked around, trying to come up with something to barter, anything but her mother's tapestry. But other than the clock on the wall from her *Ur-Ur Grossmutti,* there was nothing of value.

"Frau Klause has a garden and fruit trees of her own. A decoration is a luxury. We'll survive without it. It's more important that we have new chicks. We have to plan for the worst, Christine. I can't afford to be sentimental."

Christine offered to take the tapestry to Frau Klause, partly to save her mother the misery of handing it over, partly because Karl would be sick with terror if his mother left for any length of time, and partly because she thought she'd be able to go by Isaac's house on the way home. Now, walking past the burned-out houses and half-melted piles of keys, silverware, picture frames, and other salvaged personal belongings, set out for pickup by the Hitler Youth, she wished she'd made Heinrich stay home too. She watched his pale, wide-eyed face out of the corner of her eye.

"I'm sure everyone was in a shelter," she said.

"I know," Heinrich said.

Thankfully, the houses and shops along the rest of their route were still standing. With the relative quiet of the day, Christine could almost imagine that there wasn't a war going on. They walked another six blocks, crossed a covered bridge, then made their way along a long row of linden trees until they came to the turnoff that wound through the fallow fields of the Klause farm.

Once they were there, she was relieved that Heinrich had come, because they had to corner the rooster between the house and the barn. The bird was fast and jumpy, and after a half hour of chasing him, Christine wanted to take back her mother's tapestry. The least Frau Klause could have done was have the rooster inside the coop. Instead, she'd taken the tapestry under her arm and motioned in the direction of the barn with one bent, arthritic hand, telling them not to take the Leghorn or the rooster with the high, black tail.

Now she and Heinrich were out there, sweating and slipping in the mud, chasing a feathery, flapping bird that didn't want to get caught. Between Christine, Heinrich, and one of the Labor-year girls, it took them over an hour to corner it. Heinrich dove to the ground and caught it by one foot, the rooster squawking and flapping and turning as if it could feel the heat of a boiling pot. Finally, Heinrich stood, the bird dangling upside down in one hand, mud and chicken poop smeared up and down his trousers. Christine gripped the rooster's scaly ankles between her fingers, flipped the thrashing bird over, and wrapped her arms around its wings. She cradled the heavy fowl against her side, one hand still clasping its feet, cooing and murmuring to quiet it.

Finally, the rooster stopped panting and jerking its legs. It settled under Christine's calm but firm grasp, its red-rimmed eyes blinking in submission. At last, Christine and Heinrich started home with the exhausted rooster half-asleep in Christine's arms. Berta, the freckle-faced Labor-year girl, was at the end of her shift, so she climbed on her bicycle and rode beside them, too shy to do much more than nod or shake her head at Christine's attempts to make small talk. After a few minutes, they continued in relative silence, except for the rattle of Berta's bicycle chain and the squeak of her turning pedals. In the distance, heat rose from the earth, shimmering vapors floating above the fields like hovering apparitions.

Halfway to the village, Farmer Klause was coming toward them from the opposite direction, his horse-drawn wagon loaded down with hay. To their left, two young boys were walking across the open fields, bags thrown over their shoulders. They met up with Christine, Heinrich, and the Labor-year girl at the edge of the road, eager to show off what they had in their burlap sacks. Christine touched Heinrich's shoulder, motioning for him to stay beside her as the boys walked ahead, pulling out bullet casings, shrapnel, and hunks of scorched iron from their bags.

Just then, Christine thought she heard a buzzing noise. She looked around, puzzled because the fall nights had been too cold for wasps or bees. Then she noticed a single plane approaching from one end of the valley, headed in their direction, and a cold sense of vulnerability gripped her bowels. At first, she told herself that it was one of their own, because the Allied bombers never came alone. But the closer the plane got, the faster her heart raced. It looked different than any she'd ever seen. She put one hand on Heinrich's shoulder, feeling the need to tell him to run. But where? They were too far from the village to make it to a shelter. The plane sank in the sky, lower and lower, and then it dove straight at them. She grabbed Heinrich by the shoulders, the rooster's wings flapping in her face as it escaped from her arms, and shoved him toward the drainage ditch on the side of the road.

"Look out!" she yelled, throwing herself on top of him.

The scream of the fighter's engine and the rat-tat-tat of strafing guns filled the air. Bullets flew overhead, ripping along the grass and the road, the thud-thud in the dirt like the muted pop of toy guns. The plane growled above their heads, and a whoosh of hot air ruffled her hair and skirt, blowing dirt and grass against her face. Then, as quick as it came, the growl of the engine grew farther and farther away, until it was an angry buzz in the distance. Christine lifted her head to check for more planes, but the sky looked as empty as it had only seconds before. She pushed herself up and felt Heinrich's shoulders, back, arms, and legs. He wasn't moving.

"Heinrich!" she screamed.

Heinrich groaned and pushed himself up on his elbows, a smudge of wet dirt on his cheek. "I'm all right," he said. He felt his torso and limbs, as if to be sure, then made a move to get up. But instead of standing, he froze, his face slack, paralyzed by something behind Christine. She turned to look and put her hand over her mouth, feeling the sudden urge to throw up. She and Heinrich knelt in the ditch, staring at the carnage on the road.

Berta was on her side, her bicycle still between her legs, wheels spinning, one arm splayed on the road in front of her, ribbons of blood running from her temple and one cheek. The two boys were face down, the bags of war iron slumped at their heels, growing puddles of dark maroon staining the earth between them. Farther up the road, Farmer Klause's draft horse was snorting and struggling to get up, one front leg at an odd angle, the wagon tilting to the right behind its flanks. Farmer Klause lay crumpled in the road, his mouth open as if he were about to shout a warning, blood-covered hands still gripping the horse's reins.

Christine helped Heinrich to his feet, and they climbed out of the ditch. At the end of the road, soldiers and civilians were running toward them out of the village. Christine wrapped her arm around her brother's shoulders and led him down the center of the road, between the girl's body on the left and the two dead boys on the right. The horse had stopped struggling and lay on its side in a puddle of blood, its eyes rolling back, its life blowing out from its nostrils in shuddering, blustery groans.

Christine wanted to go to it, to kneel and stroke its warm, muscular neck, to talk to it and calm it before it died. But she had to get Heinrich out of there, away from the bodies. They moved to the right, to go around Farmer Klause and his dying horse, and then she stopped. A few yards into the brown field, the rooster lay in a scattered explosion of red and black feathers, its head cocked to one side, half its body missing.

* * *

The next night, Christine and her mother were sitting on her mother's bedroom floor getting ready to listen to the Atlantiksender, a blanket around their shoulders. Neither Heinrich nor Karl would leave their mother's side. They lay on top of her bed, dressed in layers, watching Mutti and Christine with sleepy eyes.

Heinrich hadn't said a word since yesterday, and tonight he'd sat at the dinner table unwilling to do more than nibble on a slice of rye bread. When they had first come home after the attack, Christine had insisted she was all right, moving through the rest of the day in a disjointed frame of mind. Given everything she'd seen, she should have been crumpled in a ball next to Heinrich, crying until she fell asleep in her mother's arms. But as Heinrich slept the rest of the day on the couch, she'd insisted on hanging out the laundry, pulling up the last of the leeks, and making dinner, so her mother could stay by his side. She was shocked that she felt a bit giddy, as if the fact that she and her brother had survived had ignited some kind of euphoria at the thought of just being alive. The feeling was short-lived however, and afterward she fell apart, spending the night weeping in her bed.

Earlier that day, the Hitler Youth had delivered a warning of *Tiefflieger,* low-flying enemy planes that shot at everyone and anything. To avoid being shot, the paper read, people should hide and not run. *Maybe if you'd delivered this a day earlier, four people would still be alive,* Christine wanted to say to the young boy at the door. *And I wouldn't have taken my little brother with me. And his eyes wouldn't have changed into those of an old man.* She showed the notice to Oma, Opa, Maria, and Mutti, then burnt it in the kitchen fire.

Now, as they sat on the bedroom floor, waiting for the boys to fall asleep, she whispered to her mother, "Will Frau Klause let you have another rooster?"

"She might, but I'm going to wait a while before I ask. I'm not going to raise the subject while she's grieving her husband."

Christine crawled toward the bed to turn on the radio, certain that the boys were finally asleep. But then Heinrich spoke. "I thought Vater burned the old radio." Christine looked up at him, her hand frozen on the dial. He was looking at her over the edge of the bed, his old man's eyes glassy and red. Mutti got up and sat beside him, stroking his forehead.

"He changed his mind," Mutti said. "But it's a secret. And it's important that you don't tell anyone. Are you feeling better?"

"You're listening to the enemy, aren't you?" he asked. "The ones who shot at us yesterday?"

Mutti's shoulders dropped, and she looked at Christine, who was now cross-legged on the floor.

"We're listening to it because we're trying to find out everything that's going on," Christine said. "Because there are two sides to every story."

"Is that why they're shooting at us and bombing us?" Heinrich asked. "Because they think we're doing something wrong, but they don't know our side of the story?"

"Something like that," Christine said. "They're trying to make Hitler put an end to the war."

"Because he cares what happens to us?" Heinrich asked.

"Hush," Mutti said, pulling the covers over his shoulders. "Go to sleep now. We'll keep the radio low."

"Mutti," Heinrich said. "Are we bombing them too? The British and the Americans?"

Mutti hesitated, and then she said, "Don't think about it, *Liebchen;* just go to sleep. I'll keep you safe." She kept rubbing his forehead, back and forth, back and forth, until he was asleep. Then, she stood in slow motion, sat on the floor, leaned against the wall, and sighed. "How can I explain it when I don't understand myself?"

Christine shrugged and shook her head, then turned on the radio. She pulled a blanket over her mother, only half listening to the announcements. "Hitler doesn't care if we starve. Why would he care if we're bombed?" she said.

"It won't do any good to tell Heinrich that," Mutti said.

"I know. But it's the truth."

Then, all of a sudden, her mother's eyes went wide, and she put a finger over her lips.

"Conditions on the Eastern Front are desperate," the announcer said. "German troops are running out of ammunition and have no shelter, food, or medical supplies. At last report, the Sixth Army has been trapped by the Russians in Stalingrad."

Mutti clapped both hands over her mouth and stared at Christine. *The Sixth Army. Vater's unit. Trapped by the Russians.* For the next hour, they sat frozen, listening to the terrible truth about what was happening in Russia, while the boys slept, blissfully unaware of their father's fate. Christine hadn't believed the posters depicting the Russians as barbarians, any more than she'd believed the propaganda against the Jews and Americans, but now, she couldn't help praying they weren't true.

CHAPTER 13

Over the winter, fear of the *Tiefflieger* emptied the fields of hungry civilians digging for potatoes beneath the hard earth or searching for coal along the tracks. Inside the village, people still had to stand in ration lines and walk to the farms to barter for butter or eggs, but they all did so with their eyes on the horizon, ready to run and hide at the first sight of a plane.

Most of the *Tiefflieger* attacks were at the air base, but the day before Christmas, another incident of civilians being strafed in the street on the other side of town made everyone nervous. Hitler Youth were positioned in steeples and high rooftops throughout the village, working in shifts to keep watch on the daylight skies. With every report of villagers killed, Christine thought of Isaac and prayed that he was all right.

On the night of January 24, 1943, the Atlantiksender broadcast the news that, despite Hitler's order to fight to the death, the Sixth Army had surrendered to the Russians. Christine wasn't sure how to read her mother's creased face as the announcer said that even before they were trapped, thousands of German soldiers had committed suicide.

"At least they're done fighting," Christine whispered. "Maybe now he's got a better chance."

"If a prisoner of war has a better chance," Mutti said, pulling a crumpled handkerchief from her apron pocket and wiping her nose. "If he's still alive."

"Of course he's still alive," Christine said, wondering again if she was saying the words because she knew it was what she was supposed to say.

It seemed like just yesterday her mother had been reassuring her about Isaac, and now Christine hadn't seen him in how long? Had it really been years? To her it felt like last week. She hoped it felt the same for him. But now, she didn't even know if he was still in Germany, let alone still alive. And the longer this insane war went on, the less hope she had that she'd ever see him again. Was this what was going to happen with her father? Was she going to struggle with opposing bouts of grief and optimism, week after week and month after month, only to wear down until she had to say good-bye forever?

To add to her worry, no matter how much Christine encouraged her to eat, since they had found out that the Sixth Army had been trapped in Stalingrad, Mutti had lost more weight. She told Christine that the thought of eating while her husband was freezing and starving on the Russian front, or possibly dead and forgotten beneath the snow, made her stomach turn. Now, since the Sixth Army's surrender, Christine wondered if Mutti's lack of appetite was going to get worse.

A few weeks later, Christine found out how skinny her mother really was beneath her layers of winter clothes. As usual, they'd all bathed in the metal tub in the kitchen before Mutti, because, now that wood was being rationed and it was against the law to heat enough water to bathe more than once a week, Mutti always insisted on being last. Christine knew that, besides wanting to give everyone else the hottest water, Mutti cherished the few quiet minutes she had to soak. But that day, what Christine had in her hand couldn't wait. A letter from Vater had arrived. Christine ran up the stairs and knocked on the kitchen door, fighting the urge to barge in.

"What is it?" Mutti called.

"A letter from Vater!" Christine shouted, her mouth close to the painted door. She heard a loud splash and imagined her mother bolting upright in the tub.

"Bring it in," Mutti said.

Christine pushed open the door and entered the warm kitchen, the humid air dampening her arms and face. Two pots of water boiled on the woodstove, filling the room with steam. It took a second before it registered, but then Christine realized that Mutti hadn't added more hot water to her bath. The windows were closed, condensation flowing down the glass in tiny rivers, identical to the tears on her mother's face, but the steam in the room came from the pots on the stove, not the water in the tub.

"Give me a towel so I can dry off my hands," Mutti said, her voice shaking. She was facing Christine, knees to her chest, hair pulled high on the top of her head, wet strands clinging to her thin cheeks. The twin lines of her collarbones jutted above her ribs, and her elbows were bony knobs, her legs like spindles on a chair.

Trying not to stare, Christine handed her a towel, then felt the cold, filmy water in the tub. "This water is almost freezing!" she said.

"I forgot to add more after Karl was done," Mutti said, reaching for the letter. Christine went to the stove and lifted one of the steaming pots.

"Why didn't you get out and add the hot water?" Christine said, unable to hide her anger. "Do you want to make yourself sick?" She poured the hot water in the tub, careful to avoid her mother's legs. Her mother ripped open the envelope.

"I was just going to wash up in a hurry," Mutti said, her teeth chattering now. "Besides, I have laundry to do, and it would have saved me from using more wood." Shivering, she unfolded the letter with trembling hands. Christine got the second kettle of water and poured it in the tub, then watched her mother read the letter to herself. In slow motion, her mother's face fell, and Christine's stomach knotted, waiting for her to read it out loud. Finally, she did.

> *Dearest Rose and family,*
> *I pray that you are well. I think of our house and*
> *beautiful children often, and look forward to the day*

*when I can see all of you again. The enemy is shoot-
ing from the woods nearby, and I often wonder if
those men think of their wives and children day after
day, just as I do. I don't know what I look like, but
the other men in my unit look terrible, their hands
and faces a smear of stubble, dirt, and insect bites.*

*I hope you had a peaceful Christmas. At the front
every Christmas is sad. On Christmas Eve we tried
to keep our spirits up by singing songs and telling
jokes around the fire. After that, we told our favorite
memories of Christmas at home. We recalled snow-
covered villages and rooms filled with laughter and
joy. Every now and then a soldier would get up and
leave, and we would find him alone, weeping
beneath the cold Russian moon.*

*The insignificance of everyday life pales against
this. Here, we have nothing but the idea and memory of family and home. With that, we are men who
can bear everything. Don't worry, nothing can happen to me any longer. I want you to know how much
I love you all. And, if it is within my power, I will do
everything I can to see you again.*
Heil Hitler,
Dietrich

Mutti looked up at Christine, her eyes flooding. "He's given
up," she whispered.

"Nein," Christine said, taking the letter. "He said at the end he'll
do everything in his power to see us again."

"But so many men have died . . ." Mutti said.

"We can only hope that the situation isn't as bad as the radio
says," Christine said. "The enemy is bound to exaggerate. At least
we know he's alive!"

Then, out of the blue, Mutti perked up. "He talked about
Christmas," she said. "If things were so terrible, how could he have
gotten a letter out since then?"

"That's right," Christine said. "See, it's good news." Christine moved the envelope to one side and looked at the postmark. January 10, 1942. The letter was a year old. She swallowed the sour taste at the back of her throat, shoved the letter back in the envelope, and slipped it into her apron pocket.

"I'm sorry," her mother said. "You're right. He sent it after the Russians captured them, so that means they're letting them send letters. Which means they're probably giving them food and clothes too."

"That's right," Christine said, fighting back tears. She turned toward the breakfast nook and started to pull silverware out of the drawer. *Even though the letter is a year old,* she told herself, *that doesn't mean he's dead. What would be the point of telling her, especially if it means she won't eat? I'll just smudge out the date with a piece of coal, and she'll never know.* "He's probably getting more to eat than we are," she said, struggling to keep her voice even. "So, now that you know Vater is all right, how about finishing your bath and letting me make you lunch?"

"*Ja,*" her mother said. "Let's celebrate. Get everyone together, and we'll open the last jar of plum jam."

In February, the government finally made the official announcement that the Sixth Army had surrendered. Flags were flown at half-mast, and women wept in the ration lines. At first, Christine thought they were worried about their husbands on the Russian front. But then she found out that men as old as sixty-five and boys as young as sixteen were being drafted into a newly formed division of the army called the Volkssturm, without uniforms. Twelve- to fifteen-year-olds were being sent to man anti-aircraft guns in Frankfurt, Stuttgart, and Berlin. She thanked God that her brothers were still too young.

A few weeks later, the papers announced that the German troops were consolidating and realigning on the Eastern Front, but Opa said that it really meant they were retreating and that Ivan was headed their way. Herr Weiler had informed him that *Volksdeutsche,* or ethnic Germans, were abandoning homes in Prussia and the Ukraine, and now those refugees were heading toward Germany. Christine overheard Opa telling her mother that Russian soldiers were slaughtering and raping German women and children. At first, she didn't believe it, but when, with their ration cards, leaflets were handed out that showed Russian soldiers standing over the bodies of dead German women and children, Christine felt the cold fear of another threat forming in her stomach. The message was clear: This is what will happen to our women and children if we do not protect our fatherland. Christine couldn't imagine the point of handing the flyers out in the village, because there was no one left to defend them; the men were gone. She burnt the leaflets in the woodstove so her brothers wouldn't see them.

In the middle of the night on the first day of March, Heinrich fell in his rush down the stairs during an air raid. Unlike the old, stoic Heinrich, he limped and wailed all the way to the shelter, certain he was going to die. His injuries consisted only of a bruised elbow and scraped knee, but it just added to everyone's sense of trauma at having to run for their lives. To make matters worse, they were stuck in the shelter for three days, because every time they thought the raid was finally over, the bombs started dropping again. The potato bins and wine barrels were long empty, and only a few people, including Christine's mother, had had the foresight to bring food when the sirens went off. Mutti always kept a replenished bag sitting by the front door, and this time it held a jar of pickled eggs and a loaf of rye bread.

The occupants of the shelter put all their food together and divided the bread, jam, eggs, jarred herring, bits of goat cheese, and dried apples into minuscule meals for thirty-plus people. The men broke a hole in the cement wall of the shelter and dug a tunnel to the outside, so the smallest boy could crawl through to collect water from the creek. At the end of the third day, when the all clear finally sounded, they emerged filthy and hungry, certain the village had been reduced to rubble. To everyone's disbelief, the immediate area was still standing.

The next few months went by in repetitive days filled with planting the garden, pulling weeds, standing in ration lines, cleaning, scrounging for food, and running to the bomb shelter. Christine was beginning to wonder how long they could keep it up before losing their minds. *Is this the way it's going to be for the rest of my life?* she wondered. *How long can a person live in fear of dying before it becomes too much? How long before I find out if my father is dead or alive? How long before Isaac gives up on our relationship?* Tired of feeling helpless, she decided she'd give it until fall, until the same day in late September when he'd kissed her for the first time. Then, no matter what, she was going to his house again, to see if he was still there.

At the end of July, they were in the shelter again, sweating in the middle of the night as they waited for the all clear. It'd been a hot summer, and the air in the cellar was humid and dense. There was a new person in the shelter, a nephew of Herr Weiler's, a skinny soldier who'd come home from the war missing an eye and part of his left hand. He'd come to Hessental from Hamburg, where his family had been killed in an air raid two weeks earlier. Everyone sat in a semicircle listening to him, silent and looking at each other with worried eyes.

"Eight-story apartment buildings, cathedrals, museums, schools, shops, theaters, and vehicles," he said, sweat beading up on his forehead. "All incinerated in a rain of fire. They dropped regular bombs on the most densely populated neighborhoods, Hamburg, Billwerder, Ausschlag, and Barmbek, to bust open the buildings. Then they dropped the firebombs. In the end, four square miles of the city just disappeared. I was crossing the bridge over the Elbe, coming home from a late night with friends. The bombs the Allies were dropping were like nothing I'd ever seen. When they exploded, chemicals splashed over everything, turning entire neighborhoods into a sea of fire."

"Bitte," a woman said. "The children might hear."

The soldier shared a rolled cigarette with his uncle, passing it to him with the remaining fingers of his left hand, the bitter-smelling smoke making him squint. Christine edged closer so she could hear.

"All the fires joined together, forming pyres that grew hotter and hotter and roared upward for thousands of feet, sucking in the surrounding air. Suddenly there was an awful howling, and the firestorm sucked everything in, including people trying to run away.

The fire liquefied stone, and people's feet were trapped in the melting streets. I saw burning bodies jumping into the river, only to ignite again when they crawled out. I saw women running with children in their arms, then burning, falling and not getting back up. My friends and I ran inside a building and went down to the cellar. The people inside told us they could usually tell what kind of bombs were being dropped by listening to the different sounds they made—a rustling flock of landing birds was incendiaries, a sudden crack a firebomb, a loud splash was a bomb filled with liquid rubber and benzene—but they'd never heard anything like these."

"So they're using a new kind of bomb?" someone asked.

"That's what he said," Herr Weiler said.

"I can't believe it," a woman said. "You're making it up."

"I assure you," the soldier said. "I'm not making it up."

"Then why haven't they used them here?"

"I don't know," the soldier said. "Maybe they only use them in the big cities because there are more people. Maybe after they saw how terrible they were, they decided not to use them again. Maybe it was a test. It was only two weeks ago, so maybe they're making more. I don't know what their strategies are!"

"I've heard enough," the woman who had accused him of lying said. She retreated toward the back of the cellar, and several other women followed.

"Tell them what happened next," Herr Weiler said, giving the cigarette back to him.

"After a while the temperature in the cellar started to rise. The air was filling with smoke. We could hear buildings crashing all around us. I decided to get out, even though everyone told me not to go. I pushed open the shelter door, and everything was red, like the inside of a furnace. A dry wind blew in my face, so hot it burned my windpipe. The air was on fire, but I could see a clear path back to the bridge, so I ran. Halfway there, a wall of fire was headed toward me, so I ducked into an underground bunker and pried open the door. The bunker was packed, and injured people were lying all over the floor, screaming for water. Then there was a hit, and the bunker rocked back and forth. One wall started falling in, and liquid phosphorous flowed through the cracks. People became hysterical, and I turned and ran out. I don't know how, but I made it to the edge of the city, and just stood there, watching it burn. The next day, I went back to see if my family was still alive. The survivors were burning huge piles of dead bodies in the streets."

"Why would they do that?" someone asked.

"What else could they do?" Herr Weiler said. "Bury them one by one?"

"They had to burn them," a man said. "To stop the spread of disease."

"That's right," the soldier said.

"Finish your story," Herr Weiler said.

"The building where I'd hidden was gone. The streets were filled with charred bodies, their hands outstretched, their jaws opened in silent screams. Some were burnt so badly it was hard to tell if they were adults or children. People were walking around with buckets and sacks, picking up body parts. In the cellars they found shriveled, burnt corpses, or nothing but ash. Sometimes they found the victims lined up on benches, leaning against each other as if asleep, suffocated because the fires had pulled the air out of the shelters. When I was looking for my parents' house, I couldn't even tell where I was. Nothing looked familiar to me." He paused and hung his head. After a minute, he cleared his throat and looked up, his eye wet. "Then I saw the charred corner of the library at the end of my block, and I went in the direction of our building. But everything was gone. I never found my parents or my sisters. Yesterday, I heard that over a hundred and twenty miles away, people could see Hamburg burning."

"Was there a weapons factory there?" someone asked.

"Not on that side of the city. There was no air base, no factories, nothing military."

"Do you think it was a mistake?" Herr Weiler asked.

"It wasn't a mistake. It lasted three hours. Then they came back and did it again two nights later, and again three nights after that.

They're estimating over forty-five thousand dead. Hamburg was home to millions of civilians. Now it's three-quarters erased from the face of the earth."

Wrapping her arms around herself, Christine turned away and made her way toward the back of the shelter, a block of ice forming in her gut. Maria and her little brothers were sleeping in an empty potato bin. The adults had learned that giving the children cloth or cotton to put in their ears helped them relax, sometimes enough so they could sleep. Christine wondered if they were used to the explosions, or if it was easier to deal with the unending grip of fear by just going to sleep. That way, if a bomb burst through the ceiling and killed them all, they'd never know. Sleep was an escape, and she wished she could join them. Then she remembered that once in a while, someone brought homemade schnapps for the children to sip, to calm them down. Right now, Christine wished she had a whole bottle, because she'd drink it all, until she could forget what she'd just heard.

CHAPTER 14

In the middle of September, it was announced on the radio that thousands of citizens in southern Germany had been taken into custody in the interest of public security and on suspicion of activities inimical to the state. The destination of these criminals was Dachau. Opa said that with all the criminals the Nazis had arrested, Dachau probably had a bigger population than Stuttgart.

In the ration line the next morning, Christine's heart raced when she realized that there was no one in line wearing a yellow star. The Jews were gone.

"Do you know anything?" she whispered to Frau Unger.

"Nothing for sure," Frau Unger whispered. "But I saw the Kleins leaving their house in the middle of the night, with their suitcases. Someone picked them up in a black Mercedes. And this morning, when I passed by the Leibermanns', little Esther pulled back the curtain to watch me walk by. Normally, she and Frau Leibermann are in the ration line before I get here. Something's happening."

Christine made the decision right then and there that she was going to go to the Bauermans' after she picked up her family's rations. If the sirens went off, or the *Tiefflieger* came, she wouldn't know where to go, but she didn't care. If their house was empty, she'd have the small hope that they'd already left and Isaac was safe. On the other hand, if she thought that the Bauermans were still living there, she'd knock on the door. If Isaac was there, she wanted to see him. She couldn't take it anymore.

Later that morning, as she walked toward the other side of town, the possibility crossed her mind that Isaac's house might be nothing but ruins. As she pictured it, her breath grew shallower with every step. Along with the random sections of the village that had been bombed to rubble, she passed undamaged houses that looked vacant and unkempt, their sidewalks littered with dirt and leaves, curtains drawn, window boxes overgrown with weeds. Some people had left on their own, but now she wondered if the rumors were true, that the Gestapo had taken entire families away. She imagined the empty rooms, echoing with the memories of children, mothers, fathers, and grandparents, their lives forever changed or cut short.

Instead of walking around the block four times as she'd done before, she walked up the stone steps and stood at the front door of Isaac's house, her heart hammering in her chest, her throat parched. Smeared across part of the front entrance and one window were the remains of yellow paint. She could still make out what had been written. *Juden.*

She rapped lightly at first, then harder when no one answered. *I'll leave right after I see him,* she thought, running her thumb and finger up and down her braid. Finally, the handle turned, and the door inched open. A wedge of pale cheek became visible, a brown eye peeking out through a dark crack.

"Christine?" It was Frau Bauerman. "What are you doing here?"

"I need to see Isaac!"

"He's not here. You'd better leave!"

"Bitte!" Christine pleaded. "Let me in, for just a minute!" More frightened out on the steps than she would have been inside, she decided to take matters into her own hands and pushed on the handle. All of a sudden, the door flew open. Someone grabbed her by the arm and pulled her in. It was Isaac.

"What are you doing here?" he said, slamming the door behind her. "If you're caught they'll arrest you!"

"I had to see you!" she said, trying to catch her breath. Then, suddenly, Christine froze in the middle of the foyer and looked around, shocked by changes in the house since the last time she'd been there. Ratty blankets hung over windows and across doorways, making the rooms as dark and murky as the inside of a cave. Oil lanterns cast a dim yellow glow in the foyer and the living area, leaving the end of the hall and the top of the stairs hidden in shadows. Through the wide archway on the left, the marble floors were bare except for two straw mattresses next to an old cook stove and a pile of kindling that consisted of branches, rags, and odd furniture legs. Next to the stove was a tilting table made out of an old door and wooden crates, and four mismatched chairs that had been strengthened and repaired with twine and pieces of wood. Built out of scrap wood, bricks, and rough lumber, a row of crude shelves held candle stubs, chipped dinner plates, and an assortment of dented pots and pans. How was it possible that the Bauermans were living in such conditions?

Isaac and his mother stood side-by-side, their pale, thin faces floating above their dark coats, the yellow Star of David sewn to their lapels. Nina looked like she'd aged twenty years, with dark circles under her eyes, her graying hair pulled back in a matted braid. Isaac's hair was inches longer than the last time she'd seen him, slicked back beneath his gray fedora, the length of it curling behind his ears. But even though he'd lost weight and his eyes were dark with anxiety, the sight of his handsome face was almost too much to bear. When she saw him, it was as if the dead weight of all the emotions she'd been carrying over the past few years—grief, anger, helplessness, fear—passed through her chest all at once, exiting through her rib cage and ripping her breath from her lungs, trying to yank out the beating chambers of her heart. She stepped toward him, fighting the urge to run into his arms. It was then that she noticed the four suitcases, packed and waiting, beside the front door.

"Are you leaving?" she asked.

Just then, Herr Bauerman and Gabriella appeared at the end of the hall, their tense faces and the yellow stars on their coats illuminated by the light of the single candle Gabriella carried. When she saw Christine, she gave the candle to her father, ran across the room, and threw her arms around Christine's waist. Herr Bauerman blew out the flame and sat on the stairs, his head down. Christine rubbed Gabriella's shoulders and stroked the top of her head. The young girl was shaking.

"We're being transported," Frau Bauerman said.

"Transported?" Christine said, a swell of panic rising in her throat. "Where?"

"We don't know," Isaac said. "They're coming for us today. You'd better leave."

Christine felt her eyes well up. "Come with me!" she begged him. "We'll take off the star. We'll tell everyone you're my cousin."

"Nein," he said, stepping toward her. "They have our names. It won't work. You shouldn't have come." He untangled Gabriella's arms from around Christine's waist, then gently pushed Christine toward the door, his face hard. She grabbed at his hands, trying to hold them, trying to make him stop pushing her away. But he pulled his hands out of hers, as if she were stricken with disease, each of his evasive movements ripping a giant hole in her heart.

"Bitte, let me help," she said in a trembling voice. "Come to my house and hide. Don't let them just take you away."

"We'll be all right," he said, herding her backwards. "It's only for a little while. They're putting us to work in a munitions factory. You and I will see each other when this is over, remember? Right now, your family needs you, and my family needs me. If we don't do as we're told, our chances of surviving will only be worse. Go home, and stay safe." They'd reached the door, and she was leaning against it, shaking her head, tears running down her face. He looked at his shoes, at his mother, at the wall, everywhere but in her eyes. Then, all of a sudden, he took her in his arms, his strong muscles squeezing her shoulders, his face buried in her neck. He took in a deep shuddering breath, letting it out slowly and holding her for a long time.

"I still love you," he whispered in her ear. "I always will." Then, he let go and stepped away. Christine felt herself go weak, as if he'd stolen the strength from her body. She moved toward him, reaching out, longing for him to hold her again. Instead, he grabbed her by the arm, yanked open the front entrance, and pushed her out on the steps. He closed the door.

She turned and pounded on the door with her fists, but it was no use, he wouldn't let her back in. Just then, the screech and growl of an engine turning the corner at the end of the street made her spin around. The canvas-backed army truck was coming toward her, its running boards filled with SS soldiers toting submachine guns. She ran down the steps and along the sidewalk, tears blurring her vision. Two blocks away, she slowed to a walk, unable to catch her breath.

Then she saw another army truck full of soldiers, making its way along the cobblestone street in her direction. She wiped her face and kept walking, afraid they'd slow down or stop if they saw her crying. Keeping her eyes on the sidewalk, she took the next left, hurried around the corner of a stone house, and bumped into a *Hauptscharführer,* a sergeant major of the SS. He was like a black wall, the silver skull and crossbones and SS runes on his black collar reflecting in the sun. She stumbled backwards, and he grabbed her wrist, ready to come to blows. When he realized it was a female who'd run into him, he loosened his grip and smiled. She looked up at him, her head heavy, her heartbeat throbbing in her temples.

"Little *Fräulein,*" he said. "What's your hurry?"

"Um . . . excuse me, Herr Hauptscharführer," she said, trying to keep her voice even. "I'm sorry for running into you." She automatically raised her arm and started to say the mandatory greeting, but he stopped her, touching her elbow with a gloved palm. He looked down on her with steel blue eyes, his angular jaw working as he gave her the once-over. Beside him, an overweight SS *Gruppenführer,* group leader, smiled at her with fleshy lips and gray, crooked teeth.

"Is something wrong?" the *Hauptscharführer* asked. "Anything I can help you with?"

"*Nichts,* Herr Hauptscharführer, sir," she said. "*Danke.* I'm fine."

"A pretty German girl like you shouldn't be crying."

"I'm sorry, but I have to go home," she said, stepping around them. "My mother is waiting." For a split second, she thought one of them reached out to catch her arm, but then she was moving forward, escaping down the sidewalk.

"*Fräulein?*" the overweight *Gruppenführer* called in a singsong voice. She slowed, but kept moving.

Then he yelled. "*Fräulein!*" This time, she stopped.

"Come here, *bitte,*" he said.

She clasped her hands in front of her and turned, slowly making her way back to where they stood, her heart hammering in her chest. "Herr Gruppenführer?" she said.

"Tell me, *Fräulein,*" he said, his arms behind his back. "What's your name?"

"Christine."

He looked at the tall officer and smiled, as if this were a private joke they shared, then touched the buttons of her coat. "And do you have a boyfriend, Christine?" he asked.

"*Ja.*"

"Well, I don't know if you're aware of this, but the SS need strong, beautiful German women like you to have our babies. Haven't you heard? It's your sacred obligation to increase the Aryan race."

"*Ja,*" Christine said, forcing the words from her tight throat. "The Führer already told me."

The overweight *Gruppenführer* threw back his head and laughed. "The Führer already told you!" he roared, his stomach bouncing up and down. He elbowed the other officer. "The Führer already told her! And what else did our Führer tell you, *Fräulein?* Did he tell you his next strategy for winning the war?"

"*Nein,*" Christine said. "He told me that I should make our fatherland proud. That's why my boyfriend and I plan to be married as soon as possible."

"But your boyfriend, he's regular Wehrmacht, *ja?*"

She nodded.

The overweight officer lifted his double chin and touched the twin lightning bolts on his lapel. "But do you see this?" he said. "I'm SS. Did you know that to be in the SS you have to prove your German ancestry back to the 1800s? The women who are with SS are taken care of! Hitler even gives them medals for having children, bronze for three, silver for five, and gold for six or more. After we win this war, we will be the elite!" He leaned forward and sniffed her neck, pulling her scent into his nostrils like a hungry bear smelling a rabbit inside a hollow tree. Christine stood motionless, her knees shaking up and down, her legs trembling. "You could have everything you've ever wanted," he said, reaching out to touch her hair.

"I'm sorry, Herr Gruppenführer," she said. "But I must go home right away. My mother's not well and needs me to take care of my little brothers and sister. I'm afraid she might have typhus."

When he heard the word *typhus,* the officer stepped backwards and wiped his hand on the leg of his jodhpurs.

"On your way then," he said. Christine turned and ran without looking back.

She hurried the rest of the way home, her mind racing, trying to figure out what she could do to help Isaac and his family. Frau Unger had told her that the Kleins had left in the middle of the night. Maybe they were going into hiding. Maybe she could find out where the Kleins had gone, and the Bauermans could go there too. If it wasn't already too late. If the trucks she'd heard rumbling up the street hadn't already taken the Bauermans away. Whatever she was going to do, she couldn't do it alone. Even though she knew her mother would be angry with her for going to the Bauermans', she had to tell her what was happening.

When she got home, she rushed into the kitchen, where her mother was canning the last of the tomatoes for the coming winter, a stained dishtowel over her shoulder, her hands wet with red juice.

"Mutti!" Christine said, breathless. "I went to the Bauermans' today. . . ."

Her mother's face snapped up. Before Christine could finish, she dropped her knife and wiped her hands on the towel, moving toward her.

"Why?" she said. "What were you thinking? Do you know what could have happened if you had been caught?"

"I know it was dangerous, but I needed to see Isaac. I wasn't going to go in, but I did, and they're being transported. We have to do something! They're just sitting there, waiting for the Nazis to come and take them away!"

"I'm sorry," Mutti said, putting her hands on Christine's shoulders. "I know you want to help, but there's nothing we can do. They've taken Jews from all over the village. We can't stop them. If we tried, they'd take us too. I know you care for Isaac. I care for him and his family too. But I care more about you, and Maria, and Karl, and Heinrich. My job is to protect my family."

Christine wilted; her body suddenly felt like lead. "What's going to happen to them?"

"I'm not sure," Mutti said. "I've heard they're going to a work camp."

"Dachau?"

"I don't know. I hope not."

"Why?" Christine asked, her voice weak. "What have you heard?"

Mutti looked her in the eye, her forehead furrowed. "I've heard that people are dying in Dachau."

The black space in Christine's heart expanded with a painful jolt, making her dizzy. She went to the booth and sat down. "I don't think they're going there," she said, staring at the jars of tomatoes, lined up like soldiers on the table. "Isaac said they were going to be put to work in a munitions factory."

"I hope he's right," Mutti said. "Because I don't know what to believe anymore. The Nazis tell us that the war is being won, and soon we will rule the world. I don't care about ruling the world. I just want my family to have enough to eat and a roof over their heads. I know you want to save Isaac and his family, but how? We have to worry about our family right now. As long as we do what we're told, we'll be fine."

"That's what Frau Bauerman said too," Christine whispered, her eyes filling. "And now look what's happening to them."

CHAPTER 15

The next morning broke cold and gray, the streets and buildings and clouds the color of tombstones. Christine's room was so dark when Mutti shook her shoulder to wake her that she thought it was the middle of the night and she'd slept through the air raid siren. But then she remembered she had to get up early because she'd promised to work in the orchards with her sister. Farmer Erkert had hired them, along with other women from the village, to harvest apples in exchange for two bushels to keep for themselves. He'd lost two sons in the war, and now he and his wife were trying to keep their small farm running by themselves, choosing to do it without the help of a POW or Labor-year girls.

If it had been up to her, Christine would have stayed in bed. By now, Isaac had been taken away, loaded into a truck with the rest of his family and driven who knows where. Thinking she might never see him again, she didn't care if she ever got out of bed again. But she didn't have a choice, so she sat up and sighed, rubbing her puffy eyes and nodding at her mother to let her know she was awake. After Mutti left the room, Christine pulled herself from beneath the warm cocoon of her feather bedcover and got dressed, her body responding to her frame of mind with lethargic movements, as if her limbs were not flesh and blood, but water-soaked timber from a long-sunken shipwreck.

By eight o'clock, she and Maria were high on the hillside, picking apples from the same orchard where Isaac had kissed her on that sunny day when she'd thought the world couldn't be any more perfect. Now, along with everything else, the sheep were long gone, eaten by their owners or stolen by hungry thieves. Instead of sun, there was a light mist, and the clouds hung low and threatening above. Ten other women picked apples that morning, but besides the occasional call of a bird, the orchard was silent. There was no talking, no laughter, no gossip being shared by the young women. Instead, they worked like machines, intent on getting the job done before the air raid sounded or the *Tiefflieger* appeared.

The burlap bag felt heavy on Christine's shoulder. It was all she could do to reach up and pull the apples from the branches without collapsing in a helpless pile on the damp ground. Last night, she'd suffered through terrible dreams; there were none that she could remember, but they'd left her with a feeling of prickly apprehension along with a physical burden that made her legs feel like lead and her body move in slow motion. Even the swirling gray sky seemed to weigh her down.

By ten, the mist cleared, but a patchy fog hung over the wet, fallow fields below the orchards, creating the impression that they were looking down on the earth from high in the clouds. Within the hour, they'd worked their way to the last orchard at the base of the hill. Christine could hardly wait until they were finished and she could go home.

When she heard the familiar rumble of a steam train coming toward them, she didn't even bother to look, her mind intent on picking the last cluster of apples hidden within the damp leaves. But when Maria stopped picking and stared in the direction of the pump and thud of the oncoming locomotive, Christine finally turned to look. When she saw the train, she froze.

The engine was black as pitch, emerging through a patch of fog like a giant beast, its thick, round stack heaving a sooty wave of leaden smoke that collided with the low sky in slow motion, cloaking the cars in a shadowy cape. Nazi flags trembled on flagpoles that stuck out like antennas from the oily sides of the locomotive, and an oversized banner clung to the front of the round-barreled engine, a huge black swastika plowing the way. Behind the locomotive, six cattle cars rattled along the tracks, each painted with white letters reading, "Property of the Third Reich," and the spread-winged eagle standing atop a swastika inside a wreath of oak leaves. Every car had two small windows covered by barbed wire, and visible through each opening but trapped inside the cars were gray faces, solemn eyes, and human hands clawing for freedom.

Christine thought she heard screaming, but it was hard to tell. All sound was consumed by the thunder of the engine, the mad pumping of the pistons, the clack-clack of iron wheels. The rest of the women in the orchard stood staring from beneath the trees, bags of apples sliding from their shoulders, hands over their mouths.

Christine dumped half the apples from her bag and ran toward the train, hurrying along the footpath beside the tracks.

"Catch this! It's food!" she yelled, running next to the boxcars and throwing apples toward outstretched palms. Most of the apples fell back down and hit her in the face and head, but a few were caught by hands spotted with dirt and blood, then quickly pulled back through the barbed wire. The thin, pale hands reminded Christine of a picture she'd seen of eels snatching fish from a cave.

Christine tried to keep up, but the train picked up speed, bending around a long, wide curve before being swallowed, car after car, by the dense forest. She collapsed in the dirt on her hands and knees, gasping for breath, apples flying everywhere, the palms of her hands stabbed by rocks. She watched as the last boxcar disappeared into the darkness of the woods, a whirling cloud of leaves spiraling in its wake.

"Christine!" Maria shouted, running up behind her. "What are you doing?"

"Isaac and his family could be on that train!" Christine cried, pounding her fists on the ground. "What are they doing with those poor people?"

Maria helped her up, brushing pebbles and soil from her knees. "Are you all right?"

"I'm not all right! I'm never going to be all right!"

Christine wiped her cheeks, mixing dirt with her tears, trying to make sense of what she'd just seen. She couldn't string two thoughts together. Maria picked up the apples and refilled Christine's bag, watching her closely as she stood staring toward the still-rustling tunnel formed by the trees, the thud of the locomotive growing fainter and fainter. Finally, Christine headed back toward the orchard, her stomach sour and churning.

"Maybe he wasn't on it," Maria said.

Christine said nothing and went with Maria into the last row of apple trees. She tried to keep picking, but couldn't stop crying. Instead, she stood at the bottom of the A-shaped ladder while Maria handed her apples to fill her bag, trying to convince herself that Isaac wasn't on that train. But her mind wouldn't stop the image of him there, his arms around his mother and sister, his face jerking up when he recognized her voice yelling outside the barbed-wire window. *He can't be inside one of those boxcars,* she thought. *He's too smart and too beautiful to be carted away like an animal. His father is a lawyer, his mother an aristocrat. It doesn't make sense.* No matter how hard she resisted, she imagined Isaac and his family waiting at the train station, suitcases in hand, Nina and Gabriella wearing shawls around their heads and shoulders, thinking they would be riding in a passenger car to an unknown destination, and then, being shoved into a boxcar like so much luggage.

Within the hour, the women had finished the harvest, and Herr Erkert arrived with his oxen and wagon to take them back into town. The exhausted women piled the bags and bushels of apples into the farm cart and then climbed on, their eyes on the clearing horizon. Christine started to pull herself onto the wagon, but changed her mind.

"I'm going to walk home," she said to Maria. "I need to be alone for a while."

Maria shook her head. *"Nein!"* she said, her eyes pleading. *"Bitte,* come with me! We need your help with the apples, and it's not safe out here alone!"

"I'll be all right," Christine said. The truth was, she really didn't care if the *Tiefflieger* came and put an end to her suffering, but she couldn't say that to her sister. "It's safe in the woods. I'll just go for a short walk, then come right home, I promise."

Maria frowned. "Don't be long. Mutti will be worried. She'll be mad at me for letting you go."

"I'll be careful. I promise. Tell Mutti I wouldn't listen to you."

The oxen moved forward, and Christine stood watching the spoke-wheeled cart, overloaded with apples and tired women, wobbling away along the dirt road. Maria sat at the rear of the farm cart looking back at her, her thin legs dangling over the edge, her face filled with fear.

Christine blew her a kiss, then turned to walk back toward the hills. On the upper edge of the lowest orchard, she followed rutted wagon roads edged by golden leaves until she reached the bench where she and Isaac had sat side-by-side. She sat on the weathered seat for a minute, then decided to move on. Making her way past cords of chopped wood stacked between trees, she climbed faster and faster, until she reached a dirt footpath. The path narrowed into a steep forest trail, winding between bare tree roots covered with matted layers of pine needles. She pushed herself to climb as quickly as she could, going higher still, into the forests of high-skirted spruce, where the fragrant air was quiet and still, the midday sky masked by a canopy of evergreen boughs.

At the highest point in the forest, next to the oldest and tallest trees, a massive ledge of smooth granite thrust out from the hillside like the hump of a giant whale. Christine climbed to the thickest edge of the curved ridge, where she'd always imagined the whale's blowhole to be, and sat down. To the west, she could see Comburg, the "Castle of the Grail," a two-thousand-year-old medieval cathedral surrounded by high walls, nestled between the next series of autumn-colored hills like a fairy-tale palace. She was relieved to see that it was still standing. Then, like a flash, a thought came to her. Could the outbuildings and tunnels and hidden rooms of the ancient monastery be filled with hiding Jews? *I should have thought of that,* she thought. *I should have told Isaac to take his family there. I should have done something, anything, instead of just waiting to see what happened.*

From up here, the village looked the same, but she knew it wasn't. Children rarely played in the cobblestone alleys or on the sidewalks. Soldiers and tanks and motorcycles roared through the streets. Entire houses were gone, reduced to rubble. People disappeared after a knock on the door in the middle of the night. She wondered how many were hiding beneath staircases and behind closets, inside hidden rooms and tunnels normally used for storing vegetables. But from this high place, she couldn't see any of that. All she could see was the steeple of the church across from her house and the sea of orange, clay-tiled rooftops.

She could almost imagine that nothing had changed, but what her eyes recognized as familiar, and what she felt deep within her heart and soul, were two very different things. She took a deep breath, trying to breathe in the fragrance of the pines and the fresh air that used to lift her spirits and make her feel so alive, but it had no effect. She sat there seeing but not feeling, existing but not living. She closed her eyes and tried to picture Isaac's face.

Just then, the sun came out from behind a cloud, warming her forehead and cheeks. She was grateful to feel something, anything, even just a change in temperature. The only sounds were from the squirrels and birds, and the wind rustling through the tops of the pines, a gentle, shuffling whisper that sounded like distant rolling waves, as if the ocean were on the other side of the hill. But then, in the next instant, she opened her eyes and sat up, cocking her head to one side, listening. The noise was quiet at first, then grew louder and louder. Her heart began to race, the familiar, coppery taste of fear rising in her throat. It was the unmistakable wail of the air raid siren rising up from the village. She sat frozen, unsure of what to do. Then, within minutes, the monotone roar of approaching aircraft filled her ears. She scrambled to her feet. The planes were above the trees, behind her, and she pictured herself being shot and falling off the hillside, crashing into the high-skirted trees below in a shower of bullets and splintered wood. She ran back beneath the cover of evergreens and hid behind a wide spruce. The silhouettes of hundreds of bombers filled the sky, flying overhead in attack formation, like an enormous, layered flock of prehistoric dragonflies.

More and more planes appeared. The trees and the earth trembled. She watched in horror as the lead plane dropped its deadly marker over the air base, and the strong wind blew it back over the village. Within seconds, the silver of hundreds of dropping bombs reflected in the afternoon sun, falling over rooftops and steeples like used bullet casings from the chamber of an automatic gun. It crossed her mind that she might be imagining the bombs, because she didn't hear the whistle of the shells falling through the air. But then she remembered someone saying that you only heard the screaming sound when the missiles were above you. Here, she was practically even with the airplanes, and she could see their bloated underbellies giving birth to their deadly payload. Suddenly, she remembered the story Herr Weiler's nephew had told in the shelter about the attack on Hamburg. Her body went rigid. Maybe they were a different kind of bomb. Maybe that was why she couldn't hear them. Maybe they were the kind of bomb that melted stone buildings and turned humans into ash.

She gripped the tree in her arms as if the earth were going to drop out from beneath her, waiting for the first explosion. The hollow thump-thump of detonation vibrated in her feet, and the blasts made her jump. One repercussion after another echoed through the valley as her village disappeared behind black walls of fire and smoke. Now, the tumbling bombs vanished halfway down, their silver flashes swallowed by churning, rising clouds of destruction. Christine's legs felt like water, ready to trickle out from beneath her. After the first line of planes turned in the sky and flew away, the next squadron attacked the air base. When a third line of planes appeared and dropped more bombs on the village, Christine sagged to her knees, leaning against the tree for support.

For what felt like hours, she watched bombs fall, staring numbly as the valley filled with flames and smoke. The scorched smell of burning houses made her nauseous. She gagged, her empty stomach sending bile up in the back of her throat. Finally, the planes disappeared, their growling roar replaced by the crackle of fire and distant screams.

Dizzy and light-headed, she pried her hands from the tree and stumbled down the hill toward home. Branches and thorns tore at her arms as she crashed through the underbrush, not following the usual path, just headed straight down. Her arms and legs felt detached from her brain, like the long-limbed cloth doll she used to carry around as a young girl, its face nothing but blank cloth. Her mind, reeling from terror, somehow directed her numb, rag-doll body to take her home.

Half an hour later, she entered the fire- and smoke-filled village on trembling legs, her chest heaving, her face covered in dirt and sweat. The charred stench of burning buildings and the acidic, sweet smell of burning human flesh made her gag. She held her hand over her mouth and ran, forced to search for detours around flame-filled streets and collapsed buildings. There were people running, calling for loved ones and digging in piles of rubble with bare hands. Some villagers stood rooted to one spot, mumbling and staring, rivulets of blood running in their hair or down their arms or legs, clothes scorched and torn. Shoeless children wandered aimlessly, the whites of their eyes like bright moons in their soot-covered faces. A man with a scalded face and burnt arms reached out to grab Christine. She nearly fell trying to avoid his grasp.

At last, she found the corner to Schellergasse Strasse and stopped. The road was filled with a thick wall of brownish-black smoke, and she could only see halfway up the hill. Despite the heat from the burning village, she shivered, the icy grip of terror making it difficult to put one foot in front of the other. She took off her apron, wadded it up in her hands, and held it over her nose and mouth. Then she made her way forward, stepping around scattered roof tiles, broken bricks, burnt timbers, and shattered glass. A cat came flying out of the smoke and screeched across her path, its fur seared and steaming. Then, to her left, the smoke started to clear, revealing the front of the church, its steeple a smoldering pile of rubble on the front lawn, two cathedral windows filled with licking flames. Then she could see her neighbor's barn, caved in and burning. The smoke was being blown in the opposite direction, and the air in the street started to clear. A curtain was being lifted. She held her breath, waiting to see what horror would be revealed. Then, finally, she cried out. Her house was still standing. The front windows were blown out and the upper branches of the plum trees were burnt and shriveled, but the roof was intact, and the walls looked undamaged. Tears streamed down her face. She ran the rest of the way up the hill, through the open front door of her house, and up the steps.

"Mutti? Oma? Maria?" she yelled, racing through the halls. No one answered. She ran back downstairs and outside, then saw Oma standing near the woodshed, crying and holding her arm. Christine's breath caught in her throat. Oma was too close to the burning barn, her small frame outlined by a high wall of orange flames. The skin on Oma's wrist and right hand was raw and blistered.

"Come away from there!" Christine yelled over the crackle and hiss of the fire. She led Oma toward the other side of the house. "Where is everyone?"

"Maria took the boys to the store," Oma said in a monotone, her eyes locked on the burning barn. "She left before the siren started. I don't know where your mother is. I think she went looking for you."

Christine felt her chest constrict. If something had happened to her mother because she didn't come back from picking apples when she was supposed to, she'd never be able to live with herself. "Where's Opa?" she said, examining Oma's injured arm.

"In there," Oma said, pointing toward the blaze. "He tried to put out the flames because he was afraid our woodshed would burn. But the barn wall fell on him."

Christine looked at the burning structure, her gorge rising in her throat. A group of Hitler Youth had appeared and formed a bucket brigade to finish dousing the flames closest to the woodshed. She wrapped her arms around Oma, blinking back tears.

"I'm so sorry," she said in Oma's ear. Just then, Mutti came running toward them through the smoke-filled street, her hands and legs covered with soot, a trickle of blood dripping from her forehead. Christine went limp with relief.

"Is everyone all right?" Mutti yelled, her face distorted with fear.

"We don't know where Maria and the boys are," Christine

shouted. Then she paused and placed a hand on Mutti's arm, prepared to hold her up when she told her the news. "I'm sorry, Mutti," she said. "Opa has been killed."

For a moment, she wasn't sure what her mother was going to do. Would she scream, break down and cry, fall to her knees, go into shock? Christine held her breath, waiting for the words to sink in. For what seemed like forever, Mutti stared at them, her face a blank. And then, slowly, Mutti's watering eyes cleared. She took a deep breath, pressed her lips together in resolve, and said, "I'll go to the shelter to look for Maria and the boys. Stay with Oma."

Before Christine could protest, Mutti hurried down the street. Christine took Oma inside and made her lie down on the living room couch, covering her with a blanket. Neither of them spoke while Christine carefully washed and dressed Oma's burned arm with a clean cloth. Oma pressed her lips together and closed her eyes, refusing to complain even though she had to be in considerable pain. Christine tried to keep her hands steady as she worked, trying to ignore the sounds of buildings collapsing, people yelling and screaming, and the clang-clang-clang of the Hitler Youth's horse-drawn fire brigade, ringing in false hope above the mayhem.

When the house filled with smoke and the sulfuric smell of the burning village, Christine opened the back windows and the doors between the rooms to create airflow. In the kitchen, she climbed on a chair to retrieve Vater's bottle of plum schnapps, hidden in the back of a high cupboard, and took a long, deep swig, trying not to cough when the alcohol burned her throat. Then she took the bottle into the living room, where she persuaded Oma to sit up and drink two full shots of the clear liquid, the only medicine they had to ease her pain. After putting the bottle away, Christine swept the clumps of dirt and shards of window glass from the floor, wiped the film of ashes from the table, then pulled a dining room chair next to the couch so she could sit beside Oma.

"You better clean those scratches on your arms," Oma said.

"Shhh . . . Don't worry about me," Christine said, stroking Oma's cheek. "Try to rest."

Oma looked back at her with watery blue eyes, her thin, wrinkled lips trembling as she tried not to cry. Christine didn't think she could bear seeing Oma weep, and was relieved when the exhausted old woman closed her eyes and fell asleep.

After a growing breeze cleared most of the smoke from the room, Christine shut the windows in the back of the house, closed the living room door, and hung blankets over the blown-out front windows. In the near-dark living room, she turned the switch of a lamp. Nothing happened. She tried another lamp. Still nothing. She felt her way to the kitchen, found the oil lantern, lit it, and hurried back to the living room, where she set the lamp in the middle of the table and sat back down beside Oma. There was nothing else to do now, but wait.

Finally, Mutti returned with Maria, Karl, and Heinrich, in an eruption of frantic voices and filthy clothes that smelled like the inside of a garbage-filled woodstove. Maria was crying, her hair disheveled and her eyes swollen. Karl and Heinrich sat sniffling at the end of the couch, smudges of soot mixing with their tears.

"We weren't near our shelter when the sirens went off," Maria sobbed. "We went to a different one. I didn't have time to come back for Oma and Opa! I had to take care of the boys!"

"It's all right," Mutti said. "Who knows what would have happened to you if you hadn't gotten to a shelter in time?"

"I was going to leave the boys and come home," Maria cried. "But the shelter started filling with smoke, and I was too afraid to go outside!"

"You did the right thing," Oma said. "You could have been killed, and then what would we have done? Your Opa lived a good, long life. He would have given it up for any of you."

Christine stared at her shell-shocked, grieving family, barely able to comprehend what her life had become. While she was living in constant fear of bombs falling on top of her house as she slept, her father had been taken away by the war, Isaac had been taken away by the Nazis, and now Opa had been killed by some unseen enemy, an enemy who dropped fire and death from the skies. She stood and started toward the kitchen.

"Where are you going?" Mutti asked.

"We could all use something to eat and drink," Christine said, her back to her mother so she wouldn't see that Christine was on the verge of falling apart. "I'll make some tea and cut some bread."

"I'll help," Mutti said, standing.

"You stay here," Christine said. "They need you."

In the kitchen, Christine closed the door and went to the sink, where she rinsed her face and stared at the white porcelain, letting beads of cold water run down her forehead and drip from her chin. Then she made the mistake of licking her lips. Her mouth filled with the taste of smoke and ashes. She gagged and spit into the sink over and over, rinsing her mouth with handful after handful of water from the faucet.

When the tang of death was finally washed from her taste buds, she soaked a cloth and twisted it out, over and over again, wrenching it hard enough to make her hands hurt. It felt like ice against her hot skin, numbing the bloody scratches on her arms and legs. She bit down on her lip, threw the cloth into the sink, and gripped the edge of the counter, trying to fight her grief and panic. But it was no use; she was drowning, with no bottom in sight. She let go and slid into a corner, crumpling between the wall and the cupboards like a frightened kitten. The men in her life had disappeared, and now she couldn't help wondering if the Allies would succeed at wiping Germany off the face of the earth. It only made sense that Heinrich and Karl—and ultimately, she, Maria, Mutti, and Oma—would be next.

CHAPTER 16

Two days after the bombing, a wagon carrying rows of sheet-wrapped bodies passed in front of Christine's house. When she heard the creak of the dry axles and the clip-clop of hooves against the cobblestone, she pulled back the curtains to watch through the broken living room windows. Following the makeshift hearse with their heads down, a group of women, children, and elderly people walked in slow motion, their hands clasped around Bibles, crosses, or bouquets of wildflowers. She wondered if the bodies had been pulled from the rubble, or dug out of cellars, or, as she'd heard someone say, hauled from the banks of the river. So far, the casualty count from the bombing had reached two hundred and twenty-three.

But there would be no burial or funeral or coffin for Opa. The Hitler Youth and a few old men had searched for his remains, but they hadn't found anything: not a tooth or a belt buckle or a shard of bone. The spot where the barn had once stood was nothing but smoldering ash, the iron tools and wagon trusses melted into shards of twisted metal. Last night, Christine and her family had taken Oma to the cemetery on the edge of town to put black-eyed Susans on Opa's parents' graves, as a way to honor his memory. Afterward, they prayed around the dining room table, each sharing his or her favorite story of Opa. They vowed to put up a tombstone once the war was over.

Earlier bombings had wreaked havoc on the outer edges of the village, but this last raid had left half of it in ruins. In an odd pattern, every street seemed to have three or four houses left unscathed, followed by a row of dwellings completely flattened. In addition to the church and barn beside Christine's house, the destruction in the immediate area of Schellergasse Strasse included two houses behind theirs and four houses on the next street over. The ceiling of Herr Weiler's butcher shop had caved in, and the windows in the café were gone, along with kettle-sized chunks of stone from the front façade.

Within days of the bombing, a team of soldiers had constructed barracks next to the train station: three long, low buildings with metal roofs and windowless walls. Rumor had it that the structures had been built to house incoming workers, Jewish prisoners, to be used to rebuild the destroyed air base. The day after the barracks was finished, Christine was out in her family's garden, sleeves rolled up, hair piled on top of her head, working chicken manure and wood ashes into the soil with a spade. The morning was unusually quiet, except for Heinrich and Karl making engine noises as they played with their wooden trucks on the walkway between the house and garden, and the thump and wallop of Christine's spade hitting the hard dirt. Even the birds seemed to have left town. Just as the bizarre idea started to form in her mind that everyone in the village had either left or died, that she and her family were the last people alive, she heard a man yell, then again, closer this time, and then the dry, brushing shuffle of what sounded like a thousand feet, scuffing along the cobblestones. Christine froze, trying to figure out what she was hearing. Heinrich and Karl hurried around the garden fence to stand at the edge of the road, toy trucks dangling from their dirty hands. Christine set the spade in the earth and crossed to the edge of the garden.

The ragtag formation of bald, skinny men lumbered up the street, a haggard multitude of reanimated skeletons wearing mismatched shoes and ragged uniforms. There were hundreds of them, vacant eyes staring at the ground, razor-sharp cheekbones in ashen faces. The majority of the prisoners had yellow stars sewn to their gray-and-white-striped shirts, but some wore purple or red inverted triangles, or a combination of the two. The lucky ones had hole-filled shoes or tattered boots without laces, while others were bare-foot, even though recent nights had been cold enough to make the cobblestones feel like ice. The men shuffled forward in straight lines, putting one heavy foot in front of the other while SS guards walked beside them, yelling at them to keep going. Christine guessed there were about twenty soldiers in charge of four hundred men, but the SS carried submachine guns and clubs. When a guard got close, the workers moved a step or two away, trying to distance themselves while retaining formation. One of the prisoners, a short, dark-eyed man no bigger than a child, had a brown spray of vomit splashed down the front of his chest. Another left a trail of dark fluid from the leg of his pants. A few of them looked at her and the boys, their hollow, hopeless eyes unreadable. *Is this what they're doing with the Jews?* Christine thought, her knees going weak.

"Heinrich and Karl," she shouted. "Go inside, right now." But the boys ignored her, no doubt mesmerized by the ghastly specta-cle. She turned and hurried out of the garden, determined to keep them from witnessing any more of this horror. Just as she reached them, the prisoner leaving the dark trail from his pant leg fell face-first to the ground. A guard rammed the butt of his rifle into his side, screaming at him to get up. Without a sound, the prisoner curled into the fetal position while the soldier hit him again and again, pummeling his shoulder, his thigh, his ribs. Finally, the man half rolled, half crawled to his knees, then pushed himself up on shaking arms, struggling to stand. Christine grabbed the boys by the shoulders and turned them around, herding them into the house. Mutti met her at the door.

"What's going on?" she asked, stealing glances around Chris-tine as she led the boys inside.

"It's the Jewish prisoners," Christine said, breathing hard. "The workers being used to rebuild the air base."

"Why was that soldier beating one of them?"

"Because he fell," Christine said.

"He hit him because he fell?"

"*Ja,* he fell, and if he hadn't gotten up, I don't know what would have happened."

"But they need them to work, don't they?"

"I don't know," Christine said, crying now.

Mutti put her hand on Christine's shoulder, her eyes glassy. Christine knew her mother had guessed what she was thinking. Wherever those starving, half dead-looking men had come from before arriving in their village, Isaac was probably there too.

From that day on, the skeletal prisoners were marched by twice a day, at seven in the morning and seven in the evening, because if nothing else, the Nazis were organized and punctual. During the first week, Christine was caught unawares three times, twice on her way home from the ration lines, and once working in the garden. After the fourth time, she made sure she was inside during those hours, sewing, cleaning, or playing with her little brothers, anything to keep her mind off what was outside her front door. The sight of the prisoners was too much to bear, the hollow sections of her aching heart already overflowing with horror and shock. Her sleep was already filled with nightmares of their haunted faces.

She couldn't imagine those weak-looking men being able to work twelve-hour days, let alone marching to and from the air base twice a day. If one of the men faltered, the guards shoved him back into line and struck him with a club or the butt of a gun. She couldn't comprehend the reasons behind it. They were ordinary men: husbands, fathers, brothers, and sons, just like her father and Opa used to be. And just like her little brothers, who would someday be men themselves, if Allied bombs, the *Tiefflieger,* starvation, or disease didn't kill them first. Thinking of her father, she wondered, if he was a POW in Russia, was he being treated the same way? She prayed he was not. Was he nothing but a skeleton, waiting, as these prisoners seemed to be doing, for someone or something to put him out of his misery? How long could a person last in these conditions?

Then, contrary to what Mutti had said about feeling powerless under Nazi rule, when confronted with starving prisoners on her own street, Mutti agreed that they had to do something, anything, to help. After all, before rationing had come into effect, Mutti had

always been the first one to deliver food to any villager in need—
Pflaumenkuchen to Herr Weiler's ill father, *Apfeltorte* to Frau
Müller when her husband passed, oxtail soup to Herr Blum, who
"never seemed quite right." Back in the days when they could afford a butchered pig, to be boiled in the portable wood-fired kettle
in the backyard so they could make liverwurst and sausage, Mutti
always made Christine and Maria deliver the *metzelsüppe,* pork
broth, in little tin cans to their elderly neighbors. Christine had
grown up hearing her mother say "it was understood" that you
helped those in need.

"I suppose we could spare a few slices of bread every week,"
Mutti said. "And some hard-boiled eggs, maybe even some apples
or potatoes." They were in the cellar, stringing sliced apples along
brown twine, to hang like Christmas boughs from the rafters to dry.

"They march the prisoners along the retaining wall of the churchyard," Christine said. "The guards are on the other side of the
group at that point. If we wrap the bread and apples in old newspapers, write "food" on the paper, and leave them on the steps, it
should be easy for the men on the church side to pick them up
without being seen."

"But if there's one sign of trouble," Mutti said, giving Christine
a hard look, "or if we get to a point where we can't spare the food,
I'll put a stop to it."

Christine climbed on a stool to hang apple-filled twine. "I'll
take it out at night, an hour or two before the sun comes up, so no
one sees me."

Mutti froze, her brow furrowed as if reconsidering, her hand in
midair, holding up the other end of the brown string. "What would
happen if we got caught?"

"They'd arrest us." Christine took the twine from her mother
and tied it to a nail, then climbed down from the stool. "That's why
I'm going to do it, not you."

"I don't know," her mother said. "Maybe it's not worth the
risk. . . ."

Christine put a hand on her mother's arm. "How will we live
with ourselves if we do nothing?"

Mutti's eyes filled, and she rested a hand over Christine's.

"You're right. And maybe, hopefully, someone will show the same kindness to your father."

The next morning, after Christine had snuck out under the cover of darkness to leave newspaper-wrapped bread on the steps leading up to the churchyard, she and Mutti left the shutters closed so they could watch without being seen by the guards. When the time came, they peered between the painted wood slats, silent and barely breathing, waiting for the workers to appear in the street. Finally, the first row of pale faces came into view. Mutti placed a hand over her mouth.

Outside, one of the Jewish prisoners looked over his shoulder, checked the position of the guards, then picked up the package. Christine heard her mother's sharp intake of air. Her heart hammered in her chest. The prisoner worked fast, unwrapping the bread and tucking the newspaper into his pants. He took a few big bites, chewing quickly, then passed the slice of rye to the next man in line. Christine grabbed her mother's hand as a guard moved up the ranks on the opposite side, his rifle hung over his shoulder, moving closer and closer to the row of men with the bread. But then, in the next second, the bread was gone, four men having shared it before the guards could see anything. Christine and her mother gave each other weak smiles.

Within days, Christine heard rumors that other women in the village were putting food along different sections of the prisoners' route. She prayed it was true. After a while, she and Mutti decided to believe it, because even when the guards saw the prisoners picking up the food from the church steps and eating it, they did nothing to stop them. No announcements were made that the practice was to be stopped, no posters put up warning of punishments for feeding the Jews. Christine wasn't sure if a bit of humanity still remained in the guards' hearts or if they knew they couldn't stop it. After all, they couldn't arrest the whole village.

When the weather turned cold and the sky turned winter gray, Christine and Maria, with the help of Mutti and the boys, took the doors off the kitchen cupboards and nailed them over the broken windows on the front of the house, hoping that, between the shutters and a thick layer of blankets, it would be enough to keep out ice and snow.

Before the war, the first snowfall of winter used to fill Christine with a peaceful solace, the soft drifts blanketing every rooftop and tree branch in the village. It seemed like a time for reflection, a slow, quiet cleansing before the muddy rebirth of spring. But now, this year especially, the snow seemed cold and dry, reflecting the way she felt inside. Now, the icy shroud made everything flat and lifeless, like a charcoal-gray etching of a village where everyone had either vanished or died.

With no more word from Vater, Mutti's resilience began to wear thin, and she wasn't eating again. Christine watched her at every meal, making sure she finished her plate, like a worried mother hovering over a sick child. And poor Oma tried to hide her pain, but it was easy to see her relentless grief, mourning her husband of fifty-seven years. Maria, always strong like her mother, appeared to be tolerating everything better than Christine, but the strain on her face was apparent, especially when she thought no one was looking. Karl and Heinrich seemed to accept things better than everyone, possibly due to the fact that they had been so young when it all started.

As the winter wore on, the yelling and shouting from the men guarding the Jewish prisoners increased, along with random gunshots that echoed through the narrow streets. When Christine and her family heard the firing, they stopped what they were doing and looked at each other. After working all day at the air base, the prisoners were being forced to shovel snow after every storm, and it seemed as though the guards' tempers grew shorter according to the weather. The colder it was, the more likely Christine was to see patches of coagulated blood, the white banks along the streets stained a deep maroon by the blood of a man executed for a crime as slight as talking, stumbling, or falling down. It was madness.

By the end of the winter, the family's food reserves were running low, and Mutti made the decision that they had to stop feeding the prisoners. In the cellar, they were down to a couple of pounds of potatoes, some scraggly carrots, a bag of dried apples, and two jars of plum jam. No eggs were left in the salt-water jar, and it would be two months before the hens started laying again. Flour and sugar were no longer available, and the bakery had shut down. With nothing to sell, most of the stores had closed. Seeds from the garden had become precious, because no one had sold them in two years. The only seeds would be the ones they'd saved from the previous summer. Coal and wood had been declared national resources, making the fuel to heat and cook scarcer than ever. At the end of March the government cut rations in half. Now, food was all they thought of, it seemed, and all their time and energy was devoted to acquiring it.

More than ever, Christine wondered about the cities. How were those people surviving without canned and dried vegetables from gardens, pickled eggs, or an aging hen from a backyard flock? Even here, where most people were used to living off the land, rumors flew of villagers foraging the woods, digging up roots and berries, quarreling over mushrooms and nuts. The forests were nearly stripped bare of trees, and deer and rabbits were long gone. There was talk of people eating rodents. And even though the punishment for trading in the black market was death, as the long winter turned into a wet spring, Christine heard of women trading their wedding dresses for sugar, their blankets and pillows for milk and eggs, and, out of desperation, their bodies to the officers, for cigarettes or coffee, which in turn they could barter for a loaf of bread or a tin of milk to keep their children alive.

While Christine's family counted the days until planting, the month of April passed in what seemed like a continuous downpour, the streets and sidewalks running with soot and ash-filled water, the garden nothing but mud. On the other hand, the chickens—surviving on worms, insects, weeds, and grass—started laying, and her family was thrilled to have eggs for breakfast. When the hens were up to a dozen and a half a day, enough for everyone in her family to have at least two apiece, Christine went back to leaving boiled eggs on the church steps for the prisoners.

A month later, the days finally turned sunny, heating and drying the soil in the garden. The perfume of lilacs wafted through the air, alternating with the musty smell of wet ruins. It was perfect crop-growing weather, but other than the fields on the immediate outskirts of the village, hundreds of acres of fertile valley soil remained unplowed. The elderly farmers and soldiers' wives with POWs for slave labor were reluctant to send them too far into the country-side, unwilling to lose the only help they had to the *Tiefflieger*. In-stead, they kept them close to home, to grow crops and tend animals for their own use. By the end of August, some of the POWs had fled, having heard that the Russians had retaken parts of their country.

Without telling her mother, Christine decided to visit Frau Klause to see if she could get another rooster, with hopes to replenish her family's dwindling flock. If she left early enough, she wouldn't have to worry about air raids, at least for a few hours. Along with giving her family the anticipation that they could have baby chicks as soon as possible, which meant plenty of meat from the aging hens next winter, bringing home a rooster was sure to brighten everyone's mood. Her heart lifted as she imagined her mother smiling when Christine came back in the door, the big, feathered bird in her arms. For the first time in a long time, she felt a spark of purpose as she made her way to the bottom of her street.

But her stomach dropped when she saw groups of prisoners coming up the hill. She thought she'd waited long enough for them to have passed, but they were headed straight for her. She scolded herself for not having gotten up earlier. Still, she found it hard to believe that the Nazis were running behind, and wondered if one of the men had given them trouble. She knew they'd stop the entire procession long enough to take the time to punish the offender with a shot to the back of the head or a beating with the butt of a gun. The thought made her ill.

Behind the first group of prisoners, an elderly farmer driving a team of oxen pulled a wagon of sugar beets across the intersection. He halted the team on the opposite corner, climbed down from his seat, and entered a wood storage barn, oblivious to the fact that he was blocking the road and cutting off the second group of oncom-ing prisoners. Two guards stopped and turned, making their way down the hill to tell him to move. Christine thought about running back to her house, but it was too late. The first group of prisoners was on top of her, an SS guard walking straight along her path, heading right for her. She ducked into the landing of a building on her left and leaned against the door, trying to disappear into the framework. She didn't want to be this close, didn't want to see them, didn't want to look into their haunted eyes. Most of all, she didn't want them to think that, just because she was a citizen in this nation run by madmen, she too was a Jew hater.

The guard ignored her and walked past, his hands on his rifle, his face set. And then, before she could look away, she was staring, with less than two feet between them, at jutting cheekbones and rotting teeth, at skeletal legs and sore-riddled flesh. The smell of feces and urine overwhelmed her. She clapped a hand over her mouth and dropped her eyes. She wanted to get out of there, wanted to run home, but she couldn't; she was trapped.

Then the guard who had passed her was running back, in the opposite direction, yelling, "Halt!"

The prisoners did as they were told and stopped in front of her, some with heads hanging, others turning to see what was going on. She peered around the corner of the doorframe, trying to see if this was her chance to escape. A handful of the starving men had bolted toward the sugar beets, yanking the plants from the wagon and biting into the raw roots like wild animals. The guards tried to stop them, shoving and beating them with the butts of their guns. Three prisoners fell to the cold street around the wagon, then lay motionless, their heads bleeding, their bony arms skewed at odd angles. Barefoot prisoners removed the dead men's shoes and put them on, taking their comrades' misfortune as opportunity to up their own odds of survival.

A dozen prisoners took a chance and ran. One of the guards lifted his rifle to his shoulder and shot two of the escaping men, missing on the first try but finding his mark on the second. Four guards with semi-automatics began firing, shooting wildly at the prisoners who were running for their lives. Every other fleeing man fell, chest thrust forward and head yanked back, face-first to the ground. The rest ducked into alleys or jumped over fences. Three of the guards went after them.

Christine put her hands over her ears and crouched in the doorway, trying to make herself as small as possible. Adrenaline had built up in her body, and now it roiled through her shaking arms and legs. Then, all at once, the gunfire stopped. She looked up, noticed the guards were far away, and stood, ready to bolt. But just as she was about to make a run for it, she saw a familiar figure among the prisoners, about fifteen rows away. She froze. He was still in formation with the rest of the men, facing forward and staring at the ground, maintaining the position that was least likely to get him killed. For a second, she thought she might faint. Then she took a deep breath and convinced herself her eyes were playing tricks. She shook it off and readied herself to run, then looked at the pale, haggard prisoner one more time, just to be sure. His hair was shaved close to his scalp, leaving a grimy-looking skullcap of dark stubble, and his features were thin and dirty. But then, her heart stopped. She knew that jawline, those chestnut eyes.

It was Isaac.

She gripped the edge of the doorway and looked around, trying to stop herself from rushing to him. The guards were busy, fighting with the disruptive prisoners and chasing those trying to escape. They were all near the bottom of the hill, and she was near the top, close to home. She made a split-second decision, knowing she had to take the chance.

"Isaac!" she yelled.

His face snapped up, and he looked in her direction, his forehead furrowed. When he saw who had called to him, his eyes went wide.

"Go away," he mouthed. Then he lowered his head, refusing to look at her.

"Isaac!" she pleaded. "Come with me!" He stayed in formation, ignoring her. "Hurry, they're not looking!"

Then, finally, he lifted his head and gazed at her, his lips pressed together as if he was trying not to cry. She felt her heart break, but signaled him to come closer. He glanced around, as if noticing the scuffle and commotion for the first time. She could tell by the change in his face that he'd realized she was right; no one was watching. He took a step forward, making his way into the line ahead and standing there for a long moment, as if he belonged in that spot. Christine's heart raced and she thought she'd pass out, watching him move forward line by line, closer and closer, both of them stealing backward glances to make sure that the guards hadn't noticed.

Finally, he reached her and they ran along the front of the house, then ducked into the alleyway beside it. They raced behind the row of houses, climbing over fences and trampling through gardens, stumbling through backyards and chicken runs. He fell twice, his strength spent, and she helped him up. A picket fence caught on his gray and white uniform and cut his leg, but they didn't stop. They ran until they reached her backyard, where she pushed him into the chicken coop headfirst.

"Don't make a sound," she ordered, closing the door. "I'll be right back."

She hurried through the back door of her house, then went out the front door toward the street, her knees knocking together like sledgehammers. Checking her dress and shoes, trying to give the impression of a young woman on a leisurely stroll, she headed toward the bottom of the hill. She ignored the prisoners still in formation, hoping they wouldn't recognize her as the girl who had just helped someone get away. Just then, gunshots rang through the still morning air. She stopped, shoulders jerking at each report. One, two, three, four, five, six shots echoed through the streets. Then she heard the guards yelling.

"Get back in line or you're next!"

"Jewish pig!"

At the intersection, the guards shoved the rest of the prisoners back in formation. Next to the wagon of sugar beets, six men lay dead in expanding puddles of blood. Another dozen or so lay at varying distances away, face down in the street.

"We'll send a truck for these," one of the soldiers said, kicking a dead prisoner. Christine went back to her house, trying not to run. Safely inside, she raced through the first floor hall and out into the backyard. Isaac jumped when she opened the henhouse door, his face a pale oval overwhelmed by wide, bloodshot eyes.

"Where did you go?" he said, dropping an empty eggshell on the henhouse floor, a telltale film of yellow yolk on his lips. The chickens scurried over to peck at the hollow shell.

"I went back to see if they had noticed you were gone," she said, trying to catch her breath. "I don't think they did. They shot the men trying to take the beets." She was shaking and weak-kneed, leaning against the henhouse wall. "And the ones who ran. They didn't see you get away. They would have shot at us." She reached beneath a roosting hen, pulled a warm egg out from under the bird's feathers, and handed it to him. He bit into the shell and greedily drank the raw yolk.

In the tight confines of the chicken coop, she could smell the cloak of fear and odor of near-death that seemed to radiate from his pores. But it didn't matter to her. She was so happy to see him he could have been covered in pig manure and she wouldn't have cared. She moved to hug him, but he backed away.

"Don't," he said. "I'm filthy. And I probably have lice."

"I thought I'd never see you again."

"I thought I'd never see you either," he said, staring. His face was hard, almost contorted, as if he were in pain. "I was transferred here yesterday. I had no idea where they were sending me. And this morning, I had no idea we'd be marching past your house."

She felt her eyes filling. "I've been so worried! I didn't know what to think. Where's your family?"

"My father was killed three months ago," he said in a flat voice. "I don't know where my mother and sister are. We were separated the day we arrived at Dachau."

Christine felt greasy fear twist in her stomach. "What happened?"

Isaac's face filled with grief. "He worked for a while. But they worked us over twelve hours a day." He sat down hard on the floor, as if he had to sit before he fell. "It was hard labor. My father was a smart man, but his health was never good. Eventually he got sick. Even a healthy person can't dig, push wheelbarrows, swing a pickax, and lift heavy rocks for long with little food. One day, he just collapsed. I tried to help him up, but it was no use. His strength was gone. When they saw him fall, one of the guards just walked over and shot him in the back of the head. For as long as I live, I'll never forget that murderer's face."

"*Ach* Gott," she said, tears streaming down her cheeks. "I'm so sorry."

"There was nothing I could do. I wanted to grab the guard's gun and shoot him, but even if I'd been able to wrestle it away, the other guards would have wasted no time getting rid of me too. I was standing there, my father's blood all over my hands and face, and I didn't do anything. I just kept thinking, I have to survive, my mother and my sister need me."

Christine pressed her arms over her stomach to hold herself back. She wanted to hold him, to comfort him, to take away his pain. "I'm glad you did."

"It's not over yet."

"I'll hide you in the attic," she said. "But we have to wait until tonight when everyone's asleep."

"I don't know. It's too dangerous."

"Do you have a better idea?"

He frowned, shaking his head. "If we're caught, we'll both be sent to Dachau. Or, they'll just shoot us."

"They're not going to find you. Some of the other prisoners got away. They'll think you were one of them." She went to the door, pushed it open, and slipped outside. Before closing it, she leaned back in. "Just stay here. I'll get you something to eat as soon as I can."

She fastened the latch and hurried inside to the kitchen. Her mother was there, doing laundry, metal tubs of hot water filling the room with steam and the smell of lye.

"Where were you?" Mutti said, scrubbing a nightgown against the silver washboard with red hands. "I could have used your help stripping beds."

"I'm sorry," Christine said, trying to keep her voice from shaking. "I forgot today was laundry day." *I went to get you a rooster,* she almost said, then stopped herself, thinking of what she'd brought home instead. "It was such a nice morning, I took a stroll around the block."

Mutti stopped working and gave her a hard look. Christine knew how her mother felt about her wandering off without telling anyone. "After breakfast," Mutti said, "I'm going to need your help." She hunched over the tub and resumed scrubbing.

"Of course," Christine said. She set the breakfast table as slowly as she could without arousing suspicion, waiting until Mutti went out to the side balcony to hang out a load of freshly washed sheets. Careful not to take too much for fear her mother would notice it missing, she worked fast, grabbing a slice of bread from the table and a boiled egg from the pot on the stove, filling a small bottle with watered-down goat's milk. She wrapped the egg and bread in a page of newspaper, then slipped out the kitchen door.

In the henhouse, Isaac guzzled the goat's milk, thin white rivers flowing from the corners of his mouth, running down his grimy chin. He took a bite of the bread, a bite of the egg, then stopped, one cheek stuffed with food, realizing she was watching with tears in her eyes.

"It feels like we're caught in a nightmare," she said. "I don't understand how any of this can be happening."

"It *is* a nightmare," he said. "And morning isn't coming for a long time."

CHAPTER 17

At half past midnight, when she was finally certain that everyone was asleep, Christine crept to the backyard in her stocking feet. She opened the door to the henhouse and stepped inside, squinting at the feathery shapes of roosting hens high in the dark coop.

"Isaac?"

There was no answer.

"Isaac?" she called, louder this time. Still no answer. She put a hand over her heart, feeling as if the air had been knocked out of her lungs. He was gone. Her first thought was to run out the door and go looking for him. Then, suddenly, he was in front of her, rising out of the shadows.

"I was afraid you'd left," she said.

"I'm still here. But I shouldn't be. I'm putting you and your entire family in danger. I need to leave."

"You're not leaving. If you're caught, they'll shoot you. Besides, where would you go?"

"I could sneak across town and hide in my own attic."

"And what would you do for food? Go shopping for sausage and bread? You have no money. You have no clothes. What if somebody sees you and turns you in? Besides, SS officers have taken over houses in your neighborhood. They're probably having dinner parties in your dining room."

"Good," Isaac said, scowling. "I'll sneak down in the middle of the night and slit their throats while they sleep."

"You're not making sense. You wouldn't hurt a fly, let alone another human being."

"The Nazis aren't human. They're monsters."

"I know. I'm sorry. But for now, let's just worry about getting you someplace safe. Come on, follow me."

She put a finger to her lips, then led him into the house, holding the door while he moved into the first-floor hallway. After a few steps, he stopped and pointed at his ruined boots. She waited while he slipped them off, gasping when she saw the open sores and weeping blisters on his filthy feet. He held the boots in one hand, then signaled her to move forward. They padded up the two flights of stairs, crouching against the walls and keeping their eyes on bedroom doors.

In the third-floor hall, Christine opened a trapdoor in the ceiling and pulled down the folding attic stairs, cringing at every creak, her breath quick and shallow. When the steps were fully extended, she motioned for Isaac to climb up, then followed him.

In the attic, she pulled the chain on the bare, dusty bulb that hung from the timber rafters. A dim light filled the room, leaving the far corners in inky shadows and casting black circles beneath Isaac's eyes. The top story of the old house was nearly empty, except for a few boxes, an unfilled bookcase, and a lopsided chest of drawers that was missing its handles. A four-hole chicken roost sat against one wall, dried straw scattered on the floor in a patchy half circle. The air was filled with the not-unpleasant smell of old wood and warm dust.

"Step lightly," she whispered. "My parents' room is right there." She pointed toward the rear right-hand corner. "Sometimes my mother has us bring baby chicks up here so nothing will happen to them. But we don't have to worry about that this year, because we don't have a rooster. And we don't have to worry about Mutti coming up here either."

"How can you be sure?"

"She was afraid of the attic when she was little because her *Opa* told her a ghost story about one of her uncles. I guess he was run over by a wagon and decapitated, and my *Ur-Opa* told Mutti that his ghost walks around up here with his head under his arm. Now it's just a habit for her not to come up. Luckily, she didn't tell me the story until I was old enough not to be scared."

"But now I'm scared," Isaac whispered, smiling.

Christine rolled her eyes, then tiptoed toward one end of the attic, motioning for him to follow. Under the west end of the roof, the wall looked the same as it did on the east, but as they drew closer, the outline of a short, square door became visible.

"You'll be cramped in here," she said, pushing her fingertips into the crack and pulling on the edge of the door. "But during the day, if everyone is gone, or at least not on the third floor, I'll come up and let you out to walk around. You can't open the door from the inside, and I'm going to put that bookcase in front of it once you're in there. You won't be able to get out." She looked at him, waiting for a response. There was none. "If there's an air raid, I won't be able to let you out."

"I'll risk it."

The empty area behind the door was long and narrow, little more than three feet wide, and the steep slope of the roof made it impossible to stand upright. But the space ran the whole width of the house, so there was plenty of room for Isaac to stretch out.

"I brought up an old blanket, and I'll bring you whatever else my mother won't miss. Maybe I can find some rags to make the floor a little softer, and here . . ." She reached inside the door and brought out a blue metal basin speckled with black spots. "I brought this up earlier too. My mother leaves it in the garden to gather vegetables. It's the only thing I could find for you to use as a *Klo.*"

"You don't think she'll miss it?" he said, turning the basin over in his hands.

"She'll assume it was stolen."

"*Vielen Dank . . .* for everything."

"I'm sorry you won't be more comfortable. . . ."

"If you'd seen where I came from, you'd understand how wonderful this is."

"Was it horrible, Isaac?"

He set the basin on the floor next to the blanket. When he straightened, his face was tight. "It was a living hell."

"I've heard rumors that people are dying in Dachau. After seeing those starving workers being beaten and shot . . ."

"It's worse than that. It's worse than you can imagine. We thought we were being sent to work camps, but when we arrived, we saw the truth. By then, it was too late. We were trapped."

"What do you mean, you saw the truth?"

"Are you sure you want to know?"

"*Nein,*" she said, dropping her eyes. "But tell me anyway."

He sank to the floor and leaned against the attic wall, his bony wrists resting on his knees, his gaunt face a sickly, yellowish-brown in the dusty glow of the single bulb. Christine pulled her skirt around her legs and sat in front of him, her body trembling in anticipation of what he was going to say.

"When we got off the train, the guards separated the women and children from the men, the young from the old, the sick from the healthy. They pulled my mother and sister away from my father and me like they were sheep being culled from a herd. They took our suitcases, our watches, the clothes we had on our backs, the hair from our heads." He stopped talking and touched the inside of his left wrist, his brows knitted, as if he'd forgotten something. Then he went on. "When we were sent to our assigned barracks, I didn't see any of the old men or young boys from the train. I figured they'd been sent someplace else in the camp. And I was separated from my father. I didn't see him anywhere. The other prisoners tried to tell us what was going on. They said the SS in charge of guarding the camps were called Totenkopfverbände, Death's Head Units, for a reason. We didn't believe them. But in the morning, when the sun came up, we saw the chimneys. Then we knew they were telling the truth. When we saw the black smoke spewing into the sky, that's when we understood what the Nazis were really up to."

Christine held her breath, not sure she wanted him to continue. He hesitated, and she could see the strain on his face as he struggled, trying to decide if he should tell her or not. But then he went on, his whisper high and forced, as if he'd been waiting an eternity to tell someone, anyone, the terrible truth. As if he were trying not to scream.

"They're murdering thousands of people. Along with Jews, they're killing Gypsies, the crippled, the feeble-minded, the elderly. They're gassing them and burning the corpses in giant ovens. Unless prisoners can be of some use, and then they'll work them until they die."

Christine clamped a hand over her mouth, a nauseating mass uncoiling in her stomach, like an oil-covered snake climbing up from the sewers. Once the urge to vomit had passed, she swallowed and said, "*Mein* Gott. How is something like that possible? How can they get away with it?"

"They tell everyone the same thing they told us. That we're being sent to work camps. It makes sense of course; there's a war going on. Everyone knows that, to the Nazis, the Jews are nothing but free labor."

"And when you couldn't find your father, you thought he'd been killed right away?"

"*Ja,*" he said. "For months I thought my father had been sent to the ovens. I wasn't sure about my mother and sister either. We could see a section of the women's side of the camp through the fence that separated the barracks, but I never saw either one. I looked every day."

"How did you find your father?"

"For the first four months, I had to work in the fields digging stones out of the ground with my bare hands. Eventually I was moved to the quarry, and that's where I finally saw him. I wanted to run over to him, but we couldn't even speak. The guards were always watching."

"Did you talk to him at all?"

"We only saw each other at the quarry, but we'd try to reach for a shovel or a wheelbarrow at the same time, or brush each other's shoulders when we passed, just so we could touch. Every time my father saw me, he put his hand over his heart and smiled." Tears fell from Isaac's eyes. She put a hand on his arm, but he flinched and drew away.

"Not once, not once in eleven months have I taken off these clothes!" he said, jabbing himself in the chest with his fingers. "They treated us like animals! Every so often they'd hose us down and re-shave our heads, but we had nowhere to wash. There were no bathrooms, only a ditch in the yard outside the barracks. Our living quarters were filthy and overcrowded. Men died from typhus and dysentery every day. The day I arrived in Hessental to rebuild the air base was the first time I had used a real outhouse since we left home. And the rations are bigger here. Back in Dachau, they gave us one ladle of broth and one slice of old bread a day. We lived off insects and rodents. Men would fight over the shriveled body of a dead mouse."

"No more, Isaac. *Bitte,*" she said. "I can't stomach any more."

"I shouldn't have told you. It's just that I . . . I never thought I'd be here. I thought I'd never see you again. I was certain I was going to die in that horrible, stinking place."

"It's all right. It's all right. You're safe now."

He pushed the heels of his hands into his eyes. After a few minutes, he exhaled, long and loud, his shoulders dropping, as if he'd been deflated. "What about your father?" he said, wiping at his eyes. "Was he drafted?"

"*Ja.* We haven't heard from him in two years. He was with the Sixth Army in Stalingrad. Now we don't know if he's alive, if he's a POW, or . . ."

"I'm sure he'll return safe and sound."

There it is again, Christine thought. *Someone saying what the other person needs to hear.* Nevertheless, she was grateful. With all that Isaac had been through, he still worried about her feelings.

"Tomorrow morning I'll bring you more hard-boiled eggs, with bread and plum jam. I'll bring you fresh clothes, and a basin with hot water and soap."

"It sounds like heaven. You've saved my life. How will I repay you?"

"I'll think of something," she said, giving him a weak smile. Then she stood. "For now, you should get some rest."

Isaac ducked into the crawl space, then turned around on his knees, watching as she pushed the door closed.

"It's going to be really dark in there," she said. "I'll get you a candle as soon as I can."

"It's fine," he said. Then he put out a hand to stop the door, brushing her fingers with his own. "I want you to know something. It was thoughts of you that kept me from going insane. I never stopped loving you. Not for an instant."

"Or I you," she said, grasping his hand. "Or I you."

CHAPTER 18

That night, Christine's sleep was filled with nightmares. She dreamt she was being chased through a bombed-out village in the dark while fires burned and children called her name. She couldn't find any of them, and whoever was chasing her wanted her dead. The last thing she remembered was her father calling from inside a burning building, his voice crying out in agony as he burned alive. She woke up trembling and covered with sweat. It was dawn.

Unable to go back to sleep, she got up, got dressed, and went out to the chicken coop to gather eggs. Back in the kitchen, she boiled two eggs for Isaac's breakfast and sliced off her daily portion of brown bread. She made a tin of hot tea and placed the slices of crusty bread, the boiled eggs, a saucer, a fat candle, and a box of matches in a wicker basket. Then she took off her shoes and crept through the halls up to the attic, pulling the ladder door closed behind her. The empty bookcase was light and slid easily and silently, and the door opened with little effort. Isaac was still asleep, his head and shoulders near the open door, his mouth slack. *He must be exhausted,* she thought, hesitant to wake him. But she needed to get back downstairs before everyone got up and started looking for her. She knelt on the floor and gently shook him by the shoulder. He startled, unsure of his surroundings, and grabbed her wrist.

"Isaac," she whispered. "It's all right. You're safe."

His face relaxed, and he let go. "I'm sorry," he said. "I forgot where I was."

"*Macht nichts,* I've brought you some breakfast. But I have to get back downstairs before Mutti gets up." She set the basket inside the door and fished out the saucer, the candle, and the matches.

"*Danke,* Christine."

She handed him the candle and matches. "So you don't have to eat breakfast in the dark." He got up on his knees and lit the short wick, then set the burning candle in the saucer she'd placed on the floor. "Did you sleep well?"

"Better than I have in a long time."

"I'll be back later today."

"I'll look forward to it."

As quickly and quietly as possible, she closed the door, slid the bookcase back in place, and hurried down the ladder. She held her breath as she folded up the steps and pushed the attic door back in place, alert for any noise coming from the bedrooms. On her tiptoes, she gave the attic door one last shove. And then she heard it. The squeak of mattress springs in her mother's room. She flew down the stairs, her hand gripping the banister in case she slipped on the polished steps. Just minutes after Christine put the rest of the eggs on to boil, her mother walked through the kitchen door.

"Good morning," Mutti said. "How many eggs did we get today?" In one efficient motion, her mother put her apron over her head, tied the strings behind her back, and went to the stove to look in the boiling pot.

"Only ten, I'm afraid," Christine said, hating that she had to lie. "But someone else can have my share. I'm not that hungry this morning."

Mutti placed a hand on Christine's forehead. "You do seem a bit flushed. Are you feeling ill? Is that why you're up so early?"

"*Nein,* I feel fine. I just couldn't sleep, so I decided to get an early start." She turned away and reached into the cupboards for the plates, afraid her mother would read the truth in her eyes. "Will we be working outside today?" she asked, trying to sound nonchalant. "Don't Karl and Heinrich need to clean the goats' pen? And isn't it time for us to plant a second crop of peas and radishes?"

Mutti went to the sink to fill the teakettle. "*Nein,* not today. Oma wants to transplant some black-eyed Susans onto Opa's family plot this morning. You know I can't let her do it alone."

"Of course not. But I'll stay here and work in the garden. That way, we'll be sure to get a fall harvest. The weather is perfect."

"Maria can stay and help you. But the boys will want to come with me."

"*Nein!*" Christine said, her voice too loud. Her mother turned from the sink to look at her, her eyebrows raised. "I mean . . . Maria will want to go too. You know how close she was to Opa. She might be upset if you don't include her. You know I don't mind working alone."

Mutti sighed. "As you wish. *Macht nichts* to me."

Karl and Maria came into the kitchen for breakfast, yawning and rubbing their eyes. Oma and Heinrich wandered in a few minutes later. For the next half hour, the kitchen was a flurry of activity, with everyone talking and eating and reaching across the table for bread and eggs and goat's milk. Christine did her best to act normal, helping Karl peel his soft-boiled egg, passing the salt with a steady hand, joining the conversations about the weather and the latest war news.

"Did you see what happened with the prisoners yesterday morning?" Maria asked her.

Christine nearly choked on her tea. "*Nein,*" she said, coughing.

"But I saw you leave right about that time," Maria said, frowning.

"*Nein,* I went out to the backyard in the morning."

"You went out the front door," Maria insisted. "And you headed toward the street."

Christine cleared her throat. She'd been certain everyone had been too busy to notice her slipping away. "Oh, I was going to see if I could get flour, but then I remembered we'd already used our ration coupon for this month."

"What happened with the prisoners?" Heinrich asked.

"That is not breakfast conversation," Mutti said. She spread jam on her bread, eyeing Maria at the same time.

"I'm not sure," Maria said. "But I saw women scrubbing blood off the street."

"That's enough," Mutti scolded.

"I heard some of them were shot," Heinrich said. "But some got away too."

"Then let's say a prayer for those poor, unfortunate souls and put an end to this conversation," Mutti said.

"Ja," Christine said, her knees shaking beneath the table. "Let's say a prayer."

After breakfast, the others left for the long walk to the cemetery. Christine watched until they'd disappeared around the corner, Mutti and Maria carrying buckets of black-eyed Susan transplants, Oma's long skirt swaying back and forth as she shuffled along. Karl and Heinrich ran ahead, kicking a rock back and forth, happy to be loose in the streets. The minute they were out of sight, Christine ran up to the attic.

"How was your breakfast?" she asked Isaac, putting the empty tea tin in the basket.

"The most delicious meal I've ever had, *danke.*"

"Everyone left. Do you want to go downstairs for a bath? I've got the fire going for hot water, the tub is set up in the kitchen, and I'll get some of my father's clothes."

"That would be wonderful. Are you sure?"

"You'll have to be quick."

They hurried downstairs, Christine peering over the banisters and down the hallways before motioning for him to follow. In the kitchen, she drew the curtains and put a fresh towel over a chair. Isaac helped her lift the steaming kettles from the stove to fill the tub with boiling water.

"Lock the door," she said, handing him the key as she backed out into the hall. "Just in case."

Leaving him alone to bathe, she went to her parents' bedroom to search through her father's old clothes, looking out the window a hundred times. She didn't expect her family back for at least an hour and a half, but she couldn't stop checking, just in case. It made her think of Herr Eggers, leaning out his window on the day she'd first seen the Nazi poster on the weathered barn. She'd been so worried that he might turn her in if she destroyed Nazi property that she'd stopped herself from ripping the poster down. Now, that, along with the fact that today she was breaking the law by burning extra firewood, seemed like child's play compared to hiding an escaped Jewish prisoner. She could almost laugh about the irony of it all if she weren't vibrating with anxiety. She laid out her father's shirts and trousers, picked out what she was looking for, then put the rest back exactly as they had been. When she came back downstairs, she stood outside the kitchen door.

"Did you find the razor?"

"*Ja,*" Isaac said. "I'm nearly finished."

She heard splashing and imagined his thin body in the steaming tub, how it must feel to be able to use soap and hot water after so long, the dirt and grime washed from his skin, the sores on his feet scrubbed clean. She longed to go in and wash his back and the stubbled hair on his head, to shave the dirty whiskers from his chin. Her heart started to pound as she remembered the heat of their passion in the wine cellar, the hard muscles in his arms and chest, the hunger of open-mouthed kisses.

"I've got clothes," she said.

"*Ja,* I'm coming." The door opened a crack, and a damp hand reached out.

After a few minutes, he let her in. He stood next to the sink, folding up the sleeves of Vater's blue button-down shirt, an old pair of work pants hanging from his bony frame. His face was red and shiny, the dirt and stubble gone. Even with his cheekbones and jaw more pronounced, he was still handsome. She wanted to go back upstairs with him, lie down in the attic hiding place, and let him make love to her, so she could forget about everything. Then she noticed something on his arm.

"What's that?"

He turned his wrist to look at the mark on the inside of his forearm, then dismissed it and started to empty the tub. "It's a number."

"Let me see."

He turned his arm. "They numbered the workers at the camp." Christine ran a finger over the digits: 1071504.

"Why didn't it come off in the bath?"

"It's inked into the skin. It's permanent."

She looked up at him, eyes filling.

"It means *nichts*," he said. "It's not important. It changes nothing about me."

She took his hand and wrapped his arm around her waist, feeling heat radiate from his skin, the tight, hard muscles of his stomach pressed against hers. He pulled her closer and touched her face, tracing her hair, her cheekbones, her lips. Then he kissed her, and she kissed him back, pressing her body against his so hard she could barely breathe. A groan came from deep inside his chest. He put a hand on her breast, fingers probing through her blouse. She gasped and started to tremble, the years of fear and separation dissolving into passion and longing. Tears sprang behind her closed lids, and an odd reawakening, like the return of her soul, filled her parched, empty body. Finally he drew his mouth away and looked at her, his eyes wet.

"I've missed you so much," he said.

"I've missed you too."

"I love you. I always have and always will." Then he kissed her again, his mouth open and wet, his hand kneading her breast so hard it was almost painful. She put her hands on the back of his neck and pushed her mouth into his, a sudden warmth stirring deep in her pelvis. Finally, she forced herself to pull away.

"We can't," she said, shaking her head. "We have to get you upstairs before everyone comes back."

"You're right," he said, chest heaving. "I'm sorry."

"Don't say you're sorry. Just promise you'll never leave me again."

"I didn't have a choice."

"I know." She put her head on his chest. "But just promise me, no matter what happens, we won't let anything keep us apart again."

"I'd better get back upstairs."

"Promise me," she said, looking up at him.

"Don't ask me to do that. You know I can't. Nothing is up to us anymore."

After getting Isaac back to the attic, Christine returned to the kitchen and tidied up, mopping the drips and puddles of bathwater from the tile floor. She burned Isaac's uniform in the woodstove, trying not to singe her hands as she wadded the filthy, striped material into the fire, a greasy, black stench stinging her nostrils, making her think of death. She gagged and held a hand over her mouth, opening the windows, hoping the neighbors wouldn't notice the smell. After drying the kettles and tub, she made certain that every scrap of the wretched uniform had been destroyed, then went outside to plant peas and radishes.

After the last of the seeds had been spaced, covered with dirt, and tamped down, first with the hoe and then by Christine taking baby step after baby step over each row, she stuck a stick in the dirt at the end of each line and went to get the watering can. The tin sprinkling can was hidden by the woodshed, behind a stack of firewood next to a rain barrel beneath a gutter that ran from the roof. Christine ladled brackish water from the rain barrel into the watering can, then returned to the garden to soak each row of packed soil.

On her third trip back to the garden with the sprinkling can, just as she was about to open the gate, she heard something and froze. Unfamiliar male voices drifted up the street, and they were getting closer. When she saw the peaked caps and black uniforms of the SS appear at the crest of the hill, she wheeled around and hurried back to the woodshed, where she set down the watering can and picked up some logs, ignoring the scrape of bark on her bare arms. Glancing over her shoulder, she saw the blue-eyed *Hauptscharführer* and the fleshy *Gruppenführer* she'd run into on her way home from Isaac's. They were striding up the street, their eyes raised toward windows and rooflines. After four or five steps, they stopped and pointed with black-gloved fingers. Each time they came to a halt, the *Gruppenführer* wrote something down in a notebook. Then they continued.

Christine hurried toward the front door of her house, two logs slipping from the woodpile in her arms. She ignored the fallen wood and kept going, gripping the remaining kindling to her chest until she was safely inside. On the other side of the door, she leaned against the wall and waited, her heart racing in her chest. Then, she went upstairs, dropped the firewood next to the woodstove, and peered through the living room curtains. To her relief, the street was empty.

CHAPTER 19

For the next two days, as soon as everyone else was preoccupied with their daily activities on the first and second floors, or even better, if they had gone outside to the garden, Christine hurried upstairs to deliver things to Isaac: a slice of bread, a boiled potato, the first yellow strawflower of summer's end. She'd gone to see him a few times at night, but thought it best to sneak up to the attic only while no one was on the third floor. Throughout the day, she waited for opportunities to escape unnoticed. Washing dishes or sweeping the hallways, she kept one eye on her family, certain that they could sense her impatience. She forced herself to act and move normally, while her breathing felt rapid and shallow, her nerves jittery, like a small bird tiptoeing past a hungry, sleeping cat.

On the third day, she stepped out of the kitchen after breakfast, a hard-boiled egg hidden in her apron pocket, and started up the hall to see him. Three insistent knocks on the front door made her stop. She bent over the railing, peering down the stairs toward the first floor.

"Open up, Frau Bölz!" a man's muffled voice demanded.

Christine went rigid, fingernails digging into the wood railing. The man knocked again, louder and firmer with every blow. Time slowed to a crawl as the echo of each thud boomed in the quiet hallway.

Mutti came out of the kitchen, wiping her wet hands on a dish-cloth. Christine pried her fingers from the railing and walked to-ward the living room, hiding her face from her mother.

"Did I hear someone at the door?" Mutti asked.

"I . . . I didn't hear anything," Christine said, trying to hide the tremor in her voice.

The pattern of three steady knocks, followed by increasingly louder demands to open up, continued as Mutti untied her apron and hurried down the stairs. Christine went back to the railing and leaned over to watch her mother open the door. Out on the stoop, the fleshy-lipped *Gruppenführer* and two armed soldiers positioned themselves in the entrance like a blockade, as if expecting someone to flee at any moment. Christine clamped a hand over her mouth and took a step back, her armpits and forehead instantly drenched in cold sweat.

"May I help you?" her mother said in the steady voice of a per-son certain she has nothing to hide.

"We're missing a prisoner from the work camp," the *Gruppen-führer* bellowed. "We're searching all houses and barns in the vil-lage."

Acid rose to the back of Christine's throat. She edged over to the railing to watch.

"I can assure you, Herr Gruppenführer," Mutti said. "We haven't seen any prisoners."

"Nevertheless," the *Gruppenführer* said. "We're here to search your house."

"But we would have called you right away, Herr Gruppen-führer," Mutti said.

"I will warn you one time and one time only, Frau Bölz," the *Gruppenführer* said. "You are not to interfere with matters of the state. One refusal to let me enter your house will result in your ar-rest, and you will be sent to prison. Is that clear?"

"*Ja,* Herr Gruppenführer." Mutti stepped to one side.

The *Gruppenführer* brushed past her and stopped at the bottom of the stairs, glaring up the steps as if he could measure the family's guilt just by examining the color of their walls. With a wave of his hand, he motioned the armed soldiers forward. The young men obeyed, their smooth faces devoid of emotion, their bulky subma-chine guns pointed forward. They stormed up the stairway, their jackboots striking each step in perfect, deafening unison. Christine wanted to hide, but her legs had turned to stone. At the top of the staircase, the soldiers pointed their guns at her before deciding she wasn't a threat and moving on. As they advanced into the empty kitchen, she gripped the banister with one hand, for fear her legs would crumple.

The *Gruppenführer* appeared at the top of the landing, one hand on the Luger holstered at his hip. When he saw Christine, he stopped.

"*Guten Tag, Fräulein,*" he said, tilting his head and smiling at her with gray teeth, as if he were approaching her at a party or lake-side picnic. "Christine, isn't it? I see your mother has made a full recovery." He took his hand off the Luger and put it on her shoul-der. She could feel his warm, sweaty palm through her dress. "I'm sure a good German girl like you has nothing to hide." Christine held one hand over the cool egg in her apron pocket and tried to smile. It felt more like a twitch; her lips seemed to spasm and quiver.

He gave her shoulder a squeeze, then went into the kitchen, his uniform jacket bunched over his ample buttocks. Christine swal-lowed and closed her eyes, trying not to throw up. When she opened her eyes, her mother was looking at her, brows knitted together, a silent question on her face.

Before Christine could say anything, the *Gruppenführer* came out of the kitchen, the soldiers on his heels.

"Where is your husband?" he asked Mutti.

"He . . . we don't know for sure," Mutti said. "He was with the Sixth Army and . . ."

"Did he do the honorable thing and die for his country, or was he captured by the Russians?"

"I . . . I don't know," Mutti said. "I . . ."

"*Macht nichts!*" he shouted, pulling his truncheon from his belt. "Search the house!" he said to the soldiers. He motioned for Chris-tine and Mutti to follow them, then trailed behind, watching and prodding them forward with the end of his club.

In the living room, Oma, Maria, and the boys must have heard the heavy boots on the stairs, because when the soldiers burst through the door, they were huddled together on the couch. Oma gasped, instinctively putting her arms around the children. Karl buried his face in her side and cried out, his eyes squeezed shut. Maria and Heinrich stared with pale faces at the submachine guns pointed in their direction. The *Gruppenführer* sauntered over to them, his lips curled in a sneer. He lifted Oma's sewing basket and turned it upside down, the contents falling in a tangle of spools and thread and pincushions on her lap.

"Get off the couch!" the *Gruppenführer* yelled.

Oma struggled to get up, then followed Maria and the boys as they scrambled to the other side of the room. The soldiers turned the couch over, crushing the wicker sewing basket beneath its arms. Satisfied that there was no one hiding there, the *Gruppenführer* rummaged through the pile of uniforms in the basket next to it, throwing the pants and shirts and jackets into a heap on the floor. He picked up books and read each title before letting them fall from his hands, then opened the sideboard and peered between the plates and dishes.

"Stay here and keep an eye on them!" he ordered one of the soldiers. "You two come with us," he said to Christine and Mutti. Christine's body felt like liquid. The edges of her vision darkened and blurred, as if she were peering out from behind a slowly closing curtain. Mutti looked at her daughter and linked her arm through hers, her forehead furrowed with concern. Christine was certain her mother could feel her trembling.

With the two women in tow, the remaining soldier and the *Gruppenführer* went down to the first floor and into the goats' indoor enclosure, where the soldier stabbed the piles of straw with his bayonet and overturned buckets of water. In the backyard, the *Gruppenführer* ripped open the chicken coop door and entered the dusty interior with his Luger drawn. Back in the house, they dumped potatoes and apples from bins in the cellar and upended Oma's bedroom, ripping dresses and skirts and undergarments from her trunks and dressers.

Christine held on to the walls and railings as she followed, certain she would faint with every step. The only thing she could feel was the weight of the egg in her apron pocket, bouncing on her leg as she went up and down the stairs.

The soldier and the *Gruppenführer* went through every bedroom, tossing covers from the beds, ripping open pillows, throwing nightgowns and shirts from dressers and armoires. Christine's mother stiffened when one of the solders pulled the storage box with the radio hidden inside from beneath her bed. The soldier pushed the box aside so he could explore underneath the bed frame, causing the folded blanket on top to slide slightly to one side, exposing one of the radio's dials. Mutti's face went white. Then, by some miracle, the soldier and the *Gruppenführer* left the box in the corner, forgotten as they made their way out into the hall. Christine heard her mother let out a low, shuddering breath. *The radio is the least of our worries,* she thought, guilt twisting with fear in her stomach.

In Christine's bedroom, the *Gruppenführer* snarled playfully at Christine's aged Steiff teddy bear, squeezing its stomach twice, then hurled it on her bed when it failed to growl back at him. Christine had to stop herself from picking up the bear to make sure Isaac's note stayed safely tucked inside.

After ransacking the last bedroom on the third floor, they headed into the hall toward the staircase. Christine was beginning to think she might not fall into a heap on the floor after all. *They're leaving,* she thought, finally able to breathe, her palpitating heart beginning to slow. Then the *Gruppenführer* stopped halfway to the stairs and pointed at the ceiling.

"What's up there?" he asked. Without waiting for an answer, he motioned for the soldier to open the trapdoor.

"The attic," Mutti said.

For a split second, everything went black. Christine was certain that the men could see her sway as she bit down hard on the inside of her cheek, trying to stop the surge of terror that threatened to bring her to her knees. Her mind raced. *What can I do to divert them?* she thought.

The soldier opened the trapdoor, pulled down the ladder, and climbed into the attic, one hand still gripping his submachine gun. The *Gruppenführer* motioned for Mutti and Christine to follow. Christine wasn't sure if she'd have the strength to pull herself up.

For a second, the only diversion she could think of was saying she was scared of ghosts. Then the *Gruppenführer* smiled at her with fleshy lips and gray teeth, offering his clammy hand in assistance, and she scrambled up the steps into the attic, using both hands to hold the ladder. As soon as she stood, the *Gruppenführer* rose up through the trapdoor in the floor beside her, like a putrid ghoul rising from an open grave. *If I kick him hard enough in the head,* she thought for one insane instant, *he'll fall back down, head over heels, blood running from his skull when he hits the floor.* Before she could act, the *Gruppenführer* walked over and stood next to her, his forearm touching hers.

"What's this straw all over the floor?" he asked, pointing.

"It's for baby chickens," Mutti said.

The *Gruppenführer* gave Christine's arm one last graze, then he and the soldier walked around the attic, throwing open boxes and looking inside the chest of drawers. He ran a hand over the bookcase in front of the hidden door, looking up at the rafters and dusty beams. Christine tried to keep her eyes on the floor, positive they would read the sheer terror on her face. Finally, convinced that there was nothing up there, the *Gruppenführer* headed back toward the trapdoor. Christine stepped aside as he brushed past her. He motioned for the soldier to climb down first, then he climbed down after the women.

"Let us know if you see anything suspicious, Frau Bölz," he said when they'd reached the bottom floor. "It's for your own protection."

"*Ja,* Herr Gruppenführer," Mutti said. "*Danke.*"

Before they left, the *Gruppenführer* ordered one of the soldiers to go back down to the food storage room, to get the two loaves of rye bread from their hiding place in the old dresser drawer. When the soldier brought them up, the *Gruppenführer* put them under his arm with a satisfied smile, as if he'd just purchased them from the bakery and had every right in the world to take them. The soldiers went outside while he stood in the doorway, looking directly at Christine, his stare intense.

"It's your duty to report anything out of the ordinary, remember that," he said. "If you see or know something and fail to report it, that is a crime against the German state." Then he pulled his eyes away from Christine and said to Mutti, "You wouldn't want some filthy Jew to come in here and take advantage of your daughters, would you?"

"*Nein,* Herr Gruppenführer," Mutti said.

"I've been given the authority to offer a reward in return for any Jew. They can hide behind walls, you know, just like rats. You might not even know they're there until it's too late."

"*Danke,* Herr Gruppenführer," Mutti said. "Gott knows we could use the money."

"*Heil* Hitler!" he said, raising his hand. And then he was gone.

Mutti closed the door and leaned against it. "Are you all right?" she asked Christine. "You're trembling and white as a sheet."

"I'm all right," Christine said, her knees ready to give out from beneath her. "They scare me, that's all."

"They scare me too. But we have nothing to hide. Why did he act like he knew you?"

"The day I found out Isaac was being taken away, I ran into him on the sidewalk."

"You need to be careful. He's SS and can do whatever he wants."

"I know. That's why I was so nervous."

Christine hated lying, but how could she admit that she'd put the whole family in danger? Since the war had started, every ounce of her mother's energy had been put toward keeping this family alive. How could she tell her that a split-second decision, which she alone had made, could destroy all that her mother had worked so hard to protect? On the other hand, what choice did Christine have? Was she supposed to just let Isaac die?

Mutti kissed Christine's forehead, massaging her shoulders with strong hands. Christine's teeth chattered as the adrenaline left her system, leaving her weak and crying in her mother's arms. The soft skin of her mother's cheek and her faint but familiar scent of egg noodles and milky soap seemed in stark contrast to the jagged fits and starts of Christine's strained emotions.

For the rest of the day they worked together, putting clothes back in armoires and remaking beds, trying to erase the intrusion.

Christine felt drained, as if she'd gone weeks without sleep. The realization that everyone's lives now rested on her shoulders was almost too much to bear. She didn't see Isaac until that night, after everyone was asleep.

When she entered through the hidden door, he was leaning against the wall, his face a whorl of light and shadow from the glow of the candle and the silhouette of the garden stone she'd given him earlier, going round and round in his fingers.

"Are you all right?" she asked, sitting beside him. "Could you hear what was going on?"

"Ja," he said. "Are you all right?"

"I will be, eventually. I might be able to stop shaking sometime next year."

"When I heard shouting and furniture being thrown around, I knew we were in trouble. I lay flat on the floor, trying not to move a muscle. I think I was holding my breath, because I almost passed out. I just closed my eyes and prayed. I hate putting you and your family in danger."

"You didn't do it. I did." She leaned against his shoulder. "But I've thought about it all day, since the soldiers left, and I don't know what else I could've done. I had to save you. I didn't have a choice. I love you. What good are any of us if we aren't willing to die to save other people's lives, especially the people we love?"

"Not everyone is as brave as you are. Fear is what motivates most people. I should leave. I should get out of here."

"I was thinking the same thing." She sat up on her knees, facing him. "I feel terrible putting everyone in so much danger. And you'd be safer out of Germany. We could leave in the middle of the night, and we'll only travel when it's dark. We'll walk out of this war-torn country."

"You're not going with me."

"Ja," she said, her voice firm. "I am. I've risked this much already, and I've made up my mind. No matter what you say, you're not going to talk me out of it. I'll gather the things we'll need, some of my father's warm clothes for you, a little food. I'll look in Karl and Heinrich's old schoolbooks for a map, and we'll figure out which direction to go. If we stick to the woods . . ."

"Wait a minute, slow down. We need to think about this. We need a plan, or it'll never work."

"That's what I'm talking about, making a plan. But we should go soon."

"I don't know. I need to think this through. We can't just go off, on impulse."

"*Ja,* here's the plan. You think about it, and I'll start getting things together." He shook his head, a weak smile on his face. "I love you," she said. *"Gute Nacht."* Then she kissed him long and hard before going downstairs for the night.

When the air raid siren began its high, hollow cry at four-thirty in the morning, Christine thought it was part of her dream. In her mind, she and Isaac were in a sun-drenched orchard, picking the biggest plums she'd ever seen. Bees buzzed lazily in the warm afternoon, landing on the white edelweiss and pink lupine that grew wild along the edge of the grass. The buzz of the bees grew louder and louder, an erratic cycling of high and low in her ears, before it evolved into the braying drone of an air raid siren.

"We have to hide!" she yelled at Isaac in her dream. But he didn't hear her. He just kept smiling and picking plums.

Then consciousness erased his face and the sunny orchard dissolved, replaced by the dark walls of her bedroom. She saw the familiar slice of moonlight coming in along the edges of the blackout paper on her window, but it took her a minute to realize that the sound of the siren was real. When she finally did, terror tightened in her chest. She was in her bed, it was the middle of the night, the air raid siren was going off, and Isaac was trapped in the attic. She didn't have time to go all the way up there to let him out. She had to help her brothers. Besides, where would he go?

She leapt out of bed, threw her coat over her clothes, and ran into the hallway. Everyone was already headed for the stairs. She grabbed Karl's hand and followed Maria and Heinrich down the stairs and out the front door. Mutti helped Oma hurry down the steps, and the four siblings ran hand-in-hand into the night. Christine looked over her shoulder, toward the attic of her house, craning her neck to search the black sky above the roofline.

"What are you doing?" Maria yelled at her. "Come on! *Mach schnell!*"

The high-pitched whistle of the first falling bomb screamed through the night just as they entered the shelter. A full minute later, Oma and Mutti finally ducked into the doorway, the sound of explosions propelling them inside. Herr Weiler secured the entrance, and everyone sat frozen, shoulders hunched, waiting. Christine closed her eyes and said a prayer under her breath.

"*Lieber* Gott, *bitte, bitte.* Don't let any bombs find our house."

After a few initial blasts, they heard the growling engines of planes passing over, but no bombs detonated nearby. Over the next hour, they heard sporadic anti-aircraft gunfire and low-flying planes, but the explosions sounded muted and distant, as if the attack was happening on the other end of the valley.

"Does it sound like they're far away?" Christine asked Maria. "Like they've missed us?"

"*Ja,*" Maria answered. "It sounds like they missed the air base too."

After another hour, the all clear sounded, and the villagers emerged from the shelter. A light smell of sulfur filled the air. A fire burned outside the village in the direction of the air base, but the streets were clear. As Christine and her family walked up the hill toward their house, she wondered if every person on earth had only a certain number of prayers that would be answered. If so, she was sure she had almost run out.

CHAPTER 20

The next morning, Christine pulled herself from bed and looked out her bedroom window, her desperate frame of mind mirrored by the cloud-filled sky and heavy rain. The weather looked like it had settled in for the rest of the day. She thought about crawling back under the covers, but knew her restless mind wouldn't allow her to go back to sleep.

Even the prospect of seeing Isaac couldn't brighten her mood. Last night, running away with him had seemed like the right thing to do. Escaping together had seemed romantic and adventurous, the two of them sleeping in forests and the haylofts of barns, until they were free in another country. But this morning it felt utterly terrifying, and worse yet, downright foolish. The Nazis hadn't found him in the attic; maybe he should just stay there. If he and Christine left, who knew what would happen? Where would they get food? What if they were caught? They'd be shot or sent to a camp like the one Isaac had told her about.

Once she got dressed, she felt like she was moving at high speed, her nerves frayed, dried up, and coarse, like the shavings left behind after a person raked their nails across a chalkboard. Panic wound itself around the knot of fear and grief in the pit of her stomach, like something that needed to be thrown up in a toilet.

No one else was up, and the house was quiet. She thought about looking in her brothers' schoolbooks for a map, but decided fresh air would do her good. Maybe it would clear her head. Whether escaping seemed like a good idea right now or not, if she was going to run away with Isaac, she needed to be able to think straight.

She grabbed a basket from the kitchen and went out to the henhouse. By the time she opened the latch on the coop, the downpour had let up, reduced to an intermittent ping-ping on the metal roof from water dripping off the trees. It was past sunrise, but even the chickens didn't want to come out from their dry roosts. When she reached for their eggs, the birds squawked and stood up, ready to defend themselves from the intrusion. An old, skinny hen pecked at her hand, pinching the skin. Just this slight provocation was enough to make her cry—not that it really hurt, but it took only this minor fracture in the shell of her fragile state to spring the leak that allowed every other pain to find its way to the surface and overflow.

She left the coop and sat down on the back stoop, setting the basket of eggs at her feet, and let her pent-up emotions take over. A flood spilled from her eyes, and she sobbed out loud, remembering her father and Opa. She wept for Isaac and his lost family, her nose running as she thought about all the people who were dying because of this war. She was tired of feeling helpless and terrified, tired of the air raid sirens and the black cloth over the windows, tired of seeing confusion and fear in her brothers' eyes, tired of seeing her mother work so hard just to keep everyone alive. But most of all, she was tired of wondering if any of them would even survive.

After a few minutes of wallowing, she wiped her eyes and took a deep breath. To her relief, the gnawing stress had eased. She could at least function now without feeling as if she were on the edge of a great abyss, waiting to fall and disappear like a pebble dropped in a well on a moonless night. *I need to think about my family and Isaac,* she told herself. *At least he's safe for now. Oma, my mother, Maria, Karl, and Heinrich are alive. So many others are worse off than I am. The only thing I can do is keep going. If Isaac and I think we can get away safely, so be it. If not, then we'll wait for things to change. They have to change. For better or worse, they always do.*

Only a few early fruit hung low in the plum trees, but she picked one anyway, just for herself. She sat back on the stoop and ate it slowly, letting the juice run down her chin. When she was finished, she walked over to the corner of the fenced backyard, dug a hole in the loamy soil, and buried the pit. After tamping the dirt down, she closed her eyes and made a wish that the plum pit would take root and grow, and that by the time it was a seedling, the war would be over, her father would be home, and she and Isaac would be to-gether.

Feeling less jittery and looking forward to taking breakfast to Isaac, she picked up her half-full basket of eggs, stepped into the house, and wiped her feet on the straw mat. Then she froze. At the other end of the hall, the dark silhouette of a soldier appeared against the red and blue glass of the front entrance. He pounded on the door, making the entire house rattle. The egg basket slipped from Christine's fingers and fell to the floor. For a second, she didn't budge, her pulse thumping, the eggs leaking yellow into the wicker at her feet.

"*Hallo?*" the soldier hollered. "*Hallo?*"

Christine stepped to one side, hiding behind the staircase. Her mind raced in unison with her thundering heart. *Why did the* Gruppenführer *come back? Did I give Isaac away somehow? Did he notice something in the attic? We're dead!*

The soldier knocked and shouted again. "*Hallo?*"

The voice sounded familiar, but the solid door made it sound as if he were shouting from inside a thick-walled room, the soldier's words muffled and low. *My mind must be playing tricks on me,* she thought. *It's no one I know.* She didn't dare move, didn't dare peek around the corner to look.

"Rose?" the soldier shouted, louder this time.

Christine frowned. It couldn't be him. It was the *Gruppen-führer;* she was sure of it. Of course he knew her mother's first name. He knew everything.

"Let me in!" the soldier shouted. "Rose! Christine! Maria! Any-one?"

And then she knew.

Christine ran to the entrance, hands trembling as she fumbled with the lock. Finally, she pulled open the door, ready to embrace her long-lost father.

All at once, she realized her mistake.

The skeletal, flea-bitten man must have found out their names somehow, and now he was here to steal their food. His uniform was ripped and covered in grease and mud, his shredded boots wrapped in rope and filthy rags. A rifle hung over his back, one scraped and grimy hand holding the strap at his shoulder. Christine grabbed the edge of the door with both hands and started to slam it shut.

"Christine!" the soldier said. "You don't recognize your own *Vati?*"

She stopped and looked into the man's sunken eyes, trying to find something familiar behind the patchy beard, the lank hair, the dirt-covered face. Then the soldier took off his cap and smiled. And she knew.

"Vater!" she cried, throwing her arms around him. Her father lifted her off the ground, squeezing her so tight that she thought he'd break her ribs. He kissed her forehead, her nose, her cheeks.

"You're the most beautiful thing I've seen in four years," he said, leaning back to examine her, tears streaming from his eyes. "You've grown into a woman while I was away."

His hair was grayer than Christine remembered, the circles under his eyes dark as smudged coal. His lips were cracked and dry, his fingernails dirty. His uniform hung loose on his skinny frame, but it was field green, not Nazi black. He was an ordinary German soldier, not part of the SS, and not a Nazi. And now he was here. He was alive. Christine grabbed him by the hand and dragged him into the house.

"Oma!" she shouted, rapping her knuckles on Oma's bedroom door. "Get up! Vater is home!" She pulled her father up the stairs. "Mutti!" she yelled. "Wake up, everybody! Vater is home!"

Together they ran up the two flights of stairs to her mother's bedroom, reaching the door just as she was coming out, her red hair hanging in long cascades over her shoulders, free of its tight French twist. Mutti clutched her worn bathrobe over her chest, blinking against the remnants of sleep that made her look aged beyond her years. At first, the shock of seeing a soldier in the hall contorted her face, but then, when she saw Christine holding his hand and beaming, recognition transformed her. Her hands flew over her mouth, and her chin trembled.

"Dietrich?" she said, reaching out to touch him with an unsteady hand, as if he were a ghost. "Is it really you? You're alive?"

"It's me," Vater said. Then he held out his hand and she grabbed it, her knuckles going white, as if she were afraid he'd disappear if she let go. They threw their arms around each other, and Mutti sobbed. Christine's eyes filled as she tried to swallow the lump in her throat. Mutti thanked God over and over as Vater buried his face in her hair, laughing. Maria, Karl, and Heinrich came out into the hall, eyes wide as they tried to make sense of the early morning commotion. When Vater saw them, he knelt on the floor, set his rifle at his heels, and smiled. Finally, recognizing that their long-lost father had come home, Karl and Heinrich ran into his outstretched arms. Maria put her hands over her mouth.

"I can't believe how much you've grown!" he said to the boys. He stood and caressed Christine and Maria's pale cheeks. "I have the most beautiful daughters in Germany! I kept thinking of your faces. That's what kept me going: Christine's blond hair, Maria's wide blue eyes, Karl's freckles, Heinrich's toothy grin." He laughed and put his arm around Mutti, kissing her cheek. "And the picture I carried of your mother kept me sane."

Oma made her way up the steps behind them, a shawl over her nightgown, one bony hand on the railing. Vater met her at the top of the stairs.

"Welcome home, Dietrich," Oma said, her eyes wet. "What a wonderful surprise. Welcome home."

He hugged her and led her back toward the family. "And where is Opa?" he asked.

"It's not good news," Oma said in a quiet, shaky voice. "He was killed during an air raid."

"Ach nein," Vater said, shoulders dropping. His eyes filled, and he hugged Oma again. "What happened?"

"The barn was on fire," Mutti said. "He saved our house from burning."

"I'm so sorry," Vater said, hugging her. Then he stood back, pinching the bridge of his nose between his fingers and closing his eyes, as if suddenly developing an excruciating headache. "This damn war. When will enough be enough?"

"Opa wouldn't want us to be unhappy," Oma said. "He'd be so glad to know you're all right, Dietrich. That's what he prayed for every night, for you to come home, to look after your family."

For the next few minutes, the hallway filled with tears and laughter, until, as one big, noisy group, they went down to the kitchen together. Mutti lit the woodstove and filled the teakettle with water, while Vater scrubbed his face and hands in the sink.

"I'm sorry, Mutti," Christine said. "But I dropped the eggs when I saw Vater."

"That's all right," Mutti said, smiling. "I would have dropped them too."

Christine sliced potatoes and a leftover piece of *Schinkenwurst,* ham loaf, into a cast-iron skillet. Maria added onion, and Mutti set the table. It was the first time Christine had seen her mother wearing her bathrobe in the kitchen, and the first time since her father had left that she'd heard her laugh. Both Karl and Heinrich were talking at once, telling their father about the air raids, asking questions about being a soldier.

Vater sat at the corner nook with Oma and his sons, a contented smile on his face, talking and watching his wife and daughters prepare breakfast. To Christine, the eyes above his smile seemed changed. The mischievous twinkle was gone, dimmed somehow, replaced by sorrow. In the four years since he'd left, he looked like he'd aged ten.

But the grin never left his face as he ate and sipped his tea. He looked at each of them with such wonder and gratitude that it almost made Christine cry. For a little while, things felt normal, and Christine let herself enjoy the moment. Her body relaxed, and she felt a minuscule flutter of joy as the love of her family enveloped her, making her feel warm and safe. She blocked out everything else and concentrated on her father, alive and well, her family gathered around her, a cup of hot tea, a warm kitchen, a quiet morning.

"Where have you been, Vater?" Heinrich asked.

"Russland," he said.

"Were you with the Sixth Army at Stalingrad?" Christine asked.

"*Ja,*" Vater said, staring into his tea. "*Ja,* I was in Russia with the Sixth Army."

"What happened?" Heinrich said. "How did they trap you?"

"Hitler wouldn't let us retreat. So the Russians encircled us, and there was nothing we could do. We had to surrender."

"Did Ivan put you in prison?" Heinrich said.

Mutti put a hand on Heinrich's arm. "Shh . . ." she said. "Your father doesn't want to talk about that right now. He must eat."

"*Macht nichts,*" Vater said, waving a hand in the air. "*Ja,* we were sent to a prisoner of war camp. But we had to walk there. It took days, in freezing temperatures, and we had to sleep in the snow on the way." Mutti stood and refilled his cup with hot water, then scraped the last bits of fried potato onto his plate. "Thank you, Rose, I've never tasted anything so delicious." He caught her arm and pulled her down for a kiss, and Karl and Heinrich giggled beside him.

"Then what happened, Vater?" Heinrich said. "Did you have to live on bread and water?"

"*Nein.* Once a day they gave us a little bread, a little thin soup." He tilted his plate to get the last bits of browned potatoes with his fork. When he was finished, Mutti cleared the plates from the table and filled the sink with soapy water, glancing sideways at her husband, as if making sure he was really there.

"How long were you a prisoner?" Christine asked.

Vater wiped his mouth and sat back in the booth, resting his arms on the backrest. "Over a year, I think. We had no way of keeping time. I know it's nearing fall now, but I don't know what month it is."

"It's August," Maria said.

"The Russians let you go?" Christine said.

"Let your *Vati* relax," Mutti said. "Enough questions."

"*Ja, ja,*" Vater said. "The *Kinder* are curious." He sat forward and picked up the saltshaker, examining it as if he'd never seen one before. "They didn't let me go. I escaped."

A collective gasp filled the kitchen. Mutti sat down hard on a stool, a dishcloth held over her heart.

"What happened?" Heinrich said, his eyes round.

"Ach du lieber Gott," Oma said under her breath.

"Did you dig a tunnel?" Karl said.

Heinrich put a hand over Karl's mouth. *"Nein, Dummkopf,"* he said. "There's too much snow in Russia to dig a tunnel."

Karl squirmed and mumbled, trying to pry his brother's hand from his face. Vater raised a hand to quiet them, then finished the last of his tea. He set down the empty cup, then scrubbed a hand across his forehead. Everyone went silent, waiting to hear his story.

"I think it was right before Christmas," he said. He picked up the saltshaker again, turning it round and round in his fingers. "Like I've said, I can't be sure. The Russians told the men in our barracks we were being transported. We didn't know why or when. At first we thought it was good news, maybe we were being moved to a better camp. A few days later, we were on a train, hoping the longer we were on it, the closer we were getting to home. I think I was in the boxcar for five days."

"Did you jump off?" Karl shouted.

"Shh . . ." Heinrich said. "Let him finish!"

"After three days," Vater continued, "they stopped the train out in the middle of nowhere and made us get out. They told us to line up in the snow. By that time, some of the men were so weak they couldn't even crawl out of the boxcars." He paused, shook some salt into the palm of his hand, and touched it to his tongue. At first, Christine didn't understand what he was doing; then she realized he probably hadn't tasted salt in years.

"What happened next?" Heinrich said.

"We got off the train and lined up, thinking they were giving us a bit of fresh air, or letting us clean ourselves up in the snow. But then, the Russians went up the ranks and shot random prisoners. Some of the men tried to run or jump back in the boxcar, but they shot them too. I just stood there, not moving. After the Russians were done, they ordered us back on the train. They just left our men lying alongside the tracks, to die in the snow."

Karl slid closer to his father, resting his head on his arm. Vater put his arm around him and took one of his son's hands in his, looking down at the small, pale fingers resting in his large, calloused palm.

"If you got back on the train, how did you get away?" Heinrich asked.

Vater kissed the top of Karl's head and glanced at Mutti, who was still sitting on the stool, folding and unfolding the dishcloth in her lap. She didn't look up.

"The second time the train slowed, I could see trees out both sides of the boxcar. We were in the middle of a forest. And I knew what was going to happen. I had no intention of being shot, so I decided that when they told us to get out, I'd duck under the train and run into the trees. My buddy wanted to go too. When the train stopped and the door opened, we jumped down, slipped under, and ran. They were shooting at us, but we kept running. We heard a lot of gunfire, and we're pretty sure they killed the rest of the men on the train. Some of them were just boys." He stopped for a moment, took a deep breath, and went on. "We ran until we heard the train whistle blow in the distance behind us. When we heard the engine moving away, we collapsed in the underbrush, trying to catch our breath. We had to wait until sunset to get our sense of direction."

"How did you get home?" Heinrich asked.

"Eventually, we were picked up by another one of our units. They gave us food and firearms. We stayed with them for a few weeks, then left them and walked across the Ukraine and Poland. Back in Deutschland, we parted ways. His family was from Leipzig, so he headed north and I headed south."

Christine inhaled and held her breath. *It can be done,* she thought. The kitchen was silent. Mutti kept her eyes on the floor.

"And now you are home!" Karl shouted finally, throwing his hands into the air like a magician. Everyone laughed, but the smile disappeared from her father's face.

"I have to report in tomorrow," he said, watching his wife for a reaction. Mutti finally looked at him.

"Maybe they'll let you out of the army now," she said. "You've served your time. You've made your sacrifices."

"I'm sorry," Vater said. "I wish that was the way it worked. When we crossed the border back into Germany, we had to show our papers. It won't be long before news of our return makes its way to headquarters. If I don't report in, they'll put me in prison. I have no choice."

Without a word, Mutti stood, went over to the pile of wood beside the stove, and shoved another log into the fire. As the women washed the dishes, the roar of the growing flames absorbed the weighted silence in the kitchen. Vater sat at the table with the boys playing a game of "Mensch Ärgere Dich Nicht," "People Don't Get Mad," with buttons and cloth. After the last dish was washed and put away, Mutti shooed everyone out of the kitchen so Vater could bathe in the metal tub.

With Maria and Oma in the garden, and Karl and Heinrich occupied in the living room, Christine ran up to see Isaac. The only thing she had to give him was a heel of stale bread that she'd slipped into her apron pocket before her mother chased them out of the kitchen. When she opened the door to his hiding place, he was crouched in the farthest corner of the space, face rigid, eyes wide. He saw her and exhaled loudly, then leaned back against the wall.

"What's wrong?" she asked, hurrying toward him.

"I heard a lot of noise earlier, people running up the stairs and yelling. I didn't know what was going on! I wasn't sure if it was you coming in just now, or . . ."

"Oh Gott!" Christine said, putting a hand over her heart. "I'm sorry. I didn't think about you hearing all that and being scared. It was just us. We were shouting because my father came home."

"Ahh," he said. "That explains it then. Good news for a change."

"He was a prisoner in Russia. But he escaped and walked across the Ukraine and Poland! That proves it can be done."

"But he's a German soldier. He has a uniform and papers. I know what you're thinking, but we'd be fugitives without papers, trying to sneak *out* of the country."

"I realize that. But it gave me an idea. We've got a pile of uniforms downstairs. Waffen-SS uniforms, *Hauptstrumführer* uniforms. I'll find one that fits you, and we'll pretend I'm your wife. If you're wearing an officer's uniform, no one will ask questions."

Isaac furrowed his brow, thinking. Then he said, "I don't know. Maybe I should just go alone."

"If you're leaving, I'm going with you. I can't stand the thought of . . ."

"We don't have identity papers," he interrupted. "And why would a soldier, much less an officer, be *walking* cross-country with his wife? We don't have the money or the permits to take the train."

"I don't know," she said, lowering her eyes. "I don't know what to do. I don't know if you should stay or if we should go. I don't know anything."

Isaac wound his fingers through hers. "Listen, you've been through a lot. You haven't even had time to get used to the idea that your father is alive. We don't have to figure this out right now. We've got time."

Christine wiped at her eyes. "I know, and you're right. If this is going to work we need to think it through. But right now, I've got to go back downstairs before anyone notices I'm gone."

That evening, after everyone else had gone to bed, Christine and her parents were in the living room, talking about what her father had been through since he left. Christine pretended to straighten the uneven mound of uniforms in the corner, while checking sizes as she moved them from one pile to the next, looking for a jacket and pants that would fit Isaac. Mutti sat on the couch, Vater's uniform in her lap, a silver thimble and a needle with green thread in her hand.

"Most of the men in my unit are dead or in the camps," Vater said.

Christine left the pile of uniforms and went over to talk to him. "What was it like?" She sat next to her mother, the black jacket of a *Hauptscharführer* in her hands.

"You should go to bed, Christine," he said. "You don't need to hear this."

"I'm an adult now, Vater. I want to hear what you've been through. I want to know what's going on. How will we change things in the future if no one talks about what's been happening? The old tradition of denial and hard work hasn't helped anyone."

"I keep forgetting you're . . . how old now?" he said.

"Twenty-three in a few weeks."

He caressed her cheek, his eyes sad. Then he began to talk, haltingly at first, but once started, it seemed he needed to purge his memory.

"Before we were ordered to enter Stalingrad, we felt abandoned in that empty, frozen wasteland. We didn't have the proper equipment, the right outerwear, the right boots. There were constant blizzards, so our planes couldn't deliver food or supplies for months on end."

"How did you survive with nothing to eat?" Mutti said.

"Not everyone did. Thousands of men died. We tried to hunt for birds and rabbits, but after a while, they disappeared too. Once in a while someone got a wild boar. If it hadn't been for our horses, none of us would be alive."

Christine felt her stomach turn, the image of Farmer Klause's dying horse filling her mind.

"Were you able to build fires to stay warm?" Mutti asked.

"*Ja,* we cut down trees, but with ninety thousand men in the area, it didn't take long for the forests to be used up. Then, we had no fires. We couldn't melt snow to drink. We couldn't wash. We became infested with lice. At night, we took off our uniforms to freeze the parasites off. We huddled together, trying to get warm. But every morning, there were dead men on the edges of our group, frozen to death as they slept."

"*Ach* Gott," Mutti said.

"Vater?" Christine asked. "Did they tell you what is happening with the Jews?"

"*Nein.* I'm just a foot soldier, a pawn in the game. I've heard conflicting stories. As we marched from one battle to the next, we saw trains pulling boxcars full of people. Our superiors told us they were being relocated and rehabilitated, but we've heard other rumors, horrible rumors. Why? Have you heard something?"

Christine wished she could tell him the truth. "I've heard terrible things too. And the Bauermans have been transported."

Vater looked at Mutti, his forehead furrowed. "Is this true?"

"*Ja,*" her mother said. "Last year. All the Jews have disappeared from Hessental."

"*Ach* Gott," he said, shaking his head. "Christine, I want you to understand something. War makes perpetrators of some, criminals of others, and victims of everyone. Not all of the soldiers on the front are fighting for Hitler and his ideals. Just because a soldier is in the battle, doesn't mean that he believes in the war. When they wouldn't let us retreat, and when we heard the rumors about the Jews, hundreds of us wrote anti-Nazi messages and attached them to the linings of our jackets, hoping they'd be discovered upon our deaths."

He stood and took his uniform from Mutti's lap, yanked at a thread at the hem of the jacket, and pulled out a wrinkled, yellowed paper. He unfolded it and read it out loud.

> *My name is Dietrich Bölz from Hessental, Germany. Let this show that a large number of my comrades and I do not agree with Hitler's policies. Let it be known that we recognize we are doomed for failure in Stalingrad, but have been given no other choice but to carry on. Tell the world that it is the soldiers on the front lines who are burdened with the fear and guilt of the actual combat, while the guilty men hide in their bunkers and make life-and-death decisions for the world.*

When he finished, Mutti grabbed his arm. "I don't care what the army says. I don't want you to go back! I'll tell them I haven't heard anything. Let them think something happened to you!"

"And then what?" Vater said, giving her a steady look. "I stay here, hoping they don't come and arrest me?"

"*Nein!*" Mutti said, chin trembling. "You hide! You hide in the attic! There's a hidden door in the wall where you can go if they come looking for you. We'll put your uniform in with the others. They'll never know!"

Christine tightened her grip on the jacket in her lap.

"If this war keeps on as it is," Vater said, "you might need that attic to hide our sons. If anyone can stand upright, they'll put a rifle in his hands."

"Excuse me," Christine said, standing on trembling legs. "I'm exhausted. I guess I'll go to bed after all."

"Gute Nacht," her father said. "I'm retiring soon myself. I can't wait to sleep in my own bed."

"Gute Nacht, Vater," she said, kissing him on the cheek. "I'm so happy you're home. *Gute Nacht,* Mutti." She started out of the room, trying not to run. *Surely he'll refuse to go into hiding,* she thought. *Oh, Vater, I'd love for you to stay. But what would I do with Isaac if you did? I have one night at least. One night when Vater will sleep in his own bed. And then what? Will Isaac and I be forced to leave after all?* She had reached the door when her mother called after her.

"Christine?"

Christine turned, her heart hammering in her chest. *"Ja?"* she said, trying to keep the tremor from her voice.

"What are you doing with that uniform?"

Christine looked down. She was still gripping the officer's black jacket in both hands.

CHAPTER 21

The summer wind traveled in through the open kitchen windows, carrying with it the crows of a neighbor's rooster and the hourly chime of the bells of St. Michael's. The stale night air of the house had been dispelled, evicted by warm, sweet breezes, and the rooms were filled with the aroma of baking bread. Mutti had gotten Christine up before dawn to help her with the baking. She'd been saving the last of the rye flour, hoping to stretch it at least to the end of next month, but now, determined that Vater would have bread to take with him when he left, they used it all.

Christine's father stood in the morning light of the kitchen, washed and clean-shaven, his graying black hair combed back from his angular face, his hands scrubbed, his fingernails trimmed and clean. He was wearing his uniform again, spotless and mended with precise stitches. On his feet were a pair of old work boots, because even though the dry leather was cracked and the bottom of the soles worn thin, they were better than the ruined army boots he'd had on when he'd arrived. Mutti put a hand on each side of his face and gave him a smile.

"You're still so handsome!" She kissed him on the lips, then turned her attention back to the stove.

Karl and Heinrich sat at the table, studying Vater. Occasionally, they glanced at each other, and at the plates Christine was setting in front of them, but their eyes always returned to their father. Silent and hard-faced, Vater filled his battered canteen with water, slipped his *Erkennungsmarke,* dog tags, over his head, and pushed his *Kampfmesser,* combat knife, back into its leather sheath.

"Come," Christine said to him. "Sit down and have breakfast."

Vater smoothed the front of his uniform with both hands, then sat next to Heinrich. Opposite him were Maria and Karl, with Oma and Christine on either end of the corner nook.

"You behave for your mother, now," Vater said to the boys. "You've grown while I was away. Now you have to be the men of the house until I come back."

Christine placed two fried eggs on his plate, the yolks shiny and dark yellow from the chickens' diet of insects and vegetable trimmings. She filled his favorite mug with warm goat's milk and handed him a slice of jam-smeared bread. Mutti wrapped a dishcloth around the handle of a steaming pot of mint tea, set it in the center of the table, then pulled up a chair beside her husband. The family ate in silence, letting the morning sounds of the village fill in the blank spaces. The boys had already finished eating, but they remained seated, watching their father, as if waiting for him to disappear again, like a figment of their imagination.

"Where will they send you this time?" Maria finally asked.

Mutti took in a sharp breath, then stood and started clearing the table. Christine watched her mother stack the dirty plates and pick up the used silverware, surprised to find herself vaguely irritated that Mutti wouldn't just sit down.

"Mutti, sit down and talk to Vater," Christine said. "I'll clean up the kitchen later." On one hand, she felt like she should help; but on the other, she knew that the cleaning up could wait all day if it had to—until he had left, until he was gone again, until they had no choice but to return to the mundane concerns of their lives. But she knew why her mother had gotten up. Her household was the one thing she could control. Cooking meals, washing dishes, folding laundry, washing windows, scrubbing floors. She could control all of those things, and so she did. She kept busy every minute of every day, performing each job completely and flawlessly, the only way she knew how to deal with her unpredictable life.

Mutti was at the sink, running water over the plates and silverware, her lips pressed together in a hard line. She turned off the water, then stood with one hand on the faucet, her head lowered, staring into the sink. After a long moment, she came back to the table and sat down.

"I have no idea where I'll be sent," Vater said. "They could tell me I don't need to leave for a few days, but I doubt it. They're running out of men. I'm sure they'll tell me to return to duty right away."

"When do you have to go?" Heinrich asked in a small voice.

"I wish I could sit here with you all day, but I have to go now. I have to be at the station by ten to catch the train to Stuttgart." He stood, placed his mug in the sink, then turned to look at his family.

Karl sniffed and put his hands over his face, watching his father through parted fingers. Heinrich got up and faced Vater at the sink, his face serious, his right hand outstretched.

"Good luck, Vater," he said in a loud voice. "Don't worry, I'll take care of everything until you come home again." Vater smiled and shook Heinrich's hand. A flood of tears welled in Mutti's eyes, and she wrapped her arms around Karl. Christine felt a hard knot form in her throat.

"I won't worry," Vater told Heinrich. "As long as I know you and Karl are here taking care of things."

Then, like a shot, Karl scrambled out of his seat and wrapped his arms around Vater's waist, refusing to let go. Finally, Mutti stood. She was pale and trembling, but her voice was strong.

"Come now, Karl," she said. "Your father has to go, but we can walk him to the station." She put her hands on Karl's shoulders, but he spun around, ran back to the table, and buried his face in his arms.

"I'm sorry," Vater said to no one in particular.

"You don't have anything to be sorry for," Mutti said. "None of this is your fault." She hugged him for a long time, but Christine noticed she had stopped crying. Her resolve had found its way back into the square of her shoulders and the upright position of her head. "You'd better get going now. We'll walk you to the station."

"I'll stay and clean up the kitchen," Oma offered. "You don't need me slowing you down." Christine's first instinct was to say she would stay and help. She was so conditioned to looking for opportunities to visit Isaac that she was already in the habit of waiting for everyone to leave. *I'm sorry, Isaac,* she thought. *I don't know when, or if I will ever see my father again, so I must be with him for as long as I can. You'll have to wait for breakfast until I return.*

Mutti tied a worn cotton sheet into a sling and hung it over Vater's shoulder. She placed a warm loaf of rye bread on its end in the bottom and filled a lidded tin with goat's milk. She placed the tin next to the bread in the makeshift pack, then cushioned it with a dishcloth, two extra pairs of socks, and a pair of gloves. Earlier, she'd wrapped four boiled eggs in newspaper. Now, she tucked them on top of the warm bread.

"Be careful of the milk," she said. "Don't spill it."

"We'll see each other soon," Vater said to Oma, hugging her.

"Take care of yourself."

The other six went into the hall, first Vater and then Mutti, followed by the boys, Maria, and Christine. They walked single file behind Vater, like a funeral procession down the stairs, not one of them saying a word. From her position at the end of the line, Christine could see five arms outstretched, pale, thin hands holding tight to the banister.

When Christine was four steps from the bottom of the staircase, a loud knock on the front door made her jump. She jerked backwards and nearly lost her balance, her eyes flying to the red and blue window in the top center of the entryway. Three shadows appeared on the other side of the glass, pitch black in contrast to the sunlit morning outside, the wrought iron grate giving the impression that this was a silhouette of men behind bars. She stopped on the steps, her heart a thumping boulder in her chest. The *Gruppenführer* and his armed soldiers had returned.

Vater turned to face his family. "All of you," he ordered. "Back upstairs." Christine struggled to find her feet, then turned and ran back up the stairs, the rest of her family stomping behind her. She stopped in the hall, her mother and siblings brushing past her on their frantic rush into the kitchen.

"Get in here!" Mutti ordered.

"I want to hear what's going on," Christine said. She had to listen; she had to know if her father could persuade them to leave. If they were coming up the stairs again, she needed to know. Not that she had any plan. Her heart couldn't take the suspense. She couldn't hide in the kitchen and blindly await her fate. Mutti came reluctantly into the hall, closing the kitchen door behind her. Together, they stood motionless, barely breathing, listening as Vater opened the front entrance.

"*Heil* Hitler!" Vater said.

"*Heil* Hitler!" the *Gruppenführer* shouted. "*Guten Tag,* Obergefreiter Bölz. We are here to search your house—"

The rest of his words were buried beneath the thunderous heartbeat in Christine's ears. When Mutti's eyes widened, Christine knew Vater hadn't put a stop to the second intrusion. And why would he? He had nothing to hide and no reason to believe his family did either. Mutti had instructed everyone not to tell him about the first time, deciding not to burden him. She was afraid he'd become needlessly angry and more downhearted than he already was. *I should have warned him about Isaac,* Christine thought, her mind spinning. *If he'd known, maybe he would have tried to stop them. Maybe he would have known what to do.*

Now it was too late. He was letting the soldiers in, bringing them up the stairs, bringing them into his house. She couldn't fault him. He was certain this was a formality, certain that once they cooperated, the soldiers would leave. He had no idea he might be signing his daughter's death warrant. Christine put her hands over her ears as the soldiers marched up the stairs.

"What's wrong?" Mutti said, looking at her. She pulled on Christine's hands. "Christine, calm down. You don't need to be afraid. Your father is here. We have nothing to hide."

Then Vater appeared at the top of the stairs, the *Gruppenführer* and the armed soldiers behind him. One of the soldiers had taken her father's rifle.

"These men are here to search the house," Vater said. "It seems they're missing a prisoner from the work camp."

Deep in her chest, Christine felt hysterical terror destroy the brittle restraint on her heart, as if pieces of it were flying in all directions, like a ruptured machine, ripping gaping holes in her lungs and stomach. "Vater!" she said too loudly. She tried to catch her breath. "They were here once already! They found nothing!"

"Hush, Christine!" her father said, his dark eyes stern, the tendons near his temples flexing in and out.

"There's no need for us to search the entire house, Obergefreiter Bölz," the *Gruppenführer* said. "Just the attic."

Christine felt the blood drain from her face. She started to gag and reached blindly for her mother's hand.

"Feel free to proceed, Herr Gruppenführer," her father said, stepping aside. He stared at Christine, his forehead furrowed. "We have nothing to hide."

Christine struggled to stand straight and look forward. The hall began to tilt.

"We've searched every house and barn in the village and come up with nothing," the *Gruppenführer* said, his eyes on Christine. "Your daughter was extremely nervous the last time we were here. And now that we know your wife and daughter used to work for the family of the man in question . . ."

Mutti's eyes snapped in Christine's direction, her face suddenly white. She moved closer and put her arm around Christine's shoulders, her body shaking. Now she knew who they were looking for, and that changed everything. Christine's stomach cramped, and the back of her throat felt blocked, as if her airway were closing shut.

The *Gruppenführer* walked past them, then stopped and turned, standing in the center of the hall.

"Get a lantern," he ordered her father. Vater went into the kitchen. "Follow him," the *Gruppenführer* ordered one of the soldiers. The soldier did as he was told and stood in the open doorway, following Vater's movements with the end of his gun. In the kitchen, Oma, Maria, and the boys sat at the table, watching in silence as Vater lit an oil lantern. Vater returned to the hall, lantern in hand.

"Follow me!" the *Gruppenführer* ordered.

The soldiers motioned Christine and her parents forward with their guns. Christine looked at her father, eyes wide, silently pleading with him not to let this happen, even though she knew that there was absolutely nothing he could do. He looked at her, his face hard, and shook his head back and forth. Then he motioned for Christine and Mutti to move ahead of him, putting himself between them and the submachine guns.

The *Gruppenführer* continued up the stairs to the third floor, his chin held high, as if sniffing the air. In the center of the hall, he ordered his men to pull down the attic ladder, then climbed up first, with everyone else following. At the top, he took the lantern from Vater and started at the opposite end of the attic. He walked slowly around the perimeter, knocking on the thick timber and stone walls, shining the lantern into every dark corner. When he reached the low wall near the bookcase, he knocked his knuckles along the length of the wood. Then, in slow motion, he turned his head and sneered triumphantly at Christine.

He examined the bookcase from top to bottom, his arms and legs moving precisely and deliberately, like a marionette on a stage, playing to his audience. Then he bent forward, examining the floor, and paused. He shined the light onto the floorboards in front of the bookcase, then looked up at Christine again. The grin on his face looked oddly stretched and rigid, like the painted-on smile of a lunatic puppet. It was only then, as the light of the lantern illuminated them, that Christine saw the wide, arched scrapes on the floor. The bookcase had left hard evidence each and every time she had moved it, and in the end, she had betrayed herself.

The *Gruppenführer* snapped erect. "Move this bookshelf!"

One of the soldiers did as the *Gruppenführer* instructed, while the other pointed his submachine gun at the bookcase's empty shelves, as if afraid it would grow wooden limbs and make a run for freedom. The *Gruppenführer* held the flickering light of the lantern close to the wall, his head tilted to one side as he examined it. The outline of the undersized door stood out on the aged wood like a fresh scar on pale skin.

"Open this door!" he ordered the soldier.

The soldier yanked the door open and, gun first, entered the hiding place. The *Gruppenführer* drew his Luger and followed him with the light, while the second soldier kept his gun trained on Christine and her parents. Once the *Gruppenführer* and the soldier were inside, Christine could only see them from the waist down. She held her breath as they stood, motionless and silent, facing the front wall of the house, two pairs of black legs in black boots, a submachine gun and lantern suspended strangely above. After a moment, the *Gruppenführer* stepped back into the attic.

For an instant, Christine thought that Isaac had left without her, that he'd escaped through the roof or had somehow disappeared into thin air. But then she saw the satisfied smirk on the *Gruppenführer*'s face. She felt a shift somewhere deep within her, like great glaciers sliding over one another, tearing jagged edges off, burying the old landscape and replacing it with unknown territory. She felt the change in her head, as if her brain had suddenly been altered. She felt it in her chest too, a thickening, a pressure, an abnormal slowing of her heart and lungs.

The *Gruppenführer* stood erect, his chin raised and his chest puffed out, one hand tugging on the bottom edge of his uniform jacket, as if preparing to make a speech.

"Come out now!" he screamed.

Isaac came out slowly, bent double, his hands in the air as he straightened. Mutti drew in a sharp breath and stood protectively in front of her daughter, her hands reaching blindly back for Christine. The *Gruppenführer* grabbed Isaac's arm and shoved up his shirtsleeve to expose the tattooed number on his wrist.

"So what do we have here?" he asked, looking at Christine.

"They didn't know I was up here!" Isaac said.

"Silence!" the *Gruppenführer* screamed. One of the soldiers hit Isaac in the stomach with the butt of his gun. Isaac doubled over and fell to his knees, holding his middle and gasping. The *Gruppenführer* walked over to Mutti, pushed her aside, and glared at Christine.

"I believe someone knew he was here," he said. "How else would the bookcase get in front of the door?"

Isaac got up and pushed himself between them, but a soldier

pulled him away, and the other held a gun to Isaac's chest. "They didn't have anything to do with it!" Isaac shouted. The soldier hit him again, this time in the jaw. Isaac reeled and nearly lost his footing. The soldiers held him up.

"You're right!" Christine said, breathing hard. "I did it!" She stepped forward, coming nearly toe-to-toe with the *Gruppenführer,* his face a blur through her tears. "My family knew nothing about it. I hid him there. I'm the guilty one."

"Nein!" her mother cried. "It's not true!"

Vater pulled Christine back and placed himself between her and the *Gruppenführer.*

"Take me," he said. "She's just a young girl."

"Nein, Herr Bölz," the *Gruppenführer* said. "You've served your country well. It is your daughter who is the traitor. She is the Jew lover!" He motioned to the soldiers. "Arrest them both."

"I'm sorry," Christine said to her parents.

Mutti put her hands over her mouth, shaking her head back and forth. Vater held her back as the soldiers cuffed Christine and Isaac's wrists together and pushed them toward the trapdoor.

"Nein! Nein!" Mutti screamed, struggling to get out of Vater's grip.

The *Gruppenführer* went down the ladder first, a grin etched on his face. Isaac and Christine, their hands bound together, tried not to fall as they followed. Isaac stepped down first, his arm above his head to give her some slack, moving slowly for her benefit. When they reached the hallway, the soldiers shoved them forward and down the stairs, as the *Gruppenführer* and her parents followed.

"Christine!" Mutti screamed, struggling to push past the *Gruppenführer.* *"Nein!* Don't take her! *Bitte,* don't take her!" But the *Gruppenführer* blocked her way with outstretched arms, saying nothing. Vater grabbed her, holding her back.

"They will shoot you," he said, his voice hard.

Mutti either didn't hear him or didn't care. She screamed for Christine, clawing at her husband's hands like a wild animal. Oma, Maria, and the boys came out of the kitchen, pursuing the soldiers down the stairs, everyone crying and screaming Christine's name. When they reached the street the soldiers ordered Isaac and Christine into the back of a canvas-covered army truck. The black barrels of their submachine guns followed Christine's and Isaac's every move, as if there were an invisible string from their chests to the end of the soldiers' weapons. The *Gruppenführer* climbed into the front seat with the waiting driver. Ear-piercing screeches of rusted metal drowned out Mutti's cries as the gears of the truck ground together. The oversized vehicle lurched and stopped twice, releasing bursts of exhaust before moving down the cobblestone street.

Through a flap in the back canvas, Christine could see her family in the street. As the truck drove away, they grew smaller and smaller, flickering in and out of her vision like the illustrations in a picture book that one flipped through with one's thumb, making the images on the pages appear to be in motion. Oma was looking at the sky, her frail arms held up to the heavens, her mouth an open circle of despair. In stiff, erratic movements, her mother wrenched herself from Vater and ran after the truck, her face contorted. She made it halfway to the bottom of the hill before she fell, inch by inch, to her hands and knees in the street. Christine closed her eyes. She couldn't watch any longer. But the images wouldn't stop playing over and over, frame by frame, in her mind.

CHAPTER 22

Ten minutes later, they arrived at the barracks next to the train station.

"Get out of the truck!" the *Gruppenführer* yelled.

In the truck bed, Isaac grabbed Christine and hugged her. "I'm so sorry I let this happen to you."

"Get your hands off her, you filthy Jew!" the *Gruppenführer* screamed.

One of the soldiers pried them apart, undid their handcuffs, and shoved them toward the rear of the truck. Christine fell and Isaac helped her up, then held her steady as she climbed over the tailgate.

When they were both on the ground, the *Gruppenführer* shouted, "I told you to keep your hands off of her!"

The butt of the gun collided with Isaac's head. He struggled to remain upright, but his knees buckled and he fell against the back of the truck. He lifted his hand to his skull, a trickle of blood running behind his ear. Christine wanted to reach out to help him, but she didn't dare, for fear they would hit him again.

At gunpoint, they were forced into the long, brick building of the train depot. Inside, they followed the *Gruppenführer* into a brick-walled office, where an immense SS *Hauptsturmführer,* Head

Storm Leader, dwarfed a desk in the center of the room, as if it were a student's writing table. To the left of the desk, a second door led out to the train platform. The *Hauptsturmführer* looked up when they came in, his wide forehead and broad jaw like the face of a bull. A portrait of Hitler hung on the wall above his head. In it, Hitler looked regal, almost handsome. Clouds floated behind him, as if he were a savior from God. On the desk were several stacks of papers, a jar of pens, a black telephone, and a slender, brown-handled Luger lying on a folded red cloth. Isaac and Christine stood in front of the desk, the *Gruppenführer* to Christine's right, the soldiers behind them. The *Hauptsturmführer* stood and eyed them, his wide, muscular body straining the seams of his uniform.

"I have returned our missing prisoner," the *Gruppenführer* said triumphantly.

"And who is this?" the *Hauptsturmführer* asked. He came around the desk, went to Christine, and touched her face with the back of his oversized fingers.

"This is our runaway Jew's girlfriend. She hid him upstairs in her attic."

"Well, *Fräulein*," the *Hauptsturmführer* said to her. "I can certainly see what he saw in a beautiful German girl like you, but tell me, what did you see in this Jewish pig?"

Christine kept her eyes on Isaac, standing as close to him as possible and trying to pretend it was just the two of them in the orchard on the hill. But she couldn't remember the apple trees, couldn't remember the green grass and bright sky. The only pictures in her head were of gray and white uniforms and skeletal prisoners, black boots and dropping bombs, bomb shelters and boxcars full of withered people. Isaac wouldn't look at her. He kept his head down and his eyes on the floor. She could feel every taut tendon in her neck, every burning vein beneath her skin. The side of her hand, where it touched his, felt on fire. She needed him to look at her. A scream was building in her chest, ready to erupt like a swarm of hornets exploding from their shattered hive.

One of the soldiers shoved them toward a bench against the wall, instructing them to sit. The *Hauptsturmführer* lit a cigarette and sat on the corner of his desk, the thick oak groaning beneath his weight. Then he lifted his frame and walked over to Christine, taking a long draw from his cigarette, and ran a hand over her hair, his leg pressing hard against her thigh. Christine stared at Isaac. He was breathing hard, the whites of his eyes bloodshot, his forehead bulging. The trickle of blood behind his ear was already starting to dry. The *Hauptsturmführer* dropped his cigarette and stepped on it, then pulled Christine to her feet. He put a plank-thick hand on the small of her back and held her arm out to the side, humming as he began to sway, his massive body pressed against hers. Christine glanced toward the *Gruppenführer*. His fleshy face was crimson. With disbelief, she realized he was jealous.

The *Gruppenführer* cleared his throat and said in a loud voice, "It's too bad she's been spoiled by this Jew. We could keep her for ourselves. But who would want something a dirty Jew has touched?"

The soldiers started to snicker. The *Hauptsturmführer* snorted and pushed Christine down on the bench. Finally, Isaac looked at her, his face red.

"You've timed your arrival just right," the *Hauptsturmführer* announced. "The train to Dachau is coming through within the hour."

Christine went rigid. *Dachau?* For some reason, she'd assumed they'd be staying at this camp. Isaac had said there was food. And outhouses. And no gas chambers. And no crematoriums. When she heard the name Dachau, a black dagger of horror plunged deep into her chest, where it lodged and throbbed, causing shockwaves of fire and ice to shoot through her veins. She inched closer to Isaac, sweating and shivering.

"You're dismissed!" the *Hauptsturmführer* said to the *Gruppenführer* and the soldiers. "I can handle things from here."

The *Gruppenführer* glared at Christine and Isaac as if he wanted to strangle them. Finally, he saluted the *Hauptsturmführer* and exited with the two soldiers. The *Hauptsturmführer* lit another cigarette, removed his peaked cap and placed it on the desk, then sat down. For the next few minutes, he went about his business, signing papers, answering the phone, occasionally looking over at them in disgust.

Christine folded her arms across her middle, touching the side of Isaac's arm with her fingers. Isaac stared at the floor, his back against the wall, his shoulders slumped, his hands limp in his lap. Once in a while he glanced at her, his eyes hollow with regret. She looked back at him, pleading silently for him not to surrender. All they had now was the will to live. He'd survived Dachau once, and her father had survived a POW camp in Russia. She had to believe it was possible. She had to believe they had a chance. Because if they were going to give up, if they weren't even going to try, then she might as well walk over to the desk, grab the gun lying on the red cloth, and shoot them all, right here and now.

"We'll be all right," she whispered. "We have to be."

"No talking!" the *Hauptsturmführer* yelled, slamming his huge hand on the desk. The phone and jars of pens rattled.

"I love you," she said to Isaac. "And when this is over, we'll still have our whole lives ahead of us. *Bitte,* don't give up."

The *Hauptsturmführer* grabbed the gun and flew around the desk. "I said, no talking!" he yelled, barreling toward them, the gun pointed at Christine.

Christine straightened and leaned against the wall. The *Hauptsturmführer* moved closer and shoved his thick knees between hers, forcing her legs apart. He lifted her chin with one hand, squeezing her face in a vise-like grip.

"Open your mouth!" he shouted, his thumb and fingers digging into her cheeks.

"I'll be quiet."

"Open your mouth!"

Christine did as she was told. The cold, hard metal of the Luger scraped against her teeth, the long, round barrel making her gag. Isaac stiffened beside her.

"One more word out of you," the *Hauptsturmführer* said, "and it will be your last. Understand?"

Christine closed her eyes and nodded. He pulled the gun out of her mouth, leaving the taste of metal on her tongue.

"You're a lively little *Fräulein, ja?*" He traced the Luger down her cheek, along her neck, across her collarbone. She kept her eyes closed. "Now that everyone else is gone, maybe I should give you something to remember me by." He forced her legs farther apart, pushing her skirt up her thighs, running the end of the gun over her breasts. Isaac panted beside her, his frustration and anger palpable in every breath.

The hard barrel trailed downward, along her stomach, toward the top of one thigh. Then, she heard a train in the distance. The *Hauptsturmführer* grunted and stepped away, pressing his hand against the fly of his pants. He holstered the Luger, took his cap from the desk, and shoved it onto his head.

The rumble of the approaching train quickened the already turbulent beat of Christine's heart. She had to fight the urge to run. But the *Hauptsturmführer* had the gun in his hand again, and it was pointing right at them. As the train drew closer, the hiss of steam and the screech of brakes grew louder and louder. The train stopped outside the building, pistons pounding, like the giant, beating heart of a mammoth black creature fighting its way through the very walls of the building, so it could eat them alive.

"Do everything they say," Isaac said to her. "They'll shoot you without a second thought."

"Get up!" the *Hauptsturmführer* shouted. Christine and Isaac stood. The *Hauptsturmführer* motioned toward the rear of the building with his Luger. "This way!"

He pushed them out the second door onto the concrete platform, the gun pointed at their backs. Beside the platform, the train waited, exhaling great walls of steam. Eight cattle cars trembled behind the living, breathing engine. Christine saw the small openings, the barbed wire, the reaching hands, the haunted faces. She could hear moans, cries, pleading voices. Soldiers forced her and Isaac toward the last car. She felt a thousand eyes watching as they walked along the platform.

At the last boxcar, two soldiers slid open the heavy door, then motioned Christine and Isaac forward with their guns. Inside, a multitude of pale faces with dark eyes floated above indistinct bodies. The soldiers shoved Christine and Isaac inside, thrust together and stumbling, into the mass of bodies. Christine felt hands, arms, elbows, feet. She barely had a chance to get her footing before the door was pulled closed. In slow motion, the slice of sunlight narrowed, getting thinner and thinner, until it was swallowed by shadow. On the outside of the door, a bar was shoved into place, locking them in with a final, iron thud.

Christine and Isaac stood facing each other, compressed together and wedged between a hundred other bodies. Countless people were crushed into the boxcar like kindling, filling every square inch. It was dark and stifling hot, the stench of urine and feces permeating the air. Christine tried to breathe through her mouth, pressing her face into Isaac's chest, trying to inhale the scent of his body. He buried his face in her hair. The whistle shrieked. The locomotive strained, and the entire train shuddered. With a jolt, the boxcars lurched forward. There was no need to hang on because there was nowhere to fall. Bodies jostled against bodies as the cars rattled slowly along the tracks. After the train rounded the bend out of the village, it picked up speed near the edge of the valley. Christine knew they were passing below hills covered with orchards and tall pines.

As their eyes adjusted, they saw the faces of the condemned all around them. To her right, a boy clung to his mother, his freckled nose just inches from Christine's, his dark eyes watching from beneath tousled brown hair. Her own fear and uncertainty were reflected in his eyes, her own vulnerability in his desperate grip on his mother's shawl.

Isaac wrapped his arms around her shoulders. "I love you. And I'm sorry."

"We can survive this," she said. "We have to. My father survived camps as bad as this, and so did you."

"We can try." His words lacked conviction, and his face was slack. But he held her tighter, and she could hear the heartbeat in his chest growing fast and strong.

During the first few hours, the people in the boxcar wept and spoke quietly. Somewhere, a woman moaned. Christine wanted her to stop. After what felt like a thousand hours, there was only silence, with the occasional soft words, or the sound of the woman singing softly to the young boy. Christine offered to take him from his mother to give her a rest, but they refused to let go of each other.

Eventually, Christine's legs started to cramp, and her feet ached from standing in one position. Along with that discomfort, and the fact that her stomach was growling and her throat felt parched, the pressure in her bladder was almost too much to bear. She inhaled through her nose and blew out through her mouth, trying to take her mind off the pain in her pelvis.

"What's wrong?" Isaac whispered.

"Nothing," she said. "I'm all right."

"*Nein,* you're not. I can tell."

She looked up at him. "I have to go to the bathroom."

"So go."

She shook her head. "I can't."

"Listen to me," he said. "Let it go. It doesn't matter. It doesn't matter anymore."

"*Nein.*"

He stroked the back of her head. "It doesn't matter anymore. Nothing like that matters. It's all right."

She closed her eyes and buried her face in his shirt, her tortured bladder making the decision for her. The warm liquid ran down the inside of her legs into her leather shoes, where it puddled beneath her stocking heels. Tears of shame ran down her face.

"It's not your fault," Isaac said. "It's not your fault."

Outside it had grown dark, casting the interior into blackness. Christine could barely see Isaac's face. She closed her eyes and put her head against his chest, trying to drift off, to escape into the ignorance of sleep, but it was impossible. The images of where they were going, which Isaac had unintentionally painted in her mind, played like a slideshow behind her closed eyelids. Now, the cramps in her legs and the ache in her feet felt like knives. She'd never thought of herself as claustrophobic, but if the train didn't stop soon, she wasn't sure how much longer she'd be able to control the feeling of being crushed, the heavy weight that made her arm muscles tighten and her breath shallow. She had to fight the urge to bend her arm and throw her elbow into the bodies next to hers. She couldn't breathe, she couldn't move, and she might go crazy if she wasn't let loose soon.

At last, the train started to slow. The iron wheels caught and screeched, caught and screeched. As they got closer to their dreadful destination, the occupants of the boxcar grew agitated. People tried to change positions. Everyone tried to talk at once. Children cried, and men gave instructions. Isaac had been anxious and quiet during the long trip, but now he lifted his chin and yelled above the commotion.

"When we get off the train," he shouted, "we'll be separated. Women to one side, men to the other. But don't panic. They don't like it when you panic." Everyone in the car grew silent and listened. "Look calm and strong. No matter what they do, act strong. If you want to survive, you have to look like you can work hard. If you need to, lie about your age, tell them you're somewhere between eighteen and fifty."

"How do you know these things?" a man's voice shouted.

"I've been here before, and if I can survive, so can you."

Again, everyone started talking at once. Isaac looked down at Christine. "You'll survive this too. You're young and strong. Tell them you're not Jewish. Tell them you worked as a cook. That will save you. I need you to survive. Someday when this is over, you and I will be together. We'll find each other. We'll get married and have babies."

His eyes were wet with tears, but Christine felt a strange sense of joy and strength hearing his words. He still had hope. He'd found the will to survive.

"I'll be strong," she said. "I promise."

"Until we meet again," he said, taking her face in his hands. He kissed her long and hard, not taking his lips from hers until the train came to a complete stop. "I love you, Christine."

Then the iron latches lifted, the boxcars were unlocked, and the heavy doors slid open.

CHAPTER 23

Blinking and squinting against the enormous spotlights that lit up the night like brilliant fallen moons, Christine and Isaac, along with the rest of the exhausted captives, climbed down from the confinement of the cattle car. A few hundred yards from the tracks, centered between wooden watchtowers and high wire fences, the gates to the concentration camp Dachau stood open and waiting. A row of soldiers equipped with submachine guns and barking German shepherds stood prepared to redirect strays. Long, shadowy buildings and black uniforms darkened in contrast to the artificial white light. With surreal clarity, wide, dark eyes and animated mouths looked like shifting black holes in pallid faces, giving captors and captives alike the illusion that they were the dead come to life.

The smell of something burning replaced the stench of the boxcars. Christine put her hand over her nose and mouth. Recognizing the distinct odor of burning flesh, she fought back the urge to vomit. She looked along the tracks toward the hissing, wheezing engine and saw hundreds of people spilling onto the gravel beside the train. Several people fell out; some refused to come out by any means. A handful of soldiers climbed into the boxcars and pushed out women, children, and old men. On the platform, men carried suitcases and women carried small children on their hips, holding tight to the hands of older siblings. Piped over loudspeakers from inside the camp, a German waltz played into the cool night air. The music sounded metallic, abrasive, haunting, yet eerily carefree. Signs that read: *"Achtung Gefahr der Tötung durch Elektrischen Strom,"* "Warning: Danger of Electrocution," hung from high electric fences topped with coils of barbed wire. Above the main entrance, a welded iron sign read *"Arbeit Macht Frei"*: "Work will make you free."

The soldiers had started yelling as soon as the doors to the box-cars slid open, and now they continued, nonstop. "Move! Get out of the train! Leave your luggage beside the train. It will be delivered to you later, after you've settled in."

A dozen prisoners in gray and white striped uniforms handed out pieces of chalk, instructing people to write their names on their suitcases. Christine and Isaac had nothing but the clothes on their backs, but she knew it didn't matter. Isaac had told her they would take everything. She knew the soldiers were lying, trying to make the newly arrived inmates believe they could trust their captors, so they wouldn't cause trouble.

She and Isaac walked beside the boxcars within the horde of shuffling, murmuring people, and suddenly she remembered how her father had ducked under the train and escaped. When they reached a gap between the cars, she looked through the opening, toward dark fields edged by forest. A spark of hope sent electric currents through her body, and for an instant, she felt elation. But just as she was getting ready to suggest a plan to Isaac, she saw an armed soldier walking on the other side. The crush of helplessness returned. Evidently, such an escape had been attempted before.

Christine and Isaac gripped each other by the hand and entered the line of people trudging between the gates of the camp. Just inside the main entrance, six guards stood at the head of the line, pushing the men to one side and women and children to the other.

Ahead of them in line, she saw the boy and his mother. One of the guards pried the boy from his mother's arms and took him to the left with the men. Mother and son reached for each other, fighting desperately not to be separated. The other women held the mother back as the guard dragged the boy away, but she broke free and ran to him. When the guard saw her, he pulled out his Luger and held it to the boy's head. Another guard dragged the mother back into line with the women. She shrieked, each scream longer and louder than the one before, shouting his name until her cries became ragged and hoarse.

The guard kept the gun to the boy's head, eyes scanning the crowd, daring them to try something. Horror flooded Christine's esophagus, and her throat felt sore, as if she'd just swallowed a mouthful of jagged ice.

The guard was Kate's boyfriend, Stefan.

For a brief second, their eyes met, and a flash of recognition crossed Stefan's face. Before Christine could open her mouth and point him out to Isaac, Stefan disappeared into the crowd, taking the crying boy with him. Two sounds rapidly intensified in Christine's ears: the devastated mother's guttural wails of anguish and the tinny resonance of the soaring, whirling waltz. She closed her eyes and leaned against Isaac. *How can this be happening?* she thought. A block of icy terror settled deep in the pit of her empty stomach. *Maybe I'm dreaming. Maybe I'm having a nightmare.*

Christine and Isaac reached the guards. Before she knew what was happening, she was being pushed to the right with the women. They were separated, and Isaac was getting farther and farther away. She couldn't remember letting go of his hand, and she tried desperately to remember the feel of it, the warmth and width of it in hers. She berated herself for not clinging to him, for not taking in and remembering the feel and the scent of him for as long as she could. Everything was happening too fast. Sent deeper and deeper into the yawning void of the camp, they watched each other as long as they could, until long, dark buildings and high fences came between them.

Christine tried not to hyperventilate as two female SS *Unterscharführers*, "Under Group Leaders," herded the women into a large building lined with wooden benches. Emaciated female prisoners holding oversized scissors waited silently behind the seats. They wore ill-fitting striped uniform dresses, and their hair was stubble short and ratted. They looked at the newcomers with sunken, vacant eyes, the skin of their faces stretched taut over their cheekbones, their collarbones jutting from their chests.

"Sit down!" the *Unterscharführers* ordered the incoming prisoners.

Almost before Christine had obeyed, the woman prisoner behind the bench had pulled her long, blond hair into one hand. In one big chunk, she cut it off with the scissors. Christine could hear the dull blades chewing through her hair, like a rat chewing through a wall. She could feel the woman's hands shaking as she held up what was left of her hair and cut it off, just half an inch from her scalp. Then, with a razor, the prisoner shaved her head. Christine closed her eyes.

The *Unterscharführers* walked back and forth between the benches yelling orders. "After your hair is cut, stand up, move to the rear of the building. There, you will undress. Put your shoes in the pile to the left, clothes in the pile to the right, watches and glasses in the center."

Christine stood and ran her hands over her bald head, her fingers running over alternating patches of stiff stubble and smooth skin. On trembling legs, she walked to the rear of the building, toward the growing piles of shoes and clothes. There were other piles to either side, but at first, she wasn't sure what she was looking at. The towering heaps looked like giant masses of wire or tangled yarn. Then, her breath seized in her chest, and she looked away. In the two back corners of the room, mountains of human hair went nearly to the ceiling.

She took off her high, black shoes and tossed them on top of thousands of dress heels, winter boots, and pairs of leather footwear. Then, she took off her clothes and cast them on the pile of peasant dresses and tattered aprons mixed in with fur coats and silk chemises. Teeth chattering, she tried to cover herself with her arms and hands.

"Come on, you filthy pigs!" the *Unterscharführers* yelled. "Take everything off! You're going to get the first real shower you've probably ever taken! Move it! Come on! Don't be shy!"

When everyone had been shorn and had undressed, they stood there, over a hundred of them, naked and shivering, like something out of a nightmare: bald heads, wide and frightened eyes, protruding ears . . . old women, young women, fat women, skinny women, little girls, and little boys. They all stood there together, wondering what was going to happen next. *This can't be real, it just can't be,* Christine thought. *How is this possible? How did I get here?*

"Line up!" the *Unterscharführers* said. "We're going to clean you up!" They opened a wide set of doors that led into a window-less, concrete room.

Inside the long, gray space, multiple nozzles protruded from the ceiling, and metal drain tiles lined the center of the concrete floor. The *Unterscharführers* used their truncheons to herd the women through the doors, dealing blows to anyone who didn't move fast enough. Some of the women held on to one another and sobbed, their desperate cries echoing in the hollow, empty room. Some walked in without a sound, while others prayed and whimpered. Mothers with babies and small children held them in their arms and hummed in their ears, their eyes locked on the nozzles in the ceiling. Evidently, Christine wasn't the only one who'd heard the stories about people being gassed. She wanted to turn and run, but the guards had pistols strapped to their sides.

After the *Unterscharführers* had shoved the last woman into the cold, damp room, they shut and locked the doors. Shaking and covering themselves, the women and children looked at each other, silent and waiting. They heard a screech of metal. Pipes banging. Then the showers came on. Women screamed. A few clawed their way toward the doors.

When they realized it wasn't gas or chemicals, they laughed and smeared the water over their faces and heads. But it was mixed with a disinfectant that burned their eyes and made them cough. Christine held her head down and closed her eyes, the water burning her nostrils. After a few minutes, the doors on the other end of the room opened. She could hardly see as they were led into the next room, blinking and spitting. She wiped at her eyes, stumbling and colliding with the others. No one spoke, but she felt an arm link through hers, a uniform and a pair of shoes pressed into her hands.

"Do not put on your uniforms until after you've been examined," a voice shouted. Christine used the uniform to wipe her eyes and face. She pushed her feet into laceless, rigid shoes. By then, the arm that had helped her along was no longer there. She looked at the women nearby and tried to convey her gratitude with a weak smile.

On the other side of the room, two *Gruppenführers* and a man with a stethoscope waited beside a table. One by one, the women were questioned while a soldier wrote down their information and the doctor looked into their mouths, eyes, and ears.

Then the doctor pointed, to the left or to the right.

The ones sent to the right, the healthiest-looking adults, slipped their uniforms on over their heads. The ones sent to the left, the old, the sick, and the very young, were instructed to put their uniforms and shoes into a pile. Toddlers and babies were yanked from their crying mothers' arms and handed to the people being sent to the left, before they were led naked through another wide set of double doors, where they vanished.

Christine stepped up to the men, clutching her dress to her chest.

"Name?" one of the *Gruppenführers* asked.

"Christine Bölz," she answered in as strong a voice as she could muster. "I'm not Jewish." The *Gruppenführer* laughed. She looked straight ahead.

The doctor, wearing thick, black glasses that made his eyes look oversized, looked into her eyes and mouth, breathing heavily through his open lips, his face just inches from hers. His hot breath, sour with the smell of strong coffee and tooth decay, swept over her face.

"Address?" the *Gruppenführer* asked.

"Schellergasse Five, Hessental."

"Occupation?"

"I am a domestic servant, in charge of gardening, housekeeping, and cooking. I shouldn't be here. I was falsely accused of helping a Jew." The words were like acid in her mouth. But she knew Isaac would understand.

The second *Gruppenführer* came over to get a closer look.

"Can you cook proper German food?"

"*Jawohl!* Yes, indeed!" Christine answered. "I'm a very good cook, Herr Gruppenführer."

"Lift your arms," the doctor said, making a turning motion with his finger. Christine lifted her arms and turned.

"She will replace Lagerkommandant Grünstein's cook!" the second *Gruppenführer* said to the man who was taking down names and information.

The doctor pointed to the right.

Danke, Isaac, she thought, heaving a shudder of relief. She slipped her uniform over her head and went into the next room. There, the incoming women held out their arms while more female prisoners tattooed numbers on the inside of their wrists. When it was her turn, Christine stared at the girl looking intently at her work. She never felt the number being needled into her right forearm. When it was over, the girl smiled at her, her remaining teeth rotten and yellow. Christine looked down at the black and bloody number near her wrist: 11091986.

"Keep it clean, or it'll get infected," the girl said.

A female *Blockführer,* block leader, approached Christine. "Follow me!"

Christine hurriedly fell in behind her and followed her outside. They walked toward the rear of the immense complex, passing hundreds of wooden barracks and working prisoners. After a while, they came to a small, half-timbered house surrounded by a high, metal fence. The dark, soft mud that seemed to cover the rest of the camp stopped short at the outside perimeter of the enclosed space. The house, lit up by miniature spotlights from various directions, was simple and neat, but in the bleak compound it stood out like a shimmering gem in a pile of coal dust. Waiting for the *Blockführer* to open the gate, Christine looked at the yard surrounding it. In the false daylight of the spotlights, she could see smooth, green grass, purple coneflowers along the porch, and two clay pots filled with red geraniums on either side of the front door.

Inside, Christine followed the *Blockführer* to the rear of the house, past rooms filled with framed paintings, Persian rugs, and antique furniture. At the island counter in the spotless white kitchen, a middle-aged prisoner stood peeling potatoes, her drawn, thin face expressionless, her eyes fixed on the potato in her hand. When she looked up and saw them standing there, her eyes widened; the corners of her mouth turned down.

"Your job is finished here!" the *Blockführer* barked.

The woman dropped the knife and the partially peeled potato, her face contorting in fear. *"Nein,"* she muttered, starting to weep.

"You'd better know how to cook, or you won't last long, either," the *Blockführer* warned Christine. Then she grabbed the woman by the wrist and dragged her out of the house.

Christine stood in the center of the kitchen and tried to clear her head. She needed to get her wits about her if she was going to survive. She took a deep breath, walked over to the stove, and lifted the lid on a boiling kettle. Inside, a thin, watery broth bubbled around a pale chunk of brown meat. It was a piece of pork. She could tell it was missing seasonings and spices, so she searched the cupboards and found rosemary, salt, and pepper. There was a bag of onions in the lower cupboards, so she sliced one up and added it to the broth. Then she cut two strips from a side of bacon she'd found wrapped in brown paper, and added them to the pot.

Trying to ignore the cramp and growl of her empty stomach, she finished peeling the potatoes and put them on to boil. There were carrots on the counter, so she peeled and shredded them into a bowl, all except one. She hid the extra carrot in the pile of peelings and took small bites of it, keeping her ears open and one eye on the kitchen door. Then she added vinegar, oil, and a heaping tablespoon of sugar to the shredded carrots. With the carrot salad finished, she just stood there, panicked, not knowing if what she had done would be right. She had no idea what kind of person would be coming home to sit at the single place setting in the dining room.

She sat on a stool next to the woodstove and tried to collect her thoughts. She put her head in her hands, staring at her filthy, tattered shoes. She inhaled deeply and exhaled slowly, blowing her breath out through her mouth. After a few minutes, she sat upright. She pulled her feet from her too-small shoes and examined the red bumps on the back of her heels, her skin already forming raised blisters. *Maybe I should go barefoot while I'm alone here,* she thought, relieved to realize that she was still capable of rational thought.

Then she heard footsteps coming across the porch. The door handle rattled and turned. The front door opened and closed.

She pushed her feet into her shoes, got up from the stool, and wiped her face with the palms of her hands. Footsteps were coming down the hall, toward the kitchen. She heard a man sigh and mutter under his breath, and the tight creak of leather boots. She hurried over to the counter and gathered the potato and carrot peelings into a pile. The door to the kitchen swung open. She kept her head down, her eyes on the task in front of her. The heavy boots stopped beside her. A thick, age-spotted hand rested on the counter, and an overpowering scent of Kölnisches Wasser 4711 filled the room.

"Guten Tag, Fräulein," the man said, his voice low and gritty.

Christine didn't move. He put a hand under her chin and turned her face toward his, looking her over with blue, heavy-lidded eyes. His eyebrows were too far apart, as if stretched to opposite sides by his wide, high forehead. His nose was broad, his lips full and shapely, like a woman's. He wasn't old, but he was well on his way, with the thick, soft middle of overindulgence.

"My name is Jörge Grünstein," he said. "But you must always call me Herr Lagerkommandant. Just so you know, you have nothing to fear from me. If you do as you're told, and you're careful, this job could save your life." He took off his hat and unbuttoned his jacket, then removed it and put it over his arm, his medals jingling like miniature wind chimes in the quiet kitchen. Sweat had flattened his graying hair to his forehead, and his hat had left red lines on his skin. His uniform was SS black, the silver skull and crossbones shining on the lapel and hat, but oddly, Christine felt her heart slow. He seemed and looked harmless, like someone's *Opa.* To her, his eyes seemed troubled.

"What's your name?" he asked.

"Christine. I'm not a Jew. My father fights for our beloved Führer." Self-loathing twisted in her gut.

He shook his head as if he didn't want to hear it. "The only thing I can do is share a bit of my food. But you have to be careful. Don't make it obvious. And I don't want to know about it. The other officers here would turn on me. They shot an officer just yesterday, because he dared question one of their procedures. I know it's no excuse, but I'm too old to fight back. If that makes me a coward, so be it. But I have a family I'd like to see again."

Christine said nothing, but the woozy feeling started to fade.

"I'm sure you couldn't care less about my problems," he went on. "You've got yourself to worry about. But I'm only going to say this once. The better you do your job, the longer you'll live. You're to keep this house clean, cook, and tend to the garden behind the house. The garden is not just for me. It's for the other officers who work here during the day. Do you know how to garden?"

Christine nodded.

"*Gut*. I'll wait at the table for my dinner." He walked out of the kitchen, his jacket and hat under his arm. To Christine, his weary body language seemed that of a man tormented.

As she finished cleaning up the counter, her heart returned to a steady rhythm. She drained the potatoes, covered them with fresh parsley and *real* butter, put the steaming pork on a serving platter, and took the carrot salad into the dining room. The *Lagerkommandant* watched her every move. She brought in the rest of the food, trying to think only of what she needed to do next: take away the unused soup bowl, slice the meat on the platter, refill his water glass, put one foot in front of the other without falling into a mess on the floor.

"I would like wine with my meal," he said, pointing toward the cellar door between the dining room and kitchen. "A Riesling, *bitte*."

"*Ja*, Herr Lagerkommandant."

She went down the steps to the cellar, where hundreds of dust-covered bottles lined wooden shelves. The musty scent of concrete, earth, and potatoes flooded her senses with memories of the root cellar in Hessental—memories of wonderful times with Isaac and frightening times with her family. Her chest constricted. At least back then she hadn't been alone. She took a bottle of wine from the top of the nearest shelf. LIEBFRAUMILCH, it said. She knew nothing about wine, if Riesling was white or red, so she pulled out one bottle after the other, until she found one labeled RIESLING. Then she clutched the bottle to her chest and started up the cellar stairs, gripping the banister with her free hand. She didn't trust herself with the easiest tasks, and dropping the wine was a chance she didn't want to take. *I'm safe for now,* she thought. *But where is Isaac? What's happening to him?*

"I promise I'll survive," she whispered. "I'm not going to let them break me."

After his dinner, the *Lagerkommandant* finished the bottle of wine and lit a cigar. Christine cleared the dirty dishes from the table, feeling his eyes on her as she made several trips between the dining room and kitchen. Earlier, before she'd delivered the pork, she'd eaten a few slivers of the juicy, tender meat. Now, as she placed the dirty dishes in the porcelain sink, she ate the scraps from his plate, shoving the meat and potatoes and carrots in her mouth with her fingers, chewing and swallowing as fast as she could without choking. Then, running hot water over the white china, she noticed something she hadn't before. A blue edge rimmed the plates and bowl, and the SS insignia, like blue lightning bolts, decorated the center. While the prisoners of Dachau were starving, the SS were eating meat and vegetables from their own specially designed china. The stolen food soured in her stomach.

She washed the dishes, wondering what would happen next. *Where am I supposed to sleep?* she thought. *Hopefully, not here with him.* She wouldn't be able to tolerate it, his withered, age-spotted hands on her skin, his breath on her face and neck, his sweaty body crushing her. Was that what she would be forced to endure to survive? Would giving herself to him be her final sacrifice? A hot flash of panic rushed across her chest, and she prayed she was only there to cook and clean. Just then, the *Lagerkommandant* came into the kitchen behind her.

"You will sleep in the barracks with the other women," he said. "Someone is coming for you now."

CHAPTER 24

A rapid knock on the door preceded the female *Blockführer,* who was there to lead Christine to the barracks. Despite her fear, Christine was taken aback when she saw the *Blockführer*'s flawless skin and precisely coiffed hair below her peaked cap. The woman was pretty enough to be a model or an actress. What on earth was she doing in a place like this? But her beauty disappeared when she scowled, grabbed Christine by the arm, and dragged her into the night.

Christine had no idea what time it was, but the stench of burning flesh still permeated the air. She looked up at the starless sky, wondering how God could look down on this atrocity and allow it to continue. In the black night, the gray moon seemed to smolder at the edges, as if the whole world were on fire. The *Blockführer* walked fast, leading her past long rows of shadowy barracks, only looking back to make sure she followed. Christine could hear the hammering pistons and screeching iron wheels of an incoming train, and the fleeting violins of a distant, mocking waltz. When they came to the last windowless barrack, the *Blockführer* unlocked the door and shoved Christine inside, plunging her headlong into the pitch-black space.

Christine stumbled and nearly fell before she found her footing. The stench of feces, vomit, and urine made her gag and cough. She reeled backwards and clamped a hand over her mouth. Then she felt hands, on her face, neck, arms, legs—groping, searching, feeling. She could only stand, paralyzed and blind, waiting to see what would happen next. Hoarse female voices floated out of the dark. Thin, icy fingers gripped hers, pulling her forward.

"It's all right," a raspy voice said. "Don't be afraid, we won't hurt you."

"There's not much room," another voice said. "But we'll squeeze you in."

Little by little, Christine's eyes adjusted to the gloom. She could make out bald heads floating above and below her, hundreds of pairs of eyes looking her way. The barracks was crammed full of women and girls lying together on bunks made of wood, three and four layers high. With barely two feet between them, the bunks were more like bookshelves than beds, the women stacked like cordwood.

A hand led Christine toward a rack, then pulled gently to guide her in. Christine felt her way, groping in the dark, accidentally touching bald heads and emaciated ribs, wasted arms and scrawny legs. She climbed in and lay down on her back, cramped between two bony women, her arms folded across her chest. For the next few minutes, voices murmured all around her, hushed whispers in German, Polish, Hungarian, Russian, French. Then it was quiet.

"What's your name?" a voice said in the dark.

"Christine Bölz."

"Are you Jewish?"

"*Nein.* They found my Jewish boyfriend hiding in my attic."

"Did they shoot him?" someone asked with enthusiasm.

"Of course they did," another said.

"*Nein,* they probably strung him up by his neck!" the enthusiastic voice said. "Or slit his throat!"

Christine squeezed her eyes shut. *They've all gone mad!*

"So?" the enthusiastic voice said again. "Is he dead?"

"*Nein,*" Christine said, her throat burning. "He came here on the train with me."

"You'll never see him again," the same voice said.

"Don't listen to her," the woman next to her whispered.

Christine turned toward the voice, trying to make out the features of a face. It was no use. It was too dark. "Is there any way I can find out where he is?"

There was no reply.

Christine lay motionless, staring into the darkness and listening. The only sounds were coughing, mumbling, sniffling, and soft crying. Every breath was seasoned with the bitter aroma of death. With increasing alarm, she began to realize there were hundreds of women within the vast darkness of this one building. And in this part of the camp alone, there were countless more buildings just like this one.

"Does anyone know a woman named Nina Bauerman?" she asked. "Or her daughter Gabriella?"

"When did they come in?" someone asked.

"Last fall," Christine said.

"Jewish?"

"*Ja,*" Christine said.

"I've been here a year and a half," a new voice said. "Some of the Jewish women get together in the back of the barracks for Kaddish. I remember a woman named Nina Bauerman. She was sent to the quarantine camp a few months ago. Typhus."

"Was her daughter with her?" Christine asked.

"How old?"

"Twelve."

"You won't find her," the first woman who spoke said. "Or her mother."

Christine closed her flooding eyes, trying to shut out the sounds of human suffering. She struggled to breathe, feeling like she was trapped in an enormous, black coffin, the dead and dying all around her. Every thud of her heart made her head pulsate against the hard wood beneath her skull. She prayed for exhaustion to overtake her mind, to release her into sleep. Hours later, when it finally did, she dozed in fits and starts, alternating between furious nightmares and dreams of home. At times she felt like she was floating, drifting in and out of consciousness, not sure where her dreams ended and the all-too-real nightmares began.

The next morning, dawn brought her worst fears to reality. She opened her eyes to the sight of a dead woman next to her, lying on her side, the skin of her skull stretched tight over her face. The woman's mouth drooped open; only four rotted teeth were left in her gums. Her broomstick arms were folded up under her head like a pillow, her naked knees like oversized knots in reedy saplings. But then, suddenly, her lips sucked in a ragged breath and she started to stir. Christine scrambled out of the bunk.

The other women crawled slowly out of the wooden racks, wheezing, coughing, whimpering. Christine didn't recognize anyone from the train. Most of the women were bald, and others had short, ragged hair. Several were naked except for their shoes. A few came over to Christine to smile or take her hand. The rest just walked by, wearing the shocked, blank expression of the insane. Scattered throughout the immense building were a handful of women who didn't get up. Other women sat next to them—friends and sisters, mothers and daughters—crying and begging for them not to quit, not to give up, not to die.

As the prisoners walked out of the building, a woman in line behind Christine moved close and started talking.

"You're safe for now," the woman said. "But in a few months you'll be as skinny as we are. Then you'll have to be careful. When the SS hold *"Selektion,"* the doctor shows up at morning roll call to weed out the weak and the sick. He walks up and down the ranks, writing numbers down. If your number is written down, into the ovens you'll go!"

Christine recognized the woman's voice as the one who had said she'd never see Isaac again. She turned to look at her. She was short but tough looking, her face and frame slightly more filled out than those of the rest of the prisoners. Her head and one arm twitched as she walked, and her eyes were red and crusty.

The women lined up for roll call in the frigid morning air, mud sucking at their bare feet and shoes. A *Rapportführer,* or roll-call leader, walked back and forth in front of them, shouting, "Stand up! Eyes straight ahead! Straighten that line!"

An older woman in front of Christine was having a hard time standing up, her thin arms hanging useless as she swayed side to side. A guard pulled her out of formation, pushed her to her knees, put his gun to her head, and pulled the trigger. The woman fell face-first into the mud, the hem of her uniform flying up to expose her white buttocks. Christine jumped and put a hand over her mouth, but the other women didn't flinch. *Ach* Gott! she thought, *they're used to it!*

"Put your hand down!" someone whispered beside her. "Don't draw attention to yourself!"

The woman next to her had uneven tufts of dark hair on her head, enormous brown eyes, peeling lips, and a bruise near one temple. It was hard to tell with her pronounced cheekbones and gray skin, but Christine thought they were around the same age. Christine looked forward.

"I'm Hanna," the woman whispered.

Christine nodded, her eyes fixed on the *Rapportführer* and guards.

"I can find out what happened to your friends. Nina Bauerman, *ja?* And Gabriella?"

Christine nodded again. Then, when the guards weren't looking, she whispered, "And Isaac. Isaac Bauerman."

"Only the women."

After the head count, the women were led off to their various labors. Hanna gave her a small wave as she plodded away with a large group. Christine was left standing there, shaking in the cold, not sure if she was supposed to go to the *Lagerkommandant*'s house on her own. Besides, it'd been dark last night when she had been led to the barracks; she couldn't be certain she knew how to find her way back. A guard came over to her.

"Go to work!" he screamed, then slapped her across the face.

Christine reeled sideways. Then she recovered and hurried in the direction of the house, her hand to the right side of her face. To her left, a high barbed wire fence split the camp in two. On the other side, there was block after block of identical wooden barracks, and male prisoners standing in formation. A *Rapportführer* walked back and forth in front of them. Christine looked at the sea of pale faces. There were thousands of them; it would have been impossible to spot Isaac. As she neared the house, she saw great waves of dark smoke rising from somewhere deep within the camp. The *Lagerkommandant* was standing on the front porch, smoking a cigar.

"*Guten Morgen, Fräulein*," he said.

"*Guten Morgen,* Herr Lagerkommandant. Is there anything specific you would like done today, Herr Lagerkommandant?"

"Just breakfast for now, and anything else you see that might need doing."

She put a hand on the door handle, ready to go inside. But she had to take the chance. "Excuse me, Herr Lagerkommandant?" she said, her voice shaking.

"*Ja?*" He turned to face her and leaned against the porch railing, the cigar sticking from one corner of his lips.

"I came here with someone."

His brow furrowed. He pulled the cigar from his mouth and flicked the ash over the edge of the porch. "And you want me to find out what happened to him," he said, his eyes hard to read.

"I'm sorry, Herr Lagerkommandant. I know I shouldn't have asked, but . . ."

Then he was in front of her, grabbing her, his fingers digging into her upper arm. "You're right. You shouldn't have! What's wrong with you? Didn't you listen to a word I said?"

"I'm sorry, Herr Lagerkommandant. It won't happen again, Herr Lagerkommandant."

He shoved her away, his temples pulsing. She waited, legs trembling, until he had turned and moved to the other side of the porch to stand at the top of the steps, like a mad king surveying his nightmarish kingdom, before she went into the house.

In the kitchen, she made coffee, boiled an egg, and sliced brown bread for his breakfast, her own stomach rumbling. The *Lagerkommandant* drank his coffee and ate the bread, but didn't touch the egg. After he left, she watched out the front window and wolfed down the egg. She felt like an animal, chewing and swallowing as fast as she could without choking. The fear of being discovered, coupled with the guilt of having food while so many others were starving, rendered the food tasteless. She wondered if Isaac had had anything to eat since they'd arrived.

After washing the dishes, she went out the back door to find and inspect the garden. A wide rectangle of poorly tended, weed-choked earth, the vegetable patch ran the length of the fence and took up nearly the entire backyard. She walked to the rear of the overgrown plot, trying to decide where to begin. Standing next to a yellowing row of parsnips, she could see part of the compound she hadn't seen before.

In the center of the camp stood two brick buildings, one with solid, windowless walls, the other with a mammoth red chimney. Waves of smoke billowed out from the flue. Army trucks idled next to the first building, their exhaust pipes connected to makeshift ducts in the building wall. Trapped in a corridor made of high barbed wire, long lines of people were being driven into the building by the leather whips of the SS: old men, young women, children, entire families. In between the two buildings, prisoners used wooden carts to transfer lifeless cargo from the first building into the one with the billowing chimney.

Christine fell to her knees and vomited into the dirt. She'd recognized the smell of burning flesh when they had arrived, but hadn't realized it was part of the procedure, part of the operation, part of what she now knew for certain was a deliberate slaughter. She'd thought the smell was coming from a crematorium for those who had died from starvation or disease, or who had been shot like that poor woman this morning. But the people headed into the buildings were still dressed! They hadn't even been put through the selection process. They'd just been taken off the trains and sent to their deaths. Her chest constricted as she strained to stop heaving, staring at the crabgrass and dandelions spreading between garden rows.

"Is there a problem?" the *Lagerkommandant* said behind her.

Christine stood and wiped her mouth with the back of her hand. "*Nein*, Herr Lagerkommandant," she said, trying to keep her voice steady. He glanced past her, toward the waves of rolling smoke in the sky.

"Oh," he said. "I see. You saw the crematorium." She was surprised to hear a trace of pity in his voice. "I told them that the last shipment of Zyklon-B was spoiled, and ordered them to bury it. I thought it would slow them down. But they won't stop, not even for a day. That's why they're using the trucks. That's how it started, you know, using the exhaust from the trucks." He scratched his chin with his thumb, looking at her as if he needed her to understand. "The first time I saw the crematorium, I wanted to enter the chambers with them. But then I realized I'm a witness to their murders. If I'm alive when this is over, I'll be able to tell the world what really happened here."

She didn't know how, or even if, she should respond. He had to be lying; otherwise, how could he stand there and let this happen? She wanted to go back to the barracks, longed to lie down, to be swept away by sleep. She didn't want to know, didn't want to think about what was going on here. She'd come out to start working on the garden, but now she couldn't. She needed to go back in the house, to get as far away as possible from what she'd just seen. She walked past him, hoping he wouldn't stop her, the acidic tang of bile stinging the back of her throat. The egg she'd eaten earlier tasted chalky and rancid on her tongue.

She spent the rest of the day straightening, sweeping, and preparing the *Lagerkommandant*'s meals. She'd have to go into the garden sooner or later, but she wasn't going to do it today. Instead, she worked like a machine, trying not to think. Every so often, her mind assaulted her with images of the line of people walking into the building. She saw them coming out the other side, naked and lifeless, their bodies thrown on a cart like piles of livestock after the slaughter, arms and legs entwined and dangling in awkward, unnatural positions. She tried not to think about the pain and agony experienced by the thousands of people who were dying here, but she couldn't help but carry it with her, like a heavy, black chain around her heart.

The black chain occasionally came loose. Overcome by grief, fear, and homesickness, she reached for her hair, for the comfort she used to find running it through her fingers, but there was nothing there. Several times throughout the day, reality hit, forcing her to stop what she was doing and sit down, with her head between her legs to keep from fainting, until finally, she pulled herself together enough to get back to work.

By the time she went back to her quarters, night had fallen, and she was thankful for the darkness that hid the crematorium, like a shroud pulled over a decaying corpse. When she stepped inside the barracks, someone grabbed her wrist and tried pulling her down the aisle. She dug in her heels and shouted, fighting back. Then the person drew close.

"Shush . . . it's me," Hanna said in a low voice. "Come on."

Hanna pulled her into a bottom bunk, where Christine lay on her side, squinting in the dark. Hanna's face was inches from hers, a ghost mask in the gloom.

"We have to whisper," Hanna said. "Remember that woman who warned you about *Selektion?* She's the *Blockältester,* the lead prisoner of the block. She gets double rations for reporting everything she sees and hears to the *Blockführer.* The green triangle on her uniform means she was a professional criminal before she came here. In Dachau, the professional criminals will do anything to survive, and the SS know it. Watch out for her. You don't want to get on her bad side."

"Danke," Christine whispered.

"That's not all I want to warn you about. You need to know that most of the other women aren't going to trust you either."

"Why not?" Christine said, a little too loudly. "What did I do?"

"You're not Jewish, and you work for the *Lagerkommandant.* They'll be afraid you'll tell him everything you see."

"But I'd never . . ."

"Listen. People are fighting for their lives, and that changes everything. You'd be surprised what people are capable of when it comes to saving their own skin."

"Do you trust me?"

"Ja."

"Why?"

"I don't know. Maybe because you just got here and you're not that desperate yet, or maybe because one of the first things you did was ask about your boyfriend's mother and sister."

"You said you could find out where they are."

"Ja. And I'm sorry. There's no easy way to tell you this. Gabriella was gassed and cremated shortly after she arrived."

Christine felt like she'd been punched in the stomach. "Are you sure?"

"I'm sure. I work in the records department. I type and file prisoner information."

Christine turned on her back and pressed the heels of her hands into her flooding eyes. *She was just a child,* she thought. "And Nina?" she said, her voice catching.

"Typhus, three months ago."

"*Ach* Gott."

Hanna shifted on the bunk. "Welcome to Dachau." Christine felt Hanna's hand on her shoulder. "Listen," Hanna said. "If I get a chance, I'll try to find out about your boyfriend, but I can't promise anything. I used to be able to look up the male prisoners' records, but the new *Blockschreiber,* barracks clerk, watches over the files like a hawk. He'll know I'm up to something. Before he came, I found out my twin brother was still alive, working in the munitions factory. But that was over a year ago. Now, well. I don't know if he's . . ." She paused. After a moment, she continued. "Anyway, I also found out that the former chancellor of Austria is here, and the former premier of France. The Germans are meticulous about their bookkeeping. They keep records of everyone who enters, including every person they've murdered."

Christine tried to find her voice. "How long have you been here?"

"Two years. Give or take a month or two. We were hiding with nine others in a tiny room in an apartment house in Berlin. We were safe for about six months. The neighbor turned us in to the Gestapo, in exchange for two loaves of bread."

Christine groaned. "And the rest of your family?"

"My mother and younger sisters went straight to the gas chambers. The guards hanged my father outside the gates, beside the mayor of the village of Dachau and ten other men. They left their bodies hanging for three weeks."

"I'm so sorry," Christine said.

"*Ja,*" Hanna continued, her voice flat. "The only reason they let me live was because I was a secretary and knew how to type. Imagine that. Sometimes I wish I hadn't told them." Christine felt Hanna press something hard and dry into her hand. "Here, I saved a piece of bread for you. You missed mealtime."

"*Nein, danke,*" Christine said, putting the crust back in Hanna's hand. "You need it more than I do. Besides, I'm not hungry."

"Are you sure?" Hanna said, already chewing.

"I'm sure. I've lost my appetite."

CHAPTER 25

On her daily walks to the *Lagerkommandant*'s, Christine realized how lucky she was to be working in his house. Some of the women prisoners were sent to work in armaments factories outside the camp, or to the Bayerische Motoren Werke factory to build engines for planes. Some, like Hanna, had jobs inside the camp, working in the records department, cooking for prisoners and guards, sorting piles of the incoming prisoners' belongings, or filling the hundreds of other labor positions needed to keep the camp operating. Most of the men worked on construction, outside in any weather, digging, pushing wheelbarrows, moving rocks, building roads and barracks. Guards would beat prisoners for no reason, women and men, and shoot them for even less. It was a normal occurrence for prisoners to drop to the ground, from being shot or succumbing to exhaustion, starvation, or disease. Flies, typhus, cholera, and death were ever-present companions. Every night, fewer women in her sector returned to the barracks. Every day, more women replaced them.

Night after night, Christine repeated the same prayer on her way back to the barracks, that Hanna would have news of Isaac. But it was always the same. She hadn't had an opportunity to look at the men's files without getting caught. Whenever Christine was outside, she looked for him on the other side of the fence. On her way to and from work, she walked as close as possible to the barrier that split the camp in two. There were thousands of men over there, lining up, working, falling, marching. From this distance, they all looked the same: striped uniforms, thin bodies, bald heads, dirty faces.

Cooking and cleaning inside the *Lagerkommandant*'s house, she tried to pretend that she was leading a normal life. It was the only way she could survive each hour. But the reverie disappeared when she had to go out to the garden, where the crematorium was in full horrifying view.

When the *Lagerkommandant* left scraps on his plate, she ate them. She helped herself to small portions of the food she served him, but he'd warned her not to take food out of the house. Once every evening, the prisoners were fed a watery soup made from rotting vegetables and gristly tendons of meat, along with a few ounces of stale bread. Sometimes Christine was back in time for dinner; sometimes she wasn't. When she was, she always gave her portion to Hanna. And nearly every day, when she thought she could get away with it, she stole slices of bread, a rind of cheese, or a scrap of meat to give to Hanna or one of the other women when the *Block-ältester* wasn't looking. The only places she had to hide anything were her shoes or her mouth. There were no pockets in her uniform, and she was naked beneath it.

One day, when she had a crust of bread hidden in each cheek, a guard stopped her on her way back to the barracks.

"What are you doing out here?" he demanded. Christine pointed toward the barracks and started walking again. He blocked her way, lifting his rifle. "Halt! What do you have in your mouth?" She tried to chew and swallow, but the bread was too dry. "Spit it out!" he shouted. She did as she was told, nearly choking in the process. He pointed his firearm at her head, taking aim, and she felt her bowels turn to water.

"I'm not Jewish!" she said. "Ask the *Lagerkommandant!* He will tell you!"

He lowered his rifle, eyeing her. "You're coming from the *Lagerkommandant*'s house?"

She nodded.

"So you're the sweet little *Fräulein* he tells us about." He put a hand on her thigh, lifting the hem of her uniform. "Does he know you're stealing food?"

"Herr Lagerkommandant says I'm to tell him if anyone touches what's his. And I'm an expert at remembering faces."

With that, the guard stepped back, motioning for her to be on her way. Christine hurried on, her arms over her middle, trying to keep her heart and lungs from exploding, ripping through the thin skin of her abdomen, and spilling out into a bloody pile at her feet.

So far, Dachau had not been bombed. The thump of bombs could be heard nearly every night, but they sounded far away. Christine wondered how long it would be until the Allies bombed the nearby armaments factory, or the factory used for building parts for planes. Because when they did, the camp could be next.

She'd been imprisoned in Dachau five weeks when she found the *Lagerkommandant* drunk at the dinner table. She'd come into the dining room carrying a platter of *Ente mit Sauerkraut auf Nürnberger Art,* duck with sauerkraut, apples, and grapes, and found him sitting there, a bottle of cognac in one hand, a snifter in the other. He'd brought the grapes, the duck, and the cognac back from Berlin, and she'd worried that the duck was a test, to see if she knew how to prepare it. Now, he was too intoxicated to notice that she'd spent hours getting it just right. When he saw her, he raised his glass in the air.

"To Hitler!" he said. "May he outlive us all!" His eyes were heavy and bloodshot, his lips wet. He threw back his head and drained the glass, setting it on the table with a bang. Then he picked up the cognac with an unsteady hand and refilled the snifter. Christine set the serving platter on the table and reached for his plate.

"Let me fix your plate for you, Herr Lagerkommandant," she said. "You should eat something." Using silver serving tongs, she dished a perfectly browned duck breast over the SS insignia in the center of the china, spooning the apple and grape mixture over top. When she reached for the sauerkraut, he touched her wrist and she jumped.

"Have a drink with me, Chriztine," he said, his words slurring.

To her relief, he took his hand off her arm and reached for his empty wineglass. He knocked it over. "Shit."

Christine set the wineglass upright and placed his dinner in front of him, her heart pounding. She took a step back from the table and waited. The *Lagerkommandant* pushed the plate away and picked up his water tumbler. He drank the water, letting it run down his chin, then refilled the glass with cognac. "Here," he said, offering it to her. "Sit down."

"*Nein danke,* Herr Lagerkommandant. If you don't need anything else right now, I've got work to do in the kitchen."

"*Bitte,*" he said. "Sit with me, just for a little while."

"I don't think it's a good idea, Herr Lagerkommandant."

"I think you should do as I say, Chriztine. I hold the power of life and death in my hands, remember?"

Christine pulled a chair away from the table and did as she was told, her hands folded in her lap.

"*Danke,*" he said. "That's not so bad, is it?" He blinked several times, as if falling asleep, then took another swallow of brandy. "I'm sorry. I just want to talk."

"*Ja,* Herr Lagerkommandant." Despite herself, her mouth watered as she stared at the crispy duck covered with brown sauce and shiny purple grape halves.

"*Ja, essen,*" he said, motioning toward the food. "Don't be afraid."

He picked up the plate of food, set it in front of her, and pushed his knife and fork in her direction, his thick fingers fumbling across the tablecloth. Christine kept her hands in her lap, unwilling to eat at the table with her captor. The *Lagerkommandant* didn't seem to notice. Instead he slouched back in his chair, the cognac sloshing inside his glass and spilling out over his fingers. "They failed," he said.

"I'm sorry, Herr Lagerkommandant," she said. "I don't know what you mean."

"Stauffenburg, Haeften, Olbricht, and Mertz!" he shouted, his face growing red. "Senior officers, all of them! And still they botched the plan! They should have made the bomb big enough to blow up a house! That would have killed the bastard!"

"Killed who, Herr Lagerkommandant?"

"Hitler! And it's not the first time someone tried!"

Christine's breath caught in her throat. *Hitler's own men were trying to kill him?* she thought, confused and elated at the same time. *Could this nightmare finally be coming to an end?*

"Will they try again?" she asked.

"Nein," he said, shaking his head. "Hitler had them executed. Lined up and shot." Christine's shoulders dropped. The *Lagerkommandant* took another swig. "You see? That's what I've been trying to tell you. No one is safe. The involved officers' entire families, including pregnant wives and small children, have all been arrested." He fell back in his chair, as if exhausted. After brooding in silence for a moment, he sighed and said, "Did I ever tell you how I came to be here?"

"Nein, Herr Lagerkommandant."

He looked at her with watery eyes. "I joined the Nazi Party in 1933, but I was expelled for being critical of their methods. Five years later, I was arrested by the Gestapo and sent to a labor camp." Christine's eyes went wide, and he shook his head in agreement, as if he was just as surprised. *"Ja!* I was arrested! Can you believe it? And now I'm in charge!"

Christine reached for the water jug. "May I?" she asked, her throat suddenly dry.

"Ja, ja. But if you're not going to drink this . . ." He finished the last mouthful of liquor in the brandy snifter, squeezing his eyes shut as he swallowed, then reached for the cognac he'd poured for her. "In 1940, I reapplied to the SS in order to infiltrate the Third Reich and gather information. Do you know why I did that?"

"Nein, Herr Lagerkommandant."

"I did it because the Bishop of Stuttgart told me that mentally ill patients were being killed at Hadamar and Grafeneck. In 1941, my own sister died mysteriously at Hadamar. After that, I was determined to find out the truth." He slammed a hand on the table. "They didn't even ask questions about my past! In 1941, I was admitted to the Waffen-SS. After that, I was sent on a mission to introduce Zyklon-B into the camps in Poland."

She set down her glass and looked at him. "There are other camps? Camps like this one?"

"*Ja! Ja!*" he said, nodding vigorously. "Auschwitz! Treblinka! Buchenwald! Ravensbrück! Mauthausen! I could go on and on. Auschwitz is the worst. But not all of them are extermination camps. Not all of them use gas. The Nazis said the Jews were getting *Sonderbehandlung,* or "special treatment," which is Nazi code for murder. I was shocked and disgusted, but I forced myself to watch, so I could tell the world."

Christine sat back in her chair, her hunger gone, replaced by something hard and vile. "What are you waiting for?"

"I've told people," he said. "I've risked my life to let everyone know what the Nazis are doing. I've told the press attaché at the Swiss Legation in Berlin, the coadjutor of the Catholic Bishop of Berlin. I've told several doctors and the Dutch underground. But nothing has happened. Just this morning, on the train back from Berlin, I ran into the Secretary to the Swedish Legation in Berlin. We talked for hours. I begged him to tell his government about the atrocities."

Christine remained silent, trying to decide if he was telling the truth, trying to decide if the pained look on his face was from sorrow or guilt.

"I don't think he believed me," the *Lagerkommandant* said. "I sobbed like a child in front of the man. I pleaded for him to make it known to the Allies. He kept telling me to keep my voice down. I'm sure he thinks me mad." He closed his eyes, the empty glass teetering to one side in his hand. "I don't know what else to do."

Christine stared at the wineglass on the linen tablecloth, pinpoints of light from the chandelier above the table reflecting off the crystal. She thought about what this scene would look like to an outsider: her sitting with an SS officer in her dirty uniform and shorn head, dirt and grime caked to her thin legs, the room filled with expensive paintings, Persian rugs, and cherry furniture, a plate of duck on the table in front of her. She felt like she'd gone mad.

"May I be excused, Herr Lagerkommandant?" she said in a weak voice. He didn't answer. She stood and reached for the glass in his hand. He sat forward and grabbed her wrist.

"I'm telling you this for a reason!" he said, the veins on his forehead bulging. "*Bitte,* sit down! Just let me get this off my chest!" Christine did as she was told, sitting on the edge of the chair, and he let go. He took a deep breath and smoothed the front of his uniform. "Will *you* at least listen to me? *Bitte?*"

"*Ja,* Herr Lagerkommandant."

"If you survive this, you're a witness too. Tell them that not everyone agreed with what was being done here. There are men here who have been turned by the evil that surrounds them. Their hearts have been plowed open to reveal the rotten soil of their souls. On the other hand, I have guards asking to be transferred to the Russian front, where they know they would die, but they would choose that, rather than assist the insanity within these walls." He pressed his palms to his temples, as if his thoughts were already driving him insane. "It's amazing what some will do just to stay alive. I have prisoners willing to save themselves by shoving the dead bodies of their fellow Jews into the fires."

She wanted to escape into the kitchen. He looked at her, a man condemned to hell on earth, his face pleading with her to understand. Earlier, she'd placed an open bottle of red wine on the table, unaware that he'd intended on drinking the cognac. Now, he reached for it, his cheeks and forehead crimson, and filled his glass.

"For some who are committing these evil crimes, and for those of us who allow it to happen, the reality of what we are doing is obscured by the furious turnings of war." He set down the bottle and drank the wine from the glass. "It will be later, when this war has ended, when we go home, when we sit at the dinner table in our comfortable houses, after we kiss our wives good night, it will be then that we will dread the night. We know what visions will rise from the depths of our guilty minds. It will haunt us until the end of our days, and we'll surely be spending eternity at Hitler's side in hell. All of Germany will pay for our sins. You wait and see. Yet brutal actions become war crimes only if you lose."

Christine stared at him, speechless. He refilled his glass and sighed. "There. I've said my piece." He motioned toward the plate of food in front of her. "You must eat."

"I . . . I'd rather not."

"As you wish. Eat it later, then. In the kitchen."

Christine stood.

He got to his feet, swaying and hunched over like an old man. When he teetered, Christine caught him by the arm, helped him back into his chair, and took the wineglass.

"I guess I can't drink like I used to," he said.

"You drank the entire bottle of cognac, Herr Lagerkommandant."

He looked toward the table with unfocused eyes. "So I did," he said. "Fetch me a cigar, would you?" Christine went to the buffet, opened the wooden humidor, picked out a cigar, and put it in his hand. She retrieved matches and lit it for him. Stale smoke filled the room. He watched her clear the table, his eyelids heavy. When she came back from the kitchen a third time to pick up the glasses and silverware, he was half asleep in his chair. She took the cigar and put it out in an ashtray. He startled her by speaking.

"Will you do something for me?"

"What is it, Herr Lagerkommandant?"

"If something happens to me, will you promise to remember my name? Will you let everyone know that I tried to stop it?"

Christine thought for a minute, then decided to risk it. "I'll do that for you if you do something for me."

"What is it?"

"The man I love is here. Find out where Isaac Bauerman is, and if he's still alive, promise me he'll stay that way."

He sighed. "It's not that simple. I can't just search for a certain prisoner without arousing suspicion. The other officers are just waiting for me to slip up so they can get rid of me. The previous *Lagerkommandant* used to throw drunken parties in this house. He provided them with liquor and prostitutes and let them have their way with the woman you replaced. They killed the one before her."

Christine felt the blood drain from her face. If something happened to the *Lagerkommandant*, then what would become of her? All of a sudden, she felt like she had to choose between Isaac's life and her own. "But I need to know if he's all right," she said, her voice catching.

"Even if I was able to find out if he's still alive without drawing suspicion, there's nothing I can do to keep him that way."

Eventually, Christine lost track of how much time had passed. Each long day blurred into the next. A late Indian summer had passed into a chilly fall. She'd cleaned up the garden and tended a second planting of lettuce, chard, and peas. The garden flourished, and the *Lagerkommandant* told her that the other officers were pleased.

While working outside, she tried not to look toward the crematorium, but she always looked once, when she first went out, then vowed not to look again. It was foolish hope that made her look at all—hope that one day she would see empty space where the line of people had been. But day after day, the procession of victims grew longer and wider.

If nothing else, she'd seen the stealthy progression of her time in prison in the mirror above the *Lagerkommandant*'s bathroom sink. Each time she checked, her cheekbones were more pronounced and the purple rings beneath her eyes were darker. Her eyebrows and eyelashes started falling out, and her skin paled to a chalky, ashen gray. She felt it in her body too, in her weakening arms, the ache in her hips and knees, the shake in her disappearing muscles, and the raw sores on her feet.

To make matters worse, there'd been no news of Isaac, from Hanna or the *Lagerkommandant*.

Now, the long, fall days had turned frigid, and she'd already harvested the last potatoes, piling them into crates and taking them into the cellar. Outside the camp, beyond the barbed wire coils and high fence, past the fields rolling out toward the edge of the forest, the leaves were gone from the trees. The sun was high and distant, the skies a brilliant, icy blue. At night, it was freezing, and the women shivered in their bunks. Christine feared the coming winter.

The first hard frost made its appearance in the wee hours of a long night, killing off the last of the garden. The morning after was bright and blustery, and Christine shivered, working fast on her hands and knees, yanking withered tomato vines out of the soggy soil. The leaves were black and dead, and it filled Christine with sorrow to pull them from the earth. It felt like a sign, a terrible omen that Isaac was dead. When she pulled out the last wilted vine, the thought of it suddenly overwhelmed her. She stopped working and hung her head.

Then something hard hit her in the middle of her back. She sat up and looked behind her, the wind stinging her eyes. No one was there. Again, an object hit her. She flinched, then heard a flat plop as something landed in the soil. There, on the ground in front of her, was a small stone, like a round, brown egg, nestled in the mud. She stood and looked around.

A hundred yards away, on the men's side of the fence, a group of men had started working, carrying boards and pushing wheelbarrows. A solitary man stood next to the fence, looking at her. Like every other prisoner, he was bony, filthy, and bald. At first, she wasn't sure what to make of him. Then he smiled and gave a quick wave, and her legs nearly gave out. It was Isaac. Her hands flew to her mouth. Inwardly, she shouted his name, her body aching to run over, to reach through the fence and caress his face. But she only raised her hand briefly, then quickly put it back down, aware that the guards could be watching.

Isaac went back to work with the other men, building some sort of structure near the rear of the men's complex. He bent over to saw a board in half, glancing over at her every few seconds. Christine wiped her hands on her uniform, then walked on shaking legs to the edge of the enclosure that surrounded the house. She knelt, pretending to pull weeds along the edge of the fence. There were two guards with the men, but they were smoking cigarettes and trying to stay warm, their backs turned to the harsh wind, the collars of their jackets pulled up around their necks. Their backs were turned to her and the prisoners.

Christine stood, went into the house, ran to the kitchen, and took off her shoes. She put a slice of bread in one shoe and a wedge of cheese in the other, then carried them out to the front porch. She went into the yard and stood by the front gate, her eyes on the guards, her heart knocking hard against her chest. For a split second, the world reeled in front of her, as if she had just stepped off a spinning carousel and was still dizzy. She took a deep breath and let it out slowly. Now, the guards were building a fire in a barrel, preoccupied with using their bodies to block the growing flames from the wind. She put her shoes in one hand, ready to drop them and put them on again at any second, then opened the gate and walked as fast as she could without running toward the interior fence, her eyes darting between Isaac and the guards huddled around the barrel.

When Isaac saw her coming, he shook his head back and forth. She ignored his warning and pointed at her shoes, then at him, then motioned for him to move closer to the fence. He glanced at the guards, trying to decide, then hesitantly took several steps in her direction, a piece of lumber in his hand. When she was within a few feet of the fence, they were barely three yards apart. Now she was close enough to see the grayish-yellow color of his skin, the scrapes and bruises on his face and hands, the stains on his uniform. But his eyes were shining, and his smile was bright. The other male prisoners saw her too, but they kept working, trying not to draw attention. If the guards were provoked, all of them could pay.

Christine felt a charge course through her body. She pushed the bread and cheese through the wire, then turned away, her shoes held fast to her chest. Glancing over her shoulder as she went back toward the house, she saw Isaac drop the plank on the ground. He bent over, picked up the food with the board, took a bite of cheese, and shoved the rest into the ankles of his boots. Then he turned and went back to work, the guards oblivious, warming their hands over the fire. She returned to the garden and took her time pulling the rest of the dead plants. They watched each other until Christine had to go in to prepare the *Lagerkommandant*'s *Mittag Essen*. For the rest of the afternoon, she checked out the window as she worked and kept finding reasons to go outside.

When she left that evening, the men were gone, returned to their barracks for the night. She could hardly wait to get back herself, to tell Hanna that Isaac was alive. But Hanna was nowhere to be found. Christine climbed on the edge of the wooden rack to ask the women on the top bunk, one of whom worked in the records department, if they knew anything.

"Do you know where Hanna is?"

"*Nein*," the woman from the records department said.

"You didn't see anything?" Christine asked.

"You're the *Lagerkommandant*'s whore," the woman hissed. "Why don't you ask him?"

Christine felt blood rise in her face. "I'm not . . . I just work there. I . . ."

The woman moved closer, and Christine's nostrils filled with the sour stench of tooth decay. "The *Blockschreiber* dragged her out of the building. He caught her looking through the male prisoners' files."

Christine forgot how to breathe. It took a moment before she could speak. "Is there any way you can find out what happened to her?"

"*Nein*," the woman said. "Leave me alone."

Numb, Christine climbed down and crawled into her bunk, Hanna's cold, empty space beside her.

The next day, Christine carried the *Lagerkommandant*'s poached eggs into the dining room, trying to choose her words carefully. Between her elation at finding Isaac alive, and the guilt for whatever had happened to Hanna, she hadn't slept at all. Now, she didn't trust herself with the smallest of tasks, let alone trying to ask the *Lagerkommandant* for help. If she made him angry, as she had the first time she'd asked him to find Isaac, the conversation would be over. But that had been months ago; surely their relationship had changed.

He was at the breakfast table, peering over his reading glasses at the newspaper. The morning sun cast rectangles of light across the linen, illuminating the steam from his coffee and the smoke from his cigar, like wispy spiderwebs floating in the air.

"A friend of mine disappeared yesterday, Herr Lagerkommandant," she said.

The *Lagerkommandant* kept his eyes on the paper. "*Ja*," he said, moving his head up and down as he skimmed the headlines.

"I wish I knew what might have happened to her."

The *Lagerkommandant* pushed his glasses back on his nose and looked up, his face hard. "If you haven't seen her, I doubt you will."

"I'm sorry, Herr Lagerkommandant. But that's not entirely true. I saw Isaac just yesterday. After all this time, he's alive."

"So. Now you know. Good for you."

"But Hanna could be alive somewhere too."

The *Lagerkommandant* shook his head and sighed, disgusted. "How long have you been here?"

"I'm not sure, Herr Lagerkommandant," she said. "Several months."

"And have you ever known anyone to return once they've disappeared in this godforsaken place?"

"*Nein,* Herr Lagerkommandant." She lowered her eyes, knowing she had to ask him one more thing. She cleared her throat and went on. "Isaac is working at the new construction site on the other side of the fence." The *Lagerkommandant* dropped the newspaper and took off his glasses, then rubbed his eyes and looked at her, waiting, his mouth pressed into a line. "I was hoping he could be given a different job. In a factory maybe, or the kitchen, somewhere out of the damp and cold. He's very smart, a quick learner, and . . ."

The *Lagerkommandant* slammed both hands on the table. The silverware rattled, and Christine jumped. He stood, and his chair fell over. "One more word," he said, his voice quaking with anger, "and you will be finished here! I've told you once, and I'm not going to tell you again! I will not put myself on the line for anyone, let alone someone who wasn't smart enough to keep out of trouble in the first place! If you say one more thing about you and your friends to me, it will give me a reason to prove to the other officers that I'm a loyal Nazi. I'll have all three of you strung up by the front gates! Do you understand?"

"*Ja,* Herr Lagerkommandant," Christine said, stepping backwards. "I'm sorry, Herr Lagerkommandant."

The *Lagerkommandant* grabbed his hat from the table, yanked his uniform jacket from the back of his toppled chair, and walked out of the room. Christine stood motionless for a long time, staring at the sun-filled breakfast table, tears streaming down her face. Then she picked up the chair, cleared the table, and got back to work.

* * *

For the next two weeks, Christine saw Isaac working at the construction site every day. The guards assigned to watch over the prisoners were nearly always distracted. If the weather was cold, they bent over a fire barrel. If it was warmer, they played cards. When they weren't looking, she threw potatoes over the fence or got close enough to shove more bread or cheese through the wires. They didn't speak, but seeing Isaac alive reinforced her will to survive. Then, after two short weeks, the project was finished, and the men didn't return.

By that time, the biting wind spit dry snow, and the low, ashen clouds moved swiftly through the somber winter sky. Within a month, a blanket of white shrouded the countryside, and the world seemed to be waiting in an expectant, hushed silence. The pounding chug of incoming trains echoed off the snowbound hills, amplified by the cold and stillness as if transmitted through a thousand loudspeakers. As the trains drew closer and closer to the gates of Dachau, each mighty, lumbering exhale of the slowing engines sounded to Christine like the final, dying breath of humanity.

Throughout the long, cold months, Christine persevered. If nothing else, the job at the *Lagerkommandant*'s had surely saved her life. The extra food and the warmth of the house made all the difference. She was able to wash the sores on her feet and use the toilet, which meant she didn't have to wade in the filthy ditches where the other prisoners were forced to relieve themselves. As a result, she avoided the ravages of dysentery that spread through the camp. Even so, her nights were spent in the freezing barracks, and a rattling cough had settled deep in her chest by the end of winter. Her nose seemed to run continuously, and she was exhausted due to lack of sleep. But she wasn't close to death as so many others were. The majority of the women who had been in the barracks on the night of her arrival were nowhere to be found.

She continued to look for Isaac every day, and thought she saw him a few times, a man who walked like him or looked over her way. And even though she couldn't be certain, it made her feel strong and gave her the courage to survive for one more day.

CHAPTER 26

For weeks, spring fought to gain the upper hand from winter. A relentless rain turned the camp into a muddy nightmare. The grounds, the sky, the buildings, the uniforms were devoid of color. For days on end, the only colors Christine saw outside the house were the blues and greens of the prisoners' hopeless eyes. The springtime air struggled to turn clean and pure, in opposition to the never-ending stench of the crematorium fires.

As the last patches of snow melted into the slowly warming earth and the trees edging the fields were beginning to bud, more and more trains arrived every day. The blast of the whistle and the sound of wheels screeching to a halt felt like needles in Christine's ears. But fewer women arrived in the barracks, and she knew it meant that the majority of incoming people were going straight to the gas chambers. She started to wonder why they didn't try to fight back. They outnumbered the soldiers twenty to one.

Soon, everything was coated with a thin layer of fine ash, and as the ground thawed, the remains merged with the soil beneath their feet. The ground would never be the same. Ashes to ashes, dust to dust, the earth would take back the dead ... and the earth would never forget.

As spring wore on, tens of thousands of prisoners from other camps outside of Germany arrived by train. Christine was shocked to see women, already in camp uniforms, with malnourished babies in their arms. She was equally surprised to see groups of uniformed children, clinging to each other as they were herded into a separate quarters, away from the adults. The camp population swelled, and the barracks became severely overcrowded. The sick were no longer separated from the healthy, and hundreds died of typhus every day. The new inmates spread word that the Allies were closing in, so the Nazis were moving all prisoners to camps inside German borders, making sure they never made it into the hands of the enemy alive.

As usual, a certain number of prisoners were recruited to help with incoming prisoners. They were the *Sonderkommando,* or special units, responsible for searching the dead for valuables, transferring the bodies into the crematorium, and cleaning the gas chambers. In return, they were given better housing and more food. At first, Christine couldn't understand how anyone would be willing to accept the position, but then she realized it was their only hope for a few more days or weeks, their only chance of coming out of this nightmare alive. But after a few months of service, these men were killed, replaced with newly arrived, stronger prisoners. Recently, she'd heard that the number of *Sonderkommando* had been doubled, as if the Nazis needed to speed things up.

At night, the thump of exploding bombs grew closer and closer, and she could hear the distant, mournful cry of air raid sirens. In the beginning of April, the nearby armament and parts factories were bombed. Luckily, the attack happened during the wee hours of the morning, when the factories weren't full of prisoners. The trains stopped coming because the railroad tracks had been destroyed, and along with no more prisoners, there were no more supplies. The electricity and telephones went out. Water had to be brought in by truck. There were no more showers, and water rations were cut. Christine had to flush the *Lagerkommandant*'s toilet with a bucket, and heat water on the stove for his bath.

As conditions deteriorated, the soldiers and guards grew more short-tempered, needing no provocation to shoot someone. At roll call, the hitting and screaming increased. In the barracks, the women talked about the guards using them as target practice, making them run to work or to get their daily rations. The *Lagerkommandant* was gruff at the dinner table, drinking too much and barely eating.

On one of the first dry days of spring, under a clear blue sky, Christine walked slowly on her way to the *Lagerkommandant*'s house. She looked across the fields, where she could see deer near the edge of the forest, their heads bent toward the new, sweet grass. *How can the world still be so beautiful?* she wondered. *How can the clouds still be pink and blue while witnessing this horror?*

Then she noticed hundreds of male prisoners on the men's side of the camp, walking parallel to her, picks and shovels thrown over their shoulders. Twenty guards with submachine guns and German shepherds steered the shuffling group toward a side entry gate that led out of the camp and into the fields. Christine stopped, searching for Isaac among the columns of limping, stumbling men.

And then she saw him, near the front of the group, his head down, a shovel over one shoulder, his back and shoulders slumped. Something black and oily twisted in Christine's chest. He'd taken on the posture of a *Muselmann*, camp slang for a prisoner who'd lost the will to live, due to their resemblance to a praying Muslim. She couldn't let it happen. She had to do something, anything, so he wouldn't give up.

The guards, busy watching the prisoners and controlling the dogs, either didn't notice or didn't care that she was there. She hurried toward the fence. Isaac was only a few feet away, his eyes on the ground. His head came up, and he turned and looked directly at her, his eyes missing any spark of strength or hope. Then he looked away and walked past her, and she felt her heart rip from her chest. She caught up and followed on her side of the fence, staying beside him as long as she could, until the entire group was herded through the gate.

"Don't give up, Isaac!" she shouted. "I love you!" He lifted his head and smiled weakly back at her, then looked away again. Ice-cold fear flooded her body, making her chest feel frozen and hard, as if her lungs were made of the thinnest porcelain, ready to shatter if she took a deep breath.

Then two guards were in front of her, a stern look of warning in their eyes. She turned away and hurried toward the house, where she stood on the porch to watch the group move, like a dark, ragged stain, across the green fields.

The sight of Isaac in such despair felt like the weight of an anchor chained around her heart. She went through the house in slow motion, her head in a daze, trying to concentrate on her work. Somehow, moving out of habit, she made the *Lagerkommandant*'s breakfast, did his dishes, scrubbed the tub, and swept the floors. Afterward, she headed outdoors to check the garden.

When she reached the edge of the backyard, a torrent of gunfire erupted in the distance. It came from the direction of the woods, unmistakable, uninterrupted, and unending. She fell to her knees, stomach twisting, thinking she'd go crazy before it stopped. She pressed her hands over her ears, but the sound of gunfire found its way through her trembling hands, ripping into her brain. When it finally ended, she collapsed, curled up and sobbing, her head in her hands. She lay that way for a long time, wishing she would pass out. An eternity passed before she was able to pull herself upright.

On her knees in the mud, she tried to think logically. *Why would they shoot those men when they have such an efficient method of extermination right here? Maybe it's not what I think. They need them for labor. Isaac is still alive. He has to be. They were probably just cutting down trees, and the soldiers were trying to scare them so they'd work faster. But they didn't have axes. They had shovels.*

More sporadic gunfire from the woods. Then silence. Then, six shots from a pistol. She winced at every echoing blast, her stomach tight, fresh tears starting. After a few minutes, she wiped at her face and ran her hands over her head. She stood and looked out toward the fields, waiting, the world a blur before her. The silence was deafening.

After what seemed like forever, the guards came out of the woods, smoking cigarettes, carrying shovels and submachine guns. There were no prisoners, just guards. There was no Isaac, just guards. And then she knew. She knew they had shot him and all the others. He was dead, undeniably this time. And he'd known what they were going to do. So many times before, she'd thought she'd lost him. Now, finality hit her. Again, she fell to the ground, cold mud colliding with her cheek. The world went black.

Christine had no idea how much time had passed when she came to, but when she looked across the fields, the guards were nowhere to be seen. Pushing herself onto her hands and knees, she swayed upright and retreated into the house, where she stood in the kitchen gripping the counter, her head reeling. Wondering how it was possible that her legs still held her up and her lungs drew in air, she prayed for her bleeding, shattered heart to kill her, for the agony to end. Looking around the kitchen, she tried to think of ways to poison herself, but nothing came to mind. She pictured the sharp knives in the drawer, pictured herself slicing open her wrists, but knew there were easier ways to die in Dachau.

She left the house and staggered back to the barracks, then lay down on the hard bunk and closed her eyes, hoping her mind would shut down. She folded her hands over her chest and held her breath, willing her lungs to quit struggling for air. She resolved to stay there and stop eating. If she was lucky, one of the guards would shoot her for not doing her work.

For the rest of the day, Christine lay motionless on the bunk in the empty barracks. Mental exhaustion overwhelmed her, and a deep but fragile sleep kept her mind from further torture. But it only protected her for short periods. Every few hours, she startled awake, coughing, instantly assaulted by the knowledge that Isaac was dead. A hot rush of grief lit up her face and chest, and a savage twist of regret ripped through her stomach.

No one came looking for her. No one came to shoot her for not reporting to work. When the prisoners returned that night, no one spoke to her. The barracks were overcrowded with sole survivors now; women who knew that, more than likely, they were all that was left of their families. More than ever, everyone kept to themselves. The women moved slowly and purposefully, their eyes downcast, their bony shoulders sagging, each one lost in her own dark world of personal grief and torment.

Throughout the night, Christine drifted in and out of sleep, moments of misery alternating with dreams of her mother's kitchen, black-and-white snapshots of her family, and bloody images of Isaac's body lying in the mud of the forest floor. When dawn filtered down through the transoms in the barracks ceiling, she was wide awake, having waited for what seemed like hours. For what, she wasn't sure.

The other women climbed out of the bunks, mutely shuffling outdoors for morning roll call. Christine took a deep breath, searching for the strength to command her body to sit up. She swung her legs over the side of the bunk and closed her eyes, listening for the customary name-calling and shouting, the cruel, hateful voices. But they didn't come. Instead, there was nothing but an eerie silence, as if she were suddenly alone in the vast complex of empty barracks. She pictured herself sitting there, a solitary woman on a wooden bunk, the only living thing left in row after row of enormous, filthy coffins. Then, quietly at first, then louder and louder, she heard the rumble of tanks in the distance. Somewhere, people started yelling. The rattling growl grew closer. She heard people hurrying past the door. Then a woman prisoner came back inside, running and stumbling into the barracks.

"The Americans are here!" she screamed, her eyes wild. She ran over to Christine and grabbed her by the shoulders. "The Americans are here! We're saved! Get up! We're saved!" Before Christine could respond, the shrieking woman ran out of the barracks, her bony arms flailing in the air.

Christine put her hands over her face. *Oh, Isaac! One more day, that's all you needed.* She wiped at her eyes but found no tears; either she was severely dehydrated or had used them all up. She climbed down from the bunk and staggered out of the barracks.

Drizzle was falling from gray clouds, tiny drops serrating the greasy surface of brown puddles. She blinked against the rain and wrapped her arms around herself, trying to stop shivering. Her chest hurt, and with every breath, a rattle came from somewhere inside her lungs. The grounds were filled with prisoners, shouting and hurrying toward the front of the camp. She followed the other women toward the main gate, where she'd entered the prison an eternity ago. Looking past the growing crowd, she could see two tanks and a half-dozen army trucks with white stars on the doors. A line of men blocked the exit. The white flag of surrender hung from each watchtower.

American soldiers were arresting *Unterscharführers, Block-*

führers, and guards, taking away their guns, cuffing their hands behind their backs, forcing them into the backs of open trucks. To her right, a dozen Americans were shouting and pointing their guns at a group of nearly a hundred SS guards gathered between two watchtowers. The majority of the guards looked around as if lost, hands on their heads in surrender, eyes wide. The rest glared at the Americans, brows furrowed, mouths hard. Christine looked for the *Lagerkommandant* and Stefan, but didn't see them. She didn't see the *Hauptscharführers,* or any of the other higher-ranked officers she knew were in charge of the camp.

A man carrying a movie camera surveyed the compound, panning slowly across the growing crowd. Another took pictures. The rest of the Americans stood, guns drawn, staring at the prisoners coming toward them from the other side of the electric fence, stick-thin legs, bare, bony arms, living skeletons with teeth and eyes and hair. A group of male prisoners had gathered around the American soldiers and SS guards near the base of the watchtower, screaming and yelling at the guards, shaking their fists in the air. One of them picked up a rock and threw it. The rock hit one of the guards in the forehead. The guard touched his face, then looked at his fingers, forehead furrowed, as if he'd never seen blood before. Another prisoner lunged forward, grabbed a pistol from an American soldier, and shot a guard in the head. Before anyone could stop him, the prisoner held the weapon to his own temple, rolled his eyes toward the heavens, and pulled the trigger. His knees buckled, and his head spouted blood as he crumpled. The American soldier grabbed his gun out of the dead prisoner's hand and pointed it at the other prisoners, ordering them to step back. They did as they were told. An American officer stood on the back of a truck with a bullhorn.

"We are the United States Army," he shouted in heavily accented German. "We're here to help you. Before we can let you out, we need to assess the situation. We need to attend to the sick and vaccinate against disease. We will use DDT on everyone to get rid of lice. Please be patient. Don't be afraid. You're going to be all right."

Prisoners fell to their knees and held their arms up to the sky, thanking God. One woman ran toward the exit, not willing to stay even one more second. Two soldiers caught her by the arms and held her. She pleaded with them to let her pass, to please let her out, if only to step to the other side of the iron gate. Several more inmates followed, frantic to escape. When the soldiers drew their guns, the prisoners fell into each other's arms, weeping. Other prisoners wandered throughout the growing multitudes, searching for family members, hoping by some miracle they might have survived. They zigzagged through the crowd, crying out their loved ones' names, hurrying to people they thought they recognized, putting a hand on their shoulders, only to wilt in disappointment when the person turned. When Christine saw a middle-aged couple run into each other's arms, a swell of grief ignited her chest. She felt dizzy and wanted to sit down.

"Stay calm," the officer with the bullhorn said. "As soon as the tracks are repaired, we'll send trains to pick you up."

From where she stood, Christine could see a line of deserted boxcars. Four Americans pushed up an iron bar and heaved on a rusty door, their faces straining as they slid one of the boxcars open. When the grisly contents of the train were revealed, the soldiers recoiled and turned away. Two of them bent over and vomited on the ground. Inside the boxcar, five and six deep, dead bodies were piled like reams of tattered rugs, hair and hands and feet sticking from the ends of every roll. Christine closed her eyes.

Then there was an angry shout, and a torrent of submachine gunfire ripped through the air. The Americans who'd corralled the group of guards next to the watchtower had opened fire. The captured guards grimaced as bullets tore into their flesh, blood spurting from their chests and mouths and foreheads as they fell on top of each other in a pile of black uniforms. When the shooting stopped, the guards had fallen still. *Blood and soil,* Christine thought. *If that's what the Nazis stood for, then they got their wish.*

"Christine!" a voice shouted behind her. She whirled around, her hand over her heart.

CHAPTER 27

Hanna limped toward Christine, arm in arm with a thin, dark-eyed man who appeared to be holding her up. Christine swayed. Isaac? Could it all have been a nightmare? But the man coming toward her was wearing regular clothes, not a prisoner's uniform.

"Christine!" Hanna cried. "I found my brother!"

Christine swallowed. "Hanna!" she managed.

They hugged, and Christine felt thin bones jutting from Hanna's back, as if she could crush her skeleton with the slightest increase in pressure. Then they drew apart and looked at each other, tears filling their eyes. Hanna's cheeks were razor sharp, her face a kaleidoscope of purple and yellow bruises, the veins around her irises broken and red, her lips swollen and scabbed where they had split and healed, split and healed.

"Can you believe we've been rescued?" Hanna asked. "And all this time, my brother was working in the factory."

"Where have you been?" Christine asked. "I thought you were dead!"

Hanna dropped her eyes for a fraction of a second, then looked up with fresh tears. "They kept me locked in a storage room off the main guardhouse, and . . ."

"It's all right." Christine squeezed Hanna's hands in hers. "You don't have to tell me. It's over now."

Hanna sniffed and straightened. "This is my brother, Heinz," she said. "Have you found Isaac?"

"He was taken into the woods yesterday, with a group of other prisoners, and . . . they didn't come out."

"Ach nein," Hanna said. "I'm so sorry."

"Just one more day," Christine whispered, her voice breaking. "If he would have survived just one more day . . ." Hanna put her arms around Christine and made soft, murmuring sounds, like a mother comforting a crying infant. Christine pulled away and wiped at her face. "I'm sorry for what you've been through. It's my fault."

"What are you talking about?"

"They said you were caught looking in the male prisoners' files."

"You risked your life to bring me food, didn't you? Besides, I was looking for Heinz too. It was only a matter of time before the *Blockschreiber* found a reason to pull me out of there. He had been watching me for some time. If it hadn't been that, he would have pulled me out for something else."

"At least now he'll pay," Christine said, glancing toward the trucks filled with *Unterscharführers, Blockführers,* and guards.

"I'm afraid a lot of the officers and guards got away," Heinz said. "When we were getting clothes from the storage sheds, we saw a group of them running into the woods."

Hanna closed her eyes and leaned against her brother. For a second, Christine thought she was going to collapse. But Heinz put an arm around her, holding her upright, and Hanna opened her eyes again, putting all her weight on one leg. Christine looked down and gasped. Hanna's ankle was raw and swollen, ringed by an angry wound. Streaks of purple crawled up the side of her calf.

"What happened to your leg?" Christine asked.

Hanna put the injured leg forward and looked down at the wound circling her ankle like a thick, red sock. "The guards chained me to the bed during the day."

"Let's go," Heinz said, his voice a monotone. "From what I've heard, the food storage building has a stockpile. And we should go to the storeroom to get you some warmer clothes."

Mobs of prisoners swarmed the food storage building. They had broken down doors and shattered windows, breaking the frames and throwing them out of the way in their rush to get inside. Like a fire brigade, they formed lines to pass the food to the growing crowd. From one pair of thin arms to the next went box after box of biscuits, crackers, dry milk, rolls, and bread. Crate after crate of potatoes, lettuce, turnips, carrots, and beans were split open and passed around. A shout of victory went up as everyone converged on a group of men holding up hard sausages and dried meat. Before long, piles of smoked hams, cases of canned liverwurst, and towers of cheese wheels looked like the inventory of a hundred butcher shops on display in the muddy yard.

"Be careful," Heinz told Hanna, Christine, and anyone else who would listen. "Or you'll make yourself sick."

The more insightful prisoners ate only biscuits, crackers, and bread, warning everyone else that their starved bodies wouldn't be able to handle liverwurst, smoked pork, and rich cheese. But some didn't listen. They stuffed themselves, then lay bloated and sick, their bellies distended.

Christine ate four biscuits and a wedge of hard cheese, while Hanna and her brother ripped off hunks of rye bread until an entire loaf was gone. Heinz grabbed more bread and several tins of crackers, then followed Hanna and Christine to the clothes-sorting building on the female side of the camp. He waited outside while Hanna and Christine rummaged through the mountains of dresses, skirts, blouses, and shoes. Christine took off her filthy uniform and put on a cranberry-colored dress, the faint smell of perfume still clinging to the lace collar. She slipped her arms into the soft, thick sleeves of a blue knitted sweater, her shoulders and the backs of her arms covered and warm for the first time in eight months. On the edge of the pile, Hanna was on her knees in a full-length slip, pulling a brown dress over her head.

It wasn't long before they found everything they needed, including a pair of slip-on fur-lined boots that fit over Hanna's swollen ankle and a nearly new pair of black leather shoes that fit

Christine perfectly. Christine pushed her calloused feet and bare legs into a stretchy pair of brown stockings and laced up the shoes, thinking it felt strange to be fully clothed, her arms and legs snug and comfortable, like a newborn swaddled in a cozy, soft blanket for the first time.

She looked at the other prisoners taking off their soiled uniforms and putting on actual clothes, watching each other in wonder and awe, as if dresses and shirts were a new discovery or a recent invention. They ran their hands along the arms of sleeves and the lengths of skirts, as if the fabric were made of gold and silk, not simple broadcloth and cotton. And even though it was spring, Hanna and Christine each took a long, wool coat, if only to use as a blanket during their last nights in hell. Christine put her coat on, not because she was cold, but to feel the weight of it on her shoulders. A tall woman wearing a cherry-colored dress pounded her fist against the wall to hush the crowd.

"We must say *danke* to our voiceless providers," she shouted. "And we must say Kaddish for all who have died in this terrible place."

The room grew silent as everyone bowed her head to pray. Christine didn't know how to say Kaddish, but she closed her eyes and prayed for the dead in her own way. She prayed for the souls who had died there, and for Opa and Isaac. She prayed that they had at last found peace, their suffering and tears forever ceased. She said a silent good-bye to Isaac, feeling the manacle of grief tighten around her heart, locking eternally into place with a solid, final thud. Tears found their way down her cheeks. When she finished her prayer, she lifted her head and saw rivulets of moisture on every pale and sunken face.

Two days later, the growl of incoming army trucks jarred Christine from her sleep. Her body jerked awake, her skull and every joint aching. She took a deep, shuddering breath, turned her head, and opened her eyes. Her first thought was of Isaac, and her stomach twisted with grief.

"Maybe they've sent trucks to pick us up instead of trains," Hanna said.

"I don't care what they send," Christine said. She sat up and coughed, her chest aching with every bark. "As long as they hurry up and get us out of here." She crawled out of the bunk and helped Hanna to her feet. With one arm steadying Hanna, she followed the other women outside, trying not to get her hopes up that at last they would be freed.

During the past two days, the entire camp population had been vaccinated by American army doctors; once again they were forced to strip naked so they could be disinfected with DDT. Hanna's ankle had been cleaned and dressed, and Heinz had found a pair of crutches in the camp hospital. The need to get away from the camp forever was swelling in Christine's mind, at times making her feel as if she would start screaming and never stop. If the Americans didn't send the trains to pick them up soon, she'd start walking home.

Now, over a dozen U.S. Army trucks had pulled to a stop outside the barracks. Soldiers jumped down from the front seats and went around to the back, rifles in hand, to open the tailgates. As the prisoners watched, elderly men and women, adolescent females, and mothers with young children climbed out of the backs of the trucks. Nearly every person was holding something: a loaf of bread, a wheel of cheese, a basket of eggs, a tin of milk.

"What's going on?" Christine said to Hanna.

"I have no idea," Hanna said.

In heavily accented German, an officer ordered the people to line up in pairs. A familiar fear quickened Christine's breathing. *What are they doing with these people?* she thought. The German civilians looked at each other and the soldiers, confusion and fear crumpling their brows. They stared at the gathering prisoners, their mouths open in shock. The young children pointed at the ragtag assembly of emaciated captives in mismatched clothing, then looked up at their mothers for answers. After the last truck was emptied, the officer used a bullhorn to address the more than two hundred civilians.

"Leave your donations for the prisoners of Dachau with the soldiers at the rear of this truck," he said in German, pointing at two waiting soldiers. "Afterward, remain in line and follow me. Prisoners, line up behind the civilians, and my men will distribute the food to you."

"That's probably all the food those people had," Christine whispered to Hanna.

"Maybe they're locking them up," Hanna said.

"But why?" Christine said. Hanna shrugged.

The German civilians handed the food to the soldiers, then fell in line behind the officer and four other soldiers. By then, the male prisoners had joined the women, and the majority of inmates were already lining up to get food before returning to their quarters. The rest, including Heinz, Hanna, and Christine, followed the civilians as the Americans took them into the camp.

The soldiers led the civilians through the stench-filled barracks and the cement shower rooms, past the overflowing piles of shoes, suitcases, eyeglasses, hair, and gold teeth. The women held their aprons over their mouths, weeping and covering the children's eyes. The old men stared, their wrinkled faces rigid with grief and shock. As they moved closer to the gas chambers and crematorium, Christine heard the growl of a giant engine. A huge bulldozer was pushing dirt from a wide trench. Beside the trench, male prisoners had loaded horse-drawn wagons and pushcarts with rotting corpses. The civilian women screamed and moaned, pushing their children's faces into the folds of their skirts. The old men wept silently and tried to hold the women up, but some fainted.

The soldiers said nothing. They held their rifles to their chests with both hands, looking straight ahead, and took the civilians into the gas chambers. They took them past the blood-spattered carts used to transfer the dead bodies into the fires. On the carts, piles of skeletal bodies still lay naked and twisted, abandoned and forgotten on their journey to the crematorium. From there, the soldiers took the civilians into the crematorium, past the giant brick ovens filled with ashes and pieces of bone.

Christine, Hanna, and the rest of the prisoners didn't enter the gas chambers or the crematorium. Just being close to the buildings made Christine nauseous. When the civilians came out the other side, the soldiers handed shovels to the men and to any female who wasn't carrying a child.

"What are they doing?" Christine said, her heart pounding. "Tell me they're not going to shoot them."

"They're making them bury the dead," Heinz said.

Christine gasped and looked around at the other prisoners and the soldiers, unable to comprehend what she was seeing. Were they blaming the German civilians for this? For not doing anything to stop it? She thought of Oma and poor dead Opa, her mother, her younger sister and brothers, hungry and hiding in bomb shelters. Would they blame them for the camp in Hessental? When she saw the soldiers direct the old men to start unloading the corpses, she stepped forward.

"Why are you doing this?" she shouted, hoping one of them understood German. The soldiers' faces snapped in her direction.

"What is she doing?" a female prisoner asked Hanna.

"Christine," Hanna said. "Let it go."

"It's not their fault," Christine said to Hanna. "What could they have done to stop it? Any of them? What could they have done without getting themselves killed?"

"They kept quiet," another prisoner said. "They did nothing."

Someone behind Christine shouted in Polish, another in French. A rock came flying out of the crowd and hit one of the German children in the head. The boy put his hand to his temple and buried his face in his mother's apron. Christine turned and yelled into the throng of prisoners, "These people didn't do this to you!"

"Well then," a female prisoner shouted. "Where is your SS lover, the *Lagerkommandant?* He's not here to take the blame, is he?"

"He tried to tell people!" she shouted. "No one would listen. What makes you think anyone would have listened to them?" She pointed at the civilians.

"Liar!" a man yelled.

Christine turned around again. The German civilians were unloading the bodies from the wagons and throwing them into the trench, the old men struggling to hang on to the pencil-thin wrists and skeletal ankles of stiff corpses, the women shoveling dirt into the massive grave, sobbing and vomiting into the yard.

Christine's breath came in shallow bursts. She wished she could remember the few English words Isaac had taught her. But it was no use; her brief lesson had been too long ago. She moved toward the Americans anyway, hoping one of them would understand. "They didn't do this!" she said.

An American soldier came toward her, his hand up, his gun drawn.

"You don't know what they've been through!" Christine said.

Heinz pulled Christine back. "Come on," he said to Hanna. "Let's get her out of here."

"We have to tell them," Christine said to Hanna. Heinz tried to drag her toward the barracks. "We have to tell them they didn't do anything!"

Hanna stopped and turned on her. "How do I know that?" she cried. "How do I know they didn't turn in their Jewish neighbors for a loaf of bread?"

Christine stopped struggling, and Heinz let her go. "Do you think I'm guilty as well? Should I go over there and help the women shovel?"

Hanna looked away. *"Nein,"* she said, shaking her head. *"Nein."*

"The Americans have no idea how much these people have already suffered!" Christine said. "They need to know about the food shortages and the Gestapo! They need to know about the villages and cities leveled by bombs!"

"They know about the bombs," Heinz said. "They were dropped from their planes, remember?"

"I guess the *Lagerkommandant* was right," Christine said, tears running down her face. "Brutal acts only become war crimes if you lose."

Christine curled up in the back corner of a boxcar, her head resting on her coat, which was folded against the wall like a pillow. She closed her eyes, hoping the steady side-to-side wobble of the train would lull her back to sleep, even though she only dozed in fits and starts. Unlike her journey to Dachau, there was room for everyone to stretch out. The Americans had covered the floor with straw, which provided cushioning and helped mask the odor of death that still clung to the wooden walls and floorboards. Along with the straw, the Americans had provided blankets and had lined the center of the car with crates of food and water. And while all these simple things added to the comfort of their journey, nothing in the world could make up for the fact that most of the women had made their first trip accompanied by parents, siblings, husbands, sons, and daughters. This time they were alone. Contemplating lives without their loved ones, they made the trip in silence, sleeping or staring at nothing, mixed tears of grief and gratitude in their eyes.

Earlier that morning, American officers had announced that the women would be released first, the men left behind until tomorrow. A train would take them to a village, where they would be housed in a temporary barracks until the Americans could help them return home. An hour later, when the first train pulled in, a nervous hush had settled over the crowd. They watched in silence as the lumbering locomotive braked and screeched, braked and screeched, pistons hissing longer and slower until it came to a shuddering stop. Then the boxcar doors slid open, American soldiers jumped out, and everyone cheered. When the young soldiers saw their skeletal welcoming committee, they reached into their pockets for gum and candy, giving the prisoners everything they had.

Now, countless hours later, Christine pictured the thin, hopeful faces of Hanna and her brother Heinz, smiling as they waved goodbye beside the shrunken men watching silently as the women left the camp. Understandably, Hanna had chosen to stay behind with her brother so they could travel together. She'd memorized Christine's address, with promises to write when they were finally settled, wherever and whenever that might be. The only thing that she and Heinz were certain of was that they would be leaving Germany forever.

Christine couldn't get the wretched image of Dachau out of her head. The watchtowers, the electric fences, the long, dark barracks, and the soot-stained chimney would be forever painted in her mind, like a monochromatic portrait. Even if she lived to be a hundred and ten, she'd never forget the gray stone colors of Dachau, colors that reminded her of crumbling bones and ancient tombstones on a bleak and rainy January day.

Later, when they arrived at the train station, Christine woke up as the train braked and throbbed to a shuddering stop. She sat up, her throat and chest burning, her neck stiff, the hip she'd been leaning on screaming in pain. When she could breathe without coughing, she stood, put on her wool coat, and climbed down from the boxcar with the other women.

Clutching bread and clothes collected from the Dachau storage rooms, the somber, newly released prisoners exited the boxcars and lined up without complaint, waiting patiently on the platform to give their information to the Americans. Christine found herself trying to help a confused woman remember where she was from.

"My name is Sarah Weinstein," the woman cried. "My husband's name was Uri . . . but he's dead. I can't remember the name of the town where we used to live. I can't remember anything!" She waved her hands in the air as if swatting at an invisible swarm of flies. "It doesn't matter what happens to me; my whole family is dead. It doesn't matter."

"Some of your relatives must have survived," Christine said. The woman ignored her. Christine tried naming every town she could think of, but the woman kept shaking her head.

"May I help?" an American soldier asked in broken German.

"She can't remember where she's from," Christine said. She thought about adding that the woman had lost her mind, but kept quiet. There was no need to state the obvious. *Maybe we've all lost our minds,* she thought.

The soldier shrugged and shook his head, and Christine realized he hadn't understood. He spoke some German, but not enough. Again, she tried to remember the few English words she knew, but nothing came to her. She couldn't think straight. The soldier was smiling at her, but his grin looked forced, below eyes filled with un-processed horror and pity. She tried to imagine what she looked like to him, blue eyes staring out from a pale, skeletal face, a walking dead woman with only a few inches of matted hair on her head.

"English?" he said.

Christine shook her head.

"*Namen?* Name?" he asked, pointing at the older woman.

"Sarah Weinstein," Christine said.

"Sarah," he said to the woman, bending over to look into her eyes. "*Bitte, kommen,* come." He was self-assured and muscular, a perfect blue-eyed Aryan for Hitler's army. Beneath the edge of his helmet, clean, blond hair was trimmed short around his ears. For the first time, Christine noticed that the Americans filled out their uniforms. They looked nothing like her father had when he'd come home, his grimy, ripped pants and jacket hanging off his skin-and-bone frame, his cheeks sunken and pale. The Americans looked well fed, their cheeks rosy, their eyes shiny and clear.

As the blue-eyed soldier led the distraught woman toward the other side of the platform, Christine took the opportunity to sit on a nearby bench. She was light-headed, trembling, and every breath provoked a coughing fit. Gripping the edge of the wooden seat, she suddenly became aware of her child-sized legs. As if seeing them for the first time, she noticed the sharp angles and awkward protrusions of her knees, as though her brittle bones were trying to break through her skin. For some reason, seeing a dead girl's brown stockings on her skeletal legs made her heart race. The crazy woman had put horrible fears in her head that spread and festered like poison, taking off with her hope like a feather in a windstorm. *What about my family?* she thought. *How do I know if they're still alive? What if a bomb landed on our house and killed them all?*

On the platform in front of her, black army boots appeared. The blue-eyed soldier squatted down to look at her.

"*Namen?*" he asked.

"Christine," she said, teeth chattering.

"Home?" he said in English, his voice soft. Home. She understood that word. She tried to answer, but her throat seemed blocked. Her lips moved, but no sound came out. She coughed and tried again.

"Hessental," she croaked.

To her surprise, the soldier's face broke into a wide grin, his cheeks ruddy, his teeth white as snow. Somewhere in the back of her mind, it registered that it'd been forever since she'd seen a genuine smile.

"*Fräulein,*" he said, pointing at the concrete between his boots. "Home. Hessental."

CHAPTER 28

Christine stared at the blue-eyed soldier for a moment, unable to believe what she'd just heard. Did he mean she was already home? The wide grin on his face remained unchanged. She bolted upright, nearly knocking him off his feet, and pushed past the other prisoners on the platform. Her heart hammered against her weak lungs, and she coughed as she hurried toward the central wall of the railroad station. While inside the boxcar, she'd had no way of knowing which direction they were headed. And when they'd arrived, it hadn't entered her mind to look for the station sign. She couldn't have dreamt that home would be her first stop. At first glance, this train depot looked like a hundred other train depots. But there, centered in the middle of the red brick wall, was the sign: HESSENTAL.

She clasped her hands over her mouth, a rolling surge of elation and fear running through her all at once, so strong it caused her to cry out. The blue-eyed soldier appeared at her side. "Home," she cried, pushing past him.

He hurried to block her way. *"Nein, Fräulein,"* he said, shaking his head. She stopped, and he made a writing motion, pretending to scribble on his open palm. "Name and address," he said in German. She ignored him and forged ahead, trying to skirt past him, but he caught her arm with a gentle hand. *"Bitte,"* he said. He tapped his chest, made a steering motion, and pointed at her.

She groaned and stepped back, wrapping her arms around herself. The soldier trotted over to an officer and saluted, then gestured toward Christine. The officer turned and scrutinized her for several seconds, then gave a stiff nod. The blue-eyed soldier grabbed a clipboard and hurried back to where she waited.

After she wrote down her information, he took the paper over to his superior and waited. She watched, hands gripping her elbows, trying to keep herself from falling apart. When she saw him coming back, she held her breath.

"Kommen," he said. "Home."

They hurried to the other side of the station, where he lifted her effortlessly into the passenger seat of a green army truck, then took his rifle from his shoulder, climbed in the driver's seat, and started the engine. He took a pack of cigarettes from his pocket, put one in his mouth, lit it, and offered her the pack. She shook her head. He reached into his pocket again and held out a small, yellow rectangle filled with flat strips wrapped in silver paper.

"Nein," she said, trying not to scream. "Home." She sat up, straining to look out over the oversized dashboard, black spots floating in front of her eyes.

He looked at her, a question on his face, asking which direction to go by signaling with his hand. She gestured to go forward, then left.

They drove away from the train station, past the long, wooden barracks previously used to house prisoners working on the air base. The first women to get off the train were milling about, leaning against buildings, or sitting on the ground with their heads in their hands.

The American saw her looking. "Jews," he said, the cigarette dangling from his lips. He pointed at the barracks, then made walking motions with his fingers. "To Dachau."

Christine moaned and shook her head. Farther along the street, a wooden gallows had been built, tattered bits of knotted rope still hanging from the scaffold, the German word for cowards, *Feiglinge,* painted across the main rafter. The soldier pointed at the gallows.

"Boys," he said, his face solemn.

Christine bit down on the inside of her cheek, barely able to breathe, remembering the night Vater had told Mutti she might need to hide Christine's brothers in the attic. The SS would hang them for not wanting to fight. Swallowing her growing panic, she motioned for the soldier to drive over the next bridge. On this side of the bridge, the buildings were gone, nothing but pile after pile of rubble. On the other side, a long line of houses stood ripped in half and empty, like giant, black dollhouses with vacant rooms and bare windows. Ragtag groups of women and children gathered around open cooking fires along the littered streets.

"My name is Jake," the soldier said in German, pronouncing each syllable more slowly and louder than necessary, as if she were hard of hearing.

Christine said nothing, digging her nails into her palms as they pulled up a steep hill, the dull roar of the truck's engine echoing through the narrow streets. When they entered the cobblestone square, she exhaled, the knot of fear loosening in her chest. St. Michael's stood untouched, its towering steeple and cascade of stone steps pockmarked and chipped, but intact. If the cathedral was still there, other parts of the village might still be standing.

The soldier wrenched the stick shift side to side, then gunned the engine as they turned up the road next to the cathedral. She clenched her jaw and pointed right. A burning lump in her throat threatened to cut off her breathing, and the farther they went down the road, the harder and hotter the lump grew. Within minutes, she could see what was left of Herr Weiler's butcher shop, and the half-timbered barn at the bottom of her street, crumbling walls plastered with handwritten posters in red ink, warning against surrender, with threats of being hanged or shot. Christine felt like she was going to faint.

"Home," she croaked, pointing to take the next left.

Jake turned the steering wheel, one eye squinting behind a swirl of cigarette smoke. The engine stuttered, hesitated, then pulled the truck slowly up the incline of her street. Christine held her breath and sat forward on the edge of the seat, certain her heart was going to burst from her chest. Then, in the lavender sky of early evening, the familiar tile roof came into view. A cry of joy burst from her throat, and she sobbed. When they neared the top of the hill, the scorched branches of the plum trees, one on each side of the front door, appeared. Then, finally, bent over in the front garden, she saw her mother.

"Halt!" Christine yelled. Jake pumped the brakes, and the engine shuddered and slowed. She yanked open the passenger door before the truck came to a complete stop. In the garden, her mother straightened and turned toward the sound, her brows knitted together. Christine half fell, half jumped from the high seat.

"Mutti!" she sobbed, running toward home with every ounce of strength she had left. Her mother stood motionless in the garden, a long-handled hoe in one soiled hand, limp weeds in the other. At first, she only stared, her pale, thin face crumpled in confusion. Then, understanding transformed her. The hoe and the weeds fell to the ground. Her hands flew over her open mouth.

"Mutti!" Christine shouted again. "I'm home!"

Mutti shrieked and ran out of the garden toward her, hands outstretched. They threw their arms around each other and nearly fell.

"Christine!" Mutti cried, clutching her daughter to her chest. "*Mein Liebchen!* Oh, *danke* Gott! *Danke* Gott!"

Christine collapsed in her mother's arms, legs weak, the sudden surge of strength that had carried her this far slipping away. She crumpled to the ground, shaking, the muscles in her neck loosening and tightening as she struggled to breathe. Mutti knelt, trying to hold her up.

"Maria! Heinrich!" Mutti shouted. "Come help! Our Christine is home! She's alive!" She caressed Christine's face, running her fingers over her short hair. "Oh, *mein Liebchen,* what did they do to you? Don't worry, you're safe now. I'll take care of you."

Then Christine felt arms scooping her up, lifting her from the ground, her mother's hands still cradling her head. She opened her eyes and tried to focus. A net-covered helmet, the American's face, then blackness.

At first, Christine was vaguely aware of the soft material next to her cheek and the clean, acidic smell of lye soap. Then she realized she was shivering, despite the fact that she was wrapped in a blanket and fully dressed, except for her coat and shoes. She wasn't on a wooden bunk; she was sure of that. Her head was on a pillow, and whatever she was lying on was wide and cushioned. Then she heard the soft whispers of familiar voices, and warm fingers stroked her temple. It all came back to her now. She was home. She blinked and opened her eyes. Mutti and Oma were kneeling next to the couch, staring at her with worried faces.

"Are you all right?" Mutti said.

"*Ja,*" Christine whispered.

Oma put a hand on Christine's cheek and kissed her forehead. "Welcome home, *Kleinkind,*" she said.

Behind them, Karl and Heinrich were at the table, frowning and watching with anxious eyes. Dressed in patched clothing, they looked as gaunt and pale as Mutti and Oma, a quiet sadness etched into their faces by the misery of six years of war. From the other end of the couch, a stranger looked down on her. The girl's hair was dreadfully short, only about an inch longer than Christine's. At first, she thought it was Hanna, but the coloring was wrong. This survivor's hair was fair, not auburn, her eyes blue, not brown. And although this stranger was thin, she wasn't skeletal, as Hanna had been. Then the person came forward and knelt beside her. Christine gasped. It was Maria. Confused, she touched her sister's head with grimy fingers. Maria took Christine's hand in her own and pressed it against her cheek, her eyes soft and wet.

"What happened to you?" Christine whispered.

"I was sent east with a group of girls from the village," Maria said. "We helped the women and old people dig antitank trenches. But then the Russians came through and . . ." Maria stopped and swallowed, as if trying not to be sick. Her chin trembled, and she lowered her voice, the words coming high and tight. "Only a handful of us survived the first few days. We had to disguise ourselves as boys, so the Russians would leave us alone."

"*Ach* Gott," Christine said.

"I shouldn't have let her go," Mutti said, her face crumpling in on itself. "I should have hid her in the attic with her brothers. I should have done more to protect her. To protect both of you."

"It's not your fault, Mutti," Maria said, her bloodshot eyes locked on Christine. "I made it back. Some of the other girls weren't so lucky."

Christine wrapped an arm around Maria and drew her close. Maria hugged her back, shoulders shuddering as she swallowed her sobs. After a moment she pulled away and stood, wiping her face on her sleeve.

"I can't believe you're all here," Christine said, struggling to sit up. Her arms were weak, her head heavy. "I didn't know if I'd find any of you alive." She looked at her mother, bracing herself. "What about Vater? Is he all right?"

"Your Vater is alive," Mutti said, trying to smile. "We received word just a few days ago. Now lie back down. We'll get you whatever you need. Are you hungry and thirsty? What would you like?"

Christine pushed herself to a sitting position. "I'm starving," she said, pulling back the blanket. "But more than anything, I need a hot bath." Maria and Mutti tried to help her up, but she was determined to stand on her own. "Is the fire going in the kitchen?"

"Ja," Mutti said. "But you have a fever, that's why you're shivering."

Christine straightened and wrapped her arms around herself. "I'll be fine," she said. "Karl and Heinrich, I'm so happy to see you." The boys came over to give her a quick hug, then moved away, staring up at her with furrowed brows. Christine smiled at them to show that she was all right, then headed toward the hall. Mutti and Maria stayed right on her heels, as if she were going to topple over at any moment. Everyone followed.

When Christine stepped into the kitchen, she was bombarded with the unforgettable smell of cinnamon and glazed gingerbread. She had never dreamt anything could smell so heavenly. With tears in her eyes, she looked around at the stove, the sink, the cupboards, the table. It all seemed so familiar and yet strange at the same time, as if she'd only visited it in a dream until now, or in another lifetime. She had thought she'd never see this kitchen again. Now, it seemed bigger and brighter than she remembered, every color luminous and vibrant. The red canisters, yellow curtains, blue-tiled floor, green-checked tablecloth, everything looked supple and wet, as if she could dip a brush in them and paint the sky. Compared with the monotone colors of Dachau, even her mother's worn, mended apron looked dazzling white.

Mutti hovered nearby until Christine was firmly seated at the kitchen table, then rolled up her sleeves and put more logs into the woodstove. Oma, Maria, Karl, and Heinrich filed in and sat on the benches, their eyes glued on Christine as if she'd sprouted two heads. In their troubled faces, she could tell she looked worse than her father had the first time he came home. Trying to ignore their stares, she watched her mother move around the kitchen.

Christine kept her arms under the table, her left hand wrapped around her right wrist, her thumb over the tattoo, as if she had to cover the numbered skin, like a surgery patient protecting a tender new scar. When Mutti filled a big mug with warm goat's milk and honey and handed it to her, Christine pulled the sleeves of the blue sweater over her wrists and took the steaming cup with her left hand, keeping her tattooed arm in her lap.

Closing her eyes, she inhaled the warm vapors, surprised that she could smell the goat's diet of sweet grass, and the flower pollen used by the honeybees. She took a long sip and held it in her mouth before swallowing, every sweet, buttery nuance of milk and honeycombed sugar like silk on her tongue. The creamy liquid soothed her raw, irritated throat.

"Now that the war is over," Mutti said, "when your father comes home, I'll use the last can of plums for a *Pflaumenkuchen* to celebrate your safe return."

Thinking about how close Isaac had come to surviving, Christine felt the tug and chafe of shackles in her chest. She took another sip of the goat's milk, warning herself to keep a watch on the thoughts of her heart. For right now, she needed to keep her mind on the present. She was home in her mother's kitchen, sitting at the table with Maria, Karl, Heinrich, and Oma. She was alive.

Mutti positioned the metal tub in the center of the kitchen and filled it with boiling water from the woodstove, curls of steam rising into the air. While Mutti readied the bath, Oma cut two slices of rye bread, spread each with plum jam, and set them in front of Christine.

When Christine took a small bite of the homemade bread and jam, she immediately had to stop chewing. Her eyes watered, and she pushed the bread to the inside of her cheek, certain she couldn't swallow over the growing lump in her throat. The combined flavor of earthy bread and sweet jam seemed amplified by a thousand times, the taste buds on her tongue exploding. It surprised her, and she had to catch her breath before she choked on the joy of something so simple and delicious. She sat back and put her fingers over her closed lips, a tear spilling over her cheek.

"What's wrong, *mein Liebchen?*" Oma whispered.

Christine shook her head. "Nothing," she said. "I'm just happy to be here, that's all." Then, taking her time, she finished chewing and swallowing before taking another bite.

After retrieving towels, a bar of homemade soap, and a fresh nightgown, Mutti sent everyone but Christine out of the kitchen. She locked the door and helped Christine out of the blue sweater and cranberry dress, her eyes filling when she saw her daughter's pallid, skeletal body. Christine slipped her legs out of the dead girl's brown stockings and put one leg in the tub, teeth chattering. Mutti opened the door to the woodstove, ready to shove the borrowed clothes into the roaring fire.

"Don't," Christine said.

"Why not?" her mother said.

"Because that's what the Nazis were doing to the Jews."

Without a word, Mutti folded the clothes and placed them on the floor, her lips pressed together in a thin line.

Christine climbed into the tub, slowly lowering her shivering body into the nearly scalding bath. The soapy water felt silky smooth on her grimy, arid skin, the powdery smell of lavender filling her nostrils as her mother gently scrubbed the ring of dirt from her neck and ran the washcloth over her shoulders. Christine closed her eyes, taking in every blissful sensation, the moist heat penetrating deep into her muscles, reheating and thawing her frigid bones, like the sun melting icicles in the spring.

Mutti didn't ask questions, and Christine was grateful. There would be time enough to fill her in on what she'd been through. When her mother saw the number on the inside of her wrist, she stopped and stared. Christine started to pull her arm away, but Mutti wouldn't let go. She looked at Christine with glassy eyes, ran a finger over the tattooed scar, then lifted Christine's wrist to her lips and kissed it, just as she'd kissed all bruises and scrapes throughout Christine's childhood.

Tears fell down Christine's cheeks as she realized she was experiencing the exact same things Isaac had after he had escaped. He'd eaten the bread and jam she'd taken to him after months of watery broth and crusts of bread. He'd sat in this very tub full of steaming, soapy water after not washing or changing his clothes for months on end. He'd felt what she was feeling now, this tremendous relief and euphoric elation at being rescued. How devastating it must have been to be captured and imprisoned again. If she woke up right now to discover that this was all a dream, that she'd really been asleep on the hard bunk inside the reeking barracks, she knew she'd die.

Her mother lathered her grimy hair and rinsed it with fresh water. After Christine had been scrubbed clean from head to toe, she climbed out of the tub and let Mutti dry her off next to the woodstove, a clean towel over her head and around her shoulders, just like when she was small.

With loving hands, Mutti slipped a long, flannel nightgown over Christine's head, put her scrubbed feet into thick, cotton socks, then took her up to her room, where she tucked her into a clean, fluffy feather bed. Christine's bone-weary body felt like it was sinking into a supple, white cloud, her heavy head resting on the soft, goose-down pillow. She needed sleep like a man lost in the desert needed water; every fiber of her being longed for it. Mutti sat next to the bed, caressing Christine's cheek and humming softly. Christine turned on her side and looked into her mother's watery eyes.

"Mutti," Christine whispered. "Isaac is dead."

CHAPTER 29

Over the next few nights, Mutti slept in Christine's room, cooling her head with a wet cloth when she was burning with fever, comforting her when she cried out in her sleep. When Christine woke in the middle of the night, pawing at her mother's face and arms as she tried to figure out where she was, Mutti lit the beech oil lantern on the nightstand. She would have left the lamplight on, but the electricity was still out, and no one knew when it would be coming back on.

In the morning and whenever Christine napped, Oma sat on a chair in her room, mending clothes or knitting. In the afternoons, Karl and Heinrich came in to play checkers or "Mensch Ärgere Dich Nicht," and Maria read to her at night.

Through it all, Christine held the sleeve of her nightgown over her wrist with one hand, her thumb rubbing back and forth over the numbered skin. She forgot her turn during games with her brothers and had to ask Oma to repeat herself during conversations. When Maria read to her, Christine saw her mouth moving but didn't hear the words. Instead, her mind had taken her back to Dachau.

As the days grew longer and warmer, Mutti threw open the windows of Christine's room, inviting fresh air, birdsong, and the perfume of plum blossoms to immerse her in the sounds and smells of new life. As often as Christine would let her, she brought in warm bread with plum jam and hot tea, and glass after glass of goat's milk. There were only a few chickens left, but Mutti plucked an old brown hen to make chicken soup, filling it with egg noodles made from the last of their flour.

Despite the regular dark detours of her mind, Christine's constricted lungs relaxed little by little, and she felt her strength slowly returning. After her fever broke, her nightmares were less furious and violent. After a few days, she could take deep breaths without pain, and her coughing fits grew further and further apart. After two weeks, she insisted on getting out of bed for her meals.

Now that the war was over, Americans occupied the village, their tanks and jeeps rolling up and down the cobblestone streets, making the windows of the house rattle. The roads were free of prisoners, the wailing air raid sirens had been silenced, and the sky was no longer filled with falling bombs. But food supplies were scarcer than ever, and the Allies were continuing the strict rationing set in place by Hitler and Goering. There were no farmers to work the soil, no potatoes to plant, no seeds for wheat, turnips, or beets.

Christine's father came home, thinner and dirtier than the first time he'd returned, but he was alive. He sobbed when he saw Christine, the grease and grime on his face mixing with his tears. When he lowered himself to sit beside her, he moved slowly, reaching out to steady himself, as if every bone in his body were stiff and brittle. He held her thin hands in his own, and they talked about her imprisonment. At one point they both stopped speaking, their eyes locked. It was a moment understood only by them, a silent communication that some things were too horrific to say out loud, that they each had seen and done things that would haunt them for the rest of their lives. Then Mutti came into the bedroom, and the moment was over. Vater also brought news of Hitler's suicide in a Berlin bunker, and the dictator's last plans for the Fatherland.

"He intended to destroy the whole country so there'd be nothing but ashes when the Allies arrived," he said. "We heard some of the concentration camps were bombed in an attempt to get rid of the evidence. The men running the camps became targets of our own Luftwaffe because Hitler knew we were losing the war."

"The officers and some of the guards at Dachau fled before the Americans came," Christine said.

Her father shook his head in disgust. "And most of them have probably already left the country. But not all of them. We saw SS stripping uniforms from dead Wehrmacht soldiers, so they could blend in."

Under azure skies, the trees, daffodils, and tulips began to bud and bloom, and despite the continued rationing and food shortages, the village children returned to their carefree games. They referred to the Americans as *Schokoladenwerfers*, "chocolate throwers," bolting outside when their jeeps went by, hands outstretched, yelling for more chocolate and gum. Every day, Karl and Heinrich searched for patches and medals in the discarded German uniforms left in the old schoolyard, to trade with the Americans for bread or a strange meat in a blue can called "Spam."

For the last few days, the French army had been passing through on its way back to the French-occupied zone, making everyone nervous.

"Stay away from the French," Vater warned the boys. "Yesterday they went into some cellars where people were storing what few belongings they had left. They took everything of value, then relieved themselves on the rest. They slaughtered Frau Klause's spring lambs. We're lucky to be in the American zone, but avoid the French until they're gone. I feel sorry for the Germans in their zone. And the Germans in the Russian zone will have it the worst."

On the first warm day that her mother allowed her outside, Christine blinked against the bright sunshine, feeling stiff from spending so much time in bed. Standing on the stone backyard terrace, she reached toward the sky, turning and stretching the tight muscles in her back. Her body felt weak where it used to be strong, hard where it used to be soft, bone where there used to be muscle. Her old clothes hung loose, and she had to wear a pair of worn shoes that she'd passed down to Maria ages ago, her own shoes lost forever in the monstrous, heaping pile at Dachau.

She wrapped her sweater around herself and ducked beneath the branches of the pear and plum trees, heading toward the back fence to look for the plum pit she'd planted over a year ago. She knelt and placed her fingers over the round depression, now nothing more than a circle of dirt and dead leaves. With careful fingers, she pushed back the bits of grass and curling foliage. But there was nothing growing there, not the slightest hint of a tiny twig or unfurling leaf. Her eyes filled with tears. She thought about digging up the pit and throwing it away, then imagined it rotting in the ground, worm-holed and spongy from the long months of snow and rain. Just like Isaac, the plum pit hadn't survived. Instead, she stood, the weight of grief making it difficult to straighten completely, and went back to the terrace.

Sitting in a cane-backed chair, she watched Mutti dig up a new vegetable patch in the backyard. The chickens were loose in the grass, scratching at the earth, their feathers glistening orange in the sun. Frau Klause had delivered a rooster when she heard of Christine's return, and now, the handsome bird searched for bugs and worms in the yard, his red comb and high tail feathers bobbing and weaving, his taloned feet pulling and raking at the grass. When he found a beetle or a centipede, he called the hens with a low, cooing caw, then held the squirming morsel in his beak, waiting for them to scurry over before dropping it at their feet. While the hens pecked the insect apart, he crowed and preened, strutting in a circle. Since Christine's return, the world was alive with color, and even chickens were beautiful.

She closed her eyes, lifting her face toward the late morning sky, listening to the contented clucks of the hens, breathing in the perfume of plum blossoms and the moist tang of freshly turned soil. Now, every blade of grass, every insect and sparrow, every leaf and tree had become a spectacular gift. And yet, while the skin on her face and hands felt warm in the sun, inside she still felt frozen, like spring thaw running over river ice.

"*Nein!*" Mutti screamed.

Christine's eyes flew open. Her mother had dropped her spade and was standing next to the house, her hands in fists. A French soldier stood in the next-door neighbor's backyard, his rifle aimed at one of Mutti's chickens. Mutti stood her ground. She took off her apron and flapped it in the air, shooing him away, the white material fluttering in the breeze like the flag of surrender.

"Leave my chickens alone!" Mutti yelled. Christine went to her side.

"He probably doesn't understand you," she said, putting a hand on her mother's shoulder. "We're still the enemy. You need to be careful." Christine forced herself to smile and wave at the soldier.

Mutti put her apron back on, shaking her head, her hands trembling. The Frenchman lowered his rifle and laughed. He lit a cigarette and stared at them, as if trying to decide what to do. After a minute, he got bored and left. Christine let out a sigh of relief and returned to her chair. Mutti went back to the plot of newly turned earth, lifted the spade high overhead, and brought it back down with a solid swing, hitting the dirt with a clomp.

After a while, Christine got up to help her mother rework the garden in preparation for planting cucumbers and green beans. Thanks to Mutti's careful planning, they still had seeds from last year. Earlier, they'd disagreed about Christine's readiness to return to hard labor, but Christine had insisted, telling her mother that work would make her stronger. She was at the point where too much rest was making her feel listless and weak. She longed to feel her muscles stretch and contract, her heart pound from physical exertion instead of fear.

Within an hour, they were ready to plant. They worked on their hands and knees, carefully spacing the bean seeds in long, shallow furrows. The dark earth felt silky and warm in Christine's hands, the fawn-colored seeds flawless and smooth. Black dirt caked beneath her fingernails and lined the creases of her knuckles, making the skin on her hands look bone white. Each small pebble she found in the soil reminded her of the one Isaac had thrown at her.

At noon, Mutti wiped her hands on her apron and headed toward the back door.

"Come inside," she said to Christine. "It's time to eat."

"*Ja,*" Christine said, sitting back down. "I just want to enjoy the fresh air a bit longer." Christine's arms and legs were tired and sore, but it was a content fatigue, the sort of healthy exhaustion that made her look forward to a hot bath and a good meal.

"I'll call you when everything's ready then." Mutti slipped off her dirty boots and put on her shoes, then kissed Christine on the forehead and went into the house. Within seconds, she returned. Someone waited in the hall behind her, a towering figure with a pale face and wide shoulders. Her mother held the door open, anxiety lining her forehead.

"The American is here!" she said.

"What does he want?" Christine said, sitting forward.

"How do I know?"

Just then, the soldier stepped out onto the terrace, his rifle hanging from his shoulder, a bulky silver tin in one hand. He gave Christine a quick nod. "*Guten Tag.* Hello."

Mutti remained diligently in the entryway, her sweat-streaked face pale. The American was tall and muscular, blond and blue-eyed, and Christine recognized him instantly. The soldier who had given her a ride home. What was his name? Then it came to her. *Jake.* She stood, pulled down her sleeves and crossed her arms, pushing her tattooed wrist protectively beneath her elbow.

"*Sind gut?* Are you well?" he said. He tapped his chest. "Jake, *ja?*"

Christine tried again to remember the few English words she knew. It was too much effort. She nodded.

"*Gut,*" he said, smiling. He looked back at Mutti, who was watching from the doorway. "English?"

"*Nein,*" Christine said.

"*Alles gut?* All is good?"

She nodded again and he grinned, glancing down at his feet. At the train station, she'd been anxious and sick and hadn't noticed his handsome features. Now, as he stood here in the midday sun, the blue sky framing his blond head, she could see that he was striking. When he looked at her, his eyes turned silver in the sun. He looked too young to be so far from his family, fighting a war. He was probably Isaac's age. As soon as the thought crossed her mind, the familiar black mass twisted in her chest.

Jake glanced back at Mutti again, then looked at Christine, a pink hue rising in his cheeks. "Friends?"

She understood the word but wasn't sure what to say. On one hand, he'd brought her home, and she felt like she had to be nice to him. On the other hand, she just wanted to be left alone. Besides, he was a soldier in uniform, and she was tired of anything that reminded her of war.

Before she could respond, he reached inside his jacket and pulled out a handful of brown-and-silver-wrapped bars, his dog tags jangling inside his shirt. Christine recognized the word HERSHEY written across the paper. They were the same kind of candy her brothers picked up off the streets, thrown from American jeeps. Jake held them out to her, along with the silver can. She took a step backwards. Maria had told her about the rumors, that American soldiers used their food as "*Frau* bait" to get German girls to have sex with them. She clenched her jaw and looked away, then forced herself to look back at him. "*Nein,*" she said, her voice hard.

He moved toward her, holding his gifts out at arm's length, insisting. She shook her head vigorously, eyes darting toward her mother to make sure she was still there, and pointed at the back door. "Good-bye," she said, dragging the unfamiliar English word out too long, clipping it short at the end.

He understood, and the smile dropped from his face. She was surprised to see hurt in his eyes. Instead of persisting, as she half expected, he put the tin and chocolates on the ground. For a moment, Christine worried he was going to reach for his rifle. But instead of his gun, the soldier held up his hands, like a prisoner conceding surrender, then smiled, nodded, and headed toward the exit.

"Ma'am," he said to Mutti, and then he was gone. Mutti glanced at Christine with troubled eyes, then disappeared into the hall to show him out.

The next day was rainy and cold. Christine found dark days harder than most, the rain and gloomy skies reminding her of every horrible scene she was trying to forget. She sat on the couch, shivering beneath a blanket, trying to read in the dim living room. Oma was sitting next to her, darning socks. Maria and Mutti were in the kitchen cooking dinner. Vater was out looking for work. If only they had coal to burn to take the chill out of the small room, but there was none. And they couldn't use their dwindling supply of firewood, because they needed every last log for cooking. Trying to concentrate on the words on the page, Christine held the book in one hand, her thumb caressing the number on her wrist. Instead of losing herself in the story, she found her eyes drawn to Oma's wrinkled face, wondering how she continued to exist without Opa. *I wonder if I'm that strong,* she thought, *or will I always feel as if a piece of my heart has been ripped out?*

Just when she felt her eyes filling, Heinrich hurried into the room, the silver, oversized tin in his hands, Karl at his heels.

"What's this?" Heinrich asked.

Christine put the book in her lap. "I don't know. Now go put it back where you found it."

"Mutti said the American left it. We want to see what it is!" Karl said.

"We should throw it away," Oma said. "It might be poison."

Christine pulled back the blanket and stood. "It's probably food."

Mutti came into the room, a dishcloth wrapped around the iron handle of a steaming kettle in her hands. "What's going on?" she said. "We need to set the table for *Mittag Essen.*"

She set the kettle in the center of the table and lifted the lid. Long strips of brown noodles floated in a thin, yellow broth. It was Maria's favorite, pancake soup, the noodles made by cutting crepes into strips.

Heinrich set the tin on the table too, and both boys sat down, their eyes gleaming with anticipation. "Can we open it?" Heinrich said.

Oma pushed herself up from the couch and waddled over to join them. When Maria entered the living room, eyelids swollen from crying, Mutti looked at Christine, an understanding passing between them. For the past few nights, they'd both been woken by Maria's sobs.

The first night Christine had heard Maria weeping, she'd gone to her bedroom and slipped beneath her bedcovers, trying to get Maria to turn around and face her by tugging gently on her shoulder. But Maria ignored her, staying in the same position, on her side, facing the wall.

"What's wrong?" Christine whispered. "Why are you crying?"

Maria shrugged, sniffling.

"Tell me," Christine whispered. "It's all right. I'm your sister. That's what sisters are for, remember?"

"There's nothing to tell," Maria said in a small voice.

Christine rubbed Maria's upper arm, trying to think of something to say, wise words of an older sister to take away the pain. Nothing came to her. "I understand how awful the middle of the night can be," she said. "All those horrible memories are bad enough during the day. But at night, I don't know what happens. It's like evil forces have free reign when it's dark. They get inside your head and try to make you crazy. Sometimes I can barely stand it when the memories come. I try to remind myself that the sun will come up in the morning and it will be easier to push those thoughts away. It will be a new day, a new beginning."

With that, Maria curled into a fetal position, shoulders convulsing. Christine's stomach tightened; she wished she'd said something different. What, she didn't know. After a minute, Maria turned on her back, wiping her cheeks. In the inky moonlight coming in through the windowpanes, Maria's face looked swollen and purple, the color of a bruise. Christine's breath caught, but then she realized it was just an illusion. "Maybe you feel like it's a new beginning," Maria said. "But I don't."

"But why?" Christine said. "You . . ." She bit her tongue, afraid she would say something wrong again and that her sister would refuse to talk.

"Who is going to want me now?" Maria said, her voice breaking. "I'm filthy and disgusting! I wish I'd died with the others!"

"Don't say that!" Christine said. "What happened wasn't your fault! It doesn't change anything about you! You're a beautiful, loving young woman, with a kind heart and a good soul. Someday you're going to fall in love, and that man will be lucky to have you!"

Maria shook her head, fresh tears surging down her cheeks. She looked at Christine, her face contorted. "Do you know why the Russians killed some of the other women?" she said.

Christine thought of a hundred horrible answers, none that would help. *"Nein,"* she said, bracing herself. "Why?"

"Because they resisted," Maria said.

Christine reached for Maria's hand in the dark. Her fingers felt thin and cold, and they were trembling. "Wanting to survive doesn't make you a bad person," she said.

"How do you know?"

"I just know," Christine said. "I think everyone is born with the will to survive. It's just stronger in some than in others. Listen, I know it's hard, but try to remember how lucky you are. You're here, with your family. We're all together, with a roof over our heads and food on the table. It's perfectly understandable what you're feeling, and you've got good reason to cry. But, *bitte,* try to be grateful for the little things. That's what I have to do every day."

Maria put her hands over her face and started crying again. "It's not that simple," she said, her words distorted.

"Bitte," Christine said. "Talk to me. I just want to help."

Maria wiped her nose, then lay motionless for what seemed like forever. Other than the occasional sniffle, she was silent. At first, Christine thought she was falling asleep, but then, finally, she said, "I told you. There's nothing to tell." She turned on her side and pulled the covers over her shoulder. "Right now I just want to go to sleep and forget about everything. I'm sure you're right. Things will look better in the morning. I'm sorry I woke you."

Christine's heart dropped. Instead of helping, she'd caused her sister to withdraw.

"Is there someone . . . I mean, are you in love with someone?" she asked. "Someone who came home from the war? Are you afraid he'll find out what happened? No one has to know!"

Maria let out a sputtering chortle, as if that was the most ridiculous thing she'd ever heard. *"Nein,"* she said. "I'm not pining away for a secret love." Christine said nothing. After a minute, Maria turned around again. "I'm sorry. I shouldn't have said that. I know how much you miss Isaac."

"It's all right," Christine said. "I know you didn't mean anything. I'm just upset because I want to help, that's all. I don't like hearing you cry."

"I don't mean to make you worry," Maria said. "You've been through enough."

"I'll stay here if you want me to. I need you to be all right. You're the only sister I have, you know."

Maria wrapped an arm around Christine. "I need you too," she said. "But I'm fine, really."

"Are you sure?"

"*Ja,* now go back to bed."

Reluctantly, Christine gave Maria one last hug and went back to her own bedroom, hoping she'd helped in some small way. But when she heard Maria crying again the next night, her chest flushed with fear. She couldn't explain it, but hearing her sister cry made her anxious, as if they were never going to get past all they'd been through. But every time she made her way along the hall to her sister's room and opened the door, the crying stopped.

Now, in the dining room, Mutti put the lid back on the soup, and Christine sat down next to Maria.

"What do you think is in the tin?" Christine asked Maria.

Maria shrugged and sniffed, running a pale wrist beneath her nose.

"Karl," Mutti said. "Get the can opener."

"And the chocolate bars," Christine said.

Karl retrieved the can opener from the kitchen and handed it to Christine, who opened the silver tin to reveal a smooth, light brown paste. Mutti got spoons out of the sideboard, dipped one into the can, and handed it to Karl. Karl cautiously sampled the strange, sticky substance. His eyes grew wide, and he took another lick, beaming. Heinrich grabbed a spoon and joined in.

"What is it?" Christine asked them.

"I don't know!" Heinrich said. "But it's delicious!"

Christine scraped a spoon along the edge of the creamy brown paste and took a hesitant nibble. It tasted like the hazelnuts that grew wild in the hills, only sweeter, and soft like butter. It was the most delicious thing she'd eaten in years. "Mmm . . ." she said. "It's good!" She handed a spoon to Maria, then opened two of the chocolate bars and gave everyone a piece.

Soon her whole family was dunking their spoons and chocolate into the smooth paste, just like they had dunked boiled potatoes into a vat of sour milk when there was nothing left to eat. Even Oma couldn't get enough. Mutti and the boys sucked on their utensils as if they were made of sugar. And even though Maria's cheerful expression looked forced, Christine was delighted to see everyone smiling and laughing. Years of fear and uncertainty had formed a permanent hardness in their faces, a look of buried pain that changed their eyes and the way they held their mouths. But today, their features were soft and relaxed, their grins wide and real. Christine was glad Jake had left the tin and chocolates, and she felt a little guilty for thinking the worst about him. *Even at Christmas,* she thought, *my brothers never looked this excited.*

"Wait until Vater tastes this!" Karl said.

"We need to eat some real food now," Mutti finally announced, putting a plate over the tin. The boys groaned.

After they finished eating, Christine took the dirty dishes to the kitchen, realizing she hadn't thought about her own heartache in nearly an hour. *So that's how it happens,* she thought. *I'll get distracted by life. The wounds will be covered by pleasant moments, moments that I used to take for granted. Hopefully, the pleasant moments will become more frequent, and longer lasting. Because if I keep living in the past, I won't survive.*

But when she rolled up her sleeves to wash the dishes, she stopped. Her hand flew over her wrist, her thumb pressing hard on the tattoo. At first, she couldn't figure out her reaction. Then it came to her. For just a little while, she'd forgotten about the camps and the war. But then, with a sick twist in her gut, she realized for the first time that the mud-colored number would be there for the rest of her life. Every day she would see it and be reminded.

CHAPTER 30

By the second week in May, a small number of surviving men and boys had returned to the village. The lucky ones came back sane and whole. Most came home to destroyed houses and missing relatives: mothers, grandparents, or siblings who hadn't made it to the shelter in time.

The sounds of hammering and sawing echoed throughout the spring days as every able-bodied man, woman, and boy worked together to rebuild the war-torn village. They filled the winding alleys like a swarm of worker ants, dismantling centuries of masonry and intricate stonework, knocking down unstable walls of gabled shops and remnants of barns. Using picks and hammers to chip the residual mortar away from the remains of half-timbered houses, they salvaged stone and undamaged beams. They cleared rubble-filled basements, piling the charred lumber and shattered bricks along the edge of the streets until they could be loaded onto wagons and taken away. Patched together with alternating layers of fresh mortar and gray fieldstone, the gaping hole in the church across the street from Christine's house gradually disappeared.

Vater and the boys assisted with the restoration of the village, and because Vater helped with the reconstruction of the school, he earned a small amount of money. If their ration cards allowed it, the first supplies the family tried to purchase were meat, sugar, or flour. But the butcher shop and grocery store received fewer and fewer deliveries, and the everyday staples were even harder to come by than during the war. If Christine's family was lucky enough to hear about a delivery ahead of time, Mutti or Maria went early to stand in line, because it took only a few hours for everything to sell out.

Once a week, as they had throughout the last months of conflict, Heinrich and Karl worked at the flour mill, in exchange for a half burlap sack of flour swept from the floor. Christine helped Oma separate the pieces of wood, clumps of dirt, and bits of wheat chaff from the usable flour, shaking it through the sieve until it felt clean and smooth between their fingers. But then the flour mill closed down too.

Christine's family was forced to trade Oma's last pieces of hand-printed cotton—her only material for making clothes—for sugar, and Ur-Ur Grossmutti's cherry regulator for a wagonload of firewood. Karl and Heinrich got chocolate from the Americans, traded it for cigarettes, then traded the cigarettes for cooking oil.

On the first Saturday of June, Maria and Christine sat side by side on the kitchen bench shelling early spring peas, chewing on the empty pods while they worked. The deep emerald pods snapped open effortlessly, the red ceramic bowl between them filling quickly with tender green pearls. Christine never used to understand why Maria always ate the peapods, but now the shells tasted especially sweet. Ever since her return from Dachau, sugary plums and sweet berries, salted pork fat and milky potatoes, pickled onions and vinegary cabbage, every flavor exploded on her tongue as if she were tasting food for the first time.

Out on the kitchen balcony, Mutti was hanging laundry. The girls worked without talking, listening to their mother sing as she pinned clothes to the line. On top of the woodstove, kettles of leeks and a rare pork hock filled the kitchen with the sweet, tart smell of onions and vinegar.

The breeze through the open balcony doors was mild, but still, Christine shivered. Each sun-filled day since her return was longer and warmer than the one before, yet she felt the remnants of winter hidden within each current of air, like the cold, thin hands of ghosts touching her skin. No matter the temperature, she wore winter stockings and an extra sweater. The only time she took off her sweater was when she sat in the backyard in the direct sun, where the chicken coop and the house blocked all drafts. Only then did the chill that radiated from deep inside her bones seem to retreat.

Christine glanced at her sister out of the corner of her eye, suddenly picturing the two of them as little girls, running down the hall on their way to bed, in a time before they knew about war and rape and bombs and concentration camps. But she was determined not to wallow in self-pity, so she pushed the thought from her mind, concentrating instead on the perfect round peas in her hand.

Along with keeping Christine up-to-date on who had returned from the war and who hadn't, Maria knew which local girls were seeing American soldiers on a regular basis.

"Helgard Koppe is going to America with her *Ami*," she told Christine.

"I guess I can't blame anyone for looking for romance wherever she can find it," Christine said. "There aren't many German boys left."

Just then, Mutti came inside and crossed the kitchen, then hurried downstairs and outside to the enclosed backyard, where a load of whites dried in the sun. All of a sudden, Christine heard Maria sniffing, and she turned to see tears streaming down her sister's cheeks. Maria's arms were shaking, her fingers trembling as she struggled to open a peapod.

"What's wrong?" Christine asked, a cold eddy of fear opening up in her chest. She was used to Maria being weepy, but this was different. She looked on the verge of breaking.

"I saw starving women and children living in cellars under heaps of rubble," Maria cried. "With nothing but a mattress and an empty pail for a toilet. They fought so hard to stay alive! Then the Russians came and . . ." She choked on her words, sobbing now. "But I survived, and I know I'm supposed to be grateful. . . ."

Christine took the peapod from her sister's hand, moved the bowl from between them, and turned Maria to face her. "I still hear you crying at night. And I understand! But we're strong, remember? We're survivors! And we have each other! The war is over, and our slate is wiped clean. We get to start over!"

Maria's expression tightened, and she stared at Christine with bloodshot eyes, her face getting redder by the second, like a kettle ready to burst. "I'm pregnant," she said, spitting the words out as if they were poison.

Christine stiffened, a greasy mass of nausea seizing her gut. *"Ach nein,"* she said. "Are you sure?"

Maria nodded, her tears a bitter flood.

"What are you going to do?" Christine said. She tried to put her arms around her sister, but Maria pulled away.

"I've heard there are ways," Maria said, her voice quivering. "Knitting needles, or throwing yourself down a flight of stairs . . ."

Like a jolt, a series of images flashed in Christine's mind: a boy being ripped from his mother's arms; babies being sent to the left with their grandparents while their howling mothers were sent to the right; couples with newborns being pushed into gas chambers.

"Nein," Christine said, gripping Maria's arm. "You can't do that." Maria buried her face in her hands, shoulders convulsing. Christine leaned forward, speaking in a soft voice. "Maybe you can give the baby to someone who lost a child in the war." She paused, overcome by the inadequacy of her words, knowing she had to say them anyway. "And I know it seems impossible right now, but maybe you'll feel differently once you see your baby. We'll all love it, no matter what."

Christine waited for Maria to get angry and tell her she had no idea what she was talking about. And she would be right. But Maria said nothing, instead disappearing into her pain. Christine reached out to hug her again, and this time Maria gave in, arms limp at her sides. When they heard Mutti's footsteps on the stairs, the two sisters straightened, returning to the chore of shelling peas.

CHAPTER 31

With regular meals of garden vegetables and stewed chicken, home-made bread and plum jam, Christine's bony elbows and ribs began to recede. Eventually, Mutti relented and let her take lunch to her father at the school construction site. Christine was relieved to get out of the house, to stretch her legs and feel the wind in her face. She begged Maria to go with her, but Maria refused, going through her days with her hair unwashed, her clothes un-ironed. She'd made Christine swear not to tell anyone about the baby until Maria felt strong enough to share her secret.

Walking alone inside the village, Christine felt watched from behind parted curtains, by people wanting to look at the girl who had survived the camps. Sometimes, she took the long way home, through the wide-open spaces outside town, where her pace slowed and she took long, cleansing breaths, feeling free enough to hold her chin high and look out toward the hills, remembering when the fields had been yellow with sprouting wheat, and row after row of sugar beets had spread toward stone fences like the long, green ribs of a sleeping giant.

Once, she climbed to the highest point in the forest. where she looked down on the valley and saw hundreds of American tanks and jeeps crowded around the two-story control tower at the air base. From there, the Allied path of destruction revealed itself, the outer edge of the village scarred with bomb craters, blackened patches of flat, scorched earth, and splintered, overturned trees. Between the tiled rooftops of surviving buildings, the ruined houses and shops looked crushed, as if a giant, lumbering ogre had trampled through the valley and left massive footprints across the town.

Two weeks after Maria's confession, Kate stopped by to see Christine. It was her first visit since Christine's return. During the last months of war, as the air raids had increased and the other girls were being sent off to bigger cities to become air raid wardens or auxiliary firefighters, her parents had sent her to her uncle's farm in the countryside, in the hopes of keeping her safe. Christine wondered if Kate had any idea how lucky she was.

Kate entered the living room in slow motion, her hands clasped in front of her, as if visiting someone who has suffered a long, disfiguring illness.

"How are you?" Kate asked.

"As well as can be expected," Christine said.

Kate stood in the middle of the room, fingers fidgeting with the side seam of her skirt. *She's afraid of me,* Christine thought in amazement. *She acts like I have a disease.*

"I'm glad you're home," Kate said.

"Danke," Christine said. "Me too."

"What happened to your hair?" Kate said, pointing.

Self-consciously, Christine ran her fingers over the short locks above her ear. "They cut it off."

"Why?"

"They did it to all the prisoners." Christine dropped her hands to her lap, her thumb rubbing the tattooed skin beneath her sleeve.

"Oh," Kate said, looking away. "I'm glad you're home," she repeated. "My mother said your mother thought she'd never see you again."

"I thought I'd never see anyone again either," Christine said, rearranging the couch pillows so Kate could sit down. Kate lingered awkwardly in the middle of the room, eyes darting toward the windows as if she were planning an escape. Finally, reluctantly, she moved toward the couch.

"You didn't think they'd do anything to you, did you?" she said, sitting down. "You're German, after all."

Christine pulled her legs up under herself and turned to face Kate. *Has her hair always been such a scorching shade of red?* she wondered. In the shafts of sunlight coming through the window, it looked iridescent, as if tiny flames flickered within each strand. Again, Christine ran her fingers over her own sparse hair, fine and soft, like the yellow down of a baby chick. When Kate glanced in her direction, Christine put her hands in her lap, her thumb over her wrist.

"Every minute I was in that camp," she said, "I thought I was going to die. They were murdering thousands of people every day."

"Thousands?" Kate said, looking directly at her for the first time. "Why would they murder thousands of people? And how could they even kill that many at a time?"

"They gassed them, then burned them in a giant crematorium. Sometimes they just shot them." Images of Isaac made Christine's chest constrict. Beneath her thumb, she could feel her heartbeat pick up speed below the number on her wrist.

"Why would they do that?" Kate asked again, her face filled with disbelief. "They were going to relocate them!"

"They lied. They didn't want to relocate the Jews. They wanted to slaughter them."

"I have a hard time believing that. It's physically impossible."

Christine felt a hot twist of anger at the bottom of her rib cage. "I saw thousands of people murdered. I saw it with my own eyes. They shot Isaac."

"I heard," Kate said, glancing at Christine with pity and false understanding. "And I'm sorry. You were brave to risk your life for him, and I know you've been through a lot. But you're home now. You'll be better off if you just forget it." Then she patted Christine's knee, as if she were a foolish child afraid of monsters under her bed.

"I'll never forget it," Christine said, her face burning. A ringing in her ears made her voice sound as if it were coming from someone else.

Kate ignored her and got up to stand by the window. She leaned against the sill and looked out toward the street. "Remember the three-story house with the fancy balcony on Hallerstrasse that I always admired? Stefan's mother lives there and she's giving the house to Stefan and me as soon as we're married!"

All of a sudden, the ringing in Christine's ears disappeared and she could hear perfectly. She sat up straight. "Stefan came back?"

"*Ja!* And he looks *so* handsome in his black uniform!" Then Kate straightened, and her eyes grew wide. "Oh *mein* Gott! I'm not supposed to tell anyone he has it! It just slipped out. *Bitte,* don't tell him I told you. He'd be so mad. He just tried it on so I could see him in it, then he was putting it away."

Christine felt light-headed. "Kate," she said. "I saw Stefan! He was a guard in Dachau!"

"He said what he did for Germany was important. It was a secret."

Christine took a deep breath, trying to keep her voice steady. "Does Stefan's uniform have a skull and crossbones on the hat and lapel?"

"*Ja,*" Kate said, shrugging. "So what?"

"Listen. If Stefan's uniform is black, he was a member of the SS. If it has a skull and crossbones on it, he was a member of the SS Totenkopfverbände, the Death's Head Units."

"Promise you won't tell anyone he has it! His own mother doesn't even know!"

"Did you hear what I said?" Christine said. "I saw him! The Death's Head Units were the ones running the camps, the ones murdering Jews!"

Kate rolled her eyes. "The war is over, Christine," she said. "Besides, whatever Stefan did, he was only following orders." Kate moved toward the living room door, then stopped. "I should go, so you can rest. You're still not well. I don't think you remember exactly what happened. You were homesick and scared. You could have imagined all sorts of things."

"I didn't imagine any of it!" Christine said. She got off the couch and took a step toward Kate, her vision pulsating in time with her hammering heart. "I saw it all! And for the rest of my life

I'll never forget the bodies, the blood, the lines of people being led into the gas chambers!"

"I'm not going to stay here and listen to this!" Kate said. "I came as your friend, to see how you are, and this is the thanks I get?" She marched across the room.

"Kate!" Christine said, following her. "Wait!"

At the door, Kate spun around to face her. "And if that's the way you feel, don't bother coming to the wedding!" She slammed the door in Christine's face.

With her hands clenched in fists, Christine stared at the stippled grain of the wooden door, the timber knots and tree rings like frightened faces being consumed by swirls and licks of fire. She listened to Kate run down the stairs; searing fury coiled inside her stomach. The front door opened and closed. For a second, she thought about going to the window and calling out to Kate, but changed her mind. *What could I ever say to make her believe me?* she thought. *I have no proof. As far as I know, I'm the only one from the village who survived the camps. But that should prove I'm telling the truth, shouldn't it? I'm the only one who came home. Sooner or later, they'll all know the truth, won't they?* She felt herself going somewhere else, like a dropped coin spiraling toward the bottom of a lake.

She yanked open the door and hurried to the kitchen. Oma was at the sink, and Mutti was hunched over the table, kneading a mound of dough with floured hands. Mutti stopped working and looked at her, wiping her forehead with the back of her wrist.

"Are you all right?" she said.

"I think so."

"What's wrong?"

"Oh . . . Kate left because I . . ."

"She didn't stay long," Oma said, turning toward Christine. Sunlight streamed in through the window behind her, backlighting the loose wisps of gray hair surrounding her head like a downy halo. All at once, Christine felt enveloped in stillness, as if the smell of wood-fired bread had seeped into her pores and slowed her galloping heart, the yeasty aroma so strong she could almost taste the spongy bread melting in her mouth. She wrapped her arms around her waist.

"She's mad at me."

"Why on earth would she be mad at you?" Mutti asked. She folded the dough over and over on top of itself, pushing it against the floured cutting board with strong, work-worn hands, the table below creaking in protest.

"She thinks I'm making up stories about Dachau." Christine slid into the corner nook, one elbow on the table, one hand behind her ear, rolling downy hair between her fingers.

"Maybe it was too much all at once," Oma said.

"But I never imagined someone wouldn't believe me," Christine said. "Especially someone who used to be my best friend." She put her hands in her lap and hunched forward, trying to ward off the chill despite the fire-warm room. Before her thumb found the numbered skin on her wrist, she felt something soft between her fingers, like pieces of thread. She looked down and saw delicate strands of blond hair in her hand, then reached up and felt the sore, tender spot behind her ear.

"Don't worry," Mutti said. "She'll be back. She just needs time to let it sink in. People aren't going to be ready to hear what happened. They've got their own tragedies and hardships."

A stab of guilt twisted in Christine's chest. For the hundredth time, she wondered if news of Maria's pregnancy would fracture or reinforce Mutti's regained vigor. For an instant, she considered not saying anything more, but she couldn't keep quiet. "Kate won't be back," she said. "She's going to tell everyone I'm crazy." *Maybe I am crazy,* she thought. *I just pulled my own hair out of my head.*

"Why would she do that?" Mutti asked.

"Because I told her I saw her fiancé working as a guard in Dachau." Beneath the table, Christine let go of the hair, imagining the fine, wispy filaments floating toward the kitchen floor like plucked chicken feathers. She pressed her thumb into the number on her wrist.

Mutti and Oma stared at her in silence. Christine looked back at them, a rigid thickness growing in her chest. She thought she'd scream before one of them said anything.

"You might want to keep that to yourself," Mutti said finally. "This family has had enough trouble. Kate will have to decide for herself about him."

Christine bit down on her tongue, and when she spoke she tasted blood. "I won't sit back and do nothing."

Mutti frowned and turned toward the stove. She pulled browned loaves from the oven, using the edges of a dishcloth to protect her hands. Christine knew Mutti didn't dare let the precious bread burn, but she wanted her to say something, anything to let her know she understood. Mutti set the loaves on the counter to cool, her face unreadable. Oma sat down beside Christine.

"The truth has a way of coming out," Oma said. "If Kate's fiancé did anything wrong, then someday, he'll pay for it. Maybe not soon enough to suit us, but God makes the final judgment on us all."

By evening, Christine realized the heaviness in her chest wasn't just frustration and anger. The black pull detaining every heartbeat came from the reminder that she would never be with Isaac. Kate and Stefan were together again, while her own chance at true love had been destroyed. Isaac was gone. She wanted him alive, smelling lilacs and tasting bread with jam. She needed to show him the shimmering feathers of the rooster's tail, the purple and white blossoms of the plum trees.

Sometime after midnight, Christine woke up feeling as if someone were sitting on her chest. A picture formed in her mind of her and Isaac, a bouquet of white freesia in her hands, her mother's old wedding dress flowing behind her in a soft fan of lace. In a black suit and tie, Isaac linked his arm through hers, his brown eyes and dark hair as clear as if he were standing right in front of her. Then he smiled at her.

In bed, Christine turned on her side, her shoulders heavy and rigid, as if her body were turning to stone. Tears slid down her cheeks and fell on the white pillow, tiny dots that bloomed gray. In the dim light coming from the beech oil lantern, she ran a finger over the brown, crinkled number on her wrist. *I'm still back there with you,* she thought.

CHAPTER 32

The day after Kate's visit, on her way home from taking lunch to her father, Christine took the regular shortcut through a cobblestone alley that ran between rows of gabled, five-storied houses. It was unusually hot for June and she walked slowly, grateful for the quiet coolness of the narrow, shaded corridor. Above her, fresh laundry hung damp and unmoving in the still air.

Near the middle of the long passageway, the high giggles and excited exclamations of conversation floated down from an open window. She couldn't make out every word, but could tell it was two young women, laughing about an "Ami" asking one of them to go to America. It made Christine think of Jake. Maybe she should try to find him. If she could figure out a way to tell him about Stefan, he could tell his superiors, and they could arrest him.

Deep down, she envied the laughing girls, excited about going to America. She wished Maria could be one of them, instead of hating the Russian baby growing inside her. She wished it for herself too, because there were still days when she woke from nightmares filled with dirty barracks and dying prisoners, when she scrubbed the ink on her wrist until it was raw. On days like that, when Germany felt like a country filled with nothing but the remains of war-ruined people, bombed-out houses, lines of hungry, fatherless children, and empty houses once filled with Jewish families, she thought about finding Jake and begging him to take her away.

And now, with the knowledge that evil men like Stefan still roamed free, it felt as though the events she was trying so hard to put behind her would never end.

Leaving her family and going to America was out of the question, but now, as she walked, she let her mind wander, imagining herself as she boarded a ship. Would she already feel homesick? Or would the sense of adventure and excitement of a new journey overshadow any immediate regrets? Seeing America sounded wonderful, and it might be an opportunity to help her family by sending money, but she knew that missing them, and marrying someone she barely knew, was a sacrifice she wasn't willing to make. When she pictured herself saying good-bye to her mother, a painful knot formed in her stomach. But it was the thought of spending her life with someone other than Isaac that burrowed its way into her chest and settled there, like a secret wound inside her heart.

Just then, quick, hollow footsteps echoed in the corridor behind her. She turned to look, but it was too late. Someone grabbed her from behind, knocking her against the alley wall with a bone-jarring thud. A hand seized her wrist, twisting her arm against her back.

"Remember me, Jew lover?" a man breathed in her ear. He shoved his body against hers. She thrashed beneath him, using every ounce of strength to push him off. It was no use. His full weight, nearly twice hers, pinned her to the wall like a moth beneath a rock. She could barely breathe.

"What do you want?" she asked, panting.

"I want you to keep your mouth shut," the man growled. "That's what I want."

It was Stefan.

Christine twisted her shoulders and kicked at his shins with her heels. "Why should I?"

He wrenched her arm higher. Pain shot through her wrist and elbow as muscle and bone were pulled in opposite directions. "Because I'm not the only one," Stefan hissed. "There are more of us.

And if you don't keep your mouth shut, we'll make sure you pay. I know where your father and your brothers work. Ruins can be dangerous. Anything could happen."

She grimaced, squeezing her eyes shut.

"And stay away from Kate," he said. "We know how to find you. You're marked, remember?" He dug his thumbnail deep into the number on her wrist, pressing harder and harder until she was certain the skin would break. Then, grunting, he shoved his pelvis into her buttocks and grabbed her breast.

"What a waste to have a fine German girl like you spoiled by a Jew," he whispered. Then he gave her one final shove and let go. She felt him move away, the weight and heat of his body leaving her. She waited, forehead against the painted plaster, until she heard him running down the alley before daring to look up. She put a hand to the side of her face. There was no blood, but her cheek was scraped and sore. On her wrist, the red imprint of his nail divided the tattooed numbers in half.

She looked up to see if anyone had witnessed what had happened. The windows of the surrounding houses were open, but there were no shocked faces peering down, no children looking on with curious eyes. The cobblestone alley was as silent as a cemetery.

She checked behind her, to make sure Stefan wasn't coming back, then started toward the slice of sunlight on the opposite end of the alley. After a few steps, her breath caught in her chest. She stopped and raked her hands down the sides of her head, tears of rage building up in her eyes. Then, refusing to let him win, she clenched her teeth and threw her fists down to her sides, taking long, even strides until she was out of the alley, into the bright, open street.

On her way home, awareness swirled like a snarled knot of chaos in her mind, making every man suspect, every narrow alleyway a trap. Hanna's brother had seen SS guards running into the woods at Dachau. Her own father had seen SS stealing uniforms from regular Wehrmacht soldiers. How was she supposed to know who was who?

CHAPTER 33

The next day, a Sunday, the sky had a smooth, shiny quality to it, as if a sheet of glass hung above, spreading from one end of the horizon to the other, like a vast, translucent glacier. Lilacs perfumed the air, and the occasional breeze carried the aroma of freshly turned soil.

During the war, the pastor of Christine's church had been arrested, the congregation had been afraid to assemble for fear of being labeled traitors, and the church itself had suffered a hit that weakened the front wall and destroyed the steeple. Mutti said that the bomb had missed destroying the entire building by mere inches, exploding in a colossal brown shower of earth and grass that created a deep crater in the lawn. After the initial blast, the front wall had collapsed, spraying primeval fieldstone and mortar into the street. But through it all, the ceiling and back three-quarters of the church had remained unharmed.

From the market square, in honor of the first day in five years that service would be held in the partially restored church, the ancient carillon of St. Michael's rang high in the cathedral's towering sandstone steeple. For a full hour, the town's only remaining church bells' melody looped over and over, echoing through the sun-drenched streets with the soaring peals of celebration.

Christine wanted the bells to stop ringing. How could anyone celebrate, when it felt like nothing had changed? Her cheek had turned purple and crimson while she slept. It felt hot and swollen, fluid jiggling beneath the skin when she moved her head too fast. Knowing her parents couldn't do anything, and deciding not to worry them until she had a plan, she'd forced herself to laugh when she told everyone how she'd tripped and fallen in the middle of the street, her skirt up over her legs for everyone to see. Oma prescribed vinegar and honey, followed by plenty of sunshine, then checked Christine's elbows and knees for further injuries that might require her medical expertise.

"I'm fine, really," Christine had told them. "I don't know how I managed it, but I landed on my face."

Hurrying so they wouldn't be late for church, the family gathered between the garden fence and the house, the narrow corridor dappled gray and white by the sun coming through the branches of the plum trees.

"Where's Maria?" Christine asked when she noticed her sister missing.

"She's not feeling well," Mutti said, her forehead furrowed with concern. Christine knew what her mother was thinking: typhus or tuberculosis. With the ongoing shortage of medical supplies and lack of food, disease had become epidemic; either infection could be a death sentence. Christine's first instinct was to ease her mother's anxiety by telling her the truth, that Maria probably had morning sickness. But she couldn't betray her sister's trust. Maria was still too fragile. *We're going to have to tell everyone soon,* she thought.

Christine thought about going back to see if Maria was all right, but she didn't want to walk into church alone. This would be her first public appearance since her return, and her arms and legs already vibrated with nervous tension. Oma was halfway across the street, anxious to find a seat before the service started. Christine hesitated, looking up at the windows of the house, hoping to see Maria looking out, but the shutters were pulled closed.

"Hurry up, Christine!" her mother called. Christine rushed around the garden fence to catch up.

Clusters of people dressed in their Sunday best gathered like blooming sprays of wildflowers randomly sprouted in the green churchyard. Christine kept her eyes on the walkway, sensing numerous heads turning in her direction as she walked with her family toward the entrance.

Inside the sanctuary, the murmur of people talking gave way to silence, as every head turned to watch her come in. Christine looked down at her feet, painfully aware that her blue Sunday dress still hung loose on her frame. To hide her short hair and any bald spots she might have created, she wore Oma's red scarf around her head, tied tight at the nape of her neck. She kept the edge of her sweater sleeve clenched inside her fist, to hide her tattooed wrist.

Because of the construction, the first rows of pews were kept vacant for the service. The new minister stood at the head of the center aisle, the raw, freshly-mortared façade rising high above his head. At the front of the church, a dozen wrought iron candelabras stood behind a string of lilac-filled vases. The smell of burning candles and the wet odor of fresh mortar overpowered the lilacs, making the inside of the church smell like a mausoleum.

Several people left their pews and came over to Christine, some speaking a soft "Welcome home," and "We're glad to see you're all right." Others smiled briefly at her, then turned their attention to Vater and Mutti. They put their arms around her mother, kissed her cheek, and shook her father's hand. The elderly men and the few returned soldiers grasped her father by the shoulder and thumped him on the back. With trembling hands, nearly every woman held a handkerchief beneath her nose and watery eyes.

"We're still waiting for word," some sniffed.

The *Kriegswitwen,* war widows, were silent.

Christine and her family slid into a pew near the center of the church, Christine between her mother and father. Once settled, she looked around to see who else was there, then stiffened when she saw Kate sitting six rows ahead, wearing an emerald dress that shimmered like silk, her fiery red hair blazing along her shoulders. Compared to her, everyone else looked watered down and weary. Kate's mother was beside her, and she turned to wave at Christine and her family. On the other side of Kate, sitting tall and erect, his dark blond hair precisely trimmed, was Stefan.

Kate twisted in her seat to see whom her mother was smiling at. When she saw Christine, she spun around, leaned toward Stefan, and whispered something in his ear. Stefan's head slowly rotated on his neck, the rest of his body barely moving as he turned, his face flat and expressionless. When his clear blue eyes met Christine's, she held his gaze. *You can't do anything to me here.*

He turned back around, and she looked down at her wrist, at the red imprint of his nail splitting the numbers in half. She could still hear the hatred in his voice and remember the way he'd twisted her arm. She shifted in her seat. *Maybe I should stand up and tell everyone what kind of man he really is.* Craning her neck, she looked at the elderly woman sitting beside Stefan. She'd never met his mother, but she wanted to see what the parent of an SS looked like. She could see the top of her head, white hair smoothed into a braided bun. When the woman turned slightly, Christine saw plump cheeks above a sweet smile. *Now you're acting like them,* she scolded herself. *What did you expect, horns and a tail?*

It reminded her of when she had first met Stefan, how excited Kate had been because he was teaching her English and taking her to the theater in Berlin. *How does a privileged, educated man turn into a cold-blooded killer?* Christine thought. A chill passed through her as she remembered what else Stefan had said.

She sat up, pretending to be bored, and scrutinized every unfamiliar man in the church. Blood rose to her cheeks as she looked for the others he'd warned her about, searching for evidence. Maybe it was crazy, thinking she'd be able to tell SS just by looking at them, but she looked anyway, certain she'd see or feel an aura of evil radiating from their heads, like a foul, poisonous gas. She knew that if she ever got close to anyone who'd worked in the camps, she'd recognize something in their eyes: a blankness, a disconnectedness, a black flash that would reveal the contamination in their ruined souls.

Two rows behind Stefan and Kate, a broad-shouldered man had his arm around a petite, golden-haired woman, his freckled, beefy hand resting on the back of the pew. *Possibility number one,* Christine thought. A few rows farther back on the opposite side, an oily-faced man about her father's age sat with his chin raised. *Possibility number two,* she thought, her breath growing shallow. Possibility number three sat near the middle of the church; a middle-aged man with slicked-back hair and unruly eyebrows.

The air of the church grew heavy. Her vision blurred. On her lap, her pale hands swam like white fish in the blue sea of her skirt. *I have to say something,* she thought. *I have to tell everyone about Stefan. But what if they won't do anything? What if they don't believe me? I have no proof.*

Mutti linked her arm through Christine's, resting her hand on top of hers. Christine thought maybe she'd noticed her fidgeting, her thumb unable to stop moving over the number on her wrist. But when Mutti did the same to Heinrich, sitting on her other side, Christine realized her mother was just happy to have her children by her side.

Softly at first, as if the organist was unsure of either his instrument or his ability, the pipe organ started to play. Slowly and cautiously, the music reached higher and higher crescendos, filling the hushed, cool church. Since her return, Christine hadn't heard real music, only the screeching, ghoulish waltz that swirled and twisted throughout her nightmares. Now, hearing the strong, perfect notes from the organ, her neck tingled and her eyes welled up. The last time she had been in this church was the day her father was drafted. It felt like a lifetime ago. *Isaac was still alive,* she thought. *What if I'd known how bad it was going to get? What could I have changed?*

She looked down at her mother's calloused hand resting over hers. With every crease and blister, with every age spot and hard piece of skin, she saw her mother's hard work. Hard work carried out in the name of love. Her mother always did what she thought was right. *And so did I,* she thought. *But all the love and hard work in the world won't protect anyone from fate.* Lost in thought, Christine jumped when the wooden pews creaked in unison, like a thousand snapping bones, as everyone stood to sing.

She stood, and her father put his arm around her. He smiled and tightened his grip, pulling her closer. Then, with soft tentative voices, the choir and congregation began to sing. *What did Maria and I do to deserve all this pain,* she thought, *while Stefan still walks free? Was it something we did? Some unknown sin we committed as children? Or is it that the world is getting closer to the end of its days, and the devil is winning the war for people's souls, preparing for his final reign?* She'd found herself asking the same questions during her dark, hopeless time in the camp, more certain with every passing day that the entire world must be coming to an end. But then the war was over, and Hitler's diabolical plan had been stopped in its tracks. Good had conquered evil. Now she wondered if the end of the war was only a temporary pause, a stumble over an obstacle on the certain path toward complete destruction. Hitler was dead and Europe lay in ruins, yet she was surprised and distraught to find that the questions hadn't changed. *But good can still stand up against evil. And maybe the best place to do that is here.*

The minister's sermon was brief. After he finished, he asked the congregation to bow their heads in prayer. He thanked God that the war was over, that the people of the village were able to return to worship in the church. He thanked the Americans for providing assistance. He prayed for his fellow countrymen in the French, British, and Soviet zones of occupation, giving recognition to all who'd survived, civilians and soldiers alike. He prayed for the refugees who'd found themselves on the wrong side of borders, the inhabitants of communities established for centuries who were now being killed or driven from their lands by those opposed to anything or anyone German. He prayed for those who hadn't survived, expressing gratitude to the brave men and boys who'd given their lives for their country, and asked for the safe return of the tens of thousands of soldiers still missing. He prayed for the Jewish families who'd vanished.

"May they find peace wherever they are, and may the perpetrators behind their disappearance be brought to justice," he said. "And may those who know the truth speak out."

Christine went rigid. She opened her eyes and looked up at the minister, certain he would be looking directly at her. But his eyes were closed. Her heartbeat quickened. She knew the truth. Six rows ahead sat a guilty man. She scanned the congregation of bowed heads, wondering if anyone else knew there was an SS murderer in the crowd.

All at once, she was overcome by the burning desire to get up and walk out of the church. *How can there be a God when Stefan is allowed to live, while Isaac was slaughtered like an animal? How can we thank God when the innocent have been raped, starved, tortured, and murdered, while the truly evil men will probably die of old age in their beds?* She put a hand on the back of her neck, her fingers pressing against the scarf, searching for the threadlike hairs beneath the material. She needed to touch her hair, to feel the silky softness against her fingertips. *To rip it out,* she thought. With herculean effort, she pulled her hand away from her head and folded her arms across her chest. *Nein. I can't let them win.*

She gripped the pew in front of her and leaned forward, her heart thundering like a train in her chest. Out of the corner of her eye, she saw her mother's head lift and turn toward her. Christine took a deep breath and stood. She cleared her throat.

"I have something to say."

A sea of heads bobbed upright. A hundred faces turned toward her. The minister stopped praying and opened his eyes. Christine's mother grabbed her hand. Christine looked at Kate, who had turned completely around in her seat and was staring back at her with wide, shocked eyes. Stefan turned to see who had spoken, his blue eyes calm, his eyebrows raised in curiosity. *He doesn't think I'll say anything,* Christine thought. *There's not a trace of fear on his face.*

Just as Christine opened her mouth to speak, her mother tugged hard on her hand.

"*Nein,*" Mutti whispered.

Christine looked down at Mutti's frightened eyes. She looked at her father, aware of how much he'd aged, his hollow cheeks and gray hair telling the story of all he'd endured. He sat with his arms folded, staring at the floor. When she'd told him about Stefan two days ago, he'd understood her anger, but said it was too dangerous to get involved. And yet, now, he wasn't stopping her.

"Do you have something to say?" the minister asked in the quiet church.

Christine gritted her teeth, unable to feel anything but her mother's fingers crushing hers. She pulled her hand out of her mother's grasp. *I'm sorry,* she thought. *But I have to do this.*

"Ja," she said, lifting her chin. She looked at the minister, blood rising in her cheeks. Her eyes wandered over the crowd of expectant, staring faces. Then she pointed at Stefan. "That man right there," she said. "I saw him. In the camps. He was an SS guard in Dachau."

A collective gasp filled the church. Women put gloved hands over their open mouths. Old men turned in their seats to look at her. Everyone started whispering and talking at the same time. Kate jumped up from her seat, her face pale, her hands balled in fists.

"She doesn't know what she's talking about!" she said. "She's crazy! When I went to see her the other day, she was going on and on, telling the most unbelievable stories!"

"I'm telling the truth!" Christine said. "I saw Stefan in Dachau! He did this to my face because he thinks he can keep me quiet!"

"Bitte, let's settle down," the minister said, gesturing with a Bible in his hand. *"Fräuleins, bitte.* You're in the house of God!"

"You can't believe anything she says!" Kate said, wild eyes scanning the crowd. "Look at her! She's been sick! She's delusional! She risked her life to save a Jew!"

Stefan stood and put a hand on Kate's arm, trying to calm her, his face void of emotion. He looked in Christine's direction, causing anger and frustration to unfurl in every fiber of her body, like a scorching, vile wave that washed over every muscle and nerve. Christine felt her mother beside her, sniffing and wiping her eyes.

"He has a black uniform," Christine said. "She told me. He's proud of it. He showed it to her."

"A black uniform doesn't mean anything," a man said. "The Waffen-SS wore black, and they fought on the front lines."

"Stefan's uniform has a skull and crossbones," Christine said. "He was a member of the Totenkopfverbände Unit. I saw him hold a gun to a young boy's head after ripping him from his mother's arms!"

Stefan's mother slowly got to her feet, holding her son's arm for support. She smiled, the skin of her plump cheeks as pink and smooth as the underbelly of a newborn goat.

"I'm sorry, *Fräulein,"* she said in a soft, wavering voice. "You must have my son confused with someone else. He came home wearing a *feldgrauer* uniform. He was with the *Heer,* the land forces of the army. He's a decorated war hero."

"That's right," Kate spit at Christine. "He served his country well!"

"Just like your father, Christine!" another voice said.

"Then he stole that uniform!" Christine said, feeling veins pulsate in her forehead. "He's pretending to be Wehrmacht because he was a guard at Dachau!"

The minister was moving down the aisle now, toward Christine, his lips pressed together in a hard, thin line.

"Stop saying that!" Kate yelled. She started to move past Stefan, to fight her way out of the pew, but Stefan held her back, whispering in her ear.

"It will be better to let it go," the minister said to Christine. "You're home now. That's all that matters."

"We were at war," a woman shouted. "I'm sure everyone was forced to do things they didn't want to do."

"We have to stick together," someone else said. "The entire world hates us now."

Christine looked around the room, a sea of faces looking up at her, mouths hard with anger, brows furrowed in fear, eyes filled with shock and pity. "You have no idea what you're talking about!" she shouted, feeling as if she'd saved all of her pent-up rage for this moment, and now it was boiling over.

"What if you're wrong?" someone shouted. "What if you're accusing an innocent man?"

"If Stefan is innocent," Christine said, "he should tell everyone what the SS guards did." She looked at Kate. "Did he admit that to you? Or did he lie about that too?"

"He's a good man," Kate said.

Stefan's mother had pulled a white handkerchief from her purse and was using it to wipe her eyes, her hands trembling.

"Let it go!" someone said.

"You have no idea what I saw!" Christine shouted. "You have no idea what the SS did!"

The minister was talking to the suspicious-looking man with the unruly eyebrows and pointing at Christine. The man with the unruly brows came out of the pew and stood beside the minister, his chest puffed out, ready for a struggle.

"It'd be best if you go home and get some rest," the minister said. "You're welcome to come back when you're feeling better. The rest of us are here to worship. We're very sorry for what you've been through, but this is not the time or place. It's not up to any of us to decide who is guilty or innocent."

"They were murdering women and children!" Christine cried. "And Stefan was helping them!"

The people sitting next to Christine and her family emptied the bench and stood in the aisle, staring at her as if she'd gone mad. The man with the unruly eyebrows started to enter the pew, but Christine's father stood, putting an arm out to stop him.

"We'll take her home," he said, a hand on the man's chest. "There's no need for force." The man stepped back, glaring at Christine. Vater took Christine by the arm.

"You can't let them get away with it!" Christine shouted as Vater guided her out of the pew and led her out of the church, her mother, brothers, and Oma close behind. Out on the steps, Christine yanked away from her father's grasp and ran out of the churchyard.

"Christine!" her mother called.

Christine ignored her and headed down the hill. She wanted to be alone, away from all of them. Halfway down the street, she glanced back to see her family crossing the walk in front of their house, heads hanging. The overwhelming feeling of being completely alone hit her with such force that she stopped running and sobbed out loud. She pulled the scarf from her head and stood in the center of the road, wondering what to do and where to go.

Beneath her sleeve, the number on her wrist began to itch and burn. She pressed her thumb against it, then ran her fingers down the soft strands of hair behind her ear, the bone of her skull hard beneath her skin. She pictured Isaac's dead body lying in the woods, and yanked out a tuft of hair. The pain was sharp and instant, and for a few blissful seconds, there was nothing else.

Then she heard her mother screaming.

CHAPTER 34

Christine followed her mother's screams, her legs like stone as she raced toward the open front door. In the foyer, her father was sitting on the floor, sobbing, his head in his hands. Oma leaned against the wall, the boys held to her heaving chest, their faces buried in the folds of her blouse. Mutti was on her knees, howling next to Maria's crumpled body. Maria's face was bone white, her thin neck twisted at an odd angle, one stocking foot on the bottom stair.

Christine's heart went black. She entered the foyer, the floor pitching beneath her, fear filling the back of her throat like a greasy slick of oil. She fell to her knees beside her sister. *Nein!* Her mind screamed. *Nein! This can't be! It isn't real!* Her mind raced backwards, to what had just happened in church, wondering if she was being punished for trying to ruin someone's life, for taking matters into her own hands, for thinking she could make the final judgment on Stefan. Oma's words rang in her ears: "God makes the final judgment on us all." *I'll take it back!* she thought. *Stefan can go free! I'll take it back!*

"Maria?" she cried. "Maria! Get up!" She took Maria's hand in hers. It was soft and limp. Christine screamed until her throat was raw, her stomach twisting, the veins in her forehead ready to burst. When her voice gave out, she tasted blood.

Christine's beloved sister lay on the tile floor like a discarded rag doll, her red sweater gathered under her arms, her legs and arms splayed at unnatural angles. The blond, feathery lashes beneath her closed eyes were wet with tears, and a drop of maroon blood sat below one nostril. Christine squeezed her eyes shut, hoping the image would be gone when she reopened them. Like a jolt, a memory came to her. A traveling carnival had come to town, and the next day, Christine had walked into the kitchen to find five-year-old Maria next to the woodstove, holding a burning stick over her open mouth, trying to swallow flames, like the fire-eater at the carnival. Seven-year-old Christine froze in place, one hand on the door, panicked and not knowing what to do. Luckily, Mutti came into the kitchen just in time to grab the burning stick from Maria's hand.

Even back then, before she had fully understood the finality of death, Christine had wondered how she'd carry on if anything happened to her little sister. For weeks afterward, she followed Maria around, worried she'd try another trick—walking a tightrope or juggling knives—and Christine would, once again, fail to protect her.

Now, Christine had done just that. She opened her eyes and reached out to touch Maria's face, holding her breath, as if one touch would shatter it like glass. Her trembling fingers touched her sister's cheek. Maria's skin was ice cold. Christine moaned and slumped over, covering her sister's upper body with her own. She started shaking, her limbs vibrating out of control, her breath coming in short, shallow gasps. One after the other, before she could catch her next mouthful of air, violent sobs burst from her throat, each wail wrenching the strength from her body. A block of ice pressed against her heart as guilt replaced the vacuum of shock.

"I'm so sorry!" she wailed. "I shouldn't have left you alone! Why didn't you listen to me?"

Mutti looked up at Christine, her eyes like bleeding wounds in her skull. "What do you mean? What are you talking about?"

Christine lifted her head, and somehow the words came, even as her heart shattered into a million pieces. "She was pregnant! She was pregnant and I couldn't convince her that everything would be all right!"

Mutti crushed Maria's body to hers. "Oh *nein!*" she screamed. *"Nein!"*

With gulping sobs, Vater went to Mutti's side, and they cradled Maria in their arms, caressing the thin, pale cheeks of their lost child. It was more than Christine could bear. She ran to the threshold and retched on the steps, then crumpled against the open front door, her vision blurring. With what little strength she had left, she crawled the rest of the way outside and lay on the walk, shivering and hoping she'd pass out. It was no use. Her parents' sobs echoed out of the hall into the still morning air, drowning out the muffled hymn coming from the church across the road, like the dead crying out from beyond the grave.

The long days following Maria's funeral were humid and hot, and the white sky hung hazy and low. Every other night, rumbling storms jolted Christine awake, heart hammering, brow beaded with sweat. She'd throw back the covers and jump to her feet, ready to run, before realizing that the double-barreled crashes and echoing booms were rolling thunder, not dropping bombs. Relieved, she'd fall back on her bed, limp and trying to catch her breath, until, in the next instant, realization sent a hollow draft of sorrow through her bones.

Maria was dead.

Images flashed in her mind: her sister lying in a coffin; her parents sobbing over the open grave. Then the hot flush of panic would seize her all over again, and she'd stay awake, restless and clammy until morning.

In the garden beneath a blazing sun, she spent hours digging and weeding, while over and over in her mind, she replayed what had happened, wondering what she could have said or done differently. Wiping the dripping wet sweat from her face, she worked until her legs trembled, punishing herself for not staying home from church that day. When she was done, she'd stagger into the house, her red face smeared with a mixture of dirt and tears, hoping sheer exhaustion would help her forget that Isaac and Maria were dead.

At the end of the week, Vater went back to work. The family needed the money, and there was nothing more he could do for Mutti, who'd taken to spending her days in bed. On the first day of his return to work, Christine made Vater a lunch of rye bread spread thick with lard, then wrapped it carefully in brown paper. On her way to the construction site, she walked fast, glancing behind her and avoiding the shortcut through the alley.

At the site, the sounds of hammers and saws filled the air. Four men balanced precariously on the second-floor beams, hammering roof joists into place. Other men mortared stone along each cellar wall, the scrape and slap of their trowels grating at her nerves. She didn't see Vater anywhere. She held one hand over her eyes, trying to make out a familiar face in the blinding sun.

"Who're you looking for?" one of the men called down from the roof.

"My father," she yelled. "He just returned to work today."

"Some of the workers were sent to clear out the other cellar," the man told her. "Back where the kitchen and storage building used to be."

"Danke," she said, waving. A square of barren earth stretched to the back of the next block, dappled here and there with thin patches of struggling grass. Near the center of the yard, a rubble-filled cellar fell into the earth like the yawning cavity of an extracted tooth.

At the edge of the hole, two men reached down to lift out scorched timber and heavy stones, then passed the pieces to the men behind them. Like a fire brigade, the other men hoisted the charred remains toward a waiting horse-drawn wagon.

Christine edged toward the crumbling perimeter of the cellar and looked down on the men digging through the ashes and dust, the smell of damp, burnt wood drifting out of the hole like the stench of an exhumed grave. A melted jumble of blackened canisters, twisted chairs, and burnt pipes fused with the building ruins to create a gnarled, lifeless landscape.

Standing on an unstable pile of rubble below the other men, Herr Weiler wiped his face with a bandanna and looked up. He stuffed the rag in his pants pocket and made his way toward her.

"How's your father?" he said, squinting up at her.

"What do you mean?"

"I thought he was coming back today," Herr Weiler said. "Is he sick?"

"*Nein,*" she said. "I saw him leave for work this morning."

Herr Weiler shook his head. "No one's seen him all day."

The blood drained from Christine's face. Images flashed in her mind: Stefan stabbing her father in a deserted alley; her father lying there, dying and confused, sprawled in a growing puddle of blood.

She dropped the bagged lunch and ran, racing through the cobblestone streets, calling her father's name. Everyone around her seemed to move in slow motion, while her own movements felt sped up, every step insect-like and jittery. She stopped everyone she knew, grabbing them by their shirtsleeves, asking if they'd seen him. Some shook their heads, yanking themselves from her grasp as if she had a disease; others said no with fear-filled eyes, as if the war were still going on and she were a member of the Gestapo, ready to throw them in jail if they answered her question incorrectly. Only the shoemaker's wife bothered to ask what was wrong.

When she saw an American jeep lumbering in her direction, she stood in the road, putting her hands up to stop it. The Americans were her only hope. They'd want to know about an SS guard in hiding, wouldn't they? The jeep swerved around her and kept going. As it sped past, she searched the American faces for Jake, but didn't see him. A second jeep slowed and stopped, a cloud of dirt rolling up behind it as the tires skidded across the cobblestones.

"Jake?" she said to the four Americans, hoping they might recognize the name. The driver shook his head. The front passenger said something she didn't understand, then made a motion for the driver to keep going. Two soldiers in the back elbowed each other, smiling and looking Christine up and down. One pulled a Hershey bar from his front pocket and held it out, whistling as if calling a dog. Christine shook her head. The men roared with laughter, and the driver put the vehicle in gear. She hurried around to the front of the jeep and put her hands on the hood, trying to figure out how to make them understand, hoping one of them spoke German.

"My father," she said, trying to catch her breath. "The SS have him!" The passenger in the front seat motioned for her to get out of the way. "Help," she said. The driver gunned the engine and glared at her. She gasped and stood back, her hand over her heart, her mind reeling as she tried to remember the English words she needed. "Father," she tried in English, her thick German tongue making the word come out "fadder." "Help" came out "helf."

The soldier in the passenger seat lifted his rifle and took aim at her head, staring at her with steady, dangerous eyes. She moved away from the jeep, arms limp, tears streaming down her cheeks. The Americans drove away. Suddenly, she realized that even if she could get them to listen, they probably wouldn't care about a missing German. *We're still the enemy.* Then she remembered the air base outside the village, crowded with American vehicles. Maybe she'd find Jake there, or someone who could speak German, someone who would help her. She stood in the road, trying to remember the shortest way to the base, then, trembling and nauseous, she headed east.

Five blocks over, she came to the end of town closest to the air base, the ill-fated section that had sustained the heaviest damage during the war. The eastern end of the village was gone, block after block turned into rubble. Burnt, jagged timbers and melted metal pointed skyward, like broken bones. The cobblestone streets, cleared down the center, looked like red, winding rivers flowing between rutted banks of crushed brick and shattered stone. Here and there, she saw chalked messages on the fractured walls of ruined buildings: *Greta and Helmut, we are alive, at Tante Helga's. Beloved daughter, Annelies Nille, Age 4, killed January 13, 1945. Still missing: Ingrid, Rita, and Johann Herzmann, age 32, 12, and 76.*

Christine held the edge of her sweater over her nose as she ran, imagining she could still smell the smoke, burning cinders, and melting flesh of the victims, people she used to see in church, on the sidewalks, and at the grocery store. Over four hundred people from her hometown, including babies and children, had been killed by bombings over the course of the war. She hurried past the scattered heaps of stone and shards of glass from a destroyed church and an old cemetery, where headstones leaned left and right or lay split and shattered on the ground. Along the edges of the road, bomb craters looked like newly dug graves.

Finally, she was out of the village, in the open fields, where she could see the air base near the mouth of the valley. She hurried toward it.

When she saw the security checkpoint, she slowed, praying one of the guards could understand enough German to let her pass. From behind her, a convoy of trucks and tanks approached, a column of dust and dirt rolling up like a black thundercloud in their wake. Christine stepped off the road to let the vehicles pass, a pale hand held up in greeting, hoping one of the soldiers would take pity on her, or think she was willing to have sex with him in exchange for a candy bar or stick of gum. She had to get inside, no matter what.

The engines roared in her ears, the tanks' massive tracks rattling and tearing at the earth. Groups of American soldiers sat on two trucks, crowded atop the roof and open bed like a swarm of schoolboys playing on a hill. A few glanced at Christine but didn't react.

When the first vehicle stopped at the checkpoint, Christine walked the length of the convoy, searching each cab for Jake. No one looked familiar. The driver of the last truck was alone, one arm out the window, a cigarette in his hand, head leaning back against the high seat. She approached the cab and was about to speak, when she noticed the soldier's eyes were closed. Clearly on edge, he took a long drag from his cigarette and blew out the smoke in a forceful stream, mumbling what sounded like angry words. She hurried toward the rear of the vehicle, praying there weren't any soldiers in the canvas-covered bed, ready to keep running if she was wrong.

To her relief, the back of the truck was full of wooden crates. She pulled herself up and threw herself between the tailgate and the canvas flap, her heart like a runaway train in her chest. There was just enough room to lie down sideways between the boxes and the sidewall of the truckbed. She crammed herself into the empty space, banging her elbow and forehead in the process, her nose and eyes stinging with the smell of burning diesel.

The gears of the engine squealed and caught, and the truck ambled forward, jostling Christine against the boxes like a sack of flour. She put her arms around her head, praying the vehicles wouldn't be searched before being let inside. At first the truck kept moving, but then, too quickly, it stopped. Over the growling engine, she heard voices, the driver talking, a loud bang, a series of muted clunks. Someone pulled open the canvas and she jumped. She felt rather than saw a soldier inspecting the packed bed. She held her breath, trying not to move.

Just when she thought the soldier was finished with his inspection, a rough hand seized her by the arm and yanked her up. The soldier yelled, drew his gun, and stepped back. The guards and the agitated driver trained their rifles on her as she climbed over the tailgate and jumped down, knees bent to keep from tumbling forward. A bristle-faced soldier barked an order in her face. She couldn't understand what he was saying, but she knew she was in trouble.

After the guards patted her down, the bristle-faced soldier dragged her past the checkpoint and across the compound, into a squat brick structure to the left of the control tower. Inside, an officer sat behind a desk, his balding head bowed over a jumble of maps and paperwork. When the soldier addressed him, he looked up. His cheeks and forehead were pale and lumpy, as if his skin were made of porridge. Surprise registered in his eyes. He stood and came toward them, listening as the soldier explained, then sat on the edge of the desk and studied Christine, arms folded across his chest.

"English?" he said to her. She shook her head. He scrutinized her a moment longer, as if searching her mind for devious motives, then said something to the bristle-faced soldier, who saluted and left the building. The officer pulled a chair away from the wall, metal legs scraping across the concrete floor, and motioned for Christine to sit in it. She did as she was told, legs and arms trembling, wondering if the officer could hear the blood thrashing through her veins. When he went back to his desk, she cleared her throat to get his attention. He looked at her, eyebrows raised.

She pulled back her sleeve, pointed to the number on her wrist, and said, "SS." The officer's face dropped, and he gave her a stiff nod. "Father," Christine said in English.

"Father?" he repeated, forehead furrowed in confusion. She nodded, putting a hand over her heart.

"Jake?" she said, silently berating herself for not knowing his last name, angry that she'd painted all Americans with the same brush. Maybe if she'd been willing to be friends instead of believing the worst, Stefan would already be behind bars.

Just then, the bristle-faced soldier returned with a blond man dressed in civilian clothing. When the civilian saw Christine, a look of surprise flickered across his face. Then he smiled, his mouth curling into a smug, satisfied grin. Her blood ran cold.

It was Stefan.

"Well, well, what do we have here?" he said.

Christine stared at the porridge-faced officer, hoping to convey her fear and anger with her eyes. She stood, pulled back her sleeve, jabbed her wrist again, and pointed at Stefan. "This man is SS!" she said, her words rattled by fury. "He is from Dachau!"

"You're not going to get anywhere with that old trick," Stefan said to her, his expression calm while his eyes twisted with savage glee. "These men trust me. I came to them, offering my services as a translator. I'm not the enemy anymore."

The officer said something to Stefan. She understood SS. Stefan shook his head, then went into a lengthy dialogue in English, gesturing with his hands and pointing at Christine. How ironic that they trusted a murderer just because he could speak their language. She thought she understood the words: Jew, Dachau, family, father, dead. The Americans winced several times, as if parts of Stefan's story were painful to hear.

"*Nein, nein, nein,*" Christine insisted, panic twisting in her chest. She pointed at Stefan again, made a stabbing motion with her fist toward her abdomen, and said, "SS. Father."

Stefan put a finger to his temple, made a circular motion, and whistled. The officer looked at her, eyes filled with pity. All at once, she put it together. He was telling them her family was dead, and that she had gone mad from the loss.

Unable to hold back any longer, Christine lunged at Stefan, swinging at his head, her fists colliding with his jaw, his neck, his temples.

"What did you do to my father?" she screamed. With no more effort than if he were wrestling a small child, Stefan grabbed her flailing arms and held on. She tore at his hands, trying to pry his strong fingers from her wrists. The bristle-faced soldier pulled her away and pushed her down in the chair, then held her there, his hands digging into her shoulders, waiting for her to calm down. Her breath came in short, shallow gasps, the tendons in her neck stretching and pulling as she struggled to get up. She wanted to rip Stefan's heart from his chest.

"Careful, little Jew lover," Stefan said, his voice soft, as if trying to calm her. "You're playing into everything I just told them."

"Where is my father?" she cried again, the words catching in her throat. Stefan said something to the soldier, and he reluctantly let go. Christine fought the urge to jump out of the chair again, her nails digging into the wooden arms. But Stefan was right; she had to pull herself together or the Americans would never believe her.

"What did you think would happen after your little stunt in church the other day?" Stefan said, kneeling in front of her, his face a mask of feigned kindness. "I told you I'd make you pay."

"Bitte," she said. "Just tell me where he is."

"Let me see," he said. "I believe he's being questioned about his involvement in war crimes. *Ja,* that's it. I heard someone say he was in trouble."

"Questioned? Questioned by whom? He hasn't done anything wrong! The Americans are in charge now! Not you! And not your SS friends!"

Stefan stood and said something to the officer, who nodded, his lips pressed together, as if concerned for her well-being. "You're right," Stefan said. "The Americans are in charge now, and they're holding SS and Wehrmacht alike in Dachau."

Christine swallowed. "Dachau?"

"*Ja,* and that's where your father is headed because you didn't do as you were told."

"But they won't keep him there," she cried. "They'll find out he was just a regular soldier and release him!" She looked up at the Americans, who gaped as if listening to a doctor explain a terminal diagnosis to a patient.

Stefan shook his head, as if delivering bad news for a second time, his calm confidence as unmistakable as the steel-blue color of his eyes. "Did I forget to mention my old uniform fit him perfectly? Right down to the boot size? He's going to have a hard time talking his way out of that."

"But he hasn't done anything wrong," she cried. "I'll go to Dachau and tell them who the real war criminal is!"

"Go ahead and try. Because right now, all Germans are guilty until proven innocent. They're holding women in Dachau too. Maybe if I'm lucky, they'll lock you up and my troubles will be over. Try to remember, I'm the one with the power right now. I'll throw your mother or little brothers in a hidden room or underground vault somewhere, and the Americans will never find them. This is still our territory, remember? These old villages are full of tunnels, and the alleys and houses are nothing but a maze. Whoever I take next will just rot away. Like you should have."

Christine glared at him, hatred hardening inside her chest.

"Jake?" she tried again, looking up at the officer. With the mention of an American name, the officer's face went dark, and he said something to Stefan.

"Now he thinks you might be here to cause trouble for one of his men," Stefan told her. "The American soldiers have a strict no fraternization policy with adult German civilians. He wants to know if you're aware that all Germans aged fourteen to sixty-five in the occupation zone are required to register for compulsory labor, under threat of prison or withdrawal of ration cards."

Christine nodded, pretending she had complied. It was no use; she wasn't going to get anywhere with the Americans, especially with Stefan here. The officer went to the wall behind his desk, where he pulled half a dozen cans from a shelf. He put the cans in a cloth sack and held it out to her, like a dead animal hanging between them. On trembling legs she stood and took it, her burning eyes glued on Stefan.

"I don't know how," she said to him, "but I will make you pay."

Stefan made a move to put his arms around her and she shoved him backwards, spitting in his face. The officer stepped between them, scowling and motioning for Christine to leave. The bristle-faced soldier grabbed her by the arm and led her out of the building.

Christine held the sack to her chest as the soldier dragged her across the air base, trying to figure out what to do next. She glanced at him out of the corner of her eye, wondering if he would help. His face was set, his brows furrowed in determination.

"Help?" Christine said. The soldier ignored her and kept moving. She stopped and yanked her arm from his grasp. "Help," she tried again, firmly this time. He grabbed her arm and wrenched her forward.

Halfway across the compound, she saw two jeeps at the security checkpoint, one carrying three soldiers, the other carrying two. She squinted, trying to pick out a familiar face, but they were too far away, and the soldiers' helmeted heads were turned in the other direction; they were talking with the guards. Then the jeeps entered the air base, drawing closer. In the second jeep, Christine saw a white grin and a line of blond hair.

"Jake!" she shouted, pulling away from the soldier. She tried to run but wasn't fast enough. The soldier caught her by the shoulder and pushed her down in the dirt, the sack of cans colliding like rocks with her chest, knocking the wind from her lungs. She gulped for air and tried to stand, watching the jeeps as they sped past. The soldier yanked her upright and pulled her toward the exit, leaving the cans of food scattered like a child's building blocks in the yellowed grass. She twisted her shoulders, trying to get away, but he yelled and tightened his grip, his blunt-ended fingers digging deep into her upper arm.

"Christine!" a voice shouted behind them.

She craned her neck and saw Jake sprinting toward her, a rifle in one hand, his forehead crumpled in concern. The bristle-faced soldier stopped and waited for Jake to catch up, his face a sour mixture of irritation and uncertainty. When Jake reached them, he said something to the soldier. They argued for a moment. Jake rolled his eyes and reached into his pocket, pulling out several pieces of folded green paper that looked like money. He slid two bills from the fold and held them out to the soldier, who glanced back at the officer's building, then took the money and shoved it in his pocket. Scowling, he started walking again, still gripping Christine by the arm.

Jake took Christine's other arm, and the three of them hurried toward the security checkpoint. When they neared the stone ruins of a small outbuilding, Jake pulled her behind it, glancing around nervously. The bristle-faced soldier kept going. Jake said something she didn't understand. Then, certain no one was watching, the same German words he had first spoken at the train station: "May I help?"

CHAPTER 35

The creaking train, overflowing with women, children, and either very old or wounded men, shuddered and lurched to a stop, wheels screeching and whistles shrieking, like the dying screams of a giant, tortured animal. Christine woke with a start, her heart thundering beneath her ribs, her neck stiff. Again, she had to remind herself that she was on a real passenger train, with glass windows and cloth seats, nothing more.

The other passengers peered out the windows, wondering why they were stopping in the middle of nowhere again. Not that they'd be able to see the cause of the delay, but it was an automatic reaction every time the train came to an unexpected stop. With each holdup, rumors traveled through the overloaded cars about what had caused the setback. First there was a disabled tank on the tracks, then a group of refugees with a broken wagon. Once, the tracks needed repair; another time, they were out of coal. The passengers had no way of knowing what was true. The last stop had been the longest, when two American soldiers had gone through the cars with their rifles drawn, examining every face as if they were looking for someone. Luckily the problems were always resolved and the train started moving again, but no one had expected the trip to take this long.

Two days earlier, Christine had stood on the station platform, the hot smell of burning coal, the black engine, the trembling cars making her want to run away screaming. It was all she could do to climb the stairs and find a seat in the crowded car, her thumbnail digging deep into her wrist. She had tried telling herself she was lucky to find a spot when she did, because more and more passengers kept coming, filling the aisle with bodies and boxes and suitcases, until there wasn't room to walk or move. Except she didn't feel lucky; she felt trapped and claustrophobic, wishing more than anything she could get off the train and go home.

She'd waited three days for a train heading in the right direction, and it seemed as if the whole of Germany had been waiting too. When the railroad cars pulled away from the station, hordes of displaced persons still lined the platform, elbowing each other for space, their eyes hollow with desperation. Pleading with the boarded passengers, children held out their last crusts of bread, women offered necklaces and earrings previously hidden inside their clothes, all in exchange for one last spot on the cars. One woman ran alongside the tracks, handed her baby to someone on the moving train, then fell in a heap on the cement, screaming as she watched her child disappear.

Once the train was fully underway, Christine had to remind herself to breathe, watching the green and brown patchwork of the Kocher River valley lumber past her window, every mile revealing the battered countryside full of bombed-out towns and ruined cities. Survivors cooked over open fires in the streets and washed in the streams, living in tent cities made of soot-covered rugs and tattered blankets. When she couldn't take it anymore, she stopped looking, trying instead to figure out how she was going to save Vater and get the Americans to arrest Stefan. Finally, she fell into a mind-numbing pattern of staring out the window and fitful dozing, jerking awake each time a child cried or someone coughed, her heart hammering in her chest until she realized she wasn't in a filthy boxcar filled with prisoners.

Now, the train started moving again. She clutched her mother's purse in her lap, her train tickets, the change from Jake's ten-dollar bill, Vater's letters and his *Soldbuch*, identification and service book, stashed inside. Outside, it was pouring, the trees and electric poles smudges of green and brown, blurring past the rain-streaked windows. She closed her eyes and remembered Mutti's red cheeks, wet with tears as she handed over Vater's cherished correspondence, a dog-eared stack tied with brown twine like a tattered gift. She remembered the terror in her mother's eyes when she had first learned her husband had been thrown in jail, and heard Mutti's words, uneven and high, asking why, what did the Americans think he had done? The look of confusion and helplessness on her mother's face had burned itself into Christine's memory.

"It's my fault," Christine had said, the words tearing at her throat. "Stefan did this to Vater because of me." Mutti had begged to go with her, but Christine had insisted she stay home with Oma and the boys. "Besides," Christine said, "you don't need to see that awful place. I'll bring Vater home, I promise."

She told Mutti to keep the boys home from work, to keep an eye out for Stefan, and, if anyone asked, to say Christine was sick in bed. Because if Stefan found out that Christine was going to Dachau, there was no telling what he might do. Luckily, he had no idea she could afford a train ticket. Jake had understood the words *train* and *money*. Back at the base, she'd tried to tell Jake that his superiors trusted a man who used to be SS, but their language barrier was too great. She was wasting precious time. She needed to get to Dachau, and to Vater, as soon as possible. Because if Dachau was being used as a war crimes enclosure, someone there had to speak fluent German, and maybe he would listen to her. In the end, Jake had given her what she needed without question, his eyes sad, as if he'd never see her again.

Now, outside the train windows, red tile roofs and pockmarked stucco came into view, along with the long, brick building of a crowded station. Christine knew, by asking the elderly woman seated next to her, that the train would stop in the village of Dachau, and, from there, she would have to walk. The woman confirmed that the Americans were keeping POWs at the camp, warning that they chased the locals away, especially if they were trying to bring food to the prisoners. When the passengers from the train disembarked, the old woman put a gnarled hand on Christine's arm, wishing her luck before disappearing into the crowd.

On the other side of the station, Christine stopped in her tracks, her stomach twisting. The main thoroughfare was crowded, from one direction to the other, with a throng of horses, carts, and people. They were refugees, some of the millions of ethnic Germans expelled by the Allies from centuries-old communities in Poland, Czechoslovakia, and Hungary, their only crime that they were German. Now, they were trying to find new homes in what was left of Germany. The massive human procession moved slowly west, like a giant, sluggish serpent. A parade of grim-faced women, skeletal children, and the elderly trudged forward in unison, some with white armbands on one sleeve, others with heads down, pulling their possessions in farm wagons, baby carriages, and hand carts. The only sounds were shuffling footsteps and the creak of dry axles and wooden wheels. Even the children were silent. Remnants of the exiled Germans' flight littered the trampled edges of the dirt road: fragments of broken stoneware, solitary shoes, the scattered contents of a child's lost suitcase, the splintered, wooden spokes of wagon wheels, the bloated corpse of a horse. Christine heard her father's voice in her head.

War makes victims all.

She gritted her teeth and joined the procession. The narrow, one-lane road was nothing but mud and manure, its length marred and rutted by wagon wheels and tank tracks. She kept her eyes straight ahead, ignoring the mist that floated around the trees like swirling spirits. She pretended she was in some other town, far away from the oily black forest that edged the green fields, far away from the place where Isaac was murdered. She crossed her arms over her middle, wishing she were invisible and trying to ignore the lines of refugees trudging along beside her.

Despite her surroundings, it was a relief to be on her feet, after the long days and night on the cramped train. Luckily, the rain had stopped, but her stomach growled with hunger and her lips felt parched. The bread and plums hidden inside her coat were for her father, and even if she had intended to eat them herself, she didn't dare let anyone slogging along beside her know she had food. Initially, the bread and plums had been part of the provisions her mother had packed for her to eat on the train, because they were certain her father, as a POW, was being fed and taken care of by the Americans. But after talking to the old woman, Christine ate only half of what she'd brought, deciding instead to save the rest. If what the old woman said was true, the Red Cross had not been allowed to inspect the camps; the food supplies had been taken from the civilians of Dachau; the U.S. Army had warned the civilians it was a crime punishable by death to feed German prisoners; and the prisoners were being intentionally starved. Her father would need the nourishment more than she did. Still, she felt bad every time she heard a refugee child wail with hunger.

On the outskirts of the village, she left the crowded road, crossed over a dirt path through farmers' fields, then took a right on a paved thoroughfare with a sign to Konzentrationslager Dachau. She stopped and stared at the road sign, a thumbnail digging into her wrist, her breath shallow.

She bit her lip and trudged forward, every now and then stopping to remind herself to breathe, to regain her equilibrium, the wet tarmac and gray sky reeling in front of her. When the watchtowers and barbed wire came into view, she kept her eyes on the road, putting one foot in front of the other, until she came to a wide cobblestone turnoff. There, she stopped, steeled herself, and looked up. At the end of the long driveway, edged on both sides by rows of tall evergreens, was the main entrance to Dachau, a massive cement building the color of gravestones, with a center tower and broad gate.

It looked exactly as it had the day she left, minus the giant eagle and swastika above the entry. Nausea stirred in her stomach. Jeeps and tanks sat on each side of the entrance, and two soldiers smoking cigarettes, their rifles slung over their shoulders, walked slowly back and forth in front of the closed gate. Christine took a deep breath and started toward them, stepping over the train tracks that ran through the wet cobblestones, as if touching them would pull her backwards in time.

When the guards saw her, they tossed their cigarettes on the ground, took their rifles from their shoulders, and blocked her way. One of them, a tall, dark-eyed man with pockmarked cheeks, held up a hand. "Halt!" he said. Then, in German, "Turn around and go back the way you came." His pronunciation was rough, his words a mixture of high German and some other language, perhaps Dutch or Norwegian, but at least they'd be able to understand each other.

"Bitte," Christine said. "I need help."

The soldiers remained stationary, unfazed by her plea. "You're not allowed here," the tall one said. "Go back the way you came."

"But I need help. I've come a very long way."

"This is an American installation," he said. "Only U.S. military allowed inside."

The second soldier watched her with sullen eyes, his face unreadable.

Christine focused on him, on the uneven patches of stubble on his young face and the purple-gray circles beneath his boyish blue eyes. She tried to smile. He looked tired and sad, as if he too had seen things he wished he'd never seen. She hoped it meant he would be more compassionate, even if he couldn't understand what she was saying. She gripped the edge of her purse with both hands, trying to decide if she should tell the truth, or wait until she could talk to someone with more authority.

"I'm looking for someone who was sent here by mistake," she said.

The tall soldier rolled his eyes and sniffed. *"Ja,* that's what all you Germans say."

"But it's true," Christine said. "He's my father. He was a regular soldier, like you. If you'll just let me speak to someone in charge." She reached into her purse, feeling around for her father's *Soldbuch.* "Here, I can prove it to you."

Moving fast, the tall soldier pointed his rifle at her. "Stop!" he shouted, his face a contorted mask of anger and fear. "Drop the purse and put your hands in the air!"

Christine did as she was told, her heart thundering in her chest. The tall soldier kept his gun on her while the younger one picked up the purse and rummaged through it. He pulled out the wad of German marks, eyeing her suspiciously for the first time.

Christine's mind raced, wondering what to say.

"My American boyfriend gave it to me. It's the change from my train ticket. He's a soldier too. His name is Jake."

"What division?" the tall one said, glaring at her.

"I . . . I don't know," she said.

"Maybe we should throw you in with the other women," the tall soldier said. "Maybe you're part of the breeding stock for the SS, here trying to save your boyfriend from getting hanged. Maybe you have five little Nazis at home, and you've come here trying to get their daddy."

"*Nein,*" Christine said, shaking her head. "The man in the identity book is my father. I'm here to save my father."

The young soldier looked through her father's *Soldbuch,* his forehead furrowed, then said something to the tall soldier.

"Was he a member of the Nazi Party?" the tall soldier asked her, scowling.

"*Nein,*" Christine said again, still standing with her hands in the air, too afraid to move.

"You're lying!" he shouted.

"*Bitte,*" Christine pleaded. "I'm telling the truth. I will show you something." She slowly reached over, her hands still in the air, and pushed down her sleeve. "I was a prisoner here, see?"

The young soldier glanced up at her numbered wrist, then dropped his eyes for an instant, as if embarrassed. Again, he said something to the tall soldier.

"We'll let you inside, and somebody else can figure out what to do with you," the tall soldier said finally. He stepped aside, his rifle still trained on Christine. The young soldier opened the gate and led her through. Inside, another soldier waited. The young soldier said something to him and handed Christine her purse, giving her a quick nod. She mustered a weak smile to show her gratitude. The waiting soldier led her into the compound, gripping his rifle and watching her out of the corners of his eyes.

Christine swallowed and held a hand over her churning stomach. She imagined she could still smell the stench of the crematorium fires and hear the shouts and screams of the guards and prisoners. It was all she could do not to turn around and run. In the distance, she saw row after row of low, dark barracks, like coffins for giants lined up as far as the eye could see. She crossed her arms over her middle and kept her eyes straight ahead, praying they wouldn't have to go past the gas chambers and crematorium.

Thankfully, as far as she could tell, they were headed in the direction of the former SS training grounds and the guards' barracks, previously separate sections of the prison she had only heard about. When they rounded the corner of an enormous brick building, Christine stopped in her tracks.

Before her was a vast, mud-covered field, surrounded by tall electric fences and barbed wire. The fenced-in area was divided into smaller subdivisions by more barbed wire, like pens for livestock. Inside the "cages," sitting, sleeping, and standing in filth and mud, were tens of thousands of rain-soaked, shivering men, some without boots or coats, all of them without blankets or shelter of any kind. Most still wore what was left of their uniforms—black pants, green jackets, gray trousers—colors from every division and rank of what had been Hitler's war machine. It looked to Christine as if some of the men were sick and dying, right before her very eyes. All of them looked cold, wet, and miserable. Near the fence, skeletal men reached with careful, trembling fingers through the small space at the bottom of the electric wire, plucking blades of grass from the other side and shoving them into their mouths. Several called out, begging for food and water.

For a second, Christine felt dizzy, the overwhelming sensation that she was about to fall to her knees making her sway. Convinced she had just been jarred awake from a long dream only to find herself back in the nightmare of being a prisoner in Dachau, she lifted her hand to the tender spot behind her ear, certain she would feel stubble instead of the soft silk of growing hair. To her relief, she felt supple strands and tugged once, just to be sure, tiny needles of pain drawing her inwards, away from what her eyes were seeing. Then the pain disappeared and the sea of prisoners came into focus.

What is this? Christine thought, scanning the desperate, dirty faces for her father. *Are they all SS?*

The soldier barked an order, motioning with his rifle for her to keep moving.

Next to the enormous brick building stood another, smaller structure made of fieldstone and wide timber. Above the door was a white sign with a large *A* in the center of a red circle, and below that: War Crimes Branch, Judge Advocate Section, HQ Third United States Army. Outside the open doorway, a haggard line of German prisoners waited. Christine scanned every gaunt face. No one looked familiar. The line of prisoners reached inside, where the men were forced to face a wall with pictures of the camp—starved inmates and piles of corpses—hung at eye level.

The soldier led Christine down a long, damp hall lined with cells, the doors open for what appeared to be visiting journalists, who were taking pictures and making notes. American soldiers were everywhere, while German prisoners lay inside the chambers, crumpled, moaning, covered with dirt and blood. Christine paused as long as she could in front of each cell, trying to see if one of the men being interrogated was her father. It was impossible to see anything identifiable on the contorted faces.

At the end of the hall, the soldier held up a hand, signaling for her to wait outside an office door being guarded by another soldier. After the first soldier left, a shirtless man with oily black hair flew out of a cell and landed next to her, where he made an attempt to get to his feet. Christine backed up against the office door, her purse clutched to her chest. Finally, the man managed to stand, then stood there trembling, leaning against the wall for support, arms raised as if waiting to be hit. He wore high black boots and black pants, leather, fabric, skin ripped and torn. Christine searched his face for something she might recognize, but saw nothing. She looked away and found she could see directly into another cell, where an officer had just finished an interrogation.

"Up!" yelled the officer in German. "Stand up!"

The man lay in a puddle of blood on the floor, his green uniform jacket unbuttoned and covered in dark splotches. He grabbed the edge of a stool, trying to pull himself up. After a second demand, he succeeded in getting to his feet and blindly reached for the officer.

"Why don't you finish me off?" he moaned.

The American pushed him backwards and slammed the cell door.

Finally, the office door opened, and Christine was led inside, trembling and nauseous. A soldier took her purse and dumped the contents on the floor, while another pushed her hands in the air and felt beneath her armpits, up and down her entire body, including beneath her breasts and along the insides of both legs. Behind a metal desk with a nameplate that read COLONEL HENSLEY, a gray-haired officer, wearing black-rimmed glasses that overwhelmed his wrinkled face, rifled through a stack of documents. He spoke without looking up, words Christine didn't understand.

"I'm looking for my father," Christine said, trying to keep her voice steady, hoping he would understand German. "He was brought here by mistake."

Colonel Hensley looked up then, a sheet of paper in his hand.

The soldier who'd searched her said something to the colonel, then pushed her arms down and shoved her forward.

"English?" Colonel Hensley said, holding her gaze.

She shook her head, her heart dropping. How would she ever get anywhere if no one understood German? She wanted to go back to the gate, to get the German-speaking guard, but it was impossible. "My father," she said in English, her voice high and tight. "No Nazi."

Colonel Hensley put down the paper and sat back in his chair.

Christine motioned toward the spilled contents of her purse. *"Ja?"* she said, looking at him, eyebrows raised.

He nodded.

She knelt and gathered her things, then presented Colonel Hensley with her father's identity book. Colonel Hensley took the *Soldbuch* and rifled through its pages with little interest. When Christine held out the stack of dog-eared letters, he shook his head.

She tore at the brown twine around the letters, fingers trembling, trying to undo the tight knot. "I will read one to you," she pleaded, knowing he didn't understand but hoping he would hear the desperation in her voice. "Then you will see. He was just a regular soldier, praying to return to his family."

Colonel Hensley tossed her father's identity book across the desk. A cold eddy of fear opened up in Christine's chest. She had to do something to get him to listen. She lifted her sleeve. Colonel Hensley sat forward and looked at her arm, then sighed and shook his head again. He ripped a sheet of paper from a notepad and jotted down her number.

"Name?" he said, handing her the pen. After she wrote her name below her number, he said something to one of the soldiers. The soldier took Christine by the arm and led her out of the office.

CHAPTER 36

Christine waited in a foul-smelling, cement-walled room, a trio of fat black flies buzzing around the bare, dirt-specked bulb hanging from a chain in the ceiling. She sat on the edge of the only seat in the otherwise empty space, a wooden chair with wide arms and thick legs and stained straps used to tie down wrists and ankles. A soldier had locked her in when he left, the sound of the dead bolt falling into place like a gunshot. She stared at the riveted steel door, her heart racing and her knees trembling, wondering if they were just going to throw her in with the other women after all. She dug a thumbnail into her wrist, certain it would drive her mad to be locked up in Dachau again.

Maybe that was Stefan's plan. Maybe kidnapping her father was all part of a setup. After all, he'd told her that the Americans were holding women in Dachau. Having the Americans lock her up would be an easy way to get rid of her without getting his hands dirty.

She busied herself trying to find the most relevant of her father's letters, hoping the Americans were getting a translator. She scanned the smudged script for paragraphs that told her father's story of the Russian front. Every now and then, muffled shouts and yelling filtered through the stone walls, as if coming up from the murky depths of the ocean, followed by the howl of a man in agony. She concentrated on her father's familiar words, trying to block out all sound.

After she'd decided which sentences would help the most, she left the letters on the chair seat and stood. Well over an hour had passed; she was sure of it. What was going on? She paced the room, trying to ignore the stains on the cement floor. The smell of death and blood was unmistakable, and the longer she was locked up in the tiny space, the stronger the stench grew. What ungodly things had been done in these rooms?

She wondered if the Americans were looking her name up in the camp records, or summoning the interrogator used to question women. Would she be the next person screaming? And what exactly was going on here, anyway? There had to be other ways the Americans could bring the guilty to justice.

She sat down again, a lump in her throat. *The war is over,* she thought. *So why do I feel like it's still going on?*

Then, suddenly, an image of Isaac came to her. Not Isaac as she had last seen him, desperate and starving, but a smiling, ruddy-cheeked Isaac. He was laughing, surrounded by sunlight and the falling, swirling leaves of an oak tree. She tried to use the image to calm herself, but the picture kept getting interrupted, erased, and blocked out by flashes of watchtowers and electric fences, like glaring photos jerking to life in the dark corners of her mind. Everything would have been so different if Isaac had survived. Maybe he would have found a way to turn Stefan in. *Isaac is dead,* she reminded herself, *gone forever and never coming back.*

Finally, she heard a key in the dead bolt. She stood, trembling hands held over her stomach, praying it would be a soldier escorting her father, his weary face relieved and surprised when he saw her. Instead, a man in civilian clothing appeared, a notebook under his arm. He nodded his thanks to the soldier for letting him in, pulled a pen from behind his ear, and started toward her. His thin face was bristly and his short hair was dark, the same shade as his frayed leather jacket. Christine squeezed her eyes shut, then opened them again, unable to believe what she was seeing, certain her anxious mind was playing tricks on her. But the man was still there, stopped in his tracks, his eyes locked with hers in childlike astonishment. She backed away, bumping into the chair and knocking her father's letters to the filthy floor.

"Christine?" the man said.

Christine's knees gave out. The voice was unmistakable: the accent, the deep pitch, the way he said her name. She swayed and started to crumple. The man caught her by the elbows, leading her back toward the chair. She reached blindly for the seat and lowered herself into it.

"You're alive?" she croaked, her voice scarcely a whisper.

Isaac knelt and stared at her with those dark, familiar eyes. Light-headed, she drew back. Clearly, the stress of losing Maria, having her father kidnapped, and returning to Dachau was causing hallucinations. Certain if she reached out, her hand would go through him, she wondered again if her brain had finally gone over the edge. But then, the apparition spoke again.

"It's me, Christine," he said in a soft voice. He reached out to touch her face, and she was shocked to feel the warm, soft caress of his hand on her cheek. "What are you doing here?"

"But they shot you!" she said. "The soldiers took you into the woods, and they shot you! I heard it! You never came out!"

"You're right. They shot me. But I didn't die."

"How can this be?" she cried. "I grieved for you! I've cried a million tears. All this time, all these weeks. I thought you were dead!"

"I know," he said, his voice miserable. "And I'm sorry."

She put her hands over her face and tried to breathe normally, struggling to make sense of it all. Then she looked at him again.

"Where have you been?" she asked, surprised by her anger. "What are you doing here?"

"I've been hiding in the woods," he said. "There were five of us, waiting and wondering if it would ever be safe to come out. When we saw the American flag go up over Dachau, we came back to see if any of our loved ones had survived."

"Why didn't you come home? Why didn't you come back to me?"

"I've been trying to, but the Americans need help identifying former guards and officers, and they need translators. I agreed because I didn't have any other way home. They said after the trials they'd take me wherever I wanted to go, with money in my pocket and clothes on my back. But I also agreed because I want to find the guard who shot my father."

Finally, her racing heart slowed as reality slowly sank in. "I can't believe this," she said, reaching out to touch his face. "I thought I'd lost you forever." He closed his eyes and put a hand over hers, turning his mouth to her palm and inhaling deeply, as if relishing the smell of her skin. He kissed her fingers, gazing at her with soft, loving eyes. Then, finally, he groaned and pulled her into his arms.

"I've missed you so much," he said, his voice choked with tears. He crushed her to his chest, his face buried in her shoulder, his warm, jagged breath on her neck. She closed her eyes, her mouth against the side of his jaw, his skin hot against her lips. Afraid to open her eyes and find she was dreaming, she pressed herself into him, to feel his heart pounding against hers. He held her tighter. Finally, the long weeks of grief melted away beneath his strong arms. Then his lips were on hers, kissing her with a hungry, open mouth. After a few moments, he drew back and looked at her, his eyes glistening with tears.

"*Ach* Gott," he said, a gentle hand on her cheek. "Wondering if you'd survived nearly drove me crazy. It took days to find the courage to look up your name in the camp records. I couldn't bear the thought of being responsible for your death, and I couldn't live without you. When I didn't see the word 'deceased' after your number, I fell to my knees and wept."

"This whole time you were alive," she said. "I should have known. I should have felt it."

"We're together now," he said. "That's all that matters." He kissed her again, once on the lips, softer this time. Then his eyes grew moist again. "My mother and sister are dead."

"I know," she said. "I'm sorry." She put her head on his chest. "Maria is gone too."

"*Ach nein,*" he said, holding her tighter.

She wiped her eyes and looked up at him. "The guard who shot your father could be dead, you know. I saw some of them killed, beaten by the prisoners or shot by the Americans."

"I know," he said. "But I have to try. I owe it to my family to bring these monsters to justice, especially him. You still haven't told me. Why are you here?"

She pulled away and retrieved two of her father's letters, giving them to him with trembling hands. "The same reason you are," she said. "And because Vater was kidnapped. Stefan put him in an SS uniform and turned him over to the Americans so they would send him here. I have to get Vater out of this place, and I have to get someone to listen to me about Stefan!"

Isaac scanned the pages, his forehead furrowed. "I don't understand. Who is Stefan?"

"Kate's fiancé. He was an SS guard. I saw him when we first arrived at Dachau. He's hiding his identity and working with the Americans back home."

"Do you have any proof he isn't who he says he is?"

"*Nein,*" she said. "But Kate let it slip that he had a black uniform, complete with the silver skull and crossbones on the lapel. He warned me that if I tried to expose him my mother and brothers would be next. He said there are other SS hiding in the village."

"The Americans are right then," he said. "They think a lot of SS burned their party cards to blend in with the regular army. Some of them even tried to pass themselves off as inmates of Dachau by dressing in prisoner uniforms. There's an entire regiment of Waffen-SS claiming they were recruited against their will. They're all under forty, saying they were former inmates, thrown in Dachau as 'political prisoners,' 'enemies of the state,' or 'former soldiers who disobeyed orders or refused to fight,' before being forced into service."

Suddenly, she was filled with paranoia, goose bumps rising on her skin, as if at any instant they'd discover that the SS had taken over the camp and she and Isaac were once again locked up as prisoners. She shivered and put a hand on his arm. "*Bitte,* Isaac. Tell me the Americans will listen to me, tell me you can help Vater."

"All we can do is tell Colonel Hensley and see what he says," he said. "As far as your father, I'll do what I can, but I'm going to be honest. The Americans aren't inclined to show much mercy to anyone who fought for Hitler, regular Wehrmacht or not. They've only recently released the young boys and old men from the Volkssturm.

Without finding out who they are or what they did, they send thousands of POWs over to the French or the Russians, men who will probably never return home again. For now, I might be able to keep your father from getting transported to a labor camp in another country, but I'm sure he'll have to stay here until the trials are over."

A lump formed in Christine's throat. "It's all my fault."

"But they have nothing on him, right? No eyewitnesses or paper trails to tie him in with any war crimes? And having two former inmates plead his case will help." He gathered her into his arms again, rubbing her back with strong hands. "Don't worry, he's strong. I'll talk to Colonel Hensley about having him moved out of the general population."

She looked up at him. "Do you think he'll do it?"

"I can't promise anything, but it's worth a try. The men you saw being interrogated, and the ones being kept in the fields, they're not considered prisoners of war. Eisenhower classified them as 'Disarmed Enemy Soldiers.' That's why the Americans can do whatever they want. There are a few POWs being kept in the barracks. I don't know who they are or why they're being treated better than the rest, but the wives, children, and girlfriends of the SS are being kept there too, in a separate area of course. And some of the former prisoners don't have anyplace else to go. Some are staying in the regular barracks and some, like me, are staying in the guards' barracks. They all get regular meals and medical care. I'll try to get your father transferred over to the POW barracks."

"Danke," she said. "I don't know what would have happened if you hadn't been here."

He kissed her again, and she felt herself being swept away, caught up in a flood of thoughts and feelings. When it was over, she touched his face, her body trembling with relief and fear.

"You still haven't told me," she said. "How did you survive?"

He shook his head, a sad, haunted look in his eyes. "You don't want to hear about that."

"I want to know. I have to know."

"They made us dig a trench," he said. "Then lined us up on the edge of it. As soon as they started shooting, a bullet grazed my arm, and I fell in the grave with the others. I was lucky because I was in the next to the last group, so I was near the top of the pile. I played dead, holding my breath, hoping they wouldn't finish me off. Afterward, the guards hurried to cover us up. They must have been in a rush because they didn't do a very good job. Only a few inches of dirt, and above that, piles of tree limbs and forest scrub. When they were gone, I crawled out of the grave and dug for other survivors. I found four others, barely conscious and bleeding, but their wounds weren't fatal. We ran deep into the woods and kept going until we collapsed. After nearly freezing the first night, we built shanties out of timber stolen from the burnt-out ruins of a farm. At night we snuck out of hiding to steal apples and eggs, scouring the fields for dropped ears of dried corn or undiscovered potatoes." Christine stared at him, speechless. He brushed her short hair away from her temple with gentle fingers. "Every night, the earth and sky seemed to merge into one dark and heavy presence, waiting for me to die, or to give up. I felt like it wanted to crush me. Only the silent moon was there to keep us company, but thoughts of you kept me going. When we saw the American flag go up over Dachau and didn't hear any more bombs and bullets, we knew the war was finally over."

He hugged her again, so hard she could barely breathe, but she didn't want him to let go. Little by little, she stopped shaking. Finally, he released her, took the letters, and turned toward the exit. "Come on, let's take these to Colonel Hensley and tell him about Stefan."

In Colonel Hensley's office, the colonel held up a hand, signaling Isaac to slow down.

"What is he saying?" Christine asked Isaac.

"He asked me what I thought would happen if he believed every woman who came in here claiming her father, husband, or son was innocent. He's heard the same sob story a hundred times, and has a whole corral of SS girlfriends and wives in this camp saying the same thing. The SS was a criminal organization, and anyone associated with it is guilty one way or another. They're holding a military tribunal in a few months. If your father is innocent, he'll be set free then."

"What about Stefan?"

"He doesn't see how they can arrest him without good reason. Most of the men here were captured at the end of the war, and they've been here ever since. He said they wouldn't go pulling people out of their homes based on speculation. Not without proof."

Christine tried to remember how to breathe. "Tell him I worked for Lagerkommandant Grünstein, the commander of the camp, as a housekeeper and cook. Tell him I can help identify guards and officers, but only if he helps me first."

After Isaac translated, Colonel Hensley stood and retrieved a yellow file from a black wall of metal cabinets. He sat back down, opened the file, read the first page out loud, then looked up, waiting.

"Lagerkommandant Grünstein is here," Isaac told Christine. "He turned himself in and is cooperating with the investigation. He's given them a detailed account of what happened."

Christine gasped, making Colonel Hensley raise his eyebrows.

"The Lagerkommandant can identify Stefan!" she said. "They need to bring Stefan here!" Isaac translated, and the two men talked back and forth for a minute or two. Christine thought she would scream if Isaac didn't tell her what was going on. "What's he saying?"

"He thinks you should let them handle things. He'll ask the Lagerkommandant if he remembers a Stefan Eichmann, and they'll take it from there."

Christine slammed a fist on the colonel's desk. "That's not good enough!" she said. "He threatened my family! You have to bring him in!"

Colonel Hensley scowled and leaned back, his hands clasped over his middle. Isaac pulled Christine away from the desk, placing himself between the two of them.

"Calm down," he said. "We're not going to get anywhere like that."

"I'm not going to let Stefan get away with this," she said. "If something happens to my father, or my mother . . ." She sat down in a chair opposite the colonel's desk and looked up at Isaac, hot tears of rage burning her eyes. "I'll kill him myself if I have to!"

Isaac shook his head and fell into the chair beside her, his strong fingers raking through his hair. "I'm sorry, I wish I could fix this for you."

Christine stood and paced the room, teeth clenched, hands balled into fists. She could barely breathe, her throat and sinuses blocked and tight from trying not to cry. She thought about Vater, paying the price for a war he didn't believe in, while Stefan went free, his blind devotion to the Third Reich so fierce he had murdered innocents to ensure Hitler's vision. And then, all at once, the chill of inspiration raised the hairs on the back of her neck. She whirled around to face Isaac.

"If we can't get the Americans to go to Stefan," she said, "then we'll get Stefan to come to the Americans."

CHAPTER 37

Dressed in American army camouflage, with wool caps pulled over their ears and dirt smudged on their faces, Christine and Isaac crept along the alleyway, keeping close to shadows pooled next to doorways and stone walls. It was after midnight, the wee hours of night still and humid, the starless sky gunpowder black. A waning moon smoldered behind sullen gray clouds like a milky, blind eye, casting a weak, bluish glow over the streets and buildings. The windows of the houses were dark, the streets empty. A train chugged in the distance, its whistle like a banshee in the hills.

Christine followed Isaac along the passageway with her heart in her throat, feeling as if she'd gone backwards in time, back to the uncertain days during the war, back to the nights of secret meetings, when every shadow held potential danger. When they neared the end of the cobblestone alleyway, she pushed all thought from her mind, concentrating instead on the job ahead. Isaac stopped at the corner of the last building, shoulders hunched, and held up a gloved hand. Christine came to a halt behind him, her breath shallow and quick. For the hundredth time since they'd left Dachau, she felt the interior pocket of her jacket, making sure the sealed envelope was still there. She knew every word of the letter by heart, composed in unsteady but careful script by Lagerkommandant

Grünstein, under the guidance of Christine, Isaac, and Colonel Hensley.

> *Dear Comrade,*
> *I write from the appalling conditions inside the American war crimes enclosure in Dachau. To our good fortune, an ally on the inside has made our survival, and this correspondence, possible. He informs us that you have found a way to blend in with the common soldiers, and that there are other SS who have also escaped our fate. It is my hope that you will come to our aid at this momentous moment in history, when the brave men of the Third Reich will find the strength to rise up and take back what is rightfully ours, to carry on our beloved Führer's vision. In Dachau, our numbers are great, our will is strong, and we believe that, with your help, we can overpower our captors and escape. Three nights from the arrival of this letter, I implore you, gather up our mutual allies and come to Dachau's northeast gate at midnight, where our comrade will be waiting with weapons and access to the inside of the camp. God speed my loyal friend.*
> *Heil Hitler,*
> *Lagerkommandant Jörge Grünstein*

Isaac pointed at the three-story house, kitty-corner across the street on Hallerstrasse, and looked at Christine, eyebrows raised. A faint light glowed behind the closed curtains of the window in an upstairs balcony door. Christine nodded, a flush of adrenaline warming her neck. Isaac pointed to her jacket and held out a gloved hand, waiting. Christine pulled the letter from her pocket. The envelope, like the paper inside, was dirty and wrinkled, purposely made to look smuggled from inside Dachau; yet it glowed, ghostly white, in the dark. She read the black script one more time: "Stefan Eichmann." Isaac gestured, motioning for her to hurry up. She shook her head and tapped her chest.

"I'll do it," she mouthed.

Before Isaac could protest, she darted across the street toward Stefan's house, scampered up the stone steps, pushed the letter through the low mail slot in the front door, and bolted back to the alley, her pulse like marching jackboots in her ears. When she reached Isaac she kept running, glancing back once to make sure he was behind her. Together they raced out of the long passageway, hurried down a winding cobblestone street, then turned left onto a shadowy side road, where an American army truck and driver sat waiting.

Christine and Isaac clambered into the covered bed of the vehicle and tied the canvas to the tailgate. When the truck lurched forward, she lost her balance, and Isaac caught her before she fell, his strong hands on her waist. While the transport bumped along the narrow streets, they huddled together on a pile of wool blankets, their backs against the truck's cab, trying to catch their breath. Christine wanted to ask Isaac if he thought their plan would work. But what could he say? It was done. If it didn't put Stefan away, they'd have to come up with something else.

As the truck made its way out of the village toward Dachau, Christine reached for Isaac's hand. He put his arm around her and she leaned against his shoulder, trying to picture Mutti, her face relieved when she read the letter Christine had shoved under her door earlier. But the only image that came to mind was Stefan, strolling down the carpeted stairs inside his house the next morning, his hand on the banister, his face registering surprise when he saw the sealed envelope on the foyer floor. She pictured him bending down to pick it up, his back straight, the belt of his robe tied tightly at his waist. A man certain he had nothing to fear. Would he burn the letter in the woodstove right away, or would he hurry to his study to make a list of all the SS he knew? To think he might dismiss the letter's contents made Christine nauseous. She closed her eyes, praying for sleep. It didn't come.

Four days later, in Dachau's main prison, Christine stood on her tiptoes, a hand over her churning stomach, peering through the narrow opening of a steel door. After a moment, she looked at Isaac and Colonel Hensley, shaking her head. They moved along the mottled cement corridor, and she looked through the slot in the next door.

"*Nein,*" she said, shaking her head again.

When she peered through the fifth door, her heart skipped a beat. She nodded. Colonel Hensley said something to Isaac and put the oversized key in the lock. Isaac took Christine's trembling hand.

"He wants to know if you're sure," he said to her.

Christine nodded again. "*Ja,*" she said. "I'm positive."

Another door screeched open at the end of the long corridor and an American soldier entered, gripping Lagerkommandant Grünstein by the arm. Hands and feet shackled, the *Lagerkommandant* kept his eyes on the concrete floor, gray hair falling across his sweaty brow, gnarled hands shaking. Each time he slowed, the soldier pulled him forward. The *Lagerkommandant* had deteriorated since they'd seen him just days earlier. What if the old man couldn't do what Christine needed him to do?

Colonel Hensley heaved open the steel door of the interrogation room, motioning for the soldier to lead the *Lagerkommandant* inside. Christine and Isaac watched from the hallway as the prisoner tied to the chair raised his head to look at his captors, scowling as he fought the restraints around his wrists and ankles. His forehead was bruised, his blond hair matted with dirt and blood, his hands scraped and bleeding.

"Traitor!" the prisoner yelled when he saw the *Lagerkommandant,* spittle flying from his lips.

Colonel Hensley signaled Christine and Isaac to come in, then asked the *Lagerkommandant* a question. The soldier translated. "Do you know this man?"

Christine entered the room with Isaac, eyes locked on the *Lagerkommandant,* unable to breathe until he answered.

The *Lagerkommandant* nodded. "*Ja,*" he said.

"You set us up!" the prisoner yelled. "How dare you!"

Colonel Hensley motioned toward the soldier, who wrapped a gag around the prisoner's mouth. When the man in the chair saw Christine, he stopped struggling, his brows raised in surprise. But his initial shock was quickly replaced by anger, and he glared at her with cold, savage eyes. Fire rose in Christine's cheeks. She opened her mouth to speak, but suddenly Isaac flew past her and threw himself on top of the prisoner, knocking over the chair and pummeling the man's face with his fists. The soldier and Colonel Hensley pulled Isaac up, pushed him against the concrete wall, and held him there, their faces red with exertion.

"It's him!" Isaac yelled, rage knotting the lines around his nose and mouth, giving the illusion he had gone insane. "He's the guard who shot my father!"

Christine's heart cramped against her ribcage as if squeezed by a powerful fist. Her eyes burned. The prisoner was still on the floor, gasping and straining to get free. She fought the urge to go over to him, to put her feet on his neck and stand there, her full weight crushing his windpipe, until he lay still, purple veins bulging beneath the red skin of his forehead and throat. Finally, Isaac calmed down, and the Americans released him. He slid down the wall and squatted there, furious eyes locked on the man on the floor. Colonel Hensley and the soldier pulled prisoner and chair upright, then stood in front of him. They asked the *Lagerkommandant* more questions. Blood gushed from the prisoner's split brow and broken nose, gurgling like a stopped-up drain every time he took a breath. The soldier translated for the *Lagerkommandant* and the colonel, but the *Lagerkommandant*'s answers were all Christine needed.

"Ja," the *Lagerkommandant* said. "His name is Sturmscharführer Stefan Eichmann. He was a guard in Dachau, on the men's side of the camp. He was directly responsible for a number of prisoners' deaths. Killing Jews was sport to some of them, and he always won."

CHAPTER 38

Christine lifted the iron latch on the wooden door leading out to the backyard, taking a moment to relish the familiar scents coming up from the cellar stairs: cool cement, vinegar in oak barrels, onions, earth-covered potatoes. She smiled, hearing the chickens on the other side of the door, clucking and scratching in the red dirt and spring grass. Stepping out into the fragrant afternoon, she wound her way between the apple and plum trees, heading toward the back corner of the fenced yard.

And there it was, right where she had planted the pit the day before she and Isaac were sent to Dachau: a leggy, young plum tree, its slender branches filled with clusters of buds and lavender blossoms, its leaves shimmering in the warm breeze. *You survived,* she thought, her throat tight. She reached out to touch the soft petals of an open blossom, her bare toes digging in the soft grass. Suddenly, someone grabbed her from behind and she gasped, playfully fighting off the strong arms around her waist. It was Isaac.

"Come inside, Frau Bauerman," he said, pulling her hair aside so he could kiss her neck. "Your mother made all your favorites, despite the fact that I think she's still upset we got married while we were away helping the Americans. I told her we went to the next town over and had a quiet ceremony in a nice church, but she's making plans for a proper celebration."

Christine turned and pushed her mouth into his, then drew back. "Let her plan whatever she wants, as long as we get to use the tablecloth on our wedding table."

"You still have it?"

"It's been in my room this whole time. After Mutti decided we had to use Herr Weiler's root cellar for a bomb shelter, I snuck down there in the middle of the night before the first air raid, to get the tablecloth and your lucky stone. I was going to surprise you with them when you were in the attic, but I never got the chance." She kissed him again. "It's amazing and wonderful to be home, isn't it?"

"Ja," he said. "But don't forget, the Americans paid us to testify. They want us to come back to Dachau, for a few more months, until the trials are over."

"I know. And I would do it again for free." She laid her head on his chest for a moment, then looked up into his chestnut eyes. "I love you."

"I love you too."

She sighed, then turned and touched the plum blossoms again, Isaac's arms still around her waist. "Look," she said. "It's alive and bearing fruit." Then she moved his wide, warm hand down to her belly and held it there, smiling. "Just like us."

He turned her around to face him. "Any ideas for names yet?"

"If it's a girl," she said, "I'd like to name her Maria. If it's a boy, Abraham, after your father."

He kissed her once on the lips, then gazed down at her, his eyes soft. *"Danke,"* he said.

"For what?" she said, beaming up at him.

"For surviving. I never would have been happy with anyone else. You ruined everyone for me."

"Christine!" Vater called from the second story kitchen window. "Come and eat!" Beside him, Mutti and Christine's brothers smiled and waved.

AUTHOR'S NOTE

The seeds for *The Plum Tree* were planted in my childhood, during numerous family trips to visit my grandparents, aunts, uncles, and cousins in Germany. Somehow, even at an early age, I knew that experiencing another culture and seeing a different side of the world, living for weeks in the half-timbered house where my mother grew up, was a privilege that would make a difference in my life. But I had no idea it would inspire me to write a novel.

My mother's German village was like a fairy tale, with its rolling hills, tidy orchards, sprawling vineyards, medieval cathedrals, and delicious food, all set against a backdrop of church bells, cobblestone streets, and stepped alleys. Every visit was an adventure, from exploring castle ruins to sleeping beneath a giant *Deckbed* (feather bedcover). Later, as I learned about WWII, it was hard to imagine such horrible things happening in such a beautiful place. I realized my *Oma* was an extraordinary woman, having struggled to keep her children alive while her husband was off fighting and, once the war was over, somehow feeding and clothing a family of seven during continued rationing and extreme food shortages that didn't improve until 1950. Opa's stories about the Eastern Front and his escape from two POW camps fascinated me. Above all, I was awed that my Americanized mother, the woman in heels and sunglasses, chief of the firemen's auxiliary, member of the PTA, who bought her kids bell-bottoms and loved cookouts and boating, had spent her childhood living in poverty and fear in Nazi Germany. She grew up wearing dresses made from bedsheets, bathing in a metal tub with water heated on a woodstove, running and hiding in a bomb shelter for nights on end. Having lived the typical American childhood, I could hardly comprehend what she had endured. I wanted to know everything and would often ask my mother to repeat her stories, hoping she'd remember more details. There are so many I couldn't fit them all into the manuscript.

Along with my family's history, there were a great many books that were helpful to me while writing *The Plum Tree*. Among the memoirs that mirrored and expanded on my mother's stories were: *German Boy* by Wolfgang W. E. Samuel, *The War of Our Childhood: Memories of WWII* by Wolfgang W. E. Samuel, and *Memoirs of a 1000-Year-Old Woman* by Gisela R. McBride. I also relied on *Frauen: German Women Recall the Third Reich* by Alison Owings. To understand the Allied bombing campaign, which had become a deliberate, explicit policy to destroy all German cities with populations over 100,000 using a technique called "carpet bombing"—a strategy that treated whole cities and their civilian populations as targets for attacks by high explosives and incendiary bombs—I read: *To Destroy a City: Strategic Bombing and Its Human Consequences in WWII* by Hermann Knell, *Among the Dead Cities: The History and Moral Legacy of the WWII Bombings of Civilians in Germany and Japan* by A. C. Grayling, and *The Fire* by Jörg Friedrich. Among the many horrific air raid stories in these books were the firebombing of Hamburg in July 1943, dubbed "Operation Gomorrah," which killed 45,000 civilians, and the firebombing of Dresden in February 1945, which killed 135,000 civilians. All of these books include some of the most haunting scenes I've ever read about what it was like to be a German civilian during the war.

To understand what it was like for civilians and POWs after the war, I read: *Crimes and Mercies: The Fate of German Civilians under Allied Occupation* by James Bacque. For information involving persecution of the Jews and the horror of concentration camps, I read: *Night* by Elie Wiesel, *Eyewitness Auschwitz* by Filip Müller, and *I Will Bear Witness* by Victor Klemperer.

Four novels I've read and enjoyed have also helped guide me through this period in history: *Those Who Save Us* by Jenna Blum, *Skeletons at the Feast* by Chris Bohjalian, *The Book Thief* by Markus Zusak, and *Sarah's Key* by Tatiana de Rosnay.

It is important to note that although characters in this novel endure many of the same trials as my mother and her family, Christine is not my mother. Nor are any of the other characters members of my family. But I hope the fictional Christine and Mutti have at least some resemblance to my *Oma*'s and mother's monumental courage, resilience, and compassion.

Although *The Plum Tree* is a work of fiction, I strove to be as historically accurate as possible. Any mistakes are mine alone. For the purpose of plot, Dachau was portrayed as an extermination camp, while in reality it was categorized as a work camp. Undoubtedly tens of thousands of prisoners were murdered, suffered, and died under horrible conditions at Dachau, but the camp was not set up like Auschwitz and other extermination camps, which had a deliberate "euthanasia" system for killing Jews and other undesirables. Also for the purpose of plot, the attempt on Hitler's life led by Claus von Stauffenburg was moved from July 1944 to the fall of 1944.

Please turn the page
for a very special Q&A
with Ellen Marie Wiseman!

How did you come up with the idea for this book?

This is not an easy question to answer, but I'll do my best. My mother came to America alone, by ship, at the age of twenty-one, to marry an American soldier she had met while working at the PX outside her German village. Just over a decade had passed after the war, and Germany was still rebuilding. Her family was dirt poor, and the lure of an ideal life in America was powerful enough to make her leave her family and marry a man she barely knew. Alas, her American dream was no fairy tale. The American soldier turned out to be dishonest and cruel, and my mother had nowhere to go for help, living on an isolated farm twenty minutes from the nearest village and with no car or driver's license. Somehow she persevered, giving birth in quick succession to my sister, my brother, and me. Eventually my parents divorced, and my mother took me and my siblings back to Germany, hoping to start over. But it wasn't meant to be. My father insisted she return to the States, even though he had no interest in being part of our lives. Luckily, my mother met and married a caring man who took us in as his own. I grew up traveling to Germany to see my grandparents, aunts, uncles, and cousins, longing to live in their beautiful world full of tradition and culture.

Then, when I was a junior in high school, I learned about the Holocaust. To say it was difficult to wrap my head around those atrocities happening in my amazing, beautiful dreamworld would be an understatement. WWII was our history teacher's favorite subject, and he was obsessed with teaching us as much as possible about what happened to the Jews. It didn't take long for some of my classmates to start calling me a Nazi, saluting and shouting "*Heil* Hitler" in the halls. That was when I began to understand the concept of collective guilt. I asked my mother questions about what it was like during the war, about Opa's role, and about the

Jews. I soon realized that in her own quiet way, Oma had tried to help, risking her life to set out food for the passing Jewish prisoners, even though she could barely feed her own children. Opa was drafted, fought on the Russian front, and escaped two POW camps. For over two years my mother and her family had no idea if he was dead or alive until he showed up on their doorstep one day. He was a foot soldier, not SS or a Nazi. My mother took me inside the bomb shelter where she and her family had hid, terrified and hungry, for nights on end. She told me stories about food shortages and ration lines, jumping in a ditch with her pregnant mother to avoid being shot by Allied planes, and developing earaches from the constant wailing of the air raid siren. But I was too young to understand or explain to my peers that being German doesn't make you a Nazi, that protesting something in America is easy compared to protesting something in the Third Reich, or to ask them what they would have done if they had had to choose between someone else's life and their own. My American father had taught me that evil has the ability to reside in the heart of any man, regardless of race, nationality, or religion, but I didn't know how to make those points. I didn't know how to tell my friends that collective guilt as opposed to individual guilt is senseless; that retrospective condemnation is easy. Most of all, I knew no one wanted to hear that my family had suffered during the war, too.

Then, over twenty years later, after *another* conversation with a close friend (ironically one of my former high school teasers) about how much responsibility the average German held for bringing Hitler into power, inspiration struck. I needed to write a novel about what it was like for an average German during the war, while still being sensitive to what the Nazis did to the Jews. But I also knew my book needed a twist if I wanted to sell it. Then I remembered how James Cameron used a love story to tell the bigger story of the ill-fated *Titanic*. And so the romance between a young German woman and a Jewish man was born. Together with stories from my mother's life in Nazi Germany, I knew the entire novel, from beginning to end. I finished the first dreadful draft of my novel in three days, in longhand, on a legal pad. After that, it took over four years of research and revisions before it was ready. While the wartime experiences of my main character were those of an ordinary German, what she did trying to save her Jewish boyfriend is extraordinary. In reality, she very likely would have died for her efforts. But that wouldn't have made for a very satisfying story.

You said the book is loosely based on your mother's life growing up in Germany during the war. Which of the events are true?

It's probably easier to say what isn't true, which would be the main character's having a Jewish boyfriend and being sent to Dachau. The poverty, hunger, bombings, jumping in a ditch to avoid being shot by Allied planes, risking their lives to put food out for the Jewish prisoners, not knowing if her father was dead or alive for two years, his escape from a Russian POW camp—all of that is true. After the war, American soldiers occupied Oma's house, and she did throw away the can of peanut butter they left because she thought it was poison.

What kind of childhood did you have?

Thankfully I have very few memories of my real father, because none of them are pleasant. Once my mother remarried, I had a wonderful childhood, traveling extensively, boating, swimming, reading, and playing outdoors. I had a vivid imagination back then, imagining terrifying creatures around every corner: kidnappers, ghosts, vampires, monsters from the deep. One of my favorite things to do was walk to the general store to buy a nickel candy bar and a scary comic book. As a teenager I devoured Stephen King, Anne Rice, and Dean Koontz. I suppose that explains my fascination with the monsters who ran the concentration camps. I always thought my first novel would have an element of paranormal or horror, but I guess you can't get much more horrific than WWII and the Holocaust.

Did you study creative writing?

I went to a tiny school, four hundred students in K–12, and there were no creative writing classes offered. I didn't go to college either, choosing instead to be a wife and mother.

Did you have a mentor?

After years of working alone on my writing, I wanted to find out if I was wasting my time. I had no idea if I had any writing talent to speak of. After all, I'd never taken a creative writing course, there were no local writers' groups, and I don't have a college degree. The only place I had to turn to was the Internet. I will be forever thankful that my search led me to William Kowalski, award-winning author of *Eddie's Bastard* (HarperCollins). He became my editor, teacher, mentor, and friend. His faith in my work bolstered me during difficult times and pushed me to believe in myself.

How many rejections did you receive before you found an agent?

Seventy-two, over a period of two years.

What roadblocks did you have to overcome to get your book published?

In November 2008, a few months before I started sending query letters to agents, my husband and I lost our business due to some very unpleasant circumstances beyond our control. Closing our business forced us into bankruptcy, both for the business and ourselves, and we had to look for jobs for the first time in twenty-six years. It was an extremely difficult time, but I was determined to follow my dream. In between worrying about our future and talking to lawyers, I sent out queries. During the first round, the manuscript was rejected twice because of word count (280,000). I stopped querying and spent ten months cutting and revising, during which time, while we were still in the midst of financial and legal battles, my sister passed away. For a while, I couldn't write.

But then I realized I'd worked too long and hard to give up. Somehow I found a way to cut the manuscript down to a reasonable length and started querying again. Around this time we realized we had to sell our home of twenty years and began a seven-month stint of DIY renovations so we could get as much as possible from the sale. By January of 2011, I'd gotten seventy-two rejections and was about to give up. Then I thought I'd try one more time. That query was the one that got my agent, who sold my novel in three weeks, just two months after we sold our house. Now, looking back, I realize writing and trying to sell my novel is what kept me sane.

Who would you like to see play Christine and Isaac if *The Plum Tree* is ever made into a movie?

Scarlett Johansson and Jake Gyllenhaal. And I think Leonardo DiCaprio would make a great SS villain.

THE PLUM TREE

Ellen Marie Wiseman

ABOUT THIS GUIDE

The suggested questions are included
to enhance your group's reading of
Ellen Marie Wiseman's
The Plum Tree.

Discussion Questions

1. Christine and her family were not members of the Nazi Party. When the war started in 1939, the population of Germany was over 80 million, with 5.3 million being members of the Nazi Party. The party reached its peak in 1945 with 8 million members. Many of these were nominal members who joined for careerist reasons, but the party had an active membership of at least a million, including virtually all the holders of senior positions in the national government. Not all Germans or all military were party members. Does this surprise you? Did you think all Germans were members of the Nazi Party? What do you think most people believe? Why?

2. Christine works as a domestic for a Jewish family, where she falls in love with Isaac. What brings them together? What do you think it was like the first time they met? Do you think they fell in love instantly or over time? How do you think Isaac felt about her family, knowing how the Nazis felt about Jews? Do you think Christine was envious of his family's wealth, or did she give it little thought?

3. The first anti-Jewish poster Christine sees explains who is a Jew and who isn't, and forbids Jews to enter public places like banks and post offices. It is said that Hitler drew his first ideas about how to treat the Jews from blacks being denied civil rights in the South. What do you think are the differences? Why was the KKK kept in check while the Nazis were not?

4. Christine offers to hide Isaac before the Nazis take him and his family away. Would you have taken the opportunity to go with her, or would you have stayed with your family? Do

you think Isaac's decision was based on loyalty to his parents and sister, or was it made because he thought they'd be okay since he had no idea how bad it was going to get?

5. The Nazis said they were going to "relocate" the Jews. What if this was happening where you live? How far would you be willing to go to protect your friends and neighbors? Would you risk your life or the lives of your children to save someone else?

6. We live in a world where global news and information is instant. During WWII in Nazi Germany, public information was manipulated and limited. Propaganda was used to sway public opinion. There were only two Nazi-run newspapers available, and the Nazis controlled the radio. Listening to foreign broadcasts was a crime punishable by death. After the Nazis were defeated, most Germans found out by word of mouth that Roosevelt had died, that the Wehrmacht had unconditionally surrendered, and that the atom bomb had been dropped on Japan. How do you think the availability of information affects the way people think and act? Do you think the Holocaust could have been stopped if information had been more readily available? Do you think the war would have ended sooner? What differences would better access to information have made?

7. Lagerkommandant Grünstein is loosely based on a real SS officer, Kurt Gerstein, who tried to tell the world what the Nazis were doing. After the war, Gerstein turned himself over to the French and gave them a detailed account of what had happened in the camps. Before his trial, he was found dead. There is some speculation that other imprisoned SS might have killed him. If he'd been given the chance to go to trial, should he have been punished with the rest of the SS or set free?

8. Christine thinks of her mother as key to their survival and the last thread to anything familiar and normal. From food in their stomachs to clean clothes and warm baths, Mutti provided the only bits of comfort to be had. During the war, Germany was made up of women, children, and old people struggling to survive food shortages and air raids while the men were off fighting. What do you think it was like in Germany for the women left behind? What differences would there have been between single women and those with children to take care of? At one point Christine mentions that some women sell themselves to feed their children. How far would you go to keep yourself and your children alive?

9. How do you think Christine changed over the course of the novel? What about Isaac, Maria, Heinrich, and Karl? Even though siblings are raised together, sometimes they turn out differently. What differences do you see in Christine and Maria? Heinrich and Karl?

10. Christine and the *Lagerkommandant* talk about what the prisoners will do to stay alive, from spying on each other to pushing their fellow Jews into the ovens to burn. How far would you go to stay alive in a place like Dachau? Do you think you would be strong enough to keep going like Hanna and Christine, or do you think you'd give up?

11. The Americans bombed Christine's village and shot at her and her little brother. How do you think she felt when they occupied her village? Do you think she saw them as saviors or monsters? Why?

12. When Christine and Isaac are sent to Dachau, she worries that he has lost his will to live. Discuss the will to live. Do you think it's the same for everyone, or is it stronger in some than others?

13. Discuss the significance of the plum tree. What does it symbolize, both as a pit when it's first planted and later, as a blossoming sapling at the end of the book?

14. Do you think Christine and Isaac's secret meetings are romantic or frightening? Do you think fear of the future made their love stronger and more passionate? They didn't have sex because they were afraid she would become pregnant. Do you think that is realistic, or do you think the author used it to add more tension to the story? When Isaac puts an end to their meetings, Christine only tries to see him twice. Would you have agreed to wait and see what happened, or would you have gone to his house more often, Gestapo or no Gestapo?

15. Mutti agrees to put food out for the passing Jewish prisoners even though it's dangerous and she can barely feed her family. Why do you think she does it? Would you have done the same thing?

16. When the Gestapo finds Isaac in Christine's attic, they spare the rest of her family out of respect for her father's military service. Do you think that would have happened, or do you think they would have shot her family or taken them all away?

17. After the war, Christine's friend Kate doesn't believe her when Christine tells her about the camps and Stefan's role as an SS guard. Do you think Kate is in denial because she is in love and wants to get married, or do you think she really doesn't believe Christine? When Christine tries to expose Stefan in church, again no one wants to believe her. Do you think people were in denial, were too busy with their own problems, or just didn't want to talk about it? Do you think they felt guilty?

18. When Christine gets off the train from Dachau, she doesn't realize where she is. How do you think Christine felt when she realized she was already home? How do you think she felt when she saw her house was still standing and her family was alive? How do you think it feels to survive something so horrific when so many others didn't? She tastes the grass in the goat's milk and thinks even chickens are beautiful. Do you think almost dying makes a person more aware and grateful for the little things?

19. Maria hates herself because the Russians raped her. She thinks no one will ever love her. When she finds out she is pregnant, she is devastated. Do you think she died by accident trying to get rid of the baby, or do you think she killed herself? What would you have done in her situation?

20. If Christine hadn't found out Isaac was alive, do you think she would have ended up with Jake? Do you think she would have left her family to go to America? What would Christine's and Jake's future have looked like?

Please turn the page for an exciting sneak peek of
Ellen Marie Wiseman's newest novel

THE ORPHAN COLLECTOR

coming soon wherever print and e-books are sold!

CHAPTER 1

September 28, 1918

The deadly virus stole unnoticed through the crowded cobblestone streets of Philadelphia on a sunny September day, unseen and unheard amidst the jubilant chaos of the Liberty Loan parade and the patriotic marches of John Phillips Sousa. More than two hundred thousand men, women, and children waved American flags and jostled each other for prime viewing space along the two-mile route, while the people behind shouted encouragement over shoulders and past faces to the bands, Boy Scouts, women's auxiliaries, Marines, sailors, and soldiers in the street. Planes flew overheard, draft horses pulled eight-inch howitzers, military groups performed bayonet drills, church bells clanged, and police whistles blew; old friends hugged and shook hands, couples kissed, and children shared candy and soda. The eager spectators were unaware that the lethal illness had escaped the Naval Yard. They had no idea that the local hospitals had admitted over two hundred people the previous day, or that numerous infectious disease experts had pressured the mayor to cancel the event. Not that it would have mattered. They were there to support the troops, buy war bonds, and show their patriotism during a time of war. Victory in Europe—and keeping the Huns out of America—was first and foremost on their minds.

Many of the onlookers had heard about the flu hitting Boston and New York. But the director of the Phillips Institute of Philadelphia had just announced he'd identified the cause of the specific influenza causing so much trouble—Pfeiffer's bacillus—and the local newspapers said influenza posed no danger because it was as old as history and usually accompanied by foul air, fog, and plagues of insects. None of those things were happening in Philadelphia. Therefore, it stood to reason that as long as everyone did what the Board of Health advised—kept their feet dry, stayed warm, ate more onions, and kept their bowels and windows open—they'd be fine.

But thirteen-year-old Pia Lange knew something was wrong. And not because her best friend Finn Duffy had told her about the dead sailors his brother had seen outside a local pub. Not because of the posters on telephone poles and buildings that read: *When obliged to cough or sneeze, always place a handkerchief, paper napkin, or fabric of some kind before the face* or *Cover Your Mouth! Influenza Is Spread by Droplets Sprayed from Nose and Mouth!*

Pia knew something was wrong because the minute she had followed her mother—who was pushing Pia's twin brothers in a wicker baby pram—onto the packed parade route, a sense of unease had come over her, like the thick air before a summer thunderstorm or the swirling discomfort in her belly right before she got sick. Feeling distraught in crowds was nothing new to her—she would never forget the panic she'd felt the first time she walked the busy streets of Philadelphia, or when Finn had dragged her to the maiden launch of a warship from Hog Island, where President Wilson and thirty thousand people were in attendance and the water was filled with tugboats, steamboats, and barges decorated with American flags.

But this was different. Something she couldn't name seemed to push against her from all sides, something heavy and invisible and threatening. At first she thought it was the heat and the congested sidewalks, but then she recognized the familiar sinking sensation she had grown up trying to avoid, and the sudden, overwhelming awareness that something was horribly wrong. She felt like the little girl she had once been, the little girl who hid behind Mutti's apron when company came, unable to explain why she always wanted to play alone. The little girl who didn't want to shake hands or hug, or sit on anyone's lap. The little girl who was grateful to be left out of kickball and jump rope, while at the same time it broke her heart.

Looking up at the boys in worn jackets and patched trousers clambering up streetlamps to get a better view of the parade, she wished she could join them to escape the crush of the growing throng. The boys shouted and laughed and waved their newsboy caps, hanging like monkeys below giant American flags. She wanted to be like them too, carefree and unaware that anything was wrong. But that was impossible. No matter how hard she tried, she'd never be like everyone else.

When she looked back down at the sidewalk, her mother had disappeared. She opened her mouth to shout for her, then bit her tongue. She wasn't supposed to call her Mutti anymore—not out loud, anyway. Speaking German in public was no longer allowed. Her parents would always be Mutti and Vater in her head, no matter what the law said, but she didn't dare draw attention by calling her that in a crowd. Standing on her tiptoes to see over shoulders and backs, she spotted the top of Mutti's faded brown hat a few yards away and hurried to catch up to her, stopping short and moving sideways to avoid bumping into people on her way.

Finally behind Mutti again, she wiped the sweat from her upper lip and breathed a sigh of relief. The last thing she needed was to get lost. Bunching her shoulders to make herself smaller, she stayed as close to Mutti as possible, weaving and ducking to avoid the sea of bare arms and hands all around her, wishing her mother would slow down. If only she could crawl into the baby pram with her twin brothers and hide beneath their blankets. She had known coming to the parade would be difficult, but she hadn't expected this.

As far back as she could remember she'd been extraordinarily shy. Mutti said few people could hold her when she was a baby because she cried like the world was coming to an end. She used to think being bashful was the same for everyone; that it was something you could feel, like a fever or stomachache or scratchy throat.

Sometimes she wondered what would have happened if Mutti hadn't been there to protect her from men wanting to pinch her cheeks, and little old ladies waggling their fingers at her to prove they were harmless. But gradually something had changed, even more so in the last couple of months. She'd started to notice other sensations when she touched someone's bare skin, like pain in her head or chest, or discomfort in an arm or leg. It didn't happen every time, but often enough to make her wonder if something was wrong with her. Now, whenever she went to the dry goods store or vegetable market, she took the streets, dodging horses, wagons, bicycles, and automobiles to avoid the congested sidewalks. Handing coins to the peddlers nearly gave her the vapors, so she dropped them on the counter more often than not. But there was nothing she could do about any of it. Telling Mutti—or anyone else, for that matter— was out of the question, especially since her great-aunt Lottie had spent the second half of her life locked in an insane asylum in Germany because she saw things that weren't there. No matter how confused or scared Pia got, she wasn't willing to chance getting locked up too.

Now, following Mutti along the packed sidewalks, her worst fears were confirmed when a man in a linen suit and straw gambler cut across the flow of pedestrians and bumped into her, laughing at first, then apologizing. Having been taught to always smile and be polite, she forced a smile—she was so good at it that it sometimes frightened her—but then the man pinched her cheek and a sharp pain stabbed her chest, like her heart had been split in two. She shuddered and looked down at herself, certain a knife would be sticking out of her rib cage. But there was no knife, no blood trickling down the front of her flour-sack dress. The thin bodice was smooth and spotless. She stepped backward to get away, but the man was already gone, the pain disappearing with him. The strength of it left her weak.

Then a small, cool hand latched onto hers and her chest constricted, tightening with every breath. She'd have sworn she heard her lungs rattle, but couldn't be sure with all the noise. She yanked her hand away and looked down. A little girl in a white ruffled dress gazed up at her, smiling—until she realized Pia was a stranger. Fear crumpled her face and searched the crowd with frantic eyes. Then she ran off, calling for her mother, and Pia could breathe normally again.

How Pia longed to be back in Hazleton, where there were open spaces and blue skies, swaths of wildflowers and herds of deer, instead of miles of pavement, side-by-side buildings, and hordes of people. In Philadelphia, she couldn't walk ten feet without bumping into someone, and every sight, sound, and smell seemed menacing and foreign. The neighborhood alleys were strewn with garbage and sewage, and the biggest rats she'd ever seen crawled in nooks and crannies, scampering between walls and passageways. Trolleys and wagons and motorcars fought for space on every street, and more people than she had ever seen at one time seemed to crowd every sidewalk. The city reminded her of a clogged beehive, teeming with people instead of insects. Even the row houses were full to overflowing, with multiple families squeezed into two and three rooms. Certainly there had been hardships in the mining village—the walls of their shack were paper-thin, everything from their clothes to their kitchen table seemed covered in coal dust, and worst of all, Vater's job digging for coal was dangerous and grueling—but it didn't make her any less homesick. She was glad her father had found safer work in the city a little over a year ago, but she missed the chickens in the yard and the neighbor's hound dog sleeping under their front porch. She missed taking the dirt path to Widow Wilcox's shack to learn how to read and write. She missed the mountain trails and the grass outside their front door. Vater said she missed Hazelton because deep inside she longed for the rolling hills and green fields of Bavaria. And when she reminded him she'd only been four when they boarded the ship to America, he laughed and said Germany was in her blood, like her fondness for sweets and his love for her mother.

Thinking of her father, her eyes burned. If he were here with them now, she could hold his wide, weathered hand in hers and lean against his tall, muscular frame. No one would guess by looking at him that he was always whistling, singing, and making jokes; instead they tended to hurry out of his path because of his imposing presence and piano-wide shoulders. With him by her side, she could have moved through the crowd nearly untouched. But that was impossible. He'd enlisted in the Army three months ago, along with two of his German-American friends, to prove his loyalty to the United States, and now he was somewhere in France. Like Mutti said through her tears when he left, moving to the city to keep him safe had done no good at all.

Suddenly a woman in a Lady Liberty costume pushed between Pia and her mother, jarring her from her thoughts. When the woman's bare forearm brushed her hand, Pia held her breath, waiting for something to hurt. But to her relief, she felt nothing. She relaxed her tight shoulders and exhaled, trying to calm down. She only had to get through the next hour or so. That was it. Then she could go home, to their rooms on Shunk Alley in the Fifth Ward, where no one but her loved ones could reach her.

Then Mutti stopped to talk to a woman from the greengrocers' and a pair of clammy hands clamped over Pia's eyes. Someone snickered in her ear and a sharp pain twisted near her rib cage, instantly making her dizzy. She yanked the hands away and spun around. It was Tommy Costa, the freckle-faced boy who teased her during school recess, and two of his friends, Angelo DiPrizzi and Skip Turner. They stuck out their tongues, then laughed and ran away. The pain in her ribs went with them.

By the time Mutti chose a spot to watch the parade, Pia was shaking. She had begged her mother to let her stay home, even promising to straighten up their two-room apartment while she and the twins were gone. But despite knowing how Pia felt about large gatherings, Mutti insisted.

"Going to the parade is the only way to prove we are loyal Americans," Mutti said in heavily accented English. "It's hard enough after President Wilson said all German citizens are alien enemies. I follow the new laws. I sign the papers they want me to sign refusing my German citizenship. I do the fingerprinting. But I have no money to buy liberty loans or make a donation to the Red Cross. I have to feed you and your brothers. So we must go to the parade. All of us. Even your father fighting in the war is not enough to keep the neighbors happy."

"But it won't matter if I'm with you or not," Pia said. "Everyone will see you there, and the twins will enjoy it. I could make dinner and have it ready when you return."

"*Nein*," her mother said. As soon as the word came out of her mouth, worry flickered across her face. "I mean, no. You must come with us. The radio and newspapers tell everyone to be watchful of their German-American neighbors and to report to the authorities. Before your father left, a woman shouted at me, saying he stole a real American's job. She spit and said to go back where I came from. I am not leaving you home alone."

Pia knew Mutti was right; she'd suffered enough bullying at school to know everything she said was true. Rumors were flying that German spies were poisoning food, and German-Americans were secretly hoarding arms. Some Germans had even been sent to jail or internment camps. The city was plastered with posters showing Germans standing over dead bodies; churches with German congregations had been painted yellow, and German-language newspapers were shut down. Schoolchildren were forced to sign pledges promising not to use any foreign language whatsoever. And a special police group called the Home Guard, originally formed to patrol the streets with guns to ensure adequate protection of important points in the city—the Water Works and pumping station, the electric light distributing plant, the telephone service, and various power stations at manufacturing plants—now also patrolled the south end of the city to keep an eye on German immigrants. Some companies refused to employ Germans, so Mutti lost her job at the textile mill. And because she needed a permit to withdraw money from the bank, what little cash they had left was kept under a floorboard inside a bedroom cubby. Even sauerkraut and hamburgers were renamed "liberty cabbage" and "liberty sandwiches."

But knowing Mutti was right didn't make going to the parade any easier.

Three days after the parade, while her schoolmates laughed and played hopscotch and jump rope during recess, Pia sat alone, pretending to read in her usual spot, on a flat rock near the back fence of the schoolyard. The air was pale, as gray as smoke, and the breeze carried a slight chill. Luckily, she'd remembered to bring her sweater, especially since the school windows were being kept open to ward off the grippe. Her three-quarter-length dress had long sleeves and her cotton stockings were thick, but the flour-sack material of her skirt and bodice was worn and thin. She put the book down, pulled her sleeves over her fists, and tried to stop shivering. Was she trembling because of the cold, or because she couldn't stop thinking about what she'd seen and heard since the Liberty Loan parade?

Mrs. Schmidt had told Mutti that within seventy-two hours, every bed in each of the city's thirty-one hospitals was filled with victims of a new illness called the Spanish influenza, and the hospitals were starting to refuse patients. By day four, the illness had infected over six hundred Philadelphians, and killed well over a hundred in one day. Pia overheard the teachers talking about a shortage of doctors and nurses because of the war, and that poorhouses and churches were being used as temporary hospitals. More posters went up, reading *Spitting Equals Death*, and the police arrested anyone who disobeyed. Another poster showed a man in a suit standing next to the outline of a clawed demon rising from what appeared to be a pool of saliva on the sidewalk, with the words *Halt the Epidemic! Stop Spitting, Everybody!* And because everyone was wearing pouches of garlic or camphor balls in cheesecloth around their necks, the streets were filled with a foul, peculiar odor that she couldn't help thinking was the smell of death. Most frightening of all, she heard that those who fell sick were often dead by nightfall, their faces black and blue, and blood gushing from their eyes, mouth, nose, and ears.

She'd been having nightmares too, filled with ghastly images of the parade spectators, flashing in her mind like the jerky moving pictures in a penny arcade—each face with black lips and purple cheeks, and blood coming from their mouths and eyes. Every time it happened she woke up in a sweat, her arms and legs tangled in the sheets, her stomach and chest sore and aching. Just thinking about it all made her queasy. The stench wafting up from the garlic around her neck didn't help.

She took the putrid necklace off and laid it in the grass, then lifted her chin and took a deep breath, inhaling the familiar smells of fall—moist earth, sunburnt leaves, and chimney smoke. The fragranced air was significantly better than the odor of garlic, but it reminded her of her first dreadful day in her new school last year. She could still hear the voices of her mother and new teacher.

"Did you see the letter I send in to school, Mrs. Derry?" Mutti had said.

"Yes, Mrs. Lange, I received the note. But I'm not sure I understand it."

"Forgive me, I only wish to make sure," Mutti said. "My Pia is, how do you say, delicate? She does not like crowds, or anyone touching her. I am not sure why . . ." Her mother was wringing her hands now. "But she is a normal girl and smart. Please. Can you be sure the other children—"

"Mrs. Lange, I don't see how—"

"Pia needs to learn. She needs to be at school. I don't want her to . . ."

"All right, Mrs. Lange," Mrs. Derry said. "Yes. I'll do my best. But children come into contact with each other while playing all the time, especially during recess. It's part of learning. Sometimes I won't be able to stop it from happening."

"Yes, I understand," Mutti said. "But if Pia doesn't want . . . if one of the other children does not know to leave her alone . . . please . . ."

Mrs. Derry put a hand on her mother's arm, looked at her with pity-filled eyes, and said, "Don't worry, I'll take care of her. And I'll let the other teachers know too."

Mutti nodded and gave her a tired smile, then said goodbye to Pia and left.

After that first day, for the most part, Mrs. Derry and the rest of the teachers had done little to look out for Pia. And the memory of that encounter—her mother wringing her hands and trying to communicate her odd concerns to a confused Mrs. Derry while Pia cringed at her side and the other kids watched—recurred to her every time she stepped foot in the classroom. When the other children played Duck, Duck, Goose or Ring Around the Rosy, Pia stood off to the side, sad and relieved at the same time. Inevitably, when the teachers weren't looking, some of the kids taunted and poked her, calling her names like freak-girl or scaredy-cat. And now, because of the war, they called her a Hun.

Thankfully she had met Finn before she started school, while he could form his own opinion. It was the day after they'd moved in, when Mutti sent her out to sit on the stoop with strict instructions not to wander off while she and Vater talked—about what, Pia wasn't sure. She'd been homesick and near tears, frightened to discover that the jumble of trash-strewn alleys and cobblestone streets and closely built row houses made her feel trapped, and wondering how she'd ever get used to living there, when he approached from across the alley. She tried to ignore him and hoped he was headed for the entrance behind her, but he stopped at the bottom of the steps, swept his copper-colored bangs out his eyes, and gave her a friendly grin.

"Yer a new lass around here, aren't ye?" he said in a heavy Irish brogue. "I'm Finn Duffy, your neighbor from across the way." He pointed at the shabby building across from hers, a four-story brick with narrow windows and a black fire escape.

She nodded and forced a smile. She didn't feel like talking, but didn't want to be rude either. "Yes," she said. "We moved in yesterday."

"Nice to meet you, um . . . What did you say yer name was?"

"Oh, sorry," she said. "I'm Pia Lange."

"Well, nice to meet ye, Pia Lange. Can I interest you in a game of marbles?" He pulled a cloth sack from the pocket of his threadbare trousers.

She shook her head. "No, thank you."

"Would ye mind if I sit with you then?" he said. "You look rather lonesome, if you don't mind me saying so."

She thought about telling him she wanted to be left alone, but didn't want to start off by making enemies. Instead she nodded and moved over to make room, gathering her pleated skirt beneath her legs and sitting on her hands. He smiled and sat beside her, a polite distance away. To her relief, he kept quiet, almost as if he knew she didn't feel like talking. Together they sat lost in their own thoughts, watching three colored girls with braids and pigtails play hopscotch across the way. One held a rag doll under her arm, the doll's limp head flopping up and down with every jump. Snippets of laughter, conversation, and the tinny music of a phonograph drifted down from open windows, along with the smell of fried onions and baking bread. A group of ruddy-cheeked boys in patched pants and worn shoes kicked a can along the cobblestones. Line after line of laundry hung damp and unmoving in the humid air, crisscrossing the row of buildings like layers of circus flags. People of all colors and ages and sizes spilled out onto the fire escapes, sitting on overturned washtubs and kettles, looking for relief from the heat.

An old colored woman in a dirty scarf and laceless boots limped past, humming and pulling a wooden cart filled with rags and old bottles. She skirted around two boys of about seven or eight on their knees playing cards in front of a stone building three doors down. One of the boys glanced at her over his shoulder, then jumped to his feet, grabbed something from her cart, and ran laughing, back to his friend. The old woman kept going, oblivious to the fact that she had been robbed. The second boy gathered up the cards and did the same, then they both started running away.

Finn shot to his feet and chased after them, cutting them off before they disappeared down a side alley. He yelled something Pia couldn't make out, then grabbed them by the ears and dragged them back to the old woman. After returning her things to the cart, the boys hurried away, rubbing their ears and scowling back at him, muttering under their breath. The old woman stopped and looked around, finally aware that something was amiss. When she saw Finn, she shooed him away and swatted at him with a thin, gnarled hand. He laughed and made his way back to Pia, shrugging and lifting his palms in the air.

Pia couldn't help but smile. "Do you know her?" she said.

"I don't," he said, catching his breath. He sat back on the stoop beside her and wiped the sweat from his brow. "But I see her every day, selling rags and bottles on the corner. I know the lads though, and they're always causin' a ruckus."

"They didn't look very happy with you," she said.

"I suppose they're not," he said. "But they won't cause trouble for me."

"Well," she said. "It was very nice of you to stop them and make them return what they took."

He gave her a sideways grin. "Why, isn't that grand. Ye think I'm nice. Thank you, Pia Lange."

Heat crawled up her face. She nodded because she didn't know what to say, then went back to watching the girls play hopscotch. Did he really think what she said was grand, or was he making fun of her? His smile made her think he appreciated the compliment, so she told herself that was the case. Not that it mattered. Once he found out she was German he'd probably never speak to her again.

He sat forward, his elbows on his knees, and watched the girls play hopscotch too. "We came from Ireland three years ago," he said. "How long have you been in the States?"

"Since I was four," she said.

He looked at her, his eyebrows raised. "That long?"

She nodded.

"Livin' here in Philly the entire time?"

She shook her head. "We came from Hazelton. Vater . . . I mean, my father worked in the coal mines."

He forced a hard breath between his teeth. "That's a bloody hard way to make a living."

She nodded. At least he didn't react to the German word. Or maybe he didn't notice.

"This city can be a mite overwhelming when you first arrive," he said. "But you'll get used to it. My da was the one who wanted to come, but he never got to see it."

"Why not?"

"He didn't survive the voyage."

"I'm sorry."

"Aye, I appreciate it. My mam has been having a hard time of it since then, so my older brothers and I have been taking care of her and my grandfather. Then the Army took one of my brothers six months ago and my other brother had to start working double shifts at the textile mill. I'm ready to take a job, but Mam insists I finish my last year of schoolin' first. Things were hard in Dublin, but I'm not sure they're much better here. It makes ye long for home, even when you know leaving was the right thing to do."

She really looked at him then, at his kind face and hazel eyes. It was almost as if he were reading her mind.

From that day on, they were fast friends. He didn't care that she and her family were German, or ask her to explain why she didn't want to play cat's cradle or any other game that might involve close contact. After he sent her a note on the clothesline between their fourth-floor apartments that said, "'Twas nice to meet ye, lass!" they started sending messages to each other on Sunday nights when the line was empty—but only if the windows weren't frozen shut and they were able to find scraps of paper not set aside for the war effort. The notes were silly and meaningless, just hello or a funny joke or drawing, but it was their little secret. One of the few things Pia didn't have to share with anyone else.

Once school started they discovered they were in the same classroom despite him being a grade ahead. He offered to sit with her at recess, but she said she'd rather not have the added attention. While he played kickball and marbles with the other boys, he always looked over to offer a smile or a wave. And that small gesture made everything easier.

Most days she didn't mind sitting alone. But today was different. She wished he'd stop playing ball and come sit with her. Because no matter how hard she tried, she couldn't concentrate on her book, instead constantly thinking about the flu, and distracted by an overwhelming worry and dread. Chills shivered up her spine when a group of girls skipping rope began to chant:

> There was a little girl, and she had a little bird,
> And she called it by the pretty name of Enza;
> But one day it flew away, but it didn't go to stay,
> For when she raised the window, in-flu-enza.

"What are you staring at, scaredy-cat?"

Pia looked up to see who had spoken, unaware she'd been staring. A thin girl with brown pigtails glared down at her, a disgusted look on her face. It was Mary Helen Burrows, whom everyone liked or feared, depending on which day you asked, and whether or not Mary Helen was within earshot. No one had ever seen her get into an actual brawl, but permanent anger knitted her brows, and bruises marked her arms and legs. Two other girls stood behind her, Beverly Hansom and Selma Jones, their arms crossed over their chests.

"I wasn't staring at anything," Pia said, reaching for her book.

"I'm telling you, Mary Helen," Beverly said. "She was staring at us, like she was coming up with some nasty German scheme or somethin'."

Mary Helen knocked the book out of Pia's hand. "You spying on us?"

Pia shook her head. "No, I was just—"

"What's going on?" someone said. "Are you all right, Pia?" It was Finn. He was out of breath, his face red and his hair disheveled.

"Your girlfriend was giving us the stink-eye," Mary Helen said.

"She's not my girlfriend," Finn said.

"Shut up, Mary Helen," Pia said.

Mary Helen ignored her and glared at Finn. "What would your mother think if she knew you were friends with a filthy Hun, 'specially with your older brother fighting to keep you safe?"

Pia bounced to her feet. "Take that back!"

Mary Helen's head snapped around and she gaped at Pia, shocked to hear her standing up for herself. "What'd you say?"

"I said take it back!"

Mary Helen held up her bony fists. "You want a fat lip to go with that stink-eye?"

"Jaysus," Finn said. "In the name of all that's holy, shut up, Mary Helen. You're not gonna fight."

"Oh yeah?" Mary Helen said. Then her hand shot out and grabbed the front of Pia's dress. She yanked her forward, pushing her contorted face into Pia's. The stench of garlic and onions wafting up from the bag around her neck almost made Pia gag. Thinking only of escape, she grabbed Mary Helen's wrist with both hands and tried to pull her off. A quick stab of pain twisted in her chest, sharp and immediate, and she gasped, unable to get air. She let go and tried to step backward, disoriented and dizzy. Finn pried Mary Helen's fist from Pia's dress, moved Pia behind him, and stood between them.

One of the teachers hurried over. "What in heaven's name is going on over here?" she said. It was Miss Herrick. She towered above them, willowy as a flower stem.

Pia sat down hard on the ground and tried to catch her breath.

"Nothing, ma'am," Mary Helen said. "You must be balled up. We were just playing a game."

"Well, it doesn't look like a game to me," Miss Herrick said. "You and your friends run along now, Mary Helen, and leave Pia alone."

Mary Helen harrumphed, but did as she was told. The other girls followed, their faces pinched.

"Are you all right, Pia?" Miss Herrick said. She reached down to help her up, reaching for her arm.

"Don't touch me," Pia said, louder than intended.

Miss Herrick gasped and clapped a hand to her chest.

Pia instantly regretted her outburst. The last thing she needed was to get in trouble at school. Mutti would never understand. She got up and brushed off her dress. "I'm sorry, Miss Herrick," she said. "I didn't mean to be rude. I was frightened, that's all."

Miss Herrick sighed. "That's understandable, I suppose. I know Mary Helen likes to start trouble and everyone is feeling anxious these days. But are you sure you're all right? You look like you've just seen a ghost."

Pia mustered a weak smile. "I'm fine." She wasn't anywhere near fine, but how could she explain to Miss Herrick what she'd felt when she grabbed Mary Helen's wrist?